Who Lies Beside Me

A Love Lonely Novel, Book 2

By William C. Cole

Who Lies Beside Me

Limitless Publishing, LLC
Kailua, HI 96734
www.limitlesspublishing.com

Formatting: Limitless Publishing

ISBN-13: 978-1-68058-899-6
ISBN-10: 1-68058-899-0

Dedication

To Mom and Dad

Engraved in Our Hearts Forever

You Gave Us
Roots to Grow
And Wings to Fly

Chapter One

Seldom had there been a stack of cards that Sandy could not manipulate in her favor—until now. This was something life dealt her unexpectedly. Jacob, her father, sat beside her on one of the couches in his office, located on the first floor of the ranch house, voicing his opinion regarding an appointment his daughter was being vetted for.

"Sandy, as much as I would like to persuade you differently, you cannot decline this appeal."

"Daddy, I can't accept. I'm not stepping back into that world after all the sorrow it caused our family. I came very close to losing my child and my husband. I don't want to be part of that jungle anymore."

"I understand the way you feel, and wholeheartedly agree with you." Her father appeared resolute. "But when the President of the United States requests your service, you don't say no. That's not an option."

"I know."

"The deadline to announce his new Director is nearing. He's been very patient with you up to this point, but your decision needs to be forthcoming."

Sandy was having a difficult time coming to grips with the President's invitation to swear her in as the first female Director of the CIA. Never once had she questioned her own capability. If she accepted, she would once again become an absentee wife and now mother. When she came to terms with her pregnancy, she vowed nothing would ever stand in the way of that treasured time nurturing Capella, her now one-year-old daughter.

"Someone is missing her mommy."

There in the doorway stood David holding their child. They were back from their visit to the stables.

"You two look like you've been up to no good," Sandy teased while rising to her feet.

David gently handed her Capella, who was the recipient of a mother's kiss and cuddle.

"It's amazing how the horses interact with this one," David told them. "When I hold her close, they try brushing my hand to the side with their muzzle. They are very protective of her. Whatever the future holds for her, I'm certain that bond will be a part of it."

"She is special, isn't she?" Jacob said with a smile as he came to her side.

The three of them huddled over Capella for a minute, smiling ear to ear. Little in life was as precious as a moment like this.

"Sorry, did we interrupt something?" David asked, realizing their meeting might've been important. "Here, Sandy." He put his arms out to take back the child. "You guys finish up. I'll go up and give Capella a bath."

"No, we're good. I'll come with you."

"I insist. You two finish up and I will get her ready for bed. Just don't be too long."

"Okay then. We won't be."

Sandy and her father gave the baby a kiss before David took her back and made his way up the stairs to their living quarters. They returned to the sofa to conclude their evening chat.

"How in the world can I turn my back on that?"

"You know, my dear, it is eating me up inside. There's got to be a way to make this work. I'll give David full access to my aircraft. Hire the best nannies in the world. We will do whatever it takes. But you cannot say no to the President. Hell, I've never said no to a President."

"Daddy, I know I can't, but I believe I have to."

She stood and gave her father a goodnight kiss, then slipped out of the office and made her way up the grandiose staircase, uncertain what the future held.

***

Jacob returned to his desk, opened a drawer, and retrieved a mobile phone. He tried to decide whether to make the call or wait until morning. Scrolling his speed dial, he moved to tap the Andrew icon. A split second before he did so, he was startled by his wife, "slash" partner, "slash" executive assistant, "slash" best friend.

"I figured the only way I was going to see you at

home tonight would be to come and get you."

After they married, Brooklyn and Jacob took up residency at the log chalet to distance themselves from their daily routine of the office at the main house. For just over a year, there wasn't a single night that they hadn't climbed into bed together. It was a promise they made to each other. A hug, a kiss, and more often than not a sensual lovemaking session ended each day.

"By the looks of that cell in your hand, business has not yet concluded for the day."

He put the phone in his pocket.

"You're right. You're always right. I have had enough. Let's head back. Would you mind if we walk by way of the stable? I'm in need of a dose of revitalization, and those animals never fail to provide it."

Soon, they were holding hands as they walked down the path toward the light escaping the barn doors.

"You were calling the President, weren't you?"

He nodded.

"Then Sandy's not going to take the appointment, is she?"

"She's adamant about declining and I can't blame her."

They strolled through the stable, stopping at the stalls so Jacob could brush the mane of each horse. He spoke to them in a quiet tone. The innocence these creatures were blessed with was mystifying. To saunter through the barn any time during the day, but more so in the calm of night, put a person in a state of tranquility. Jacob would enter one door and exit the other with a cleansed soul.

"Jacob, as much as we want the best for her, she needs to be the sole proprietor of her decision. It is the only way she will be capable of living with it."

"Again, you're right, my voice of reason."

They exited the stable and walked to their residence. Once inside, Brooklyn put on a pot of tea, and Jacob cracked open a cold beer. The plan was to sit up for an hour or so talking or reading, then bedtime. As they settled on the couch, the phone in Jacob's back pocket chimed. Any communication on this device was reserved for a select few. An incoming call could not be ignored. Brooklyn was well aware of the significance of such a call. Jacob answered.

"Please hold for the President of the United States," a sophisticated voice on the other end said.

He pulled the receiver away from his ear to whisper, "The President," to his wife.

"Jacob, my dear friend, how are you keeping? I hope I haven't caught you at an inconvenient time."

"Andrew, I always have time for you." He addressed the President by his first name.

"I appreciate that. I've been fighting an inclination that you might be contacting me today. So, I took the bull by the horns and called you."

"Andrew, I'm resigned to the fact my daughter won't be accepting your proposal. We've had a number of heart-to-hearts and she believes her focus at this point in her life should be solely on family."

"Considering everything she has been through, I understand her hesitation, but she will come around. My belief is that Sandy will not only make this country a better place to live in, she will make the world safer for all. Unfortunately, I cannot go into details, but what your daughter has already achieved on behalf of this country will not be forgotten."

"Andrew, I will speak to her again."

"Thank you. Now for the key reason of my call. I've insisted my two lovely daughters find more time to spend with their father. To my surprise, we came up with a mutually agreed upon activity that we seldom find time to enjoy. A weekend of horseback riding."

"Sir, I think that is a wonderful idea. Sandy and I have spent many hours riding at the ranch. Some great memories were had."

"That's exactly what I'm seeking with my daughters. I boasted a bit and told them I had a good friend who happened to house the most exceptional array of thoroughbred horses in the country. I mentioned to them that the next time I spoke to you, I would ask if you would be kind enough to harbor the three of us for a weekend on the trails."

"Absolutely. It would be my honor. You name the time and we will provide the girls with a day they won't soon forget."

"Perfect. Would this upcoming weekend work for you? Addison will be on one of her few college breaks. I trust this short notice won't be too much of an imposition. I'd understand if you would prefer to schedule for a later date."

Jacob smiled and glanced at Brooklyn. His success was achieved in part by having an uncanny ability to discern between what is being voiced and what is being said. He knew full well the real purpose of the President's visit was to court Sandy.

"That would be ideal. I look forward to a relaxing sit down by the fireplace. Last time we saw each other, I was not myself."

Jacob was referring to his storming into the Oval Office in a rage, demanding the head of the person responsible for the injuries inflicted on his daughter.

"No need to apologize, Jacob. I would have reacted as you had, probably worse. So, good, we have a date. The girls will be ecstatic. We will see you Friday evening."

"I'm looking forward to it."

"Unfortunately, they're going to want to send up a prep team, which I will insist be kept to a minimum. Your wife will know how to cradle them. Please say hello to her for me. You're a lucky man, Jacob. They only made one Brooklyn."

"Thank you. We will see you Friday."

The conversation came to an end. Brooklyn was sporting a smirk. Without hearing the opposite side of the conversation, it was clear she knew exactly what had transpired and the preparation required in accommodating such a visit. After all, this was what she coordinated on a daily basis during her years at the White House.

"We should get to bed. You have your work cut out for you tomorrow."

"That's what I do. Besides…" She took him by his hand and led him to the bedroom, then pushed him onto the bed. "…this."

***

Sandy emerged from the baby's room. The bright little star was down for a couple of hours, or at least that was the hope. While she read to Capella, her husband showered. Now, she found him lying on the bed sporting a blue bath towel.

"You care to join me?" Sandy stripped out of her clothes.

"I just got out."

"I think you should," she repeated.

"Sandy, I just finished, hence the towel."

Slipping off her panties, she stood at the end of the bed, naked.

"Well, I think you should have another. Certain parts of a person's body require a little extra attention."

Sandy glanced down below her belly to her clean shave. Turning, she walked in the direction of the bathroom. Then she moved toward the bathroom, knowing that with each defined step, David was watching the muscles in her bum flex. He wouldn't decline the invitation. Sandy was not only a master of martial arts, she was adept at seduction. He soon pushed off the bed and followed.

The water sprayed from above, below, and on the side of the huge shower. Sandy was already soaked when he entered, sitting on one of the benches with water pounding on her body. Her legs were spread, presenting David with a view of what she was offering.

In silence, he bent to his knees and eased between her legs. With her eyes closed, Sandy rested the back of her head on the wall and moaned softly. David continued until she eased him from the hollow and pushed him into the center of the rainfall before arching and placing him in her mouth. After a half hour of foreplay, they retired to the bed where the main course was served up.

The satisfaction of the evening's session left the couple spent. David laid flat on his back with one arm around her and the other propping up his head. Sandy cuddled as she rested her head on his chest.

"Motherhood has thrust you into a whole new level of beauty, which I thought was beyond attainment. You are no longer the most beautiful woman in the world. You are the most beautiful woman in the universe."

"I bet that's what you said to all your bedmates."

She gave him a little jab in the ribs. He retaliated by climbing on top of her and tickling her with both his hands. Sandy laughed while struggling to free herself. The playful moment was cut short by a whimper from the baby's room.

"At least she was kind enough to give us a couple of hours," Sandy said.

"Saved by your child. You got lucky," he teased, knowing full well if she wanted to he'd be thrown off and hogtied on the floor within a split second.

Both went to check on Capella, who was again sound asleep. They returned to the bed to rest, as morning was quickly approaching. Before they drifted off, Sandy felt the need to test the waters.

"David, if I accepted the directorship, would you consider making the move to Washington with me?"

"Sandy, I'm a small town guy. I was raised on a farm in Alberta and my whole life was split between being in a hockey arena or a barn. I don't think I could survive that lifestyle."

"When you were playing in the NHL, you lived in large cities."

"That's different. We were on the ice or flying off to the next game. Being here with the horses is what I love. Besides, I thought we agreed this is where Capella should grow up."

"Washington has a team. Maybe they have a coaching job available. You could hang out with all your Canadian buddies."

"It doesn't work like that, Sandy. Listen, I've said it before, whatever your decision is, you have my support. We will be fine."

"I love you."

***

By six in the morning, Brooklyn and Jacob had settled into the office.

"Brooklyn, would you buzz Sandy and David? We need to enlighten them about our upcoming guests. I'd like to take care of it before all hell breaks loose with the arrival of his team."

"It's a little early. Let's give them a few more minutes of sleep. I'm sure the baby will have them up soon enough."

"Okay, but not too much longer."

At seven sharp, Brooklyn called.

"Brooklyn, it's quite early. Is there something wrong?"

"All is fine, Sandy. However, something of importance has transpired and your father would like to discuss it with you and David."

"David is still sleeping. We can meet with him around lunchtime."

"Sandy, he would like to get together soon. He wanted me to call you at six, but I talked him into giving you more time to rest. Do you think you could wake David and gather in his office within the hour, please?"

"What is this about, Brooklyn?"

"Sandy, your father would prefer to discuss it with you in person."

"We will be down shortly."

"And please bring Capella with you. I would love to spoil my step-grandchild for a while."

"She's your grandchild, Brooklyn, not step."

"Thank you."

A short time later, when Brooklyn heard them coming down the hall, she was up and around her desk instantaneously. She would sit out of the meeting and babysit. It would definitely be the highlight of her day.

They handed over their daughter and entered the office.

***

Jacob rose from his seat. "Good, you're here. I see my grandchild is in good hands. Please, come in."

They took a seat on the sofas. Jacob offered coffee or tea, but both declined.

"Daddy, what's wrong? I can count the times you've shown such urgency on one hand."

"I wanted to discuss something with the two of you before it was made obvious by other means."

"Well, Jacob, we are all ears," David said, sounding a little perturbed at the early hour call.

"We are entertaining guests this weekend."

"Who are we entertaining, Father?"

Jacob took a sip of his coffee while contemplating how best to tell them. He knew his daughter's immediate reaction would be negative, as the President was the last person she wanted to see.

"Last night, I had a call from a good friend of mine who would like to bring his daughters here for a weekend of riding."

"Who is this friend?" Suddenly, the answer dawned on her. "No, don't tell me."

"What?" David interjected.

"The President. It's Andrew, isn't it, Father?"

"Yes, it is. But, my dear, the sole purpose of his visit is bonding time with his daughters. He didn't even ask if you were going to be here. I didn't offer up your plans to him, so if you prefer to disappear for a couple of days, I would understand. The plane is fueled and ready to roll."

"I'm not going anywhere. I'd love to take the girls for a ride."

Jacob had been prepared for more resistance, so he was pleased the chat went so smoothly. The three of them knew all too well the underlying reason for the visit.

"Is there anything else you would like to go over?" David asked. "I need to get on with my day and head to the track."

"There is one thing. If I'm correct, we have no races scheduled for this week."

"That's right."

"Good. I would like you to invite Renée over for the weekend. We will accommodate her here at the ranch. It will take the pressure off you two. She will get along great with his children. After all, she is a little closer to their age."

David displayed a fleeting paranoid look in his eye at the reference to his trainer's age, and he didn't seem sure how to react. Jacob noticed his son-in-law's discomfort but didn't put much thought into it.

"I don't think that will be necessary, Jacob. Sandy and I will enjoy taking the kids out on the trails. We don't do enough of it ourselves. Besides, I think Brooklyn would love some quality time with Capella."

But after a quick reconsider, not wanting to raise any further suspicion, David tensed his closed lips, then exhaled. "I'll let Renée know."

"I apologize for getting you two up and around so early," Jacob said. "We can now get back to the business of the day."

They left the room to find Brooklyn beaming like a kid in a candy store. She would have made a wonderful mother. The grandparents stole a few more minutes with their bundle of joy before everyone settled into their daily routine.

David and Sandy would provide the young girls with a weekend packed with special memories.

Meanwhile, Jacob and Brooklyn began preparation for the Secret Service's arrival.

13

***

Sandy secretly reveled watching her husband squirm at the point of the meeting when Renée's name was mentioned. She knew how uncomfortable it would be for him having their trainer sleep under the same roof for two days. Although it was only once a topic of conversation, and the affair was stagnant at the moment, she was well aware of his indiscretions.

During the conversation, she was thinking to herself, *David just agree and say it's a great idea or you're going to put your foot in your mouth.*

When he did, she thought, *Good boy.*

***

Once at the track, David's first order of business was to inform Renée of his father-in-law's request. He wasn't expecting a positive response. But when you're being paid over a million dollars a year, sometimes there will be unpopular demands made of you.

After a quick look around, he phoned her only to receive a message: "Bonjour, I will call you soon."

The staff soon informed him that she was riding a training session. He walked to the track's outer fence. There were a number of owners and trainers watching a handful of horses being put through their paces. Renée was mounted on one of their choice thoroughbreds.

"She looks good out there," a voice to his right said.

Turning, he was startled by Gabriela standing next to him.

Watching Renée brought on a feeling of emptiness in his chest and stomach. He repeatedly asked himself if he would ever be completely over her. The answer was no. The attraction was too deep. He was resigned to the fact that he would always care deeply for two women, although he had no plans of rekindling the affair.

"Yes, she does look good. How long has she been out there? I would like to talk to her."

"She should be done soon."

"Good."

They fell silent and continued watching the thousand pound animals stride around the turf.

"I meant the horse, David." Gabriela gave him a slight wink.

"Of course." He stumbled with the reply, knowing she was aware his reference was to Renée.

Soon the training came to an end. Renée dismounted at the fence, where her friend and boss stood. She handed the horse off to one of the walkers and vaulted her whole hundred pounds over the barrier.

"David, I'm surprised to see you here so early. I thought you were coming in later."

"Something has come up. We need to talk."

Gabriela took the hint and excused herself, promising to catch up later. David and Renée remained at the fence until no one was within earshot.

"What's going on, boss?"

"I need you to spend the weekend at the ranch."

Caught off guard, she didn't immediately reply. She wasn't sure what was behind such a request.

"Why would you want me at the ranch? Better yet, why would I want to spend the weekend? David, this better not be—"

"No, Renée, that's not it. Jacob is entertaining for a couple of days and he has asked me to invite you to spend some time riding with his guests. It's very important to him."

She seemed curious, but being that it was one of the few weeks without having horses on a race card, she had some work and social life to catch up on.

"David, I really prefer not to. I have a lot planned. I'm sure the ranch hands can show his guests the trails."

"Renée, Jacob's insisting you be there."

He knew she could read the urgency in his voice and wouldn't be prepared to bite off the hand that fed her.

"Okay. When would you like me there?"

"Friday night will work. You'll have a room at the ranch."

It had been over a year since they'd felt each other's bodies. It would be an uncomfortable situation, and they both felt it.

"David, sleeping in the same house is going to be a bit awkward. This will remain strictly professional, I hope."

David's heart skipped a beat or two. From the moment Jacob presented the idea, a pleasurable but guilty feeling came over him. The thought of them being together again put him in a fogged state of mind. Her remark had sparked the pilot light.

"So, who are these special guests we will be entertaining?"

"The President and his two daughters."

Chapter Two

Early Friday evening, the restrained activity of the advance Secret Service team amplified. The first indication of the President's arrival was evident by a flyby of two pairs of F-16 fighter jets, enforcing a no fly zone. Soon after, the fluttering of Marine One could be heard in the distance. It wasn't long before the helicopter came into sight. The entire family, including Renée, took in the spectacle from the front porch of the ranch. All the animals were safely huddled away in the stable with the doors closed to muffle the sound of the aircraft.

"I've witnessed this play out hundreds of times, but it never fails to bring chills to my spine," Brooklyn said.

"So true. There is something magical about seeing that Presidential seal," Jacob agreed. "Oh, listen to me, getting all patriotic."

The chopper landed on the immaculately manicured lawn centering the wraparound drive. Two Secret Service agents moved in to assist the passengers. There was the President and his two daughters. No First Lady, no additional staff.

The two groups began to walk toward each other.

"Girls, this is…" The President hesitated, turning his attention to the host. "May we use first names?"

Everyone nodded.

"This is Brooklyn, Jacob, Sandy, David…and you must be the acclaimed horse whisperer, Renée. I was hoping you would be here. I believe the girls can learn a lot from you."

Renée blushed. To think the President knew your name was overwhelming.

"And these are my two little bundles of joy, Addison and Layla."

Addison gave him what could be described as a yucky look. She was nineteen, and her sister, sixteen, but her father still referred to them as he did when they were in elementary school.

"Girls, we did meet a long time ago, which you probably don't remember," Brooklyn said. "I must say, you have grown into beautiful young ladies."

"Brooklyn used to work at the Oval Office before we took up residency," the President explained. "Her picture is still on the wall. Jacob here scooped her up for himself and then married her."

With the introductions taken care of, they made their way to the common room of the ranch where the staff served up beverages. Most selected a soda, water, or juice except for Jacob and the President, who both opted for a beer.

"Can I have one?" Addison asked her father.

"No, Addison, you're only nineteen."

"Dad, I'm in college."

"My dear, I'm aware of your schooling level."

The rebellious exchange ended quickly. It was noticeable to everyone that the teenager was trying to push her limits, but also clear that she had been groomed to behave in public the way a child of her eminence was expected to.

They sat around chatting for an hour or so before a dinner was offered up. The change in rooms didn't dampen the conversation, which pertained mostly to the following two days on the trail. The banter created an excitement for all. Even Sandy and David were eager for the morning, somewhat of a forced relaxation. As selfish as it felt, Sandy was thinking how nice it would be to take a few hours' break from motherhood.

"We've been talking so much about horses I have forgotten to enlighten you about your accommodations," Jacob said. "Brooklyn and I have vacated the chalet to provide your staff with private lodging. The Secret Service has accepted our suggestion for your accommodations here at the main house. Girls, you will each have your own separate room."

"That sounds perfect, Jacob. I hope we haven't caused too much of an inconvenience," the President replied.

"Anytime, my friend."

Dinner was served. The chatter soon returned to the animals. Addison was sitting next to Renée and they were hitting it off well. Actually, David took notice that the two were having their own little exchange, zoned out from the remainder of the guests. Dinner soon came to an end.

"Girls, I think we should call it a night. We have a lot planned for tomorrow," the President said as he stood and stretched.

"Dad, Renée has invited me for a walk down to the stables to say goodnight to the horses."

"Only if it's okay with our hosts." When they nodded, he said, "Sure, I don't see why not. Layla, will you be joining them?"

"No. I'm tired." She declined in lieu of resuming her social media obligations.

Everyone bid each other a good night. Jacob convinced the President to have a nightcap with him in his office. Brooklyn passed up the invitation to join them for some quiet reading time. David and Sandy were looking forward to getting their little one to bed. She had been fast asleep in her child seat halfway through dinner.

***

Once they were settled nicely into the office, it was Jacob who spoke first.

"Would you like me to coordinate a one-on-one with Sandy?"

"Absolutely not, Jacob. I'm here for the girls. That is the main focus of our visit. Actually, I believe the idea of this trip may originate from my admiration of your relationship with Sandy. I recall you telling me how therapeutic these rides were for the two of you while going through some difficult times.

"Although we lead different lives, we are similar when it comes to the time we have to spend with

21

family. Sandy's frequent absence must tear you apart. In my case, it's my responsibilities that are the culprit. But yet, you two have found a way to foster such a wonderful connection. I want that with my daughters. That's why we're here."

"I'm sure your children are very proud of their father and understand the magnitude of his achievements. You being here is evidence in itself that the three of you are on the right track."

"I hope that's true, Jacob."

Both took a drink and remained silent for a while, contemplating the direction of the conversation.

"Andrew, you need to spend some time with Sandy this weekend. Deep down, I believe she does want to accept the position. Her reluctance stems from exactly what we have been discussing."

"Let's see how tomorrow unfolds. But tonight we sit back and leave our business behind. Seldom do we have time to revel in the nonattendance of our duties."

***

Renée and Addison entered the stable. They talked about tomorrow's ride and Renée gave her guest her choice of horse.

"Renée, you have such a cool job being around these horses all day. It sure beats being in college."

"College must be fun. I regret not going. My life took a different path."

"It's not. I can't wait for it to be over. Everyone seems so immature. The guys act like little boys and the girls aren't much better."

"Well, Addison, you need to stick it out. It will be in the past before you know it and you'll probably wish you were still there."

"I don't think so. But when I do finish and start working, I hope my boss is as hot as yours. How can you keep your hands off him?"

Her comment came out of the blue. Renée wasn't sure how to respond, but she felt it was best to bring the tour to an end.

"Addison." Renée smiled at the teenager's bluntness. "I think we should call it a night."

Addison, who was already standing near, positioned herself to face Renée's side. She gently caressed the back of Renée's shoulder with one hand and brushed up against her with her knee while replying.

"I guess not all of us are into guys."

Startled, Renée immediately pulled back, thanking her lucky stars the Secret Service agent had positioned himself outside the stable entrance. She wasn't sure if Addison was referring to her or herself. She began to make her way to the opened door.

"Let's go, Addison. I think what you need is a cold shower and a good night's rest. We have a big day planned."

The young girl just grinned and followed Renée back to the ranch.

***

Morning arrived quickly. By eight, everyone had

eaten and now gathered at the stables, saddling up for a day on the trails. Ten horses were being prepared by the staff for David, Sandy, Renée, their three guests, and four Secret Service agents. Renée paired the animals the best she could based on the riding ability of each individual.

Jacob, Brooklyn, and Capella watched all the activity. There would be no work today. The grandparents were relishing the idea of babysitting and spoiling their grandchild, *check*.

Soon they were saddled and paraded out of the stable. Sandy led the way, followed by the two girls, with the President behind them. Renée and David took up the rear. The Secret Service would float in and out of the grouping, trying their best to stay low key. Food, drink, and first aid supplies were tucked away in a couple of packsacks.

"Well, there they go. We have this little one all to ourselves for the next few hours."

"That we do. Let's head back to the house, pack a bag, and take Capella down to the pond for a picnic."

***

For the first part of the ride, which took them through the trails, they rode at a slow pace in single file. The last twenty minutes, though, they galloped at a good speed through an open field.

It had now been a few hours of continuous riding so a break was in order, allowing everyone with the exception of Renée to walk off the numbness in their bums. She was on these animals so often, her behind was as tough as the saddle she sat on.

Everyone dismounted and began stretching their legs. They tied all the horses except one to the small trees bordering the grasslands. The lone free mare, named Beaches, was Sandy's. She'd been with her at birth and was the only person to ever ride her. The horse would not let her mistress out of sight. It was as protective as a dog to its keeper.

Mindful that the true reason for the President's visit was to procure a conversation relating to his offer, Sandy felt it would be best to address it. She approached her husband and spoke low so as not to be overheard.

"David, do you mind if I take the President up to Willow Meadows alone? Maybe you and Renée could take the girls down to the lake."

"Okay. What are you going to tell him?"

"David, this conversation is going to take place this weekend one way or the other, so I would prefer to get it over with now."

"Sandy, whatever you decide, we will make it work for us. I promise."

"Thank you."

"Renée, girls, let's head down to the lake," he called out. "I believe your father and Sandy would like a few minutes of private time."

The President appeared caught off guard by the invitation.

They climbed back on their rides and the two groups headed off in separate directions, throwing the Secret Service into a quick repositioning. Protocol dictated they split into two pairs.

***

David, Renée, and the girls found the lake. Renée assisted Layla off her ride and they were quickly at the shoreline, allowing their horses a drink. David did the same with Addison, except her dismounting was slower. She swung off the horse, balancing her hands on David's shoulders. Instead of vaulting to the ground, she locked her arms around his neck, pressing her front snuggly against his. Purposely, she slid her feet to the soil while rubbing against him. David felt every curve of her slender body. He was not prepared for the blandishment of the nineteen-year-old, which delayed his reaction of putting his hands on her waist, then gently lifting and placing her a couple of feet in front of him.

"Addison, you can't do that."

"I couldn't resist it. You didn't like it?"

"You're nineteen. I'm married and almost old enough to be your father."

"I'm going to be twenty in two months."

"That's enough. Let's get these horses some water before your Secret Service agent shoots me."

With the horses on the outside of them, they walked beside each other, leading the animals to the water. Just before they reached the other two, Addison gave David's butt a quick tap as one athlete would do to another. Again, he instinctively brushed it away, but due to the proximity to the others, he didn't say anything. He did throw her a cautionary look, which she returned with a leer. David didn't notice Renée had taken in the interactions from a distance.

The sisters removed their shoes and rolled up their jeans. They walked knee-high into the water with their horses. David and Renée stayed on shore.

"What are you doing, David? She's a kid," Renée whispered.

"I didn't do anything. She's all over me. Let's get the girls back to the ranch as soon as we can. I need you to stay between us."

"I don't think that will help much. She came on to me last night in the barn."

"Oh, boy. We have our hands full."

***

Sandy and the President perched on top of the cliff overlooking the grassland. A mesmerizing view even to those who had the pleasure of experiencing the most spectacular scenery the world offered. The magnificence commanded one to just breathe and sit in silence for a few minutes. They did so until the President initiated his pitch.

"Sandy, I would like for you to listen to my reasoning one final time."

"Sir, please go ahead."

"As you are aware, Christopher will be retiring on the planned date. He was tough as nails and did whatever it took to keep our people safe. We all owe him a great deal of gratitude. But, he was old school with a Cold War mentality. I have a number of capable individuals with stellar track records campaigning for this position. Obviously, I will soon name his successor.

27

"I would like that to be you. We have covered my reasoning in past conversations, but bear with me if I repeat some of the major points once again." He waited a second or two, allowing her the opportunity to respond.

"Our threats today come from many different mindsets. At the moment, the world's most significant challenge is terrorism, those who will strap a bomb around their waist and kill as many innocent people as possible, all in the name of some godforsaken belief.

"The person I need at the helm is one who can achieve success with brains, not brawn. We need to understand how these groups think, where they think, why they think this way. You've spent so much time in the Middle East and abroad, more than any other candidate. This, I believe, puts you in the unique position of identifying the telltale signs of this war, and believe me, they haven't labeled it the Third World War, but make no mistake, that is exactly what it is.

"But more importantly, my hope is your friendship with the leaders of these countries will pave the way for an unprecedented onset of cooperation. Today this collaboration is imperative to purge these extremists. You command an enormous amount of respect and trust with these regimes, more so than any other single person I know. Acquiring an alliance with your close friend, Fyad, will further our ability to stabilize this unrest. That in itself would be a great achievement, and Sandy, you have so much more to offer. I need you, and your country entreaties you to champion this cause."

He took a deep breath and stared at the lowland. Sandy remained silent. It was time for the President to bring his solicitation to an end. A moment of silence was in order as he prepared to encapsulate his plea in a sentence or two.

"Sandy, I understand you wish to focus your energies on providing Capella with a loving upbringing. This can still be accomplished if you accept. Your father is the busiest person I know, and after your mother's passing, God bless her, he singlehandedly raised you. And believe me when I say this, Sandy, you are an extraordinary human being. If my daughters realize even a fraction of your character, I will deem my parenting a success. When Capella grows into the amazing young lady I know she will be, she will understand and respect your choices. That's all I've got for you, Sandy. I will never speak of this again. It's in your hands."

"Okay."

The President assumed she needed time to absorb his explanation, so he leaned back, resting his arms behind him and staring into the glistening landscape once more.

"Well, we should get back," Sandy said.

He had been hoping for finality before the distraction of joining the others. More importantly, he was certain that once back at the ranch with Capella in her arms, his chat would become inconsequential.

"You're probably right." He pushed himself into a standing position.

As they untied his horse, he added, "I was

hoping for a resolution one way or the other before we met up with the others."

"Andrew, I said 'okay.'"

He was confused. He thought when saying okay, she was acknowledging his pledge of not mentioning it again.

"Okay, what?" His heart skipped a beat or two in puzzlement.

"Okay, I'll take the job."

Once the answer sank in, his actions were similar to a sports fan whose favorite team had won a championship in the last second of the game. With an ear to ear smile, he gave her a big hug. "Thank you."

"There will be some conditions. We will work out the details later this evening or in the morning. For now, this remains between the two of us. Promise?"

"I pinky swear on it."

They did, both breaking into an ebullient laugh.

If only the world could have witnessed the President of the United States solidifying the appointment of his new Director of the CIA on a pinky swear.

With the resolution of the matter at hand, the President suggested they sit back down for a bit so he could take in the splendor of the land with a clear mind. They spent the next hour or so discussing such subjects as family and their shared vision of peacefulness throughout the world.

***

Around the same time as history books were being etched with the inclusion of the first female CIA Directorship, Renée, David, and the girls were at the stables dusting off from the ride.

"Why don't you girls head back to the house and clean up for dinner? Renée and I will finish up here," David said.

They thanked their hosts for the day's activities, then went on their way.

"Wow, the President has his hands full with Addison," Renée said.

"I'll be glad when she's aboard Marine One on her way back to college. She's one dangerous young lady," he agreed.

While they were discussing the teen's carnal appetite, they were removing the saddles from the remaining two horses. David then directed the one he had a hold of into a stall. In the adjacent opening, Renée attempted to do the same with hers. As she tapped the animal on its backside, giving it a little encouragement to enter its resting place for the evening, it resisted and backed into her. The nudge caught her off guard, forcing her back into David, who put his arms out to assist.

There they stood, her back to David with his arms wrapped around her. It had been over a year since they'd touched like this. With one hand resting on her belly, and the other above, his thumb touched the bottom of her breast and David felt his heart pounding in his throat. All the suppressed feelings resurfaced for both of them. Neither made a move to unlock the hold. The horse settled nicely into the stall by himself.

"It's been a long time."

Without attempting to break free, she replied, "David, we can't do this."

He slowly lowered his head and gave her hair a gentle kiss, then inched his hand up and cupped the lower portion of her breast. She sighed and leaned back into him, succumbing to desire. Her bottom made contact with one of his legs and began to ever so slightly rub back and forth. He turned her to face him. Staring fixedly at one another, they recognized and interpreted what was transpiring. They could not deny the drawing power that cultivated in the past which was now re-emerging as they reached for each other, embraced, and closed in for a kiss. Renée pulled away.

"We can't do this. I can't do this. Please, David, let's stop. Please."

"I miss you this way, Renée. I will never get over how good you feel."

They knew a kiss would lead to a fervent lovemaking session. It may have felt right emotionally, but in reality it was the wrong place and the wrong time. Sandy would be arriving shortly and a few out of sight staff were still close by, so they pulled away and fought off their desire.

***

Once all were nestled in back at the ranch, dinner was served. The conversation centered on the day's ride. Brooklyn gave David and Sandy a recap of their day with Capella. It was an enjoyable time for all, a few hours of putting the country and business aside. Even the President's daughters showed no signs of social media withdrawals as they partook equally in the talks.

"Father," Addison said. "You know how you're always telling us we should strive to lead as normal a life as possible?"

Everyone went silent, allowing the father-daughter exchange to take place without interruption.

"That is true," the President said, then addressed the others. "As difficult as it is, I've advocated the girls pursue a typical lifestyle. What is it you're getting at, Addison?"

"You've been suggesting I find summer employment after I graduate this year, allowing time to decide what career opportunities are available to me. I was wondering if it would be possible to work here at the ranch. I love this land and the animals. Renée and David have been so kind. I think I could learn so much from them."

She then shifted her position so she could direct her next comment to Renée.

"Renée, I feel I could gain a great deal of knowledge being around you and the ranch. I realized today we have similar interests."

Renée seemed unable to produce a response. David nearly choked on the slice of cherry cheesecake he was enjoying. Sandy gave her father a quick glance, indicating the proposal was an interesting one.

"If Mr. McGinnis approves, would you let me, Father? This lifestyle might be good for me."

She was a smart girl to direct the onus to Jacob,

who had no idea of her earlier interactions with Renée and David.

"We can consider your idea, although there are ranches closer to home. I'll have my staff seek out some opportunities for you."

"Nonsense," Jacob said. "Andrew, we would love for your daughter to spend the summer. We are always in need of an extra ranch hand. I'm sure Renée can find some time to show her the ropes. What do you think, Renée?"

Renée was sitting to David's immediate left, close enough for him to kick her leg under the table.

"It's a tough job, Addison," David said. "Up early, late to bed, and the cell phone stays in your room when working."

Where would she stay? Under the same roof, of course. The cell phone rule could be enough to discourage her.

"Honestly, there is so much your ranch has to offer," Addison said. "I won't need my phone. I'll leave it at the White House."

"A healthy choice," Jacob commented. "Andrew, we would be honored to employ a young lady with such an appreciation for nature. She can reside in the room she presently occupies. Renée, I know you're busy, but I'm sure you can find the time to develop a program for Addison."

Renée did her best to try to justify what was being asked of her, though she wished she could get out of it. *Merde! Well, you pay me a million dollars, I'll figure something out.*

"Absolutely. We'd be happy to offer you a student apprenticeship this summer." This produced another under-the-table kick.

"Settled, then," Jacob confirmed.

"Thank you," the President said. "Addison, I don't believe I've seen you so passionate about something for a long time. If you promise to pull your weight and not get in anyone's way, I'll agree."

"Thank you, Father."

The day was nearing its end with most making their way to their respective accommodations. The President and Jacob repeated the previous night's sit down in the office.

***

Capella again fell asleep in her carrying seat during dinner. David and Sandy were successful in switching her to the crib without the baby waking. They both showered after the day's ride and it wasn't long before they lay beside each other on the bed.

"What did the President have to say?" David asked.

"He's not going to take no for an answer."

"You really don't want to say no, anyway."

The conversation went on until the wee hours of the morning. The pros and cons were discussed in detail but were irrelevant because the outcome had been determined months before—by those who don't take no for an answer. Sandy was truthful about wanting to decline until that moment at the meadows. Yet, everyone close knew deep down that her acceptance was inevitable.

"Can we survive this?" she wondered.

He had run through the scenarios many times. Should he move with her? Should he stay at the ranch? Could a nanny provide a stable environment for their daughter? How often would they see each other? The questions were endless.

"We can survive anything. Our daughter will be just fine. I knew you would eventually agree to the position, but you seemed so adamant about declining. What changed your mind?"

"It was the exact same reason I wanted to decline. Capella. I had full intentions of informing the President today that my final decision was an unequivocal *no*. That's why I wanted to be alone with him. It wasn't until we sat there looking out into Willow Meadow that my reasoning changed. I was listening, but not hearing the President's rationalization of why I should say yes, because all I could think about was our daughter. My only thought was, if I pass up on an opportunity to influence the safeguarding of this country and assist in the preservation of our freedom, to ensure our daughter can sit right here on this very hilltop without fear, I couldn't live with myself."

"I'm proud of you," he said with a reassuring tone.

"Thank you."

Sandy rolled to face him, then gave him a hug and kiss. She knew she was instantaneously thrusting the majority of the responsibility of Capella's upbringing on her husband, at least for the near future. She made herself a pledge to spend every one of the few spare hours she expected to have with them.

David was supportive of her decision. Not being privy to her covert accomplishments, he didn't fully grasp her qualifications but knew she would make a difference. The world would be a better place with his wife at the helm.

What was catching him off guard was part of his applaud had nothing to do with Sandy's attainment but rather a selfish one—Renée. After last night's encounter, as twisted as it seemed, his wife's return to frequent absenteeism fueled his desire to rekindle the affair with his employee.

He was genuinely proud of his wife's accomplishments and the entrustment the administration was offering her. However, the contradictory cognition of his newfound eagerness to once again pursue Renée was bothersome—very real, but bothersome.

The feeling was so pleasurable he had little desire to analyze it. He didn't want it to go away.

***

During breakfast the following day, the destination of the ride was mapped out. Sandy and the President would join up with the group after lunch. The morning was reserved for the airing of the conditions Sandy would be insisting on. The foundation of her reign was about to be laid out. Brooklyn would also remain at the ranch babysitting Capella. Jacob decided to spend the morning with his wife and grandchild, then enjoy the remainder of the day by joining the afternoon portion of the ride.

The President and Sandy walked to the stables to see the posse off and soon after, they were alone in Jacob's office. No Secret Service, no recordings, the door locked.

"Did David persuade you to change your mind?" the President inquired.

"On the contrary, he was very supportive. Over the years, David's become accustomed to my being away. I believe my omnipresence has cramped his style a bit."

"Sandy, this will work out. Your family will be fine."

"I know."

"So let's have it. What are these preconditions that come with your acceptance?"

Sandy stepped over to the bar, opened the refrigerator, and snatched up a bottle of water.

"Would you like a drink? I can put some coffee on."

The President took a quick glance around the room, subconsciously validating their isolation from all others. It was an old habit that had saved him from embarrassment on more than one occasion.

"What time is it?" he asked. "Oh, the hell with the time. Crack open a beer for me."

A smile came across Sandy's face as she set the water bottle back and took out two beers. "Prerequisite number one. Never let the President drink alone."

"You see, that in itself authenticates my choice in you."

Their disposition quickly shifted to a more

serious one.

"I will commit for the remainder of your term. It will be on the incoming Commander's shoulder to prove our agendas are similar. Second, I take direction from you and you alone. I will apprise each and every department according to protocol but I will not take orders from your Chief of Staff, Homeland, Secretary of State, or any other branch of the administration."

They simultaneously took a drink of their beverages. The President listened closely and wasn't prepared to interrupt.

"You've made reference to the benefits of my association with other leaders, in particular the Middle East," she continued. "I will be the sole proprietor of what intelligence will be shared. If you are serious about bringing the Agency into a new era, then we must begin to trust our allies. We will need to hand over information that at present would not be thought of. It is the only way this 'scratch my back' mentality will succeed."

"My staff is not going to be pleased."

"I don't need a cheering section. I'm not taking this job to make friends."

"Fine. I'll make it work your way."

He stood up and walked to the window, deep in thought. "Can you make the call?"

"Have I ever not been able to?"

"This is different. You're not in the field. You're in an office, directing an operative to bring an end to someone's life. I want this new way of thinking instituted, but there's going to be occasions when you sign off on someone not making it home."

"Safeguarding our country with a pacifism methodology will be my main focus. But on the other hand, any person who is a threat to our nation's security will be dealt with swiftly, void of repentance."

"I'm relieved I'm in your good books."

They both had a chuckle before Sandy spoke again.

"Andrew, seriously, how are you going to spin this? The world knows me as a philanthropist, the rich little girl from Kentucky."

"I have campaigned from day one to rid this administration of the old style of rule. The people believe in me and support me. When I appointed Madison to head up the FBI, I was faced with resistance from hardliners and now they're running off with their tails between their legs. The same scenario will repeat itself with you. You're educated, bright, connected, and fearless. You have access to statesmen that even I don't. I have quietly reached out to some of our allies and they are ecstatic about the possibility of this new wave of cooperation. Your appointment is a matter of going through the motions. We will face little opposition."

"What about experience? We know the extent of my involvement, but that can't be made public. That alone would deflate support from these leaders. They would not be too happy learning some of my visits had ulterior motives."

"Your covert existence will not come into play. Any and all files that connect you have been destroyed. The explanation of this offer will be based on your education, your exceptional leadership qualities. Nobody can argue your unique global positioning, which I believe is unparalleled. It will take time for some to rationalize my agenda, but they will come around. What we need to stress is our present day challenge not of the Cold War epoch, but rather the threat of terrorism. We can go it alone and I have no doubt we will triumph. Although with the collaboration of others, which you will introduce, the end result will be forthcoming in a more acceptable timeframe. With you as Director, this will be achieved."

"Okay, let's do this."

"Done. Now let's go for a ride."

The President stood and gulped down the rest of his brew.

"You know, I think I'm going to pass," Sandy said. "I'd like to spend the remainder of the morning with Capella. To be honest, my butt is a little tender from yesterday's outing. I suppose I have become a bit soft during the past year."

They both had a laugh, knowing Sandy's definition of slipping out of shape was equal to an Olympian a hundredth of a second slower than a world record.

"To tell you the truth," the President began, "I've had a hard time walking straight this morning. That being said, I can't remember the last time I've felt so relaxed and in touch with this great land we spend most of our lives nurturing."

With that, they said their goodbyes, one going to the stables in search of Jacob, the other remaining in the office, settling into the leather chair positioned behind the desk.

She pressed an icon on her cell, one of the few contacts set for speed dial.

"Fyad, we need to talk."

***

Back on the trail, the others dismounted for a break. David stuck with the younger of the two sisters. He left the lascivious Addison in the hands of Renée, and from what he was witnessing, he knew it was the right decision. Although being out of earshot, he noted an intense conversation taking place.

"Renée, you're sleeping with David, aren't you?"

"No, I'm not, and if I were, it is none of your business. Listen, I know things can be a little confusing at your age, but you really need to filter what comes out of that mouth. Focus on your own life, not others. Talking like that will only find you trouble. Being so young, you don't want to start burning bridges, especially around here. If you want to be treated like an adult, it's time to start acting like one. Just a word of advice, but do what you want with it."

"I'm just saying, and you can deny it all you want, but I see the way you two look at each other."

Renée wasn't expecting such frankness from the young lady. She knew this needed to be rectified immediately or the upcoming summer would be a fiasco.

"Listen up, Addison—"

"I know, I know, don't worry. I won't touch him.

Your secret is safe with me. You know I wouldn't want to be you if his wife was to find out."

"Addison, zip it! Here's how it's going down. You go back to college. Hook up with some guy or girl, whatever your preference, and get this coming of age stuff out of your system, so by the time you return this summer, you will want nothing to do with it. Once here, the only thing getting into those tight jeans of yours is your own fingers," Renée snapped. "I'm sure you've developed a skill for that by now. If I believe for even a moment that you've made an advance to *anyone* at this ranch, I will send you packing before you can speed dial Daddy. I really don't care whose daughter you are. Now grow up and start acting like the President's daughter, or for that matter, anyone's daughter. Understand?"

"Yes. You know, Renée, I believe this summer is shaping up to be a memorable one."

"Saddle up, guys, we should be going," David shouted. "We need to meet up with the others."

After mounting their horses, Layla leaned toward David and quietly spoke.

"Mr. Watson."

"Yes, Layla."

"Please forgive my sister's actions. She's going through a stage. Our parents taught us from the time we were very young to set a goal and pursue it full speed ahead. 'Never let anything stand in your way,' they would say. My sister has a hard time deciphering the true meaning behind their wisdom."

"Everything is good, Layla. Are you sure you're the younger sister?"

They both had a laugh.

Soon the group was on its way to the predetermined rendezvous location. The sisters were quick learners, so they rode at a brisk pace. Putting aside Addison's not so subtle advances, David was fostering an appreciation for her exceptional horsemanship. When it came to the animals, she seemed to retain and execute direction with ease—her personal life, maybe not so much. There were signs that she really cared for the horses. He began to consider she may end up becoming an asset to the ranch during her summer apprenticeship.

The party was soon joined by the President and Jacob. David was disappointed that Sandy opted out on the afternoon ride. Disappointed but not surprised.

"David and Renée, I would like to let the girls experience Willow Meadow. It's too beautiful to describe. Would you mind if we head up there?"

"Mr. President, we certainly can. A ride on this ranch would not be complete without that vision," David said.

With that, they made the trek to the eighth wonder of the world. David knew that no matter what the future held in store for the President's daughters, one thing was for sure: They would always have Willow Meadow etched into their minds.

***

Back at the ranch, Sandy and Fyad were nearing

their second hour of the telephone conversation, each voicing their opinions and concerns regarding Sandy's appointment. Although Fyad was not a fan of the United States, he was an aficionada of Sandy. Their ties were similar to those of twins. Their time together was so intense it shaped a unique bond, one that demanded the support of the other void of any ambiguity.

"Sandy, don't get this wrong, I think you and I can make great strides in reducing the aggression of these groups."

For the past half hour, she had been mostly listening to her best friend warn her of the dangers that she was about to dive into. Nothing he said was unfamiliar to her and he knew it. But it had to be told.

Sandy understood the inner mechanism of terrorism better than most politicians. She had been there. She had done that and more. But she listened, hanging on to every word he spoke, until she felt he was finished.

"You're not getting a little chauvinistic on me, are you?" she teased.

"I might be. My world is still a far cry away from yours."

"Fyad, we are going to change the face of the world, you and me. This is what we have dreamed about since we were kids. It's now all come to fruition. Let's get to work."

"Okay then. I'm all in. But we must move cautiously. We have already intercepted chatter signifying displeasure with the possibility of your appointment. Some are nervous the international relationships you have forged may be a formula for success. It will come as no surprise to you that the majority of these rumblings come from within your own country."

Both had a grasp of the economics of war. A country without a war to fight is a country experiencing a grave fiscal period. There must always be a battle to fight justifying military spending, or a security threat to rationalize a country's invasion of privacy on its citizens. Those who felt their profit may be jeopardized would go to great lengths to eliminate obstructions.

"Fyad, I'm aware of the ramifications of my acceptance. But believe me when I say that they have no idea what I am capable of."

"Sandy…" He hesitated, then took a deep breath before continuing. "These people will not come after you. They will come after those you love."

Chapter Three

Shimmering sunshine reflected off the man-made pond south of the ranch. Brooklyn sat at the edge with Capella safely snuggled on her lap. With one hand she supported her granddaughter and with the other she effortlessly skipped small stones into the still water. Capella laughed at every hop of the pebbles. They would stay put until the arrival of grandparent number two.

***

Jacob occupied the leather chair sitting behind his desk. The business of the day was gnawing away more of his time than he first anticipated. His priority was to join his wife and enjoy time with Capella while the child's mother and father were in Washington. But as the resolving of one situation led to another, time was fleeting. So he picked up the phone and dialed Brooklyn.

"Hi there, how are you two doing?"

"We're good. I presume you are still bunkered

down."

"Well, without my assistant, my sense of duty expands."

"Jacob, it's quite warm out, so I think we will head back soon. Maybe you can break for lunch."

"That's too bad. I really wanted to spend some time out there with you guys."

"We will be in soon."

A few minutes later, Jacob had his fill of business for the day and his body was stiffening, a reminder of the throbbing injuries attained by way of his college football days. In hindsight, knowing what he knew now, he would have eased off the roughhousing a bit in preparation of days to come. But he didn't, and now all the little aches and pains became a partner to his daily routine.

Standing up, he stretched out. In need of companionship, he headed to the kitchen expecting to join the others for a luncheon and an afternoon of pure joyfulness. His wife and grandchild had yet to arrive, so he took it upon himself to probe the immaculately systematized refrigerator and cupboards in search of ingredients to prepare lunch.

Soon, sandwiches and salad occupied the breakfast bar. There was still no sign of them and uneasiness pitted in his belly. He had never allowed his gut feelings to go unheard, and what they were saying at this moment was that something had gone wrong. Call it intuition, or clairvoyance, or ESP, or whatever else, but he *knew*.

Jacob left the kitchen with urgency in search of his loved ones.

Who Lies Beside Me

***

On the South Lawn of the White House, the grouping of accredited media huddled like school children anticipating the recess bell. All of them were jockeying for best camera angle or the ideal positioning to have their questions acknowledged. Most knew in brief what the news conference was pertaining to, yet it had been a closely guarded secret. Although the subject of the gathering was newsworthy, the reporters were provided with a list of the current topic subjects by their editors. Each outlet was seeking to expose the next scandal or secret that would propel them into a momentary superiority over their colleagues.

Gathered in the Oval Office was the President, his Press Secretary, Chief of Staff, outgoing CIA Director Christopher Young, Sandy, and David.

"The President will address the reporters first," the Press Secretary instructed. "He will speak for approximately ten minutes, thanking Director Young for his years of service. Then he will introduce you, Miss McGinnis-Watson. Mr. Watson, I would like you to stand next to me, behind your wife. Please smile, look enthusiastic, signifying your full support of her appointment."

Unlike Sandy and her father, David had never been privy to the inner workings of the administration. What took him by surprise was the orchestration going into every second of the production. They would like the public to believe the President speaks freely, from the heart, but in reality when he commandeers your television screen each syllable has been scripted.

It was time. The group was led to the South Lawn. With the Secret Service falling in place, the original grouping doubled in size. At the opening of the doors, the clicking of cameras pecked at their eardrums as the strobe light effect from the flashes put some seventies' discos to shame.

"Ladies and gentlemen, the President of the United States." The Press Secretary, Sophia Foster, made the introduction.

The Commander in Chief stepped up to the podium amidst an array of arms trying to outreach the competitors in anticipation of being selected to put forth that singular question that would become the trending hashtag of the day. But today there would be no queries.

"Thank you all for attending. This is a special day," he began while holding up both hands, fending off any questions.

"I made a promise to the American people that I would institute a new age philosophy into this historic building that sits behind us, and I have strived to do so. This transformation has been ongoing and I would like to believe that my successors will see the benefits arrived from the abolishment of our old school mentality. Today will go down in the history books as another pivotal moment in that quest." He paused for a moment and everyone remained hushed.

He motioned to the outgoing CIA director to join him.

"I would like to take this moment to express our sincere gratitude to Director Christopher Young for his irrefutable devotion and loyalty. After a great deal of soul searching, it is with a heavy heart that I announce that I have accepted the director's retirement plans. Mr. Young has so passionately put the well-being of all of us at the forefront of every breath he has taken."

He turned and offered a handshake. "Sir, it has been my honor to have stood by your side for all these years. We all owe you a debt of gratitude. The world is in a much healthier position thanks to your dedication."

The director smiled and nodded in acceptance but offered no words. This wasn't in the script. He then dropped into the background, clearing the way for the official presentation of his somewhat surprising replacement. There had been some rumblings as to whom would head up the most powerful intelligence agency in the world, but for the most part it was going to be a shock.

On cue, Sandy nestled her way to the side of the President, who was acknowledging her with a beaming smile. It was another piece of the puzzle, another spoke in the wheel, each part being strategically placed, etching out the legacy of his years in office.

"Most of you are familiar with Mrs. Watson and the peerless philanthropist undertakings which she has championed."

Under his leadership, the administration had made great strides implementing equality for all regardless of race, gender, and religion. The most competent applicant was awarded assignments. But he was a touch traditional about acknowledging

Sandy's maiden name hyphened to her husband's.

"What you might not be aware of is the incomparable alliance Sandy Watson has shaped with many governments we regard as our unyielding allies. She has fostered relations—"

A Secret Service agent suddenly whispered in the President's ear, stopping him mid-sentence. When the information sank in, he locked eyes with Sandy, at which point everyone in the party knew a matter of significance had materialized.

Ms. Foster replaced him at the podium. "A matter which requires the President's immediate attention has emerged. That will be all for today. We will advise you as to when and where this press conference will continue. Thank you."

The grouping walked hurriedly toward the Oval Office, ignoring a flurry of questions being shouted: "Is Sandy Watson the next CIA director?"

"Can you explain her qualifications?"

"What is the reason for cutting this conference short?"

"Does this have anything to do with our country's present military actions?"

Ignoring the reporters, they reached the office and the Chief of Staff entered, followed by the President, Christopher Young, and Sandy. As Ms. Foster and David started to enter, a Secret Service agent blocked them and the door closed, leaving them to ponder the urgency of those inside.

***

Prior to Jacob placing the emergency call to

Director Taylor, who in turn contacted the White House, he gathered all available staff at the barn. Brooklyn and Capella were nowhere to be found. He and his residence staff had searched every nook and cranny of the sprawling ranch house with no sign of his wife and grandchild. So now, with all available personnel, the search expanded to the grounds of the estate.

With a calming demeanor, he coordinated a methodic grid search of every square inch. But what churned inside was a completely different emotion. His stomach knotted. What if—? Considering the situation gave way to the possibility that harm may have come upon his family. It broke his heart. He would find them. There must be a reasonable explanation for their absence.

Twelve men and women were divided up into four groups of three, each with a specific chunk of land to search. The thirteenth member of the group happened to be an avid scuba diver. He retrieved a wet suit and snorkeling gear from his vehicle. There was little chance they had fallen into the pond, but it was deep enough to swallow up a body. No stone would be left unturned until some sense was made of this mystery. One of the employees returned from the stable with six two-way radios she had fetched from the office. With the channels set at the same frequency, they were instructed to report anything out of the ordinary, no matter how minute the discovery may seem.

***

Word of the situation at the ranch spread quickly to the team caring for the horses at the racetrack, including Renée. She instantaneously made the decision to designate one of the grooms to tend to the thoroughbreds and then instructed the others to immediately join the search at the ranch. They would be there within the hour. An employee of Jacob's became part of a family, a job for life if you took pride in your work, had a passion for the horses, and cared for your co-workers.

Renée and the team arrived just as the crew was reevaluating the grid search. All the buildings had been checked over and over again. The only occupants of the pond were the fish it had been stocked with. There was no sign of Brooklyn and her granddaughter.

Jacob appeared relieved at the arrival of his lead trainer. After a quick private word with her, it was decided she would take some of the staff with her and ride the nearby trails. Jacob would lead the others into the wooded area to the west of the main house. The investigation continued with an increased urgency, all knowing the longer it took to locate them, chances they'd just wandered off dwindled away. The day was nearing its twilight and Jacob was distraught at the idea of his loved ones being lost in the darkness.

Once Renée was saddled up, she decided to ride up to Willow Meadow. Although it was far too great of a hike to make on foot with the baby, she decided to have a look since it was one of the family's favorite destinations. The remainder of the group would be concentrating closer to the main ranch, areas within reasonable walking distance. She rode fast, not wanting to fritter away any precious time.

Emerging from the arching tree domed trail, Renée's breath was taken away by the sight of the majestic scenery. David had described the tranquilizing hideaway, but she had never been presented the opportunity to visit until this weekend. She thought it was in part because this was David and Sandy's special place. As strange as it was, she probably read more into it than she should've, but it felt meddlesome stepping into their sanctuary.

It didn't take long to snap out of her trance, given the severity of the present moment. She scanned the area repeatedly with no sign of Brooklyn or the child. Renée walked to the edge of the overhang, and looked down at the gently sloping grasslands, but no individuals could be seen. Realizing this was not the area accommodating the missing pair, she jumped onto her horse to assist the others.

The instant she gave her ride a slight tug with the right rein to turn him toward the path, a glittering caught her peripheral vision. She pulled back on the horse, stopping him, and dismounted. The reflection was similar to someone sending an SOS with a mirror. The brightness of the sun made it difficult to decipher what was causing the glistening. It was coming from what looked to be a pile of grass or twigs. As she got closer, the realization of what she had discovered weakened her legs and chilled her head to toe. There in front of her sat Capella's baby bag with a smiling teddy bear stitched on it. Peeking out of the infant's satchel was a yellow rattle mirror, which had caused the flickering.

Renée was so taken aback that it took a moment to focus on what was partly wedged under the bag. It looked so out of place. She struggled, uncertain whether she should touch anything. Once the initial surprise began to wear off, she noticed something written on the front of an envelope. It read: *Jacob*.

Renée dropped back on her butt and yelled "*Merde!*" in her mother tongue. It echoed throughout the valley. She took out her two-way, and instead of pressing the activation button, she stared at it. How was she going to put her unearthing into words? "Jacob, this is Renée, please come in." She let go of the button, giving way to a split second of static. "Jacob, please come in." She repeated the process.

"Renée, this is Jacob. Have you found something?"

"Jacob, can you get here to Willow Meadow? *Tout de suite*."

Although she was now very comfortable with the English language, her thoughts were in French, and under pressure some words just wouldn't translate correctly.

"Renée, please tell me what you have found."

She explained exactly what she was looking at. There was a short period of silence after she was finished before the hissing of the two-way resonated back to her.

"Read the letter to me."

"But Jacob—"

"Now!"

Renée eased the letter from underneath the bag, careful not to make contact with the other items. To her relief, the envelope was not sealed, so slipping the paper out required no tearing.

"Renée, now, please." Jacob was uncharacteristically impatient.

"Dear Jacob, I can no longer stand by and witness your daughter throw her life away by accepting the Directorship of the CIA. I will return Capella to the ranch once your daughter has publicly declined the position. Should she choose her career over her family, I will have no alternative but to provide Capella with the love and nurturing she so deserves. I am sorry for this, but I see no other way. Loving you dearly, Brooke."

Renée listened to Jacob's instructions carefully. "Do not move from your location. Do not take your eye off the bag. If for one second you feel there is anyone else near you, radio me immediately. I'm on my way."

"Yes, sir."

That's when he made the call.

***

The head of the Secret Service was being brought up to date through the tiny headset in his right ear. The four remained in silence as two other Secret Service personnel stood guard at the door. The gravity of a matter important enough to disrupt a press conference was one of grave concern to all. The agent standing in the center of the room was receiving some sort of instruction. He would brief them in detail once finished.

He oddly turned to address Sandy instead of the President.

"Mrs. McGinnis-Watson, we have a situation at your estate. We have just been informed that your stepmother and daughter cannot be located at the present moment."

"What exactly are you saying?" Sandy cut him off.

"From what we understand, they were outside this morning and failed to rendezvous with your father. He and your ranch hands have been searching for them the better part of the day."

"There must be a simple explanation." Sandy was not one to panic.

"Ma'am, one of your staff members located your daughter's baby bag, which had been placed at Willow Meadow."

"What else do we know?" She was analyzing the situation void of emotion the best she could.

"There was a note."

The agent went on to explain the details known to him.

"What actions are in place?" the President asked.

"Prior to us learning of the situation, the Director of the FBI was notified by Mr. McGinnis. She has an elite SWAT squad and a specialized rescue group headed there as we speak. All air traffic in the state has been grounded. A no fly zone is in effect. My understanding is she asked the military to provide air support to enforce it. I have Marine One manned and ready to transport Mrs. and Mr. Watson to the ranch."

All eyes were on the Special Agent during the briefing, so no one noticed Sandy as she eased herself next to the outgoing Director. In a split second, she had Christopher pushed up against the wall with her right middle finger pressed into the highest point of his jawline, just below the ear. The harsh pressure caused him excruciating pain, limiting his speaking to a low gurgle. With one quick move she could have easily dislocated his jaw. The two Secret Service Agents guarding the door jumped to the aid of Mr. Young, only to be waved off by the President.

Sandy addressed the man she had in her grasp. "If you had anything to do with this, I will bury you with my own hands."

Then she let go, walked over to one of the couches, and plopped herself onto it.

Christopher cleared his throat. "Sandy, you have my word that I was not involved in this. Actually, I have been warming up to the idea of retirement. I would never put Capella in harm's way."

"You expect me to believe that after almost killing me in an attempt to abort my child?"

"Sandy, you would have done the exact same thing, and you know it."

The Director moved toward the President. "Enough of this. We need to put all our energies into the recovery of Sandy's family members. If nothing more is required of me today, I would like to return to Langley and see what we can learn."

He got his nod of approval and left the room. At that point, the President invited in his Press Secretary and David. Sandy regained her composure and took it upon herself to explain everything to him in a reassuring manner, which didn't help. He flipped out and demanded they return to the ranch immediately. Being told his daughter's wellbeing was in jeopardy caused him to nearly throw up on the Presidential Seal. Nothing could prepare a parent for the shock of learning their child was in danger.

"Sandy, I believe David is correct. Marine One will return you to the ranch. That is where you belong right now. I'm certain we will resolve this promptly. Everything else can be put aside until then. Now please go. The media has been removed from the grounds."

He ordered the Secret Service to escort the couple to the South Lawn, and with that they were on their way. That left three people in the office. He directed the next set of instructions to Ms. Foster, his press secretary.

"Sophia, I want this contained. No one, and I mean no one, gets wind of it. Inform the FBI and CIA. Make damn sure they understand you are in charge and their response will be no comment, unless you authorize it."

"Absolutely. Yes, sir."

"Now, would you be kind enough to give me and Mr. White a few minutes?" he asked, speaking of his Chief of Staff.

Alone with his number one, he let his guard down.

"Joshua, do think Christopher is behind this?"

"Not a chance. He has nothing to gain in this particular situation."

"I hope you're right."

***

Jacob traded in the saddle for a four-wheel quad. He asked the others to keep looking for clues before he took to the trail, leaving a cloud of dust in his wake. Within a half hour of his being advised of Renée's discovery, he was standing next to her, positioned in front of his granddaughter's belongings, neither knowing exactly what to do.

Go through the bag, or leave it alone until the authorities arrived? So many stirring emotions clouded their customary good judgment.

They decided to leave the bag sit there undisturbed and began combing the area looking for other clues. Their unavailing efforts went on until the yelping of helicopters momentarily seized their attention. With their arrival came hope in anticipation that the teams were the very best, that they knew exactly how to coordinate this effort and bring his family back together. Jacob had organized the search the best he knew how, but it took all the restraint he could amass within to not break down.

"Renée," he called out. "We're spinning our wheels here. We can expect the search and rescue team shortly."

He asked her for the two-way and radioed the ranch, giving them instructions to guide the agents to Willow Meadow. To his surprise, they were already on their way, being led by two of the ranch's senior hands. Whether from exhaustion, shock, disbelief, or just the realization that he wasn't adept at guiding this devastating ordeal, he sat, or rather dropped to the ground. Viewing the countryside through the haziness of teardrops didn't carry its usual solace, but rather an antipathy for those responsible. Renée eased to his side in an attempt to console him.

Without turning to her, in an eerie wraithlike tenor, he said, "Whoever is responsible for taking my family will pay dearly."

"But Jacob, what about the note?"

"She's not responsible for this. During our trip to Europe last year, we thought it best to have a code recognisable by us but one that an outsider would consider of the norm."

He wiped the tears from his cheek with the cuff of his denim shirt. "She is so smart. She will find a way to give us hints as where to find them. I originally thought the whole idea was silly, but she insisted. Her justification was that with our stature in the business world, it made us targets for a handsome ransom by the likes of radically inclined groups. The thing is, I never thought it might be the clue that saves us here on our own ranch."

He finally turned to lock eyes with her. "Renée, our code was to sign off, whether in writing or verbally, by saying, 'Loving you dearly, Brooke.' They've been abducted."

Renée was momentarily relieved that Brooklyn did not lose her mind and make off with the child. But it only took a minute to realize the severity of what Jacob was saying. They had been kidnapped and Brooklyn had been forced to write the note. Their lives were certainly in jeopardy.

It wasn't long before they were surrounded by a squadron of men fitted in full battle fatigues. Orders were barked, helicopters flew over top, and two F-16 Fighter jets kept making a pass.

If he wasn't before, he was now confident that they would locate his family in short order. How could they not with the wrath of the most powerful military in the world at his service?

Chapter Four

Behind his flamboyant gold trimmed desk—a world away from the issues his best friend Sandy was encountering—sat Fyad, engulfed in the management of his country's security. His task was far from unproblematic, as the country his family ruled for many years was situated in the center of so much conflict. The players in the region changed on a daily basis. Being the largest member of the Arab League, and the largest oil exporter, bequeathed upon them a reasonable assurance that little aggression would be directed at them.

But keeping up-to-date absorbed the majority of Fyad's time, so if one was to disturb him they had better have a justifiable reason, as did the man who had just entered.

"Your Highness, you need to look at this."

"Can it wait? As you can see, I'm busy.

"To be honest, you need to review it now. It's related to our friend, Sandy."

That was the last name Fyad expected to be brought to his attention with urgency. Terrorists, kings of other kingdoms, Middle East coups, but not Sandy.

The messenger backed off but remained inside the office in preparation of forthcoming orders. He was correct in doing so. After Fyad read the short briefing, he spoke with the authoritarian manner royalty possessed.

"I want every—and I mean *every*—person within the walls of the compound on this. Updates will be emailed to me each quarter of the hour. You will oversee this. Hamza, this is family."

All communication waves bouncing off the twenty-five hundred satellites orbiting earth were being monitored in the control room. Certain words, voice recognition, sentence structure, and so on were programmed into FS11, allowing it to spit out a massive amount of suggested threats.

The supercomputer was housed in its own building on the grounds of the estate. Its power was only surpassed the by Tianhe-2, a supercomputer at China's National University of Defense and Titan A Cray XK7 system at the U.S. Department of the Oak Ridge National Observatory in Oak Ridge, Tennessee. Oil revenues afforded Fyad and his father, the King, the luxury of surrounding themselves with the best technology the world had to offer and the finest personnel to operate it.

Fyad was outraged at the thought of Sandy's daughter being forcefully separated from her mother. He knew the government of the United States would be going above and beyond, deploying their resources in search of Brooklyn and the child. Sandy had become an integral part of the U.S.

intelligence agency, but sometimes they didn't quite grasp the convoluted workings of his side of the world and it was possible the abductors were associated with the Middle East.

During the last few weeks, his network had intercepted what they believed to be references of displeasure pertaining to her rumored appointment from various groupings in the region. This type of chatter was ongoing daily, and it was the burden of the intelligence world to decipher between discontentment and a bona fide threat. So far, it was determined most were only voicing an opinion. He couldn't settle in to the other tasks at hand, so he made his way to the control room.

Upon entry, he questioned the senior analyst. "Have we had a hit as of yet?"

"No, sir, quite the opposite. The appointment of the incoming director has logged substantial dialogue over the past week, but for the past two days there has been little mention. Sir, if someone even thinks of her or the ongoing circumstances, we will hear them. I assure you."

"Thank you."

Fyad stood for a short while, taking in all before him. He prided himself on having a solid understanding of the workings of this electronic brain. The people occupying the room were recruited from MIT, Stanford, Harvard, Cambridge, Oxford, and other universities world renowned for their technology curriculum. These men and women were some of the brightest minds, making four times what Silicon Valley had to offer. Money was no object to Fyad and his father. The employees spent every waking moment absorbed in analyzing information.

Once he snapped out of his trance, Fyad decided he could be of no service and returned to his office.

***

"Madison, please listen carefully." Jacob had the FBI Director on the line. "Your agents are not warming to my informing them the letter confirms we are dealing with a kidnapping by some unknown persons. We cannot let this ill-conceived notion that Brooklyn may have meant what she wrote divide our resources. Am I making myself clear?"

"Jacob, you are one of the most successful entrepreneurs in the world, but I am the most competent law enforcement officer you will ever know. We will find them. Please let me do my job. Our time would be best spent doing what is required of us rather than arguing. Please cooperate with my personnel and we will have your wife and grandchild back in no time."

"You'd better know what you're doing, Madison."

"I will be in touch frequently, Jacob."

The call ended without niceties.

He sat at his desk in silence, considering initiating his own investigation when the sound of Marine One came into range. Jacob made a beeline for the front door. It was comforting knowing Sandy was home. She understood this corrupt world and would be kept abreast of the FBI and CIA's developments. Seldom in his lifetime did he feel relieved turning over control, but in this case he knew his daughter was equipped to lead this charge even if she was the mother.

Sandy ran up to her father and gave him a hug. David followed at a slower pace and was greeted to a gentleman's embrace.

"Daddy, we have the very best people from every agency searching. We will find them and they will be okay. I assure you whoever is behind this will not harm them. The evidence presenting itself thus far indicates this was a professionally orchestrated abduction. Someone or some group is attempting to intimidate me. But I promise you that whoever is behind this does not want the wrath of my agency at their heels for the remainder of their existence, which will be a reality if they are not returned safe and sound. I've been receiving real-time updates of all FBI communications. We have activated every available operative to explore their resources. Daddy, believe me, we will find them soon."

"How the hell can you just stand there and act like this is just another assignment or whatever you call what you do? This is our child we're talking about. I can't stand here and listen to you. I need to go do something."

"David," Jacob called out.

"Let him go. He needs to deal with this in his own way. He'll be fine."

"Actually, Sandy, I can relate to what he's saying. It's alarming how composed you are. This is your daughter and my wife we're talking about and it terrifies me. What if…" He stopped, not able to talk about the possibility of a hostile outcome.

Sandy had been schooled most of her life in preparation of managing calamities. This was when she was most composed, bordering on a state of tranquility, void of all emotion. Her train of thought was zeroed on resolution, nothing less, nothing more. She understood David and her father had not been exposed to this side of her, except for the incident she regretted her husband had to witness last year. The heartlessness she portrayed was difficult for someone on the outside to comprehend. But at the moment, that was the least of her concerns.

One hundred percent of her focus was on the safe return of Brooklyn and Capella. And she would be successful. There was no other outcome.

***

David saddled his horse and headed out in the direction of Willow Meadows. He knew the acreage better than any of the law enforcement team on site. Soon after he left Sandy, she contacted the agent in charge to request he be given full access to all areas without interference. Although this was an official FBI investigation, her stature assured any request from her would be met without resistance.

The evening's full moon guided David's solo search well into the wee hours of the morning.

***

Hamza entered Fyad's office without knocking, passing on the formalities. "Fyad, I believe we may have something. You should have a look."

After reviewing the document, Fyad looked slightly perplexed. "I'm not making the connection. Would you be kind enough to expand?"

"I happened upon this in an unrelated interest, but something struck me as abnormal. I believe we have intercepted a pattern that lends itself to a few years ago with the Brit's introduction to new leadership of The Circus."

"I don't know how that fits into the quandary at hand," Fyad said, looking down at the document.

"If I may, sir." Hamza stepped behind the desk. "As you know, leading up to these leadership and senior appointments, we see an abnormal shift in investment and trade earmarked for the allies of the subject country. Maybe to smooth the waters, show their support, to reflect suspicion from them until they can establish an influence with the incoming. In this case, we are seeing the opposite. There seems to be a dramatic injection into the hands of America's adversaries. What this indicates is these influential groupings believe Mrs. Watson is going to have a real impact. They're not trying to cuddle up, they're running scared. An acceleration of this kind makes me believe they are hastily moving much more than the norm with the intention to lie dormant during her tenure. Once the President's term comes to its end, word is most are expecting Sandy to step down as well."

"I understand this, Hamza, but I am not connecting the abduction."

Fyad's man pointed at something on the page. "As you know, during times such as this, we pay close attention to the movement of those we suspect being participants of this kind of activity. A private aircraft, one belonging to a person of interest, landed in Cuba earlier today. First report has a subject cleared via a shoe, a woman, and I'm certain once our ghoul completes his search we will learn the others are traveling with false documentation. We have an unconfirmed report that one of the passengers was a child."

Hamza was suggesting the group used forged documents to gain entry to Cuba. The identity of one was already confirmed to be that of a person who had long ago passed away. An agent referred to as a ghoul, specialized in cross referencing obituaries and graveyards for names of the deceased, which were then often used as identities for undercover agents.

"It is unlikely the States would have picked up on this just yet. Our asset happened to be in the right place at the right time. It appears all were U.S. citizens."

"Assemble the team and prepare the aircraft. I want to be airborne within the hour."

"Yes, sir. One more thing. It may be difficult to accept as imaginable, but combined with our latest elint we may have to consider this is being micromanaged by the Bonanza Club. There are many similarities to their past involvements."

Fyad's gaze pierced through his agent as he reiterated with greater urgency, "One hour. Have the crew file a flight plan to Cuba. That will be all."

Now alone, he was tempted to call Sandy but curbed the urge, as he wasn't yet prepared to discuss his suspicions. He would leave that until being airborne. That would allow extra time to obtain and confirm the influx of data coming his way. It was going to be an interminable flight, leaving a great deal of time to connect with her.

There was little preparation required as the plane was stocked with duplicates of all required equipment, clothing, weaponry, and supplies. So instead of making the call, he reached out to locate his father, the King. Soon he was sitting with him in the elegance of the library. He was brought up to date, and Fyad asked if he could find time to oversee his other palace responsibilities during his absence.

"Fyad, I would like to contact Jacob to pledge our support and resources."

"Of course, Father, but I think it best not to mention my excursion. I would like to remain under the radar until we can establish confirmation of our suspicions."

"I understand. The man must be devastated."

"I am sure it is a trying time for their family."

"Fyad…" He stopped him before he departed. "Should you resolve this before the others, please promise the ones responsible for violating our good friend's family are incapable of repeating their atrocity."

"You have my word, Father."

***

Sitting up on the bed with her back leaning against the concrete wall of the dorm room, Addison was focused on the screen of a decal-clad Mac propped up on her lap, preparing for an upcoming exam. It was her second to last, and once she aced the finals, the plan was to waste no time finding her way back to the ranch. Since that weekend's visit, every single evening at the onset of slumber land, she reflected on the short stay. She had read about the serenity being around horses could offer but never experienced it, until now. She was hooked.

Her iPhone chimed, nudging her from daydreaming back to the present. A quick glance indicated it was a text from her sister, Layla. She placed the cell back on the night stand. The message would have to wait, as she needed to get back to studying. There had already been too much lost time. Besides, most of her sister's communications were words of wisdom, which for the most part made complete sense. Layla had the uncanny ability to be the voice of reason. Sixteen going on twenty-five was how her father characterized it. On more than one occasion, the President hinted it would be wise for the elder sister to take a lesson or two from the younger. And he was correct, but at the moment, Addison needed to study.

The smartphone repeated the chime. Once again, her sister was showing persistence. This text showed only a bold question mark. Addison considered this short form of communicating rude, so Layla could wait until tomorrow. Before she could refocus, the ringtone played the course of an

Ellie Goulding song. Frustrated, she answered.

"What do you want, Layla? I'm studying."

"Did you not look at my text?"

"No."

"You need to see this."

"Why, Layla? I'm really tied down here."

"Don't say I didn't try to fill you in on what's happening." With that, she hung up.

Now she had no choice but to open the text. It took a couple of seconds to focus in on the image the tiny screen was displaying. Her sister sent her a screen shot of a news story that was trending. The picture was of a yellow taped police barricade cordoning off a country road. The photograph concentrated on the heavy presence of reporters.

The picture had a caption imposed on it:

FBI swarms billionaire Jacob McGinnis's ranch.

She tossed the cell on the bed and began a search on her computer. It didn't take long. All the major news outlets were reporting from the scene, each with relatively the same story.

FBI is tight-lipped about the present situation at billionaire Jacob McGinnis's ranch, the home of what is believed to be our next director of the CIA. No one on this side of the barricade has been provided with any information other than, "no comment." But the vast presence of what seems to be FBI swat teams, military helicopters, and the sighting of fighter jets indicates we are dealing with a serious matter.

"Oh my God," she blurted out.

As her heart rate rapidly increased, she rummaged around the covers for the discarded phone. Once she cuddled the device in her trembling hand, she could barely touch the number two on the speed dial. Nobody was assigned to the number one; it was reserved for someone she had not met as of yet. The designation of the digit two was reserved for her father. He answered after the second ring. He always answered. The world could be on the brink of disaster, and if one of his girls called, he would be the voice on the other end.

"Addison, it's nice to hear from you. I was under the impression you would be bogged down in your books. When you run for President, your grades will become a topic of discussion."

"Father, what is happening at the McGinnis ranch?"

He would never belittle a question from her and reply that it was nothing to be concerned about, but there was a limit to the security clearance of a family member.

"My dear, we do have a situation at the ranch. We are doing everything in our power to resolve it quickly."

"What exactly is the situation?"

"Addison, this is one of these circumstances that I can't discuss with you, at least not right now."

"Father, I suggest you disband with protocol and enlighten me as to what is going on or I will blow off my finals and drive to Kentucky right now. I hope your Secret Service is proficient in fixing speeding tickets."

Her urgency merited a straightforward reply.

"Addison, give me five minutes to deal with something here and I will call you back, I promise."

"I will be at the gas station in twenty filling my tank if you don't call back." She paused, adding, "Father, I love you."

She knew whenever she told him she loved him, he was reduced from the most powerful man in the world to a softhearted gentle giant.

After a few minutes, he called her back. Addison answered without saying hello. "Father, I want to know what's happening."

"Of course, and I think you should. But first, Addison, this is a very sensitive situation we are dealing with, so I need your promise that what I am about to tell you is not repeated. We are trying to keep a tight lid on this and any leak, even in its smallest form, could put lives in danger. Before I continue, please remember it is how we handle ourselves in times like this that help define us."

"Mr. President, I understand you're required to caution me on the consequences of my exposing sensitive information, but hey, I'm your daughter, and you schooled me well. Now please explain what is going on at the ranch. I am so worried."

Addison addressed her father as Mr. President whenever she was trying to drive home a point and wasn't in the mood for political jargon.

"I will get to that after I have your promise you won't, as you might say, blow off your exams. I need your word. There is nothing you can do at the ranch."

"Okay, I promise."

"All right. We believe Mrs. McGinnis and Capella may have been abducted. We are not a hundred percent certain at this time, but there is a good chance. We have the best recovery teams in place at the ranch and are confident they will be located soon."

Addison remained silent as her eyes became glassy. She was by herself. Her roommate had completed her finals and was on her way home to spend the summer with family. Addison had four days remaining until she was to return to the White House. A couple of weeks with Mom and Dad, and then it would be time to relocate to the country. She was a bright person and knew what this meant with regards to her summer plans. The droplets paving a glistening pathway down her cheeks weren't brought on by the possibility of altering her summer agenda. She just couldn't fathom the thought of that beautiful child, Capella, being in jeopardy.

"Dad, I want to come home."

"Addison, I thought we had a deal."

Now the crying was perceptible. Her father would be able to hear the loneliness, a true distress being transmitted.

"Addison, please listen to me. The best thing for those of us who so dearly care for our friends is to be strong. Let the men and women who train every single day do what they do best. We should pray for their safe return, but we have to find a way to continue with our responsibilities. You take your tests, then come home. I will call you with updates daily. Are we okay?"

"Daddy, I want to come home now. This scares

me."

"I have an idea. What if I speak to your mother and see if she will allow Layla to miss a few days of school? If she agrees, your sister could come up and bunk with you until your exams are over. After all, she will be attending there in the fall, so it wouldn't hurt for her to have a look around. If I get the okay, I will make arrangements for her to leave in the morning."

Addison knew she had to stay and finish school, but she was letting her emotions get the best of her. Having her sister visit was a nice idea. Her father always held that magical remedy.

"I would like that. I'm going to give Layla a call," she said. "You promise to keep me updated? The McGinnises are the kindest family I have ever met."

"I will take care of everything and be in touch often. Now please get back to studying."

"Thank you, Father. I love you."

***

Nightfall had vacuumed the light offered by the daytime. David was still frantically combing every inch of the property one person could possibly cover alone. The darkness did not hamper his efforts as he could pretty well guide himself throughout the estate blindfolded. There was nothing, absolutely nothing he wouldn't do to make sure their child was safe and sound.

He checked in with Sandy a few times but he must not have listened to the last message she sent.

It informed him the FBI made a discovery, and now Sandy, Jacob, and Renée, along with a number of agents, were gathered in the office for a briefing.

***

Sandy instructed the staff members—who out of concern for the family wouldn't have left until the situation was resolved—to search for her husband.

It was well into the early morning, so the law enforcement agency's discovery could not wait for his arrival to be explained. There was little time to spare for the necessity of a briefing; time was better spent resolving. They had been missing for more than fourteen hours.

"We are now fairly certain the kidnapping theory is actually what has transpired here," FBI Special Agent Miller began. "Our dogs led us to an area approximately four miles south of the ranch. At first we were a bit torn as to what direction they were heading. We believe your family's belongings were purposely dragged in various directions, such as to Willow Meadow, to confuse the search by scent. It took a couple of minutes, but our animals are good and couldn't be fooled.

"At this point, we believe they were transported by helicopter. This is good news, as we are reviewing all aircraft movement for the past week. We expect an update shortly. If they were airborne, we will pinpoint the destination.

"Mr. McGinnis, did you see or hear a helicopter during the time your wife was outside?"

"No, I was here in the office. However, if I had, I

wouldn't have paid much attention to it since a number of our neighbors have been air surveying their properties this past year. It is not an uncommon practice in this part lately."

"Our canvassing of your neighbors confirms this. It has been a month or two since any of them have contracted this kind of work, yet a black helicopter was spotted in close proximity about the same time your family went missing," Agent Miller continued.

"The silver lining is we have not received a ransom call. Sandy, your thought about this being utilized as a scare tactic because of your upcoming placement is faring well. If this is the case, your family members are most likely being treated well and will be returned unharmed after a short period of time. This abduction has the markings of someone demonstrating their far-reaching influence as a warning to you to play ball. They're not amateurs, but it is unlikely whoever is orchestrating the kidnapping wants to be on the receiving end of a joint FBI-CIA military hunt.

"We expect to nail down the air traffic shortly. Our recovery teams are strategically placed and ready to deploy at a moment's notice. They are highly equipped to deal with any situation that presents itself. That's all I have at this time. But please rest assured we are not going anywhere until your wife…" He made eye contact with Jacob. "And your daughter," he said, looking at Sandy, "are home." He concluded his clinically toned briefing.

It was late and with the meeting over, most in attendance silently contemplated their next step.

Sleep was not on anyone's agenda. The thought of it wouldn't be entertained by anyone touched by this until those responsible were captured.

Renée was the first to break the silence. "If we're done here and there is nothing further required of me, I'd like to send the staff home. I'll take a ride and see if I can track down David. It shouldn't take me long. I'm pretty sure I have a good idea of where he might be. He needs to be brought up to date."

She didn't look at Sandy after making the comment, but it could have been construed as taking a jab at her. In Renée's mind, she was far too calm for a mother whose child was being held hostage. Renée received no response other than a few nods of approval.

***

Sandy ignored the little dig, aware of Renée's disapproval of her absenteeism lifestyle. Most people on the exterior of the callous world she had been thrust into couldn't possibly comprehend the state of mind of those inside.

Nevertheless, in some eccentric way, Sandy was comforted by the thought of Renée being there for David. An attribute she herself should be more attuned to, but couldn't, nor at the moment did she necessarily want to be.

She knew David and Renée had slept together in the past, but that was sex, a physical gratification. She recognized Renée would keep the emotional facet of the relationship in check. Sandy could read them like a book. Renée fulfilling her desire, and David in search of the companionship he was lacking due to her exhaustive absence...which was soon to become more extensive.

She watched Renée leave the room, banishing these thoughts from her mind.

***

Renée made her way to the barn, where she would saddle up and set her sights on locating her boss. The moon would provide all the luminosity necessary to her search. David was most likely holed up at one of his favorite refuges, feeling at a loss about what to do next. Putting aside the personal aspect of their relationship, it was David who steered her in the right direction and maybe tonight she felt she could return some words of wisdom.

First she radioed the employees on site and instructed them to go home, as it was now confirmed Brooklyn and Capella were not on the property. As insensitive as it might seem, she had to consider the well-being of the horses, so it was imperative her staff found their beds for some rest before resuming their regular duties in a short few hours.

***

Lost in the nightmare and not knowing what to do, Jacob went to the kitchen in search of fresh coffee. Not that he could drink it; his stomach was upset. He wanted to pick up the telephone and bark at someone, but that wouldn't solve anything. Within the hour, should more information not be presented, he would begin his own investigation by way of a friend's influential private security firm.

Something about the attack on his family was all too familiar. He couldn't fathom the possibility. *It couldn't be.*

He decided to make one call—to Fyad's father, the King.

***

Meanwhile, the other FBI Agents retreated to the chalet, which had been made available to them as a Central Command Post. Special Agent Ethan Miller found himself alone in the room with Sandy, an opportunity he would have eventually requested.

"Mrs. McGinnis-Watson, could I have a private word?"

"Absolutely. Please close the door."

He glanced down the hallway for any sign of Jacob before shutting it.

"Unofficially, have you reached out to Christopher Young?"

"We have been in contact a number of times today. Why do you ask?"

"As I said earlier, we do have our teams on standby. However, should the circumstances be…" he paused, searching for the correct words. "How should I put this…if a situation arises whereby political correctness becomes part of the equation, we may require the CIA's services with a not-so-permissible method of extraction. I am certain Ms. Taylor will not take to my way of thinking, yet it is a real possibility the orchestrators of this abduction reach far beyond our borders…places your people would be more familiar with."

"Agent Miller, rest assured Christopher and Madison have been communicating. Both are on board should the CIA's resources be considered necessary. Is there anything else?"

"No, Ma'am. I've been doing this a long time and I sense a positive outcome here."

"Thank you. I will inform Christopher of your concerns. If we learn anything new from our side, I will inform you. Please keep me updated real-time."

Chapter Five

The occupants aboard the private aircraft, in the air for half a day now, were very quiet. The two pilots were securely locked into the cockpit and excursions such as this did not require the service of flight attendants.

Fyad and the five members of his team were barely visible in the dimly lit cabin except for the flickering of their laptops. Unlike other groupings such as this, where every member would have their own specialty, each one of Fyad's players were adept in every aspect of what was required of such an elite entourage. All of them could snap a person's neck in a split second or walk into a bikers' bar and be the only person left standing if challenged.

Every single one had proficiency in technology superior to the majority of MIT graduates. The minimum number of languages spoken by any of them was five.

Hamza walked down the aisle, touching each of the luxury chairs with his left hand, carrying an iPad in his right.

"Fyad, may I…?" He gestured to the empty seat across from his superior.

"Please. What do you have?"

"The bona fides of all six were negative. Their documents were not forged, though. They were official USA issued. This plays into our suspicions of a privileged organization similar to The Bonanza Club being involved. The group has taken up residency at the Bay of Matanzas. I've placed an asset on surveillance and he has confirmation of your friend's family's presence. Sir, the Cuban authorities have granted us carte blanche on the extraction."

Hamza thought he saw a slight smile on his superior's face, or at least a look of relief.

"We are cleared for landing at Juan Gualberto Gómez Airport, which puts us right on top of the target. Transportation is in place."

"Good, brief the men. Priority: Brooklyn and Capella, without a scratch. We will appease our reprisal for those responsible in due time."

"Yes, sir. Fyad, we will return your friends."

"We will. How are the Americans progressing?"

"Our elint indicates they are closing in, but at best they will be a few hours behind us."

"Good. Thank you."

***

Now sitting alone in her father's office, Fyad's number lit up Sandy's silent cell.

"Fyad, I'm so glad to hear from you. You've

been on my mind."

"Sandy, I'm so distraught to hear about Capella and Brooklyn. How are you holding up?"

"I'm okay. We will get them back."

"You will, I promise."

"Fyad, this was kept on a need to know lock down. How is it you learned of their disappearance?"

"Sandy, you're talking to me. Need I say more?"

"No. I shouldn't have even asked."

"Sandy, I so understand how our discipline suppresses our true emotions, but you need to allow yourself room to ache. They will be returned to you in short order."

"How can we be that certain?" She stopped as that little bulb above her head snapped on. "Fyad, are you in possession of information which could assist us?"

"I would trust the authorities are capable of bringing this to an end."

"You didn't answer my question."

"I have my team administering every resource available to us. I will not rest until Capella is sleeping once again in her own crib."

"What have you heard so far?"

"I have to go. I will be in touch shortly. Take care." He disconnected the call.

She knew he'd be one step ahead of the FBI. There was little need for her to be apprised by him of any knowledge on the matter. Every single move he made would be the exact method she would've used, given the same intel. He was the only person on the face of the earth who understood her completely.

At times, she wondered whether Fyad's father was right.

What would it be like if Fyad had been her life partner instead?

***

It took Renée about fifteen minutes to locate David. His horse moved at a leisurely pace in the direction of the ranch house. Through the luminescent sky, she could see a weary man in a state of despair. Once they were riding side by side, that depiction of his mindset was confirmed. His head slanted toward the ground and he spoke in an incoherent nature. He was a beaten man who felt he'd failed his family, was incapable of protecting them, and didn't know where to turn.

Renée hurt for him, knowing this was the most gut-wrenching experience he'd faced. She would have to choose her words carefully to inject some hope, but not lead him into a false sense of security.

She pulled the reins to halt her horse, and he followed her lead.

"David, the police may be closer to getting them home. They are very good at what they do."

His eyes brightened. "Did they find them?"

"No, David, but they will. Let's put our faith in them. They really do care."

"What the hell am I suppose to do?" he snapped. "I can't sit in that office acting all cool and collected like Sandy."

"She's hurting very much. We all wear our

anguish differently. You might not recognize it, but she needs you by her side, so why don't we head back and Sandy can bring you up to date?"

Without responding, he gave the horse's crest a gentle stroke. Renée was pleased to witness him instinctively guiding the animal with the deep-seated respect she had become accustomed to. He was not letting his frustrations lessen his admiration for the companion he'd mounted. It touched her heart.

This is a good man.

They rode beside one another at a canter while Renée briefed him of the authorities' findings. Within twenty minutes, they dismounted. David started to unsaddle when Renée stopped him.

"Go to Sandy. I'll take care of these guys." She rubbed her horse's forehead.

"You sure?"

"*Oui*, David. Go."

As the remainder of the staff went home, she would brush the two horses down before heading back to the main house, where she'd been offered a room.

David turned and hurriedly walked toward the barn door. Renée stood still and watched his disappearance into the framed darkness. Seeing him in such a vulnerable state tore her apart. What caught her by surprise was the escalation of her desire to bed him once again. The yearning was accompanied by guilt, not from her attraction, but rather the timing of it.

She had always been capable of suppressing her emotional attraction, but had zero control over the physical draw. This early morning was no different except for the fact the arousal from his presence was so intense that she was wet. So impassioned, she decided to crash in the stable's bunkroom for the remainder of the night to allow the flush of the sensation to wear off.

It was best to avoid his family as she envisioned being astride him.

***

"David!" Sandy jumped up from behind the desk and welcomed her husband with a tight hug.

By this time, Jacob had returned and was sitting on the tanned leather couch, watching in silence.

"Sandy, Renée said they have a lead. Are they okay? Have we found them?" His tone betrayed his panic.

"No, we haven't located them. Please, let's sit." She motioned to the sofa.

"No, I'm not sitting down. I have no clue how you can be so composed. For God's sake, this is our daughter we're talking about."

"And my wife," Jacob interjected.

In his state of mind, David hadn't noticed his father-in-law settled in behind him. Then again, he actually didn't care who heard him vent his frustration.

"Yes, Jacob, and your wife. You're also sitting there so calmly. What is it with this family? How can you be so relaxed? Where's the anger? We should be somewhere pounding someone's head in, making them pay for this."

"David, believe me when I say whoever is responsible for this will pay dearly," Jacob said, trying to reassure him. "But we can't run off half-cocked and jeopardize the FBI's investigation."

"Father is right," Sandy said. "We expect to learn of their location shortly. The FBI has determined they were transported by private aircraft to a site in the Caribbean. We have the finest extraction teams in place and ready to mobilize within seconds of securing their whereabouts. They will be home soon."

"Sandy, can't you talk to me as a mother, not the Director of the CIA? Scream, yell, cry! Show me you have a heart."

"This is the proper protocol to follow," she said, raising her voice. "*This* is how we get our daughter and mother back unharmed."

"So what do we do in the meantime? Sit here and sip tea?"

"No, David, we—"

"I can't be here right now," he shouted, throwing his hands in the air. "I'll be in the stables. The second we locate them, I want to know."

"David, wait!"

He disappeared out the door and slowly walked alongside the rustic fence line, making his way to the barn. A lost soul with no idea which way to turn.

He presumed Renée would've retired to her room by now and he didn't recall seeing any staff lingering, so he was alone. Perhaps he would find some solace in the company of the horses.

William C. Cole

***

After brushing and settling the rides into their respective stalls, Renée made her way to the room adjacent to the office. It was a small area housing two sets of bunk beds. Often a ranch hand would sleep over if an animal was close to birthing, or if sick, and especially the nights leading up to important races. Tonight she was alone with all others retired to their respective residences. She was exhausted, and the couple of hours remaining until daylight were best used wisely to recuperate from today's tragic events.

Renée chose the bottom bunk. She fluffed a pillow, then plopped herself down on the mattress. Fully clothed minus the cowboy boots she had slipped out of, she was soon snuggled under a woolen blanket with the ranch's logo imprinted on it.

Sleep was imminent but not immediate. The arousal from bouncing in her saddle for the past hour, coupled with being in the company of her boss, didn't subside. The degree of her desire became more evident as she lay there. Her Victoria's Secret panties were sodden, as was the inner center crease of her denims.

She decided there was only one way to resolve this hunger, so she unbuckled her jeans. With the knowledge of being alone, she unzipped them an inch or so, then slipped in her right hand. She was certain to find fulfillment quickly after the intensity of the early morning ride. With laser-like precision, she placed her index and middle fingers at the spots they needed to be, then began to caress the moistened skin.

***

David was just about to enter the dimly lit barn when his cell vibrated. Whenever he rode, he silenced the phone, not wanting to be interrupted. He'd forgotten to reset it. Once he read the display, he felt like kicking himself in the butt for not calling them sooner, as every major news station was speculating the reasoning of the heavy FBI presence. Since most of the television viewing in Canada was of American channels, it was only a matter of time before his parents would become aware of the commotion around the ranch.

He delayed making the call, as he hoped his daughter would have found her way home by now and he didn't want to worry them. Seldom did his parents watch TV, let alone the news. His father believed it a waste of time unless it was Hockey Night in Canada, which had been airing since 1952, seven to ten every Saturday evening.

But of course his siblings would have seen the broadcasts and immediately informed their parents. There was no upside of ignoring the call.

He stepped back to the fence and leaned on it with his left leg curled, resting his heel on the bottom rail.

"Hello."

"David, it's your mother."

No matter how innovative technology became, his mother felt the need to identify herself each time she called.

It normally made him chuckle, but today nothing seemed entertaining.

"I know it's you, Mother. It is a bit early in the day to be calling, even for you. Is everything okay?"

"Oh yes, David, all is well here, but your brother called and told us the police have surrounded your house and it's on the news."

He was quite certain the kidnapping had been contained and no one outside the immediate investigating teams had knowledge of it. So he elected not to tell his family in hopes it would be resolved and never made public. The last thing he wanted was for his parents to go through what he was experiencing.

"Mother, everything is okay. If anything was wrong, I would have called you right away."

"That's what your father said. But why are the police there?"

"With Sandy's new position, we felt we needed to secure the area. There are some unstable people out there and we wanted to be cautious. I did mention to you there would be discussions about her in the media. Today was supposed to be the announcement of her appointment but it had to be delayed. All the media attention will die down soon."

"Okay, that's a relief. How is my little bright star?"

It was a tough question to answer, one he hoped to avoid. He tried to clear the lump in his throat and put his best foot forward.

"She's fine, Mother. Listen, I have to tend to a couple of horses, so I need to say goodbye. Say hi to Dad for me."

"All right, but we would like you three to come for a visit soon. We miss our little granddaughter."

"Soon, Mom, I promise."

He ended the call and choked back tears. Exhausted to the point of collapse, he felt it was best to check on the horses. Failing the revitalization they typically yielded, he would take refuge in the bunkroom and possibly close his eyes for a couple of minutes.

The stable was calm, aside from the rustling of a couple of animals, but most were settled in nicely. As it turned out, they weren't going to provide much consolation as all showed little interest in any interaction, including his own. Maybe they were picking up on his despondency or perhaps they were also tired, but not one of them wanted to socialize at this hour. He headed for the bunkroom.

The full moon and the night lighting of the stable provided a sufficient glow to guide his way to the bunks. When he reached the doorway, he froze. Being under the impression that all the staff had been sent home, at least for the next few hours, he was startled by the outline of what seemed to be someone occupying the bottom bunk.

His heart started to race as he realized it was Renée.

Not only had he found his bedmate of the past occupying the bottom bunk, but she was engaged in the passionate art of self-fulfillment.

He stood there, not stepping back, not stepping

forward, and not quite knowing how to react. Six feet away was Renée, completely absorbed, oblivious to his presence. There he quietly stood, centered in the doorframe, anchored to the barn wood flooring, allowing her the delicate time to continue undisturbed.

With the blanket partly drawn off, he saw that her jeans were unzipped, and were slightly inched down to reveal the contour of her bare hips. The hand which disappeared into them was feverishly busy while the other rode up under her white sweater, presumably cupping one of her breasts. As his eyes adjusted, it became clear that she was nearing an orgasm. Her pelvis thrust upward as she began to quiver.

At that moment her head turned toward him and their eyes locked. She had entered a point of no return. Her puppy eye look was one of a child getting caught stealing candy—shocked, intense, yet so innocent. It was an expression he wouldn't soon forget.

If he hadn't been overwhelmed by his daughter's abduction, he might've been enticed. But instead he remained fixed in place, allowing her completion of the blissful sphere she had entered. She was climaxing and couldn't have reversed the eruption within her even if she wanted to.

All she could do was look at him and wait until the spasm subsided.

When she collapsed back onto the bunk, David entered the room and sat on the mattress at the base of the bed. Renée curled her legs up to her chest, then covered herself with the blanket. He could feel her sporadic jerks from the reverberations of the orgasm. He didn't look at her right away but rather gazed straight ahead at the wall. She pulled the cover slightly over her head, composing herself before uttering a word.

Finally, Renée caught her breath, then broke the silence.

"David, I thought I was alone."

She didn't seem embarrassed. It was an awkward situation, yes, but she wasn't embarrassed. Having been raised by opened-minded parents, it was embedded in her at an early age to embrace such desires without shame. To cherish those times of being in touch with one's inner needs. This, tonight, an act discreetly played out in countless bedrooms throughout the world was quite natural for her.

He turned and saw those sultry eyes peeking out from beneath the blanket. "To be honest, Renée, I thought I was alone."

He sat on a bunk, leaning his back against the wall with his legs straightened.

Renée did not attempt to pull up her pants and remained in a fetal position under the bedding. The ease with which the intrusion was handled showed the lifelong affinity rooted within each of them the second they crossed the line into intimacy.

They held each other's gazes as she slowly uncovered the remainder of her face. David then witnessed the most transcendent seductive look he had ever seen.

It would be etched in his memory for life.

Chapter Six

Fyad and his team sat in a black SUV two hundred feet from the villa where Brooklyn and Capella were being held. Each member had a specific role and was now running through one final take of the anticipated scenarios.

The Cuban authorities had blocked any access to the roadways, so there'd be little chance of an intrusion. Once the pair had been rescued by the team from the Middle East, the villa would be seized by the government as a property used in crime. It would be sold as a vacation home to some rich foreigner.

The search of the property's existing ownership showed it registered to a fictitious company based out of Malaysia. No paper trail existed and the legal owners couldn't care less if the Cubans took possession, as they made more money in a blink of an eye than most made in a lifetime.

As for the four soldiers holding the captives, looking into their backgrounds would be useless. Their identities didn't exist. Fingerprints, dental records—no documentation would be recorded in any database and no one would come looking for them. They were expendable assets, which played well into Fyad's plans.

He would like to leave one of them alive for questioning, but it really didn't matter, as he was most certain which organization was behind this cowardly act. Chances were the abductors had seen their last sunrise.

It was time.

Fyad and one of the men remained in the vehicle as the others stepped out. They had three minutes to strategically place themselves front and back of the residence. Fyad sat in the driver's seat as the other team member sat in the rear with his laptop resting open on his knee. The three minute mark was reached. He eased the SUV down the street and parked by the curb directly in front of the villa. The luxury vehicle didn't look out of place, as the area was home to many well-to-do vacationers.

Dressed like a tourist, he popped the hood and stepped out of the truck. He then pressed the panic button on the remote clipped to a key chain. With a metronome pattern, the alarm began to sound off. Fyad then unlatched and lifted the hood to make it appear as if he was examining the engine. Anyone witnessing his performance would presume he was some rich guy who could probably manipulate the stock market to his favor, but when it came to a simple alarm system, he was clueless.

Exactly as planned, one of the kidnappers stepped outside to see what all the commotion was about. He wouldn't be the one in charge. The last thing the abductors wanted was to have any type of tumult drawing undue attention to the house. The team was counting on this. At the very least, one of the men would come to their aid.

Fyad locked his hands behind the back of his neck and began pacing a little back and forth, depicting a wealthy vacationer who shouldn't have been allowed to drive.

"What the hell is going on here?"

"I'm so sorry for disturbing you, sir. This is a rental, and when I stopped to take in this stunning view, the alarm went off and I have no clue how to stop it."

"You need to get back in your vehicle and get out of here."

"I'm so sorry I have interrupted you. As soon as I figure out how to turn this off, I will be on my way. Sir, would you happen to know how to make it stop?"

The man shook his head in disbelief. "You're kidding me. Just hit the panic button."

"What panic button? I'm sorry, sir. I normally have a driver."

"Give me your keys," he demanded, growing impatient.

Fyad looked clueless and started patting his pockets, looking for the keys, then motioned to the SUV.

"I think I left them in the vehicle."

Both of the men turned in the direction of the driver's door when one of the other abductors stuck his head out of the arched doorway.

"What's going on out there? Is everything

okay?"

"Yes, boss. This jackass doesn't know what a damn panic button is."

"Take care of it."

Being hand selected for such a delicate assignment apparently didn't require an IQ test. He wasn't surprised, but more disappointed in his adversary's selection process. These guys were the muscle, not the brain.

Two things came to his mind—serious mistakes the man had made. First off, the extricating of the family just got easier after now knowing the identity of the person in charge. Secondly, up to the point of calling Fyad a jackass, his fate was at best spending a lengthy stretch in a Cuban jail cell. But unfortunately, when he spoke the word *jackass*, he'd assured himself a worse fate.

Fyad opened the driver's side door and within a split second, abductor number one had his neck snapped and was dead. He pushed him into the passenger's seat, where he would remain until the mission was complete.

Simultaneously, the horn stopped honking, and Hamza, who was positioned in the rear seat, tapped an icon on his laptop which turned off all utility services into the villa. As mediocre as this group was, Fyad's team knew the interruption of services would be recognized as a telltale sign of an attack. One of the Middle East squad would have been sufficient to take out the remaining three. When they blasted their way in, the abductors had zero chance of defending themselves.

Two of the team entered through the unlocked

front door, another by way of the sliding poolside door. Two of the abductors were ready with their weapons pulled, but were put down with two quick shots straight to the forehead.

That left one kidnapper—the female of the group—and she sat there looking ever so confident on the sofa, with her gun boring a crease into the baby's head. The room fell silent and nobody moved an inch. To the right of the couch, Brooklyn was taped to a chair with her mouth gagged.

"If anyone so much as sneezes, the baby is dead. Sure, I'll die. But I don't care."

Nobody moved.

Through the window behind the sofa, Fyad and Hamza were witnessing the standoff and knew precisely how delicate the situation had become. Without a word, they knew what the other was thinking.

Hamza remained at the window, his gun trained directly at the back of the woman's head. He alone would make the call if he felt it was warranted, and he wouldn't miss. Fyad ran around to the poolside entrance. He wanted to enter the home in front of the gun wielding female, so as not to startle her.

This was an unexpected turn of events which required a heightened alertness by all involved.

***

Sandy's cell chimed. It was outgoing CIA Director Young.

"Christopher," she said.

"They're being held in Cuba. I just spoke with

Madison, and the recovery teams are in the air. Sandy, it's only a matter of hours and they will be home. The Cubans have agreed to collaborate with our group and will guide the teams once they arrive. We have an asset on the ground and I have authorized him to coordinate surveillance of the location until the extraction teams arrive. They will keep the FBI updated in real-time."

"Thank you, Christopher. I owe you. I'm sorry for—"

"Enough of that. Now, I'm suggesting you and David stay put but I know that's not going to happen. So, here is the agenda. Once your daughter and Brooklyn are safely in our care, they will be transported to NAS Key West Navy Base. If you're going anywhere, go there. Do not fly into Cuba."

Being a bit anxious to leave, she agreed by raising her voice. "Fine."

"I understand your urgency, Sandy, but please remember you are about to become the Director of the greatest intelligence agency in the world. Aside from the President, you might be the second most powerful person in the world. You can't go off half-cocked. I'm appreciative of the fact you are probably the most qualified person on the face of this earth to single-handedly execute this assignment. However, that is no longer in the cards. We've had our difficulties justifying your appointment without exposing your true experience, so please let the team do their job. Capella will be safely in your arms when you land at the base. I've filed your flight plan and cleared your aircraft for priority take off and landing."

"Thank you, Christopher."

"I do have a heart," he added. "Most days I need to hide it. You will find that balance. Now go."

Before she could say goodbye and thank her predecessor, Agent Miller and two other agents tumultuously entered the office, followed by Jacob. With the phone still pressed to her ear, she held up her index finger, asking for a second.

"Goodbye, Christopher," she said.

Director Young had already ended the call.

How could she expect anything different? She couldn't recall a single communication with him that ended with pleasantries. A slight smile came across her face but quickly disappeared. This was no time for the portrayal of amusement.

As she lowered the cell, the FBI agent didn't waste a second and began to update her, but didn't get more than a few words out when she rose and cut him off.

"Thank you, Agent Miller. I have been notified of the current developments." She turned to Jacob. "Father, we will be flying to Key West. Agent Miller, please inform your chopper pilot he will be transporting us to the airfield."

Agent Miller put a call in to the helicopter pilot who was bunked up in the chalet. Jacob contacted his crew, who were on call twenty-four-seven to prepare his jet.

And the third connection was Sandy ringing David. She presumed he was held up at the stables.

***

Being in a state of slumber, he didn't notice the vibration repeated itself a few times before it caught Renée's attention.

David had removed the device from his back pocket and tossed it on the bed when he sat down. It somehow found its way under the covers and snuggled up against her. He remained sitting upright, but had dozed off with his arm resting above the covers on her feet.

While he was lost to the world, Renée stayed awake. She stared at him, daydreaming about their liaison with the realization that it would most likely never be rekindled.

"David."

He didn't respond to her nudge. He just readjusted himself and remained asleep. She gave him a little more forceful push with her foot and spoke a little louder.

"David, your phone is ringing. David, it's probably Sandy. You'd better answer it."

This time, he heard her, and in a semi-awakened state, he began to fumble his way under the covers, trying to retrieve the phone as it continued to buzz. Renée threw the blankets aside to assist in the search. As they were both reaching for the device, she hooked her leg behind David's backside to assist in wedging herself up into a sitting position. While trying to locate it, the warmth from their arms and hands brushing up against each other coaxed another subtle reminder of the past.

"Hello," David hastily answered, not bothering to look at the call display screen.

He listened.

"I'll be there in a second."

He flew off the bed, tripping over his own feet in the dimly lit room, searching for the cowboy boots he had removed earlier before sitting on the bed. Hopping on one foot, he fell back first against the wall, ungainly pulling a boot on.

"They found them. They found them!"

Excited to hear the news, Renée jumped off the bed, grabbed the second boot, then handed it to him.

"Renée, they found them," he said again, unable to contain his relief.

"David, go, go! Don't worry about anything here. I've got it covered. Now go."

With that, he started for the exit, but quickly turned, pulled her close by the shoulders, and gave her a feverish kiss. It took her breath away. She stood speechless, assuming she'd later shrug this off due to his current emotional state.

David then ran out of the barn and up the narrow roadway toward the ranch. Before he was halfway to the imposing veranda, he was whisked in the direction of the black helicopter's fluttering rotors by two burly FBI agents. Coming from the other direction was Sandy, with the child's fresh baby bag strapped on her shoulder, and her father, along with additional special agents.

As they met up, David demanded, "Where are they? Are they okay?"

No one answered him as he was hastily pushed into the opened door of the helicopter, followed by his wife, his father-in-law, Agent Miller, and one other FBI agent.

"Give us one second to get in the air, David, and

I will explain everything," Sandy said.

"No, you explain it now. Are they okay?"

All the occupants slipped on their headphones except for David, so when Sandy began to reply to his request, he couldn't hear a thing due to the noise from the rotors. She grabbed his set, which was sitting between them, and handed it over, motioning for him to put it on. Giving him a second to adjust the apparatus, she then began speaking through the microphone attached to the arm of the headset.

"We found them. They are being held in Cuba, and from every source of information we received, we strongly believe both are being treated well and unharmed. The FBI has a Special Force extraction team in the air and they should be landing momentarily."

"Where are we going? Are we going to Cuba? We need to be there, Sandy."

"No. We're flying to Key West. Once a team has safely secured their freedom, they will immediately be flown to the NSA Key West Navy Base. By the time we arrive, they will most likely already be on the ground."

"That's bullshit. I want to go to Cuba. These guys should be looking over their shoulders for the rest of their lives, because if it's the last thing I do, they will pay dearly."

"Our goal here is to reunite with our family as quickly as possible, and that means Key West."

Sandy leaned toward him, laying her head on his shoulder, and locked her arms through his. Other than the *thwup, thwup, thwup* of the aircraft's blades, the remainder of the short flight to the airport was relatively a silent one.

They were soon setting down on the tarmac close to Jacob's eighty-five million dollar Gulfstream 650. Once the rotor had slowed to a safe speed, the side door slid open. One by one, the occupants began to briskly run to the waiting aircraft. Halfway there, Sandy slowed while she retrieved one of her cell phones, then tapped once on the contacts.

"Sandy, I was actually just going to call you with an update," Director Young answered on the first ring.

"I'm listening."

"Our feet on the ground have been delayed in securing a visible on the location. It would seem the Cubans have blockaded the roads accessing the property. Our personnel will utilize an alternate route. However, knowing the FBI team has just landed, it's concerning to see such a Cuban attendance so early into the mission. I will get a grip on this shortly and get back to you. Are you good?"

"We are boarding now. Christopher, we need our asset in place. I want real-time on this starting yesterday." As usual, the line went dead with no goodbyes.

Something was not sitting well with her.

There should not have been any Cuban presence. The operation was to be led by the FBI specialty team. She had expected the local government to act solely in a backup capacity, providing information but staying away from a hands-on role. Although the two countries were working toward easing the tensions between them, the relationship was still strained. Yet, she doubted they would be so brazen as to go alone and renege on their original commitment.

When the execution of an exercise of this magnitude, or for that matter, any level of importance was altered—even in the slightest—the successful outcome became jeopardized. Sandy's concern for Capella and Brooklyn amplified.

With everyone now seated in the aircraft, the jet engines began to slowly inch the airplane backward, moving away from the hangar in preparation for takeoff. Agent Miller walked up the aisle until he came to where David and Sandy sat. Leaning toward them, he spoke in a quiet voice.

"We've just received word that our team has landed and is estimated to be on site within a half hour."

"Thank you, Agent Miller," Sandy said.

"Who were you on the phone with?" David asked.

"I was speaking with Director Young."

"Do you have any new information?"

"Only what we just heard from Agent Miller. David, she will be in our arms soon. I promise."

Damn, another lie, she thought.

Sandy had once made a promise that she would never lie to him. Bend the truth, yes, but no lying. And here she was blatantly withholding the truth from her husband in fear of his overreaction.

David had not been trained, hardened as she had, and she felt it best to contain his emotional backlash by being selective on what and how information was passed on. In this particular case, she could forgive herself for the deception.

Whether or not David could forgive her would have to wait.

***

After his briefing from the FBI, the President knew everyone in need of being advised of the current situation would have been, or would be, except for one. So as soon as he found himself alone, he called his daughter, Addison.

"Sweetheart, as promised, I have some information for you with regards to the kidnapping. We have located Mrs. McGinnis and her granddaughter and have the best FBI unit on the ground preparing to rescue them within the hour. I will get back to you as soon as I get word they are safely in our hands. Everything is going to work out fine. I promise."

"Father, I will hold you to that. Please, please, make sure this goes well."

"You have my word, Addison. Did your sister arrive?"

"Yes, she's here. I appreciate you allowing her the break from classes. If anyone can keep me grounded, it's Layla."

"I have to run. Call me. I'm always here for you. I will be in touch the moment I learn anything."

"Goodbye, Father. I…" She paused and looked at her sister. "We love you."

***

Fyad entered the house with his hands in the air. As planned, he was careful to walk in and portray a calming aura. The last thing he wanted was for their one remaining abductor to be startled. All the men were well-versed on making Capella's safety a number one priority. Brooklyn was as important, but would become secondary to the child if necessary.

"I'm unarmed and entering through the patio doors," Fyad said in a soothing tone.

Everyone remained silent and still. The woman holding the baby did not reply as she watched him walk into the living area.

"Gentlemen, please lower your weapons," he said to his men in an effort to secure the trust of the young woman.

Fyad took a split second to analyze the room, taking in everything from lighting, to windows, to doorways, to the demeanor of the woman holding the baby, and he especially concentrated on her trigger finger.

When he took a quick glance at Brooklyn, he sensed her relief once she recognized him. They had met a few times through Sandy and she knew well of his capabilities.

"May I ask for your name?" Fyad asked the woman.

"What name would you like me to give you? The one I'm using today or the one I used yesterday? What does it matter?"

"Do you mind if I sit?" He motioned to the chair directly across from her.

She shrugged as if to say she couldn't care less.

111

This was a bad sign. He had seen it many times when an adversary had given up hope, knowing there was to be no good outcome. In that state of mind, quite often the subject would try to harm others before their battle was lost.

Fyad realized he must instill a glimmer of hope if the baby were to survive.

"I understand where you're coming from and admire your dedication to your trade. You must be very accomplished at what you do to have garnered the trust of those you serve. It is something that I look for in all the men and women who are within my employ."

He noticed a slight change in her facial expression. He had complimented her and also established that he himself was not one for hire, but was the one in charge.

"As you can tell, my men are very well-trained." He motioned to her lifeless comrades lying on the floor. "They are very good at what they do, so let's try to understand each other and resolve this peacefully."

"My instructions are to hold the baby and this lady captive until advised to release them unharmed. Your intrusion was premature, as they would have been returned without a scratch. But now, based on my colleagues' deaths, the way I see it, this child is my only bargaining tool. So if this is it, I may as well go out in a blaze of glory."

"I couldn't help overhear you telling my men you were not afraid to die. Neither are we. Yet, I believe it true that none of us want to. So why don't we bring this to an end now?"

"Yeah, sure. I hand her over and you put a bullet in my head."

"What would you suggest we do? I came a long way and I assured the mother that her child would be returned safely."

The woman was beginning to speak more confidently, thinking she had the upper hand.

"I think we will sit here and wait for the arrival of my people. Then she is yours and you can discuss your displeasure with them."

"That doesn't work for me...more unnecessary deaths. Out of curiosity, do you recognize me?"

"I can't say I do."

"I am Prince Fyad. You may have heard the name."

His power and influence was recognized throughout the world, especially to those who dealt in questionable commodities. "I take it from your facial expression that my name may have evoked some uneasiness. I am now running out of time, and trust me when I say I have little to spare. Enough with the niceties. I am now going to get up and walk over to you. You will lower the gun from the child's head and hand her over to me."

"Why don't I just put the gun to my own head? At least it will be my bullet, not yours, that ends my life. The way I read this, today is my last whether you get what you want or not."

"Feel free to do as you please. But if that baby comes out of this with even a scratch, you will die the worst death imaginable. I will take your body back to my country and have my medical team search every record until I learn of your true identity, and I will. Not only will you die today, I will hunt down and put to death every living relative of yours, every person you have ever been close to, every special teacher you had, every colleague who stood by your side. I will make certain that everyone knows you had the opportunity to save them. Are you prepared to sign their death warrants? If you recognize my name, you know I am one to keep my promises. On the other hand, give me the child and I give my word I will not harm you or those close to you."

There was little time to spare. The Americans would have landed by now and would be en route. The blockade would buy a few minutes, but they needed to leave soon.

Fyad rose and inched his way to the sofa. He put his arms out, but the gun remained pointed at the baby's temple. Being a Grandmaster of several martial arts disciplines, he would trust his lighting speed to disarm the abductor. He was certain this could be achieved without bringing harm to the baby. A split second before Fyad was about to lay a Mae Geri kick, which would have sent the gun flying in the air and most likely break her arm or wrist, she lowered her weapon. He paused as she ever so gently slid the Sig Sauer across the coffee table toward him.

In seconds, Fyad had Capella safely in his arms. One of his team pounced on the abductor and had her instantaneously incapacitated. Another member was at Brooklyn's side, cutting away the tape securing her to the chair. Once freed, she jumped to Fyad's side.

"Thank you, Fyad. I have no idea how we will repay you for this. Please…" She opened her arms, gesturing for him to hand over the baby.

"Brooklyn, you owe us nothing." He placed Capella in her arms. "Should the circumstances have been reversed, your family would have done the exact same thing."

When Hamza witnessed the rescue from outside, he knew what needed to be done. He ran to the SUV to retrieve the body, which was propped up in the passenger seat. He carried it through the front door and laid it beside the other two. Two of his men began to escort Brooklyn and the baby out to the poolside while the others remained inside.

As Brooklyn passed Fyad, she stopped and whispered to him, "Let me do it."

"Brooklyn, that is a line you do not want to cross. Please go with my men. We will have you home soon."

She looked back. If a stare could bore a flame into someone, the woman who had minutes earlier held a gun to her grandchild would be smoldering.

Fyad would keep his word not to bring harm to her family. He promised that he would not kill her, but made no reference to one of his men, Hamza in particular, bringing her life to an end. The thought had crossed his mind, but he believed another method would achieve the same result.

All were instructed to exit the room, leaving Fyad and the woman alone.

"Get it over with."

"But I promised."

"You said you wouldn't kill me. There was no

mention of what your men would do."

"I gave you my word. Taking your life seems like the easy way out. Once your superiors learn of your failure, I believe you will wish I killed you, because they will hunt you down and will not be kind. I trust it will be a long, drawn out affair ending with you begging for death." He let his words sink in before continuing. "Personally, I would never allow them such pleasure. This is my gift to you for releasing the baby unharmed. You do as you feel needs to be done."

With that, he slowly slid her loaded gun back across the table, turned, and walked out to join the others. Brooklyn was upset that she hadn't overheard a gun being discharged.

"Fyad, please, she has to pay. Let me."

He held up his index finger, silencing her and stood still, angling his ears to the open patio doors. They all remained stationary until suddenly, a single gunshot was heard.

Their escape plan needed to be altered. If they were to return to their aircraft with Brooklyn and the child in hand, it was highly probable they'd encounter the American recovery team. Explanations would eventually get sorted out, but Fyad had little patience for being accountable to others.

The quickest way to unite the family became suddenly clear. Swaying in the waves at the end of the dock was a yellow 1200 HP Baja Outlaw 35 speedboat.

Fyad nodded to Hamza. A new plan was born.

The keys for the boat were easily found,

although any of the men could have started it in less than a minute by hot-wiring.

Fyad, Hamza, and one of the other men accompanied Brooklyn and the child to the dock. Fyad and the two others would remain. Quickly aboard, they would travel NNW to the nearest point of the USA—Key West.

The Baja would top out at eighty-five miles per hour on a smooth day like today. However, Hamza would not jeopardize the safety of his passengers in lieu of an early arrival.

The ocean seemed tame at the moment. He would push speeds of up to forty miles per hour, at least until they reached international waters, which were twelve nautical miles from shore.

There was a trust with the Cuban government, but one could never be cautious enough. After that point, he would adjust his speed according to conditions. Given the common high swells of the straits of Florida, there was a good chance the ninety-one nautical mile trip would take close to three hours. Fyad would advise the authorities so the expectation was the Coast Guard would intercept the group as they neared U.S. waters.

The boat began to gurgle as it inched backward away from the dock. With ease, the long yellow nose of the craft slowly turned toward open water. Once pointing in the correct direction, Hamza shifted the throttle to begin the journey.

Fyad stood alone on the wooden pier, watching the powerful vessel slice through the water like it was cutting glass. As the craft began to speed off, Fyad experienced a stillness brought on by the

117

diminishing noise and the knowledge the endeavor had been successful. He raised his secured satellite phone and with one finger touched the screen. It wasn't answered in the timeframe he was accustomed to.

He then began tapping the words **urgent answer** into the screen with his index finger, then sent the text. With the phone lowered to his side, he watched as the yellow boat faded into the indigo of the briny deep. A minute passed before he raised the phone halfway and again gently touched a single number. This time it was answered after one ring.

***

Tranquilized by the low hum of the jet engines, Sandy and her husband, along with the rest of the group, sat in silence, each contemplating their own private thoughts. The cell she used for her government business sat to her side on vibrate only, with the screen facing away from David. Any call coming in to this phone was of the utmost importance and required her to answer it, yet as it pulsed against her thigh, she momentarily ignored it.

Whether it was good or bad news, she did not want to answer it in front of her husband. She excused herself and made her way to the lavatory, then locked the door and before she had a chance to look at the screen to see who had been trying to call, it began to vibrate again. This time she saw it was Fyad.

"I wasn't expecting to hear from you," she said.

"Sandy, I require your unconditional trust with what I'm about to tell you. I do not have time to explain, but please follow my instructions."

"You know that goes without saying."

"I do." He paused, then said, "Capella and Brooklyn are fine. They are being transported to Key West by way of a yellow Baja speedboat. They are unharmed and in the company of Hamza and one other of my men. Please advise the Coast Guard to intercept the boat at the twelve mile zone. I prefer he not have to enter U.S. waters. I would suggest you and David now make your way to Key West, as they are only hours away.

"Sandy, I promise to explain what transpired in detail soon, but first your priority should be to reunite with your daughter. There will be some confusion on the part of your extraction team when they arrive at the site, so I would suggest you have the mission immediately aborted. One final request: I need your assurance that my men will not be questioned, as they will refuse to speak with your authorities. Once your family is aboard the Coast Guard vessel, Hamza will be returning to Cuba."

Sandy felt relieved the abduction came to an end in a favorable manner and her family was safe. There was little need to be briefed by Fyad, as she understood exactly what had taken place. He had arrived there before the Americans and she knew those responsible would no longer be breathing.

The poise in his voice, his far-reaching supremacy, all reaffirmed her belief that once she took office, their newly found collaboration might well propel them to become the two most powerful

119

people in the world. Only good could come of it. He was the one person who truly understood her, as she did him.

"I will take care of it. Thank you. Soon."

"Soon."

Nothing more needed to be said, so the call was ended. Before advising those on the plane, she called the outgoing Director. He answered without giving her a chance to talk. "I was just going to contact you. Our asset is reporting activity at the site but has yet to complete a full assessment. Something is off. The FBI team's ETA is ten minutes. He will attempt to close in and report back shortly. I must emphasize nothing negative is being reported, just unpredicted movement."

Sandy knew there was no sense in trying to cut into his conversation, aware it would be brief and to the point.

"Christopher, I don't have time to explain, but I have just been informed my family has been recovered."

"Explain," he demanded. After all, he was still the one in charge.

"Fyad," she said simply.

Then she ordered no communications with Hamza and relayed the coordinates of where they were to rendezvous. She also insisted he immediately notify Madison Taylor to abort the mission. He agreed on the condition she explain Fyad's infringement on the U.S. undertaking. She assured him it was forthcoming.

Sandy unlocked the door, then walked down the aisle.

"May I have everyone's attention?" She startled a couple who had dozed off. Everyone glanced up at her. "Capella and Brooklyn have been freed. They are safe and unharmed." She turned to the FBI agents. "We are so grateful to everyone for putting their heart and soul into my family's recovery."

David jumped out of his seat, as did Jacob, both repeating Sandy's words at the same time: "They found them."

They looked at each other, repeating, "They found them."

"Yes, they are safe and on their way home," she said, showing little signs of emotion.

Sandy needed to remain placid. It was imperative she brief Agent Miller immediately and have him follow up on having the operation aborted, as she wouldn't put it past Christopher Young to delay it, enabling a report of the scene by U.S. personnel. He most certainly wouldn't rely on receiving credible information from the Cuban government and knew Fyad would not be calling him for a chat.

The whole situation would be cleaner if the Cubans purged the mayhem. Fyad's country had a good rapport with the local government and the bodies would be disposed of without examination.

"David, Father, if you would allow me to speak with Agent Miller first, I will then explain everything to you."

Her husband and father barely heard her, they were so elated. They sat together, hearts racing, smiling ear to ear in anticipation of seeing their loved ones. Sandy nestled beside Agent Miller and spoke to him at a low volume, not wanting the others to overhear. She first asked him to confirm the recovery plan with the Coast Guard, then turned to the next set of instructions.

"I want you to contact Director Taylor and immediately abort the mission."

"I don't understand. I thought you just said we recovered them."

"I said they had been freed, but not by our teams. I can't explain right now. Please call Madison."

He did just that, but Sandy didn't wait for the outcome. She preferred not having the team exposed to the location, but it wasn't the end of the world if they observed the aftermath. Actually, on second thought, she wouldn't mind knowing the condition of the site as she would never expect Fyad to paint the full picture. As the agent began his calls, she walked back to join her family. She took a seat facing both of them and began a brief explanation.

"I have few details, but they are safe and being transported to Key West, where we will meet up with them. I'm told they are in excellent health. They are being moved by boat, as it is the quickest mode of transportation from the location they were being held."

"Why didn't they just fly them out? Use one of those damn helicopters our tax dollars keep in service," her father snapped.

"I don't understand, either. It doesn't make sense," David added.

"I think it best that we concentrate on their freedom at the moment and delve into the specifics after we are safely home."

It was clear there was more to the story. If everything transpired as it was supposed to, the group on board would be applauding the team's success. Her father was willing to let it slide for the time being. On the other hand, David wasn't.

"What's going on, Sandy? The private conversation with Agent Miller, the lack of jubilation of the FBI's good work—something doesn't add up. There's more to this than meets the eye. I think your father and I have a right to know. As much as I want to see my daughter, reality is I can't until we land, so there is plenty of time to explain."

She knew he wouldn't give up—a quality in him she adored except in a case like this. The only reason she was withholding the information was she didn't want to get into a lengthy briefing without knowing the complete details, which would be forthcoming in the near future. But she decided there was really no good time.

"The FBI's team did not rescue them. It was Fyad."

"What the hell does Fyad have to do with this?"

"To be honest, I have no idea. When I was in the washroom I got a call from Fyad and he didn't elaborate on what went down. It would seem his intelligence agency somehow intercepted conversation pertaining to the abduction. He and his team were able to free Capella and Brooklyn before we could get to them. Their decision was to find the quickest route of freedom, so they elected to utilize a boat which will rendezvous with the Coast Guard. Our family is in good hands and we should be thankful. That's all I know, honestly. Fyad will bring me up to date on everything that has transpired in due time."

David and Jacob sat there in disbelief of what they just heard. All along, it was thought that the FBI special group would be the savior.

"I'm really confused here, Sandy," David said. "But for now I…or rather, we…will follow your lead for the sake of our family. However, we will expect an extensive accounting of how this developed."

***

They soon touched down at Boca Chica Field, the NAS Base in Key West. There was no sign of their family. Two young military police officers escorted them to the operations center, where the base commander awaited them. They were soon shuffled into a private office before being briefed.

"Let me voice my disapproval of being ordered to put my base on high alert status without an inkling of reasoning," the base commander said. "Our orders are to authorize the docking of the Coast Guard, who will deliver two subjects, who will then be handed over to you.

"ETA is one hour. The boarding was successful and the subjects have been examined by a physician, who has determined they are in excellent health. That is all I have. Any questions?"

David was about to spring an inquiry, but Sandy cut him off.

"Thank you, Captain. I assure you we will be on

our way shortly and your base can return to normal. We do appreciate all you are doing for us."

"Well, then, I do have a base to command, so if there's anything you require, my officers will be more than happy to accommodate you."

The Captain left the room after Sandy thanked him again. There was nothing left to do now but wait.

***

Fyad and his two men returned to the airport, taking a number of back routes to avoid an encounter with the Americans. They sat aboard their luxury private aircraft and awaited word from Hamza. Once it was confirmed everything was complete, they would return home.

Hamza and his partner would make their way back to Cuba, leaving the boat at Marina Hemingway, where the Cuban authorities would impound the vessel as property used in crime, then auction it off to some rich part-time resident of the island.

Then, Hamza and his associate who'd gone with him, would board a commercial aircraft and also return home.

The mission was complete.

***

Forty-five restless minutes after the Captain left the room, he returned with Brooklyn and Capella in tow. Tears of joy trickled down everyone's cheeks. Even though the Captain was not privy to the details, he was a smart man and knew the meaning behind an emotional gathering.

After the initial elation of the reunion, David held his daughter with a steadfast demeanor, warding off any who dare try to separate them. Sandy understood his need, and although she would have loved to be cradling her child, at the moment it was best to leave father and daughter together.

They were whisked off to their jet and in the air within thirty minutes of reuniting. Capella was firmly positioned on David's lap. Sandy sat next to them, talking to her daughter while her index finger was being squeezed by the baby's tiny fingers. Brooklyn and Jacob sat across the aisle, arms locked, shoulders pushed up against one another, not speaking, just smiling and reveling in the moment.

A few minutes passed before David and Capella were slowly drifting off. Sandy knew she had little time to spare before her phone would begin ringing. The patience of those presently in charge would be wearing thin in anticipation of a debriefing. Because of the irregular recovery, it had been agreed upon to let Sandy debrief Brooklyn.

No time like the present. She slid into a chair that she swiveled to sit face-to-face with her stepmother. "Father, if you don't mind, I have to go through some details with Brooklyn."

"That's fine, but I'm not moving. I want to know everything that happened, but only if you're ready to speak about it," he said to his wife.

126

"I'm fine, Jacob," she assured him.

"I'm so happy to have you back with us, Brooklyn, and I'm sorry to have to put you through this. Tolerance levels will be running short, so if I can't appease them, we may have an unruly crowd upon landing. I've been given a little latitude here due to the delicacy of the matter, so it would be best for us all if I was the one to be briefing the President and the FBI."

Brooklyn went on to explain everything in detail, right from the very inkling she recognized they were in danger. Sandy listened without interruption as Brooklyn clarified every minute detail.

She explained how she made herself visible to every security camera possible. Sandy interrupted to say these actions were certainly a key ingredient in leading Fyad to their location. Brooklyn reassured them they were treated well, leaving out the visual of the gun against her granddaughter's face. There was no upside in describing it, yet it was certainly going to revisit her in her nightmares.

"Sandy, I believe what got me through this is the realization that Capella will have no memory of the ordeal," she finished.

"I need you to tell me exactly what happened from the second you realized Fyad and his men were present."

She again described every element of the encounter after her rescuers' arrival, including the death of all four abductors. At that point, she stopped talking, as there was nothing further she could add.

"In your opinion, was Fyad justified in ending

the lives of all four kidnappers to protect your safety?"

"For God's sake, Sandy, they kidnapped my wife and your daughter," her father interrupted. "What other ending would be justified?"

"Father, please, I need to provide the FBI's Director and more than likely the President with answers to these questions. Please let me continue. I would rather Brooklyn be interrogated by me than other authorities. When we land, I will insist all communications be directed through me, but I need to provide them with a minute to minute reconstruction of the events that took place."

He nodded, though he was clearly uncomfortable with his daughter grilling Brooklyn. Deep down, he knew she was right.

"Yes," was all Brooklyn offered.

"Can you expand on that? What were the threats to you and Capella at the time your captors were killed?"

"Sandy." Brooklyn's gaze locked with hers. "Fyad had no choice. To be honest, if he hadn't killed them, I would have."

Jacob had heard enough. He couldn't hold back, hearing his wife speak with such vengeance. She was a soft-spoken, intelligent, rational person without an ounce of vindictiveness in her bones.

"That's enough," he said angrily.

"It's okay, Jacob," Brooklyn continued. "There's nothing more to tell. I can't think of another detail we haven't covered."

"Good. Are we done?" He directed the question to his daughter.

"I believe we are, for now."

Jacob stood up, slowly stretching his legs. "Would you two ladies excuse me?"

They both nodded as he turned and made his way to the washroom.

Sandy also rose to her feet, preparing to rejoin David and the baby.

"Thank you, Brooklyn. I'm sure there will be more questions, but all communications will come through me. Thank you from the bottom of my heart for protecting our daughter. It may not seem like it at times, but she is my life."

"I know she is, Sandy."

"That is a comforting thought. We should be landing soon, so try to get some rest."

"Please sit back down. I did tell you everything, except…"

"Except what?" She took a seat.

"I honestly don't believe they had knowledge of who hired them. From everything I can gather, they were soldiers following orders passed down from many levels above. Just pawns who wouldn't dare make a move without being instructed to do so."

"What did you hear?"

"Capella was resting on me and I had my eyes closed, so I presume they thought I was also napping. In an undertone, I heard two of the men debating on who they thought might ultimately be signing their paychecks. These guys were playing a guessing game and there is little merit to their conjecture."

"The name, please."

"I didn't mention it in front of your father. He's

been through enough for one day, and I will speak to him tomorrow once he's had a chance to rest. You have to promise you won't talk about this to him until I get a chance to."

"The name?"

"I've heard of this organization referred to during my White House tenure. I also believe it may be familiar to your father, so you have to promise…"

"Yes, Brooklyn, you have my word."

They kept eye contact for a couple of seconds before Brooklyn spoke again.

"The Bonanza Club."

Chapter Seven

Fyad and his crew arrived home safely, pleased to be advised that the extraction mission by the Americans was aborted prior to the team physically reaching their target. By now, the Cuban officials would have disposed of the bodies and put the villa on the market.

It was back to the country's business at hand, except for Hamza. Fyad reassigned his duties with the sole purpose of identifying the members of the Bonanza Club after Brooklyn advised him of what she overheard during their walk to the dock.

Most governments, along with the world's power players, knew of their existence and the influence they wielded. However, those in the secret club—if it actually did exist—remained in the dark for many years.

Fyad wanted names.

***

Sandy and her family were once again returned

to the ranch via helicopter. This time they found the atmosphere relatively subdued compared to the police presence when they left. There were no more roadblocks, just a few agents packing up their gear, ready to be off site by sundown. It was felt by all concerned that the threat had been nullified and there would be little chance of any further assaults on the family. The point had been made. In the meantime, the FBI would leave two agents at the ranch to wander about as a precaution.

David and Sandy were quick to retire to their suite, and it wasn't long before Capella was nestled in her crib, unaware of what she'd been through.

"When do you leave?"

"Soon." Sandy sat down beside him on the bed. "The plan was to leave the day after tomorrow, but I've delayed a couple of weeks. David, are we going to survive this?"

"We have no choice. You know I'd rather you stay, but it is what it is. I just thought it would be nice if you could find a little more time for Capella, that's all."

She moved herself up on the bed, positioning herself half resting on the pillow and half on the wall. Trying to avoid a rehash of their opposing beliefs, she took a moment to evaluate her reply before speaking. Not wanting to initiate a debate, she felt the less said at this point, the better.

"David, I understand where you're coming from, but we have talked this through many times and we've had to make a difficult decision. I would love to have you and Capella move to Washington with me, yet I fully understand you wanting to stay here.

Just know that it will always be an option. Who knows? Maybe someday you'll want to get back into hockey, and Washington does have a team. Actually, I believe the Verizon Center is just down the street from the White House."

"We're good. We will make it work for Capella's sake."

The path to the future was set. It was time to move on. No sense dwelling on the past. They certainly weren't going that way.

***

Morning came quickly. The suppressed exhaustion festering within had got the best of them once their eyes were closed. There were no comforting hugs, no intimacy, just the stillness of sleep.

Uncharacteristically, David awoke first. He made his way to their daughter's room and to his surprise, Capella was still fast asleep. She made it through the night without waking. David checked the baby monitor to make sure it was working. It made him think that the ordeal which had unfolded within the last couple of days affected his daughter more than they all thought.

On his way to the bathroom, he glanced over at his wife, who was still resting. It was time to get back to work. He needed to move forward. A quick shower was in order and then he would make his way down to the stables. The hope was to find Renée, who he was feeling bad for because of the additional responsibility thrust upon her. It was difficult enough to oversee their facility at the racetrack, let alone the stables at the ranch, not to speak of the fifty-some staff members manning them.

He was anxious to be updated on the business happenings of the last two days and resume his ranch duties, which would allow Renée to once again concentrate on the track stable. Truthfully, he wasn't sure how to act. His daughter had been kidnapped and safely returned. His wife was moving to Washington. Options swirled in his mind. But for the time being, he felt moving back into his responsibilities as quickly as possible was for the best.

As he was drying off, in the fogged mirror he saw Sandy's blurred naked body appear behind him. She put her arms around him, placing her opened hands flatly on his lower belly with the bottom of her finger resting on the base of his member. She pushed herself snuggly against his backside.

"Capella's still sleeping. We should take advantage of these times," she teased, while rubbing that little finger gently along the top of his growing manhood.

David quickly pulled away, turned, and gently put his hand on her shoulder. "Not now, Sandy. I have to get going and spend the morning regrouping. I need to find time with Renée and bring myself up to speed so she can get back to the track."

Sandy pushed off him, grabbing a bath towel to cover her perfectly carved frame. Always so emotionally contained, the new Director of the CIA broke into tears. She made a beeline for the bed, falling face down. She couldn't hold the tears back. A lifetime of stifling despair, joy, sadness, fervor, along with the full gamut of emotions poured out of her with the authority of a typhoon.

With the realization those few precious moments, already sparse, would soon become a rarity, at least for the next few years, she had been hopeful of a different reception. The last, the very last thing she or any other women wanted at a time of intimacy was her partner making reference to another woman.

David didn't even take time to dry off. Her reaction terrified him. He'd never seen her in this state of mind. He sat at her side, placing his hand on the back of her head. She pushed his arm away.

"Sandy, please. I just meant—" The baby began to cry.

Sandy instinctively tried to compose herself, lifting herself up to care for her child.

"I've got it," he told her, motioning with his hand.

She was numb to his bid of fatherhood. As her feet hit the ground, she a little too aggressively shoved him back onto the bed.

"I can take care of my daughter. Go find your little Renée," she said forcefully.

"Sandy, please!"

Her face stiffened in anger. "Just go. Get out of here. I don't want this right now."

With that, she disappeared into the baby's room and he sat there contemplating what to do next. His gut feeling was to follow, but good sense told him to make a quick exit. In addition to what he had learned, or rather witnessed the past couple of years, seeing this episode actually frightened him, so that's exactly what he did.

***

Halfway to the barn, he pulled his cell and tapped the number two. His wife was one, Renée two. The call went directly to voicemail. Not leaving a message, he pressed end. His phone immediately chimed, indicating a missed call. When he read the screen, it brought a smile to his face. He and Renée were trying to reach out to one another at the exact same time, sending both calls to their respective voicemails. He hastily held back the grin, questioning his ability to experience an uplifting reflection while his wife was so upset with him.

The smile suddenly reappeared as he looked up and noticed Renée watching him. There she stood in denims, leaning her right shoulder on the corner of the barn, arms crossed with her left leg bent and tucked in behind the right, the toe of her cowboy boot tapping the dirt. The vision gave rise to him becoming weak-kneed. It happened every time he saw her. He'd given up trying to fight it. The reaction seemed out of his control.

It is what it is, he'd tell himself. They had found a way to keep their longing in check and focus solely on the professional relationship. What was stirring inside was a different story.

As he neared, Renée spoke first. "You back, boss?"

He nodded. "I'm back."

"Yay!" Her grin widened as she pumped her fist.

"You got time to bring me up to speed?"

He motioned toward the door of the barn, so she pushed off the rustic wooden structure and turned to the opening. After a few steps, Renée stopped. David took a couple more strides before realizing she wasn't at his side.

"David, before we go in, um…" Unsure how to continue, she cursed in French. "*Merde!*"

He faced her, flipping his palms upward, questioning her without speaking.

"David, about the other night…I thought I was alone."

"That's what's bugging you? It's fine. Don't give it a second thought. We're good here, kid. Under different circumstances, I might have joined you."

"Don't go there, but thank you. It was a tiny bit awkward." She bashfully tensed her facial expression, squeezing one eye shut.

He put his hands on her shoulders. "Seriously, Renée, we're good here. I think us North Americans could rid ourselves of a few sexual hang-ups by hanging out with you for a while."

She gently removed his arms and touched his hands a second longer than would be proper for friends or co-workers. As he was about to turn back toward the barn entrance, he caught sight of the ranch house. Standing in the upper large oval window stood his wife, holding their daughter. He knew she'd taken in the exchange, which looked less innocent than it was. The bump in the road just got a little steeper, but any restoration of harmony would have to be set aside, as it was time to focus on running the multi-million dollar McGinnis farm. Life was going to move ahead, and he was done trying to manufacture the perfect household.

It didn't take long for Renée to bring him up to date on the past few days.

"David, I need to get back to the track. Gabriela has been holding everything together and we didn't hire her as a ranch hand. She had to sit out a couple of races and we need her back in the saddle."

Gabriela, North America's leading money-winning jockey, had always been the McGinnis stable's biggest threat. Her rides crossed the finish line first more often than not. Over the years, David tried to woo her services to no avail. When Jacob and David hired Renée, it didn't even cross their mind that she wielded the influence to mastermind what they could not. Within six months of Renée's placement as lead trainer, Gabriela was exclusively mounting the finest thoroughbreds the McGinnis stable fielded.

"I agree. I've got this. You should head out as soon as we are done here."

"*Bon.*"

"Actually, I guess that pretty well wraps it up." He paused. "Renée...Sandy will be home for the next couple of weeks, so I've decided to take advantage of it and join you at next weekend's race in Florida."

Her heart fluttered, but she managed to remain composed.

"David, when you say *join me*, do you mean...?"

"No. Once Sandy leaves for Washington, I will have little time to enjoy race day, and to tell you the truth, this past year I have missed those trips. Strictly business, I promise."

She was relieved and disappointed at the same time. David read it in her face. Yes, life would be a little less confusing for both if the embers weren't still smoldering, but they were, and that was a reality. It wasn't going anywhere soon.

"To be honest, it would be nice to have you there to take care of business. We have two breeding contracts to deal with and they want to discuss them in person the day of the race."

"Okay, I believe we have it covered. You should be on your way. Please thank Gabriela, and thank all our staff for their support. Tell them we do appreciate it."

"I will."

Renée headed for the ranch pick-up she'd been using. David planned to stay and spend some time with the horses. As they were beginning to distance themselves from one another, something crossed Renée's mind.

"David," she called out.

He turned and once again they approached each other.

"It slipped my mind, but this morning I received a call from the White House. They asked if it would be okay if Addison could come out two weeks from now."

"Damn, I forgot about her. Well, if I have learned anything recently, it's that you don't say no to the President, so tell them it will be fine."

"Is she going to apprentice here or the track?"

"You do what you want with her. Just keep her away from me," he instructed Renée with a smirk on his face.

"I really don't have time to be babysitting."

"You'll think of something."

"Thanks, boss."

***

Back at the chalet, Jacob insisted they take the morning off so Brooklyn could rest. She protested, but not very forcefully. Her train of thought was she should get back to a regular routine sooner rather than later, a distraction from the recent distress of the past few days. It threw her off her game a little, but she knew last night's nightmare about Capella was going to be repeated many times over, and the images would be difficult to control. She would keep those mental pictures to herself for the remainder of her life. There would be no benefit to anyone in sharing them. But before she attempted to return to the office, the morning would be the perfect opportunity to discuss what was overheard during her capture.

At the breakfast table, they sat adjacent to each other, rather than the customary opposite sides. Little was said and Jacob made a conscious effort not to discuss the kidnapping. Brooklyn then suggested they retire to the living area. Holding hands, they eased onto a sofa.

"Jacob, I appreciate you're not asking me to replay the ordeal, I do. We need to put it into the past as soon as we can. I will say again, knowing Capella will have no recollection is a blessing. However, before we put it to rest, there is something I wish to discuss with you."

"Brooklyn." He squeezed her hand tightly. "I believe you're right. Let's get on with our life. As we have discussed many times, this reaffirms that our longevity is far too short. We know those who committed this atrocity have paid the ultimate price for their actions. I will trust the authority's certainty that it was an ill-advised attempt to drive home some meaningless intimidation practice directed at Sandy. I also want to accept as true that at no time were you in harm's way. Have mercy on those dunderheads who ordered this violation when my daughter finds them out."

"Dunderheads?"

"Yes, dunderheads. Would you prefer my actual description, the one I think best remain in my head?"

"Dunderheads, it is."

"Brooklyn, maybe you're right. It might be best for you to forge ahead." He reversed his thinking after hearing the tone in her voice. "Why don't we make our way to the office and get on with it? It will also give us a chance to check on Capella."

"Yes, but first, that subject I want to discuss," she began. "During my years at the White House, I was privy to many conversations that I believe might even surprise you. While our abductors thought I was asleep, a reference was made about an organization, a name I recognized. In the past, on the few occasions I overheard it being referenced to, an eerie hush came about the room. It seemed no one, including the President, wanted to address the subject."

"What is it they referred to that raises such a concern?"

"They knew nothing of the identity of their employer. They were sitting there guessing who ordered the abduction. How far up did their payoff come from? I'd venture to say they had no idea who they were working for."

"We really don't have to do this right now."

"Yes, we do."

"Have you mentioned it to Sandy?"

"I did, but I felt it was best that I advise you. She agreed. Jacob, my concern is that you may have had some form of business with the association throughout the years. I don't want you running off trying to track them down and put yourself in danger. As you've said, let's leave it to the authorities to see how much substance is behind these suspicions."

"Who did they make mention of?"

"The Bonanza Club."

Jacob face drained to white and his piercing stare troubled his wife.

"That can't be…"

***

David felt his stay at the barn had been as long as he could justify. It was time to return to the ranch house and face the music. Should he just come clean? Tell his wife that although he wished away his feelings for Renée, they weren't going anywhere? Sandy would never put him in a position where he had to lie or formulate any sort of explanation. She was above that, a class act. How in the world could he have dishonored her goodness?

After finding their suite empty, he went in search of his family, prepared to face the music. Coming down the grand staircase, he spotted her headed out the door with their daughter.

"Sandy."

With one leg out and the other inside the entrance, she stopped and turned to face him. There she stood sporting a gleaming smile. Not what he was anticipating. She looked beautiful, a woman who had everything, not a worry in the world. Not knowing what to say, he froze, allowing her current state of mind to manifest. What he was witnessing was completely throwing him off.

"Baby, look, it's Daddy."

He recognized it was a sincere smile, not fabricated.

"Well, are you just going to stand there or come join us?"

David was puzzled by her transformation, but wasn't going to reverse it by saying something stupid.

"Sure, where are we off to?"

"Actually, we were taking a walk down to the barn. We thought we would tear you away for a while. You must have slipped by us when we were in the kitchen."

David stepped down the stairs, gave Sandy a kiss, grabbed Capella, and lifted her into the air.

"Does my little girl want to go see the horses?"

Off they went as if life was ideal, laughing, joking. No mention was made of the earlier confrontation. David was okay with that. He figured the saying "leave well enough alone" fit the scenario perfectly.

After a half hour or so of being entertained by the animals, or possibly the opposite—Capella entertaining them—the family began a slow walk along the white fence toward the ranch.

"David, I was thinking, since I'm here for a couple more weeks, why don't we jump in the plane and go visit your parents? We're all so busy, so little time for them to get to know their granddaughter. Besides, I'm sure they've heard all the speculations being reported and are probably worried."

"Wow, I didn't see that coming. That's a great idea. When did you want to leave?"

"Let me talk to my father to see if he has any travel plans, and if not, I'll have the jet fueled and ready for tomorrow. I'm looking forward to some of your mother's home-cooked meals."

"Okay." He hesitated.

"What?" Sandy gave him an inquisitive stare.

"It's not important."

"What?"

"I was planning on taking in our race in Florida this weekend. I've missed so many cards this past year and there is some pressing business that would be best taken care of in person. Once you take up residency in Washington, I will have few opportunities."

He was careful not to mention that Renée requested his assistance. He would be cautious to not refer to Renée under any circumstances.

"David, I'm taking on a new career, not dying."

"I didn't mean it that way."

"What did you tell your parents about the police presence at the ranch?"

"I told them it was protocol on the day of you being sworn in, a precautionary measure, which they probably didn't buy into but won't question."

They paused for a bit, paying more attention to Capella than each other before Sandy, the voice of reason, broke the silence.

"We will leave Monday. Go to the race, and the little one and I will have a girls' weekend. Maybe we'll go shopping."

David shook his head. "You've got to be kidding. Might I remind you that you hate shopping?"

"Oh yes, but this little girl…" She gave Capella a tickle. "She needs to look her best for her grandparents. Should we be picking up a parka for her?"

"Nice. Actually, the igloo can get cool at night, so that might be a good idea."

They both laughed. Sandy liked to tease him about his Canadian roots, but truth be told, she loved everything about the country. She wished they could spend more time with his parents. They were such an unassuming couple with strong values. Family and land were above all else. The only drawback to their infrequent visits was that she always packed on an extra few pounds. The food was so plentiful and delicious.

"So you good with Monday?"

"Absolutely."

"Okay then, I will give my parents a call today."

"Why don't we just show up and surprise them?"

"My mother would have a heart attack if we arrived unannounced. Meals need to be planned. Bedding needs to be prepared and on and on."

"Well, you give her a call and I'll talk to Father about the plane."

"We can fly commercial."

"We could, but we have so little time, let's not waste it sitting at the airport."

"You win." He didn't want to argue.

The remainder of the afternoon was spent puttering around the grounds of the ranch. With a child, the awareness of nature's offerings became more noticeable. Butterflies, tiny little pebbles, puddles and thousands of other things which adults most often passed right by without a thought, the young eye found intriguing.

The ranchland provided no lack of wonders.

***

The minute Brooklyn gave details of what she'd overheard, Jacob excused himself, suggesting to his wife she take her time and they would catch up at the office. His heart rate and blood pressure peaked as he hurried to the main house. Once inside, he shut the office door and had the telephone receiver at his ear before his fingers punched out the ten digit number. It was answered.

"I'm flying in tomorrow. Just you and me. The others are not to be advised of the meeting."

He listened to the short reply before speaking again, this time with an authoritarian manner.

"Oh, you'll be there. You have some explaining to do. I will arrive at noon. Do not disappoint me."

The receiver reconnected on its base with force as Jacob fell back into his chair. Opening a desk drawer, he searched for his blood pressure pills and doubled the prescribed dose. Probably not a good idea, but he was uncharacteristically allowing his emotions to take control.

***

Brooklyn was quick to follow him to the office, as she suspected the reasoning behind Jacob's swift departure was her mention of the Bonanza Club. A man of his stature, considered to be in the elite one percent of the world's most wealthy, would at least in one way or another cross paths with members of such a club, if it even existed. She believed it was best to be in close proximity in case a nudging of common sense was necessary. She presumed her husband's plan to allow the authorities to complete their investigations without interference was a thing of the past.

Once at the office, Brooklyn tapped on the door before slipping in. It was next to impossible, but they did try to retain some form of office formality pertaining to boss and assistant.

"That was an abrupt exit."

"Come in, sit." He motioned to one of the chairs

in front of the oak desk. "I'm sorry for that. Your conversation rattled me. I hope what you overheard is not factual."

"I have no idea who was behind it, but let me be very clear, Jacob." Her tone commanded his undivided attention. "I don't care. It's over. We are home safe and sound and I want nothing more than to put this behind us. From this point on, it didn't happen, so please respect my resolution. Please, Jacob."

He leaned back into the leather chair, joining his hands together, lifting his index fingers into an upside down V shape and rested them on his face. He took a deep breath. "I understand. There will be no further mention. We move on."

"Thank you." She stood and began to make her way to the outer office. "Do we have issues that need to be dealt with before I begin to bring myself up to date?"

"No, I don't believe there are any pressing matters." He seemed to stumble with his words before adding, "Actually, that's not true. I had a call from Kristof just before you arrived and there seems to be a pressing issue that we feel is best discussed in person. I plan on flying out for the day tomorrow morning. Would you arrange for the jet to be readied?"

She gave him a curious smile. "All right. Now there's a name I haven't heard mentioned in a while." She left the room.

***

148

Once back in their suite, Capella settled on the floor to entertain herself.

"She seems quite content. Maybe this would be a good time to go down and talk to my father about our travel plans," Sandy said.

"Sounds good. I will give my parents a call to give them a heads up."

After a short time, Sandy returned from the visit with her father. She was a little suspicious, learning of his last minute travel arrangements. Seldom did he attend meetings out of the country anymore. For the most part, his associates made their way to the ranch for such gatherings. Although she was curious, she thought better of prying into his business, as he must have his reasons. He did, however, give his assurance that the aircraft would be available for their trip up north.

When entering the suite, she heard David say, "Love you too, Mom. Say hi to Dad."

"Did your mother seem happy about our visit?"

David didn't reply. He seemed to be processing something from the conversation.

"Father said the jet is all ours. Is there something wrong?"

"No. Yes…I don't know. My parents are going on a vacation."

"That's wonderful. They work very hard and a vacation will be good for them. You've always urged them to make time for themselves."

"You don't understand. My father doesn't take vacations. He hates traveling. The thought of sitting in some resort with hundred degree weather is his worst fear. He loves the farm. A walk in the bush is his definition of a holiday."

"Maybe he's doing it for your mother."

"Probably, but it's weird. The only time I can honestly say I remember him leaving our property was for our hockey or my sister's activities. He wouldn't even stay overnight, electing to drive hundreds of miles home at some godforsaken early morning hour." He paused, giving it some more thought. "I guess you're never too old for a change of heart."

"Well, I'm sure you'll find some time alone with him when we're there and get his side of the story."

"That's the thing. They don't want us to come. They are leaving next week and my mother feels it best if we reschedule for when they return. She went on about how much they had to prepare before the trip. This is so out of character for both of them. I'll get in touch with my brother later and see if he can fill me in."

"It does seem odd, and coincidently my father just informed me he is taking a day trip out of the country tomorrow, which is also peculiar. David, we're not their keepers and they are adults, so we really shouldn't be questioning their decisions, at least not out loud."

"You're right. So what now?"

"You go to Florida and we will figure out something special for us to do when you get home."

***

Early the next morning, Jacob landed at Grand Bahamas International Airport in Freeport. One of his companies held an ownership interest in the airport and he owned a private hangar on the property. An ideal location when the occasional meeting demanded the utmost secrecy.

As they taxied near the hangar, there sat a private aircraft. It was a bit bigger, a bit more showy, and a bit more extravagant than his, which made him smile. It was owned by the only other invite to the party, a man who felt the need to flaunt his cavalier lifestyle—Kristof Hoffmann.

Once safely inside the structure, confident no one was within auditory range, Jacob skipped the niceties and began to voice his discord. A sweeping of the hangar for listening devises was conducted earlier in the day, so holding back his antipathy wasn't in the cards.

"My wife, my grandchild—what the hell were you thinking? Have you lost your mind?"

"Jacob, please, the modus operandi…" He shrugged and spread out his hands. "No harm came to them and never would have."

"It's over. As of this minute, we are done. Inform the others I have brought our association to an end."

"You know that is not possible. This is bigger than any one of us. Please, my friend, you are upset. We all understand this. It was discussed in length prior to our order. We wish your daughter had declined, as you led us to believe she would, but it was a necessary evil. She needed to discover that we—and Jacob, I do mean *we*—have far-reaching influence. We trust she now understands, so should the need arise, we can count on her."

"Open your ears, Kristof. It's over. We are done."

"Jacob, after your call yesterday, I spoke to the others and we are in agreement that we will leave any further encouragement of your daughter solely in your hands. We can count on you, can't we?"

"Oh, Kristof, you ostentatious ass, must I remind you who *made* you? You would be nothing without me. If I for one second I believe you've made any attempt to forge forward with the others, you will be panhandling at your favorite Russian street corner. Understood?"

"Jacob, I will speak to the others, but I do not believe this can be halted."

"You do not want me to take matters into my own hands. That, my friend would not be in your best interest. It's over. Have a wonderful life, Kristof. You never know when the end will sneak up on you."

Jacob left without offering a goodbye or a handshake. This would be the last meeting of this kind. He should have ended it years ago. Power, wealth, influence took on a life of its own. But now the time had come for him to rid himself of these iniquities.

For most of the flight back home, he gazed out the window at the brilliance of the sun. In the not too near future, he would admit the purpose of the trip to his wife, apologize and promise never to twist the truth again.

Brooklyn was a perceptive person who in all probability knew the true meaning of the meeting. It was time for him to begin the rest of his life, time to squeeze every last moment out of it with his wife and family at his side.

First, he would commence the downsizing of the business. Hell, maybe they would hike around Australia, go back to Europe, sit on the couch reading—it didn't matter as long as Brooklyn was at his side. He didn't need the rest. He was over it.

***

David and Renée boarded the flight to Florida, but they weren't alone. Gabriela was the third person. He wasn't sure why, but Brooklyn had reserved four first class tickets. Maybe she anticipated Sandy joining them or possibly to avoid either of them being forced to converse with a stranger who might have been seated beside them. As it turned out, he sat alone in the first row and the women occupied the two seats directly behind him. It was nice to have the extra room. He would have to thank Brooklyn upon his return.

"Have you two girls worked out a game plan for the race?"

"We have. Would you like us to walk you through it?" Renée asked in a business-like matter.

Gabriela had probably picked up on the overstated formality.

"Nope, it's in your hands," David said. "You two have been doing just fine without throwing my two cents in."

Renée and Gabriela chatted for the remainder of the flight. David closed his eyes and let his mind wander as the music pulsed through the earphones of his iPhone.

It was an awkward check-in for David and his lead trainer. The hotel was the same one they'd spent the weekend in just over a year ago, an amorous memory for both. The recollection of it clouded their minds, but would not be mentioned, at least not unless they were alone, and maybe not even then.

"Why don't we clean up and grab a bite?"

"Sounds wonderful," Renée replied a little too enthusiastically.

"You two go enjoy yourselves. I have a weigh-out tomorrow and I've been eating a little too much lately."

Both David and Renée blurted out at the exact same time, "No, I—" They laughed at the synchronization of their words, then added, "We insist."

Having Gabriela accompany them was their safety net, a preventative measure fending off any flare-up of temptation.

"Join us, Gabriela. Have a small salad. You have to eat something," Renée said.

***

They wrapped up dinner, and with a little clumsiness, all three made it to their respective rooms, which were located on the same floor. At some point during their night's isolation, each found themselves reflective of one another.

There was zero reference to any personal matters during the evening. However, what went through each person's mind was a different scenario. David visualized Renée naked, lying next to him, the way it was a year ago, wondering if they would give in to their desires this weekend.

Renée's thoughts were similar, but she was reliving the spontaneity of their last Florida stay. The sex was amazing but the playfulness of the affair was what she recalled most. Being tossed into the ocean, the concert, the joking, all brought a smile to her face. She felt curious as to how the relationship would play out during the next couple of days.

Gabriela's hopes of snuggling up beside Renée were dwindling away. It was obvious from the prepensely restrained behavior of her co-workers that she would remain alone. Since she agreed to exclusively ride for the McGinnis stable, she and Renée shared a bed during their out of town races on more than one occasion. Not every trip, but on a few. Tonight wouldn't be one of them.

***

The weekend was a success. Gabriela's riding was brilliant, crossing the finish line first in both of the races. David solidified a lucrative breeding deal, and all made it through without surrendering to their longings.

The flight home was a repeat of the initial trip. The seating formation remained the same yet the girls were less talkative as they were exhausted by the effort expended realizing the wins.

***

Upon his return, Jacob assured his wife all went well and the business at hand was concluded. Brooklyn had her suspicions that the trip did relate to her abduction but was prepared to let it alone.

Exhausted from the few hours in the air, and his tenacious confrontation, he dispersed any further business for the day. After their hellos, Brooklyn suggested he retire to the chalet and that she would wrap things up, which she did within an hour or so. "How is life treating Kristof these days?"

"Oh, he's still pretentious as ever, but I don't believe we will have many future dealings. Speaking of business, there is something I would like to discuss with you after dinner."

She was surprised, as seldom had they conversed about the company's dealings at the chalet. Both preferred to reserve those discussions for the office.

"Maybe we should put business aside until tomorrow."

"I would prefer to get it off my mind sooner rather than later."

"Well, let's have dinner first, then see where it takes us."

***

When David arrived home, his wife and child were all smiles. The shopping spree didn't come about, but plenty of bonding time was had by the two of them, and also Brooklyn.

"Congratulations, David."

"Thanks, but our trainer and jockey made it all happen. I can't take any of the credit." He wanted to avoid saying Renée's name.

"Those two are going to set the racing community on fire."

"That they are."

The attention soon shifted to Capella, and there would be no more questions with regard to his weekend.

"David, I have an idea. Your parents will be vacationing for two weeks, right?"

"I believe so."

"I'm going to be in Washington by then, but why don't we send the jet, pick them up, and bring them here for a few days? You know Daddy would love that. He enjoys your father's company. I will try to sneak back while they're here, but at least this way they get to spend time with their granddaughter."

"I'm not sure they will go for that."

"Sure they will. You fly down and meet them. They're not going to refuse flying home with their son on a private plane. We just have to make sure you get there on the morning of their scheduled departure. Brooklyn's offered to watch Capella."

"As crazy as it sounds, I like it. Let's do it."

***

With dinner complete and the kitchen tidied up, Jacob and Brooklyn made themselves comfortable in the living area. Nothing was said for a couple of minutes until Brooklyn broke the silence.

"What's on your mind, Jacob?"

"Maybe you're right. We should wait until tomorrow. We did promise no business at home."

"No," she pressed. "This seems important, so let's make an exception this evening."

He wanted to explain himself, but didn't want to go on and on about it, so he tried to select the proper way to discuss it.

"I believe the time has come to downsize our business. I no longer want us trudging off to the office every single day. Our focus should be discovering more time for us."

"Jacob, we do spend the majority of our days together. I would think more so than most couples."

"I don't mean at the office. What I have in mind is selling our interests and just living life, you and me. We have more money than ninety-nine percent of the people in this world. Hell, we have more money than most countries do. My hope was Sandy would take the helm someday, but that's not likely to happen now. We'll hand over whatever portion she and David wish to continue to manage and designate the remainder of the control to the board.

"Brooklyn, look at us. We're not getting any younger, and I just don't want to do this anymore. I want us to wake up and go for a walk on the shores of some island down in the Caribbean. Spend afternoons swinging in a hammock together, fly to Paris for lunch, go parachuting, go hiking, make a bucket list, click one off every day, and just live. I want to spend whatever time I have left with you."

Brooklyn read between the lines, suspecting his recent meeting sparked the new mindset. The prospect of permanently getting out from behind the desk was a wonderful vision, but she would let the idea settle in for a couple of days before allowing herself to indulge in the concept.

"What brought this on, Jacob? You're painting a lovely picture, but I'm not quite convinced you're ready to give up on the business. It flows in your blood, it's your life, always has been. Let's give it some time to sink in, think about it a bit before we make any harsh decisions. If in a few weeks, maybe a month, if we still feel the same…then we go for it."

"Brooklyn, I've made up my mind. I want us to begin the remainder of our lives right now."

"Has this been on your mind for a while, or is it something that happened recently?"

"I've been mulling it over for quite some time now. The truth is, it has occupied my mind since the day we have found ourselves together. And with everything that's been going on recently, it only bolsters my decision. I'm excited about you and me just relaxing. We'll arrange a board meeting and I will put the plan into action."

"If this is what you want, let's strive to make it a reality. And, Jacob, to be honest…it does sound amazing."

"Do you remember the first night I knocked on your door?"

"Of course I do. One doesn't forget the most important day of her life."

They moved closer together on the couch. She laid her head on his shoulder as their arms intertwined. He gave her a kiss on the forehead. A pleasant smile appeared on both their faces, recognizing the momentousness of their resolution.

"Do you recall what you told me?" He didn't give her a chance to answer. "You said sometimes it appears our life is fulfilled but in actuality our careers, our daily routine, substitutes for true affection. We fall in love with all the bells and whistles money provides us, the power, the chase. But so often we don't truly know the meaning of love. What was the phrase used?"

"Love lonely."

"Yes, that's it. Without realizing it, we fall in love with being lonely. I've given that a great deal of thought since you summed up my life with that saying. Look at what Sandy and David are going through right now. We are fortunate to have the means to say we've had enough. Let's do this. Are you with me?"

"I'm all in." Her smile got brighter and she gave him a kiss.

"You asked what brought this on. As I said, I've been thinking about it for a long time. On the flight home, I was staring out the window at the incandescent sun. The warmth of it sneaking into the tiny windows had such a calming effect on me, like a drug. It was a beautiful sight, one I've never paid too much attention to. And you know what came to mind?"

Brooklyn looked at him curiously.

"As strange as this may sound," he continued, "I started to wonder about how many more sunrises and sunsets I have left. I should say, we have left. For a minute, I started doing the math, calculating and predicting the number of days remaining in my life. It really didn't take me long before I gave my head a shake and realized this is crazy. I want to live each sunset and sunrise, not count them."

He was so passionate about his plea that ever so slightly Brooklyn's eyes began to water as both of them remained silent. She knew his mind was made up and the downsizing would commence in the morning.

"No more being in love with lonely. It's time to love us, love life," Jacob concluded.

"Okay, let's embrace the many suns to come."

"Sounds delicious," he replied.

"Then, my dear husband, we begin praying for suns."

Chapter Eight

A couple of weeks seemed to fly by in a snap of a finger. Sandy had taken up residency in Washington with the promise to spend every second weekend at the ranch. David and Capella would visit the D.C. condo as much as possible.

Jacob and Brooklyn began the downsizing of their business interests. It wasn't going to be accomplished overnight. A machine of such grand scale would require time to phase down. They did, however, commit to introducing a three-day weekend and to allocating one full week per month off.

David oversaw the ranch's stable while Renée did the same at the racetrack. After their recent close encounters, it was decided Renée would revert back to taking care of all out-of-state races alone. But today she was back at the ranch awaiting the arrival of the new summer intern, Addison. Neither David nor his trainer wanted the babysitting responsibility, yet it was the President's daughter, so they would devise a plan to make it happen.

162

Who Lies Beside Me

***

An unassuming black SUV eased its way down the drive. Once the vehicle came to a stop, the front doors opened. A woman dressed in denim and cowboy boots stepped out of the driver's side. A second later, Addison appeared from the passenger's door, white headphones covering her ears, feet snuggled into a pair of black Converse All-Star Shoreline Slips, not the recommended footwear for a ranch. Her jeans were tight and an unbuttoned flannel shirt covered a white halter top.

"Should I get her to muck out the stalls before she gets a chance to change her shoes?" Renée whispered in David's ear.

They both had to hold back their laugh but it did register a smile.

"Be nice, now," he teased.

They stepped down the porch stairs to greet their two guests.

"Addison, it's nice to see you again," David said.

"I'm so glad to be back. This is Ava, my assigned Secret Service agent."

"It's a pleasure to meet you." They shook hands.

"It's very nice to meet you, sir. I will do my best to remain in the background. However, Addison's safety is my first priority."

"Well, we welcome both of you. I'm sure we will have a great summer. The staff has prepared your rooms." David gestured toward the entrance.

Once inside, the staff carried the luggage to their assigned accommodations. David wanted to give them a quick tour of the main floor, in particular the kitchen, as for the most part the visitors would be fending for themselves as the family rarely gathered for meals. Renée was anxious to head home, as it had been an early morning at the track before driving to the ranch to be a part of the welcoming committee.

She made a decision to keep Addison as far away from David as possible, so the guest's training would take place at the track.

"Addison, I need to be leaving soon, so if you don't mind, I would like a private moment with you. If you can spare a few minutes, I'd appreciate it."

Renée was somewhat asking for the agent's permission, but in a manner which she hoped would set the tone for the remainder of the summer. It was going to be difficult enough finding time to oversee Addison's duties without having to seek permission before every task. So the ground rules needed to be laid out right from the get go. At least that was her intention. There was no objection, so Renée and Addison found their way to the porch swing.

"I know, Renée," Addison began. "I'm not going to mess up. You don't have to worry."

"I'm not worried. I am, however, very busy, and travel a great deal, so I don't have time to be overlooking your every move. You need to understand you are the low person on our seniority list, and duties will be assigned by other staff members. I need you to follow those instructions to a tee. Do you understand?"

"Yes."

"Good, I'm happy we understand each other."

"So when do I start cleaning out the horse stalls?" Addison asked, presuming she would be designated to the dirtiest farm duties right away. She seemed prepared to accept the challenge without protest.

"Oh no, Addison, you have to work yourself up to that task."

"Then what will be my job?"

"We have decided to start your training at the racetrack, since that's where I am most days. I or one of my assistants will delegate duties daily or weekly. I don't want to hear you balking at any of the jobs. If you're serious about this, you have to work hard, listen, and learn. We employ the best people in the industry, so take advantage of it. Only a select few are invited to join our family."

"I'm here to learn, Renée. You can rely on me."

"Okay, then. One more thing, if I even hear a rumor about you making an advance at any of my staff, you will be sent home before you can speed dial your father. So it's one chance only. I will give you two days a week off. What you do with them outside the McGinnis properties is no concern of mine. You are welcome to hang around the track on those days, but you will not be paid for it."

"I get it." Addison sounded a bit agitated from the ongoing lecture.

"I've decided to train you on feeding duty first. It's not as simple as it may sound. You'll be assigned to one of our assistant trainers."

Addison was surprised at the assignment, having expected much worse.

"I can do that."

"I know you can. Did you bring proper clothing? If not, we can arrange for some."

"I'm good."

"Perfect. The first feeding is at four, so you and Agent Ava will need to be on the road by three."

"Can I come earlier? I would like to have a look around."

"You could, but you won't see very much, as it's fairly quiet at that time."

"You said four…" She suddenly realized she'd meant four in the *morning*.

"You don't have a problem with that, do you?"

"Ah…no, I will be there."

"Okay then, I should be on my way. I will see you in the morning. The staff is expecting you, so introduce yourself and they will set you up. Be sure to advise Ava of the plans. I'm sure she will be excited about the early start."

They got up, Renée jumped into a company truck, and Addison entered the house with one thing on her mind—bed. She was determined not to be late, although the thought of getting up before she normally went to bed didn't seem humanly possible.

***

On the other side of the world, Fyad was settled into his daily routine of securing his country's safety. He would soon be visiting the United States and planned to touch base with Sandy as he did most times when in close proximity. He appreciated that Sandy kept to her word about not pressuring him for a detailed discussion on what transpired in

Cuba.

During the intense stand-off procuring the safety of his friend's child, a chilling awareness came over him about how much he really did care for Sandy. He shook it off as a weak moment. He was now married, and so was she. Yet, no one knew him as well as she did.

Sitting in his office, he found himself reflecting on the emotions but was soon relieved of the thoughts by a knock at the door.

"Come in."

"Sir, can you spare a minute?" Hamza asked.

"Please, come in."

His main lieutenant sat in a chair in front of the imposing desk.

"As per your instructions I have concluded an in-depth analysis with regards to possible members of the Bonanza Club. Utilizing intercepted communications, a shift in political powers, coups, arms deals, world wealth, transactions, travel arrangement, and a number of other factors, I have prepared a list of nine persons we believe make up this group. There is a slight possibility there may be one or two additional members and a few of these names may just be associated with but do not participate within the inner circle."

"Good job, my friend. May I have the list?"

Hamza hesitated in handing over the document.

"Sir, I will continue interpreting our findings, but I'm seeking your instructions on how to proceed with two names we have assessed as high probabilities."

He handed Fyad the document, who took a

moment to review it before replying to his assistant's request.

"Hamza, remove my father's name immediately. We will leave Mr. McGinnis's name for the time being. Please include him in your continued probe. However, his inclusion will remain between you and me. I need an unwavering certainty of these identifications before we decide on how to proceed. Also, please confirm the arrangements for my upcoming trip to the United States."

"Yes, sir. Will that be all?"

"Thank you, Hamza."

The inclusion of his father, as well as Sandy's, did not come as a surprise. He knew their influence touched most parts of the world. Eventually, a discussion with the King would take place, but not until the findings were verified over and over again. Then, and only then, would he seek out his father's advice with regards to the steps required in avenging the group's actions.

***

The alarm on her iPhone rapped out a tune alerting her to the time of day, or in this case, morning. She found a way to flop her legs to the floor. She hadn't really slept, just laid there in a vague state of rest, not wanting to be late on her debut. It was the first time she could remember waking at such an hour, and she was hurting.

Addison removed her pink striped thermal pajama bottoms and tossed them on the bed. Sporting only the tightly fitting top, she found herself leaning over the bathroom sink, splashing cold water on her face in an attempt to wake up. Once realizing she wasn't succeeding, she leaned in and adjusted the taps of the shower to the chilly temperature necessary to revive the walking dead back to life.

Snuggled into a pair of jeans, denim shirt, jacket, and cowboy boots, she walked out the front door at precisely three in the morning. Ava stood leaning up against the SUV, surprised her assignment presented herself on time.

"Sorry about this, Ava. I'm going to be at the racetrack all day and there will be a lot of people around, so if you want to go back to bed, I'll be fine."

"Can't do that, Addison. I'll keep a low profile. You won't even know I'm there."

The agent smiled and offered a cup of coffee she'd brewed in the main kitchen. It was black and strong, just the way Addison liked it.

"Thank you. I think I'll need a few more of these before the sun comes up."

They had a laugh, then set out to the racetrack.

***

At this time of morning, the staffing at the track was minimal, but soon it would be a bustling complex. The thoroughbred industry was not modeled after a typical business. People scheduled their days around the needs of the horses. Many of the animals were worth millions of dollars to their owners, so these athletes' well-being trumped all else.

The formalities of introductions were quick and polite. Renée arranged for Savannah to guide Addison through the first stage of her internship. Being that they were only a few years apart in age, Renée felt the communication between them would ease Addison into demands she wasn't accustomed to.

"Addison, would you like to change into a pair of rubber boots?"

The rookie looked down at Savannah's feet and noted a pair of cowboy boots, so she was fairly confident hers would suffice.

"No, I think I'm fine. I'll be careful."

"Okay then, let's head to the feed room."

Off they went to a detached building adjacent to the stable. What was inside took Addison by surprise. It looked more like a lab, one she might have taken a chemistry class in. The room was as clean and shiny as any five-star restaurant. The endless rolls of the food for the animals had been piled in immaculate order. Scales, large and small, were placed throughout the building. But what caught her most off-guard were the charts on the wall. The only writing on them she understood was a map of which horse was in which stall. Beside each name were a number of equations which she knew related to the animals' diets, but she had no clue what they meant.

"I sense you're a little taken back by the elaborate set-up."

"I wasn't expecting this. I thought when Renée told me I was on feed duty, I would be tossing a few bales of hay to the horses."

"Well, that you will be doing, but each of our animals has a specific diet that Renée and our veterinarian team has developed for them," Savannah explained. "Actually, I'm surprised Renée gave you this assignment. Under normal circumstances, an apprentice wouldn't be placed here until they had been with us for months. And that's only a select few she's developed a lot of confidence in."

Addison was surprised by the comment. She was an intelligent girl and knew the only reason her summer employment request was approved was because of her father, and she was okay with that. It touched every aspect of her life, so she could either embrace it and reap the benefits, or struggle with it. She chose to take advantage of the opportunities it presented.

"To be honest, I think she is testing me with the early mornings."

"That might be true. You never really get used to functioning properly at this time of day."

Addison followed the trainer to the far end of the building, where she put a number of items on an electric pallet jack. Each bag of feed and supplements had a control sheet on which she documented her name, quantity, date, the horse it was meant to feed, among other details which were foreign to her.

"Addison, for the next couple of days, how about you follow me around and I will briefly explain each step of our process? It does take quite a bit of time to fully understand every aspect of what we do here."

"Sure, whatever you think is best. What is that room over there used for?"

Addison was pointing to a door with a sign centered on its window labeled ***International Feed Room.***

"That's where we prepare feed for the horses we race outside the United States. Every ingredient requires approval for importation into each respective country, which by the way, all have different guidelines of what can or can't be brought in," she said. "It's a very tedious process, as on top of having each ingredient approved, we have to make sure each individual horse's diet is adequately supplied to cover the duration of their stay. Sometimes I think there're more forms to be filled out than there is in the amount of oats we prepare. Also, each country has their own quarantine regulation, which means a horse could conceivably have to spend up to two weeks in a country to run one race. I'm not sure if Renée will have you involved in that process before the end of the summer, but you never know."

Addison spent the remainder of the day becoming educated on the many steps of the preparation required before the horses actually got to eat. She and Savannah prepared and fed both the morning and afternoon meals. There was little time for anything other than making ready and delivering the food.

It was seven in the evening before Addison and Ava found their way back to the ranch. A meal had been prepared by the house staff in anticipation of the guests being hungry after their first day on the job. Ava grabbed one of the premade dishes and took it to her room, which was located directly across from her assignment's quarters.

Addison, on the other hand, opted out of the meal for some extra shut-eye. She was beyond exhausted, but throughout the day she'd disguised her tiredness. Within the seclusion of her room, it was a different story. She dragged herself to the shower and in record speed was curled up underneath the covers of the bed. Soon, she was asleep, only to dream about once again being wakened by her alarm at two in the morning, ready for a repeat of day one.

***

Sandy was settling in nicely at Langley as the transition of leadership seemed to be moving along smoothly and near complete. Christopher Young would be making all final decisions until the day he vacated his office, although Sandy would be apprised of all matters up to that point. On the other hand, she was experiencing a cool reception from many of the higher level members. Everyone wanted to know, why Sandy? Why not an internal placement?

The Assistant Director was well-respected, a life-time CIA employee, so why not him?

Many questions were being asked in regard to the President's choice, yet all knew whether they blessed her appointment or not, she would soon be the one with the power to alter their future at the snap of a finger.

For several years, Sandy's inclusion into the agency and government's inner circle prepared her well for the responsibility which lay ahead. Yet, it was difficult not to be amazed by the far-reaching arm of the CIA. Simply put, no one on the face of the earth was excluded from its grasp if the organization took an interest in them. The average citizen would have nightmares for the remainder of their lives if they were aware of what Sandy had knowledge of.

One of the first items on her agenda was to conduct a search and purge any past activities which might have made reference to her. The investigation came up empty. The President was good to his word. She would conduct a more in-depth exploration once the outgoing Director had officially handed in his credentials. The next item was to pull all information pertaining to Fyad. What she found was not surprising, but the classification the organization labeled him was disturbing. This review solidified the vastly different train of thought between her and Mr. Young.

Sandy was confident her modus operandi would see the Agency modernized to the necessities of today's world. The remaining personal item on her list was to commence an operation to uncover those persons or group responsible for ordering the kidnapping of her daughter and stepmother. However, that would be a personal, low-key undertaking which was best left for when she had settled in and knew who she could trust.

***

During her absence, Sandy and David kept in touch on a daily basis. The first three weeks passed in the blink of an eye. She missed her husband and daughter immensely. The plan was to spend every second or third weekend together at the ranch. In addition, David would try to visit Washington with Capella as often as possible. They would strive to make both residences feel as much like a home as possible. But, the initial few months of transition would absorb the majority of Sandy's time. The shift in power was not a simple one. The weight of the country's safety rested on her shoulders.

She had just concluded a meeting with a handful of senior staff members when her mobile vibrated. It was David and she wanted to talk to him. She dismissed the group.

"Hey, you, I miss you guys so much."

"We miss you too."

"Seriously, David, I wish you two were here."

"So do we, but the weekend will be here before you know it."

"David, I hadn't planned on coming home this weekend. I need to work straight through. I think Christopher is becoming anxious for his retirement, so we are pushing hard to complete the turnover."

"Well, this is the weekend I'm flying to Freeport to intercept my parents' return and bring them here. My brothers organized a plan to take care of the farm for another week. I'm hoping I can convince them to stay for a while."

"I'm sorry, David, I forgot. I can't see how I can

make it work."

"Come on, Sandy, you have to spend some time with them, and us. Christopher is still there. The world's not going to fall apart if you disappear for a few days."

She leaned back in the chair, held her breath for a few seconds before exhaling.

"David, did we make a mistake here?"

"Listen to me, and listen closely. I am extremely proud of you. You are immensely talented, and with you at the helm of the agency, we can all sleep better. We can do this, you can do this. Let's move forward, not look back. We're not going that way."

"You go get your parents. I'll find a way to slip out for a couple of days."

He was relieved she would make an appearance. Although his parents were supportive of their family's choices, they were a bit old-fashioned and he would rather not be justifying her absence.

"How's Capella holding up?"

"She's great. Your father and Brooklyn have made it their mission to spoil her rotten. All kidding aside, she's happy, Sandy, and always smiling. She's been sleeping through the night. I know when she is old enough to understand your choices, she will be very proud of you."

Tears began to materialize on her cheeks. She didn't reply, and David knew the difficulties she was experiencing not being with her child. He thought it best to end the call so she could once again bury herself into her work.

"Listen, babe, I need to go. I will talk to you tomorrow."

"Okay, give Capella a kiss for me. I love you two."

"We love you."

***

David woke up thirsty around two in the morning only to find his refrigerator barren of dairy, so he grabbed the baby monitor, and set out in the direction of the ranch's main kitchen. He'd put little thought into his attire, as he wasn't expecting to meet up with anyone. He was barefoot, shirtless, only wearing a pair of loosely fitting flannel pajama bottoms.

The only glow in the room came from the refrigerator light as he held the door open, contemplating his refreshment of choice. It came as a surprise to him when the ceiling light suddenly illuminated the kitchen. Being that he was leaning deep into the appliance retrieving a carton of milk, his hasty reaction caused him to clumsily bang the back of his head on the upper shelf of the unit, while simultaneously bumping his arm on the door. He dropped the container.

"Sorry. I didn't mean to scare you," Addison offered.

Slightly embarrassed and not certain how to respond, it took him a few seconds to reply. "I wasn't expecting to bump into anyone at this hour."

"Well, technically you didn't bump into anyone. The way I see it, your adversary is the refrigerator," she teased. "I'm sorry. I didn't see you and I didn't mean to startle you. Let me clean that up." She

177

nodded to the white liquid filling the tiny crevices of the floor.

"What are you doing up so early?"

"I was going to brew a cup of coffee for me and Ava." She placed a pod in the coffee machine, then a mug on the holder. At the touch of a button, the gurgling began. "I need to be getting to work soon. We don't want those horses to go hungry."

David searched the room for something to absorb the mess. Before he knew it, she tossed him a towel and they crouched down opposite of each other, wiping up the spill.

"Renée still has you on feed duty?"

She gave a long drawn out answer. "Yup."

David hadn't taken notice, but as he looked across at her, her terry cloth robe had eased open, revealing a pair of sheer laced panties that didn't do a good job of concealing what they should. He forced his eyes upward, only to catch her staring at his chest. Not sporting a shirt hadn't crossed his mind in the minute or two they had been fumbling about. Addison didn't seem fazed by the interaction and made no attempt to readjust her housecoat.

Once the floor was dried, they stood up, and although at that point Addison did pull the upper part of the robe closer, the v-shaped opening of the bottom half clearly continued to reveal her see-through yellow undies. While she acted innocent, oblivious to her display, it remained uncovered by design, and he knew it. Although she hadn't planned for the encounter, she was aware her actions were achieving the result they were meant to.

To his surprise, the crossing of paths sparked an arousal. Thinking about her in that nature never crossed his mind. She was a kid, just turned twenty. Actually, the further away she stayed, the better. It wouldn't have bothered him in the least if they never laid eyes on one another for the rest of his life. Yet, here he was, momentarily seized under her spell. The one thing he would give her credit for was the ability to get what she wanted. He had no doubt she would conquer whatever she set her sights on. Her methods might be unconventional, but she would triumph.

Suddenly, he realized she'd noticed his manhood was slightly enlarging. Since he wasn't wearing any underwear, his phallus was becoming more noticeable as it slightly began to pressure the front of his pajamas. He turned away from her to pour a glass of milk and decided to drink it on the way back to his room.

"Have a good day, Addison," he offered as he tried to keep his lower half shielded.

"I will now." She held up her mug.

He hoped her reference regarded the coffee, not his arousal, but he knew better. David nodded his goodbye and exited the room, but not before he noticed the nice little grin on her face.

Once back in his suite, David first checked on Capella, who was still fast asleep. He couldn't shake off the image of Addison kneeling in front of him with her legs partially spread apart, exposing her panties, which she might as well not have been wearing, as they left little to the imagination.

It had been nearly a month since he was last with

his wife and his stimulation was getting the better of him. He stepped in the shower in anticipation of the urge subsiding. That didn't work. If anything, it made it worse. He couldn't rid himself of the visualization. Once again, a guilty feeling came over him.

She was only twenty years old, but her mind and body was one of a matured woman twice her age. He gave in to the craving, rested one arm on the shower wall, and took a hold of himself. He wanted to purge his mind of what had transpired, but creative thoughts of Sandy and Renée were eclipsed by the curvature revealed through Addison's panties. Within a couple of minutes, his physical needs were fulfilled.

***

"Renée, I won't be available Saturday or for much of next week. Can you take double duty?"

"Sure, what's up?"

The stable had a couple of local races scheduled, and nothing out of the ordinary, so Renée's workload would be manageable.

"I'm flying to Freeport to surprise my parents, who are on a holiday. They don't know it yet, but I'm going to hijack them and extend their vacation."

"When will you be back?"

"I'll only be gone for the day. I want to intercept them before their return home and convince them to spend a week or so here at the ranch."

"That's nice. I'm sure they are going to love seeing Capella."

"I think they will. So you've got me covered?"

"*Oui*, David."

"Good. By the way, how is Addison doing?"

"Actually, she's been doing fine. I'm pleasantly surprised. I haven't had to tear her off anybody yet."

"Hmm."

"David, is there something you're not telling me?"

"No. I'm just surprised, that's all."

"Are you sure? I'm not going to tolerate any of her childish behavior. So if something's going on at the ranch, I want to know."

"Everything's good. I rarely see her."

"Okay. Is there anything else you want to discuss?"

"I will call you when I get back."

"*C'est bon. Au revoir.*"

David ended the call, then tapped the number one. After a couple of rings, Sandy answered.

"What up, Wattsy?"

"You're in a good mood. I can't remember you calling me that for long time."

"I am. Things are coming together nicely. I should be back at the ranch by Sunday. I can't wait to see you guys."

"That sounds good. Hopefully nothing comes up."

"I'll be there."

"I'm going to fly out early tomorrow morning. I've decided to leave Capella here with your father and Brooklyn. I think it best."

"I agree. Listen, sorry to cut you off, but I need

to run. I have a meeting in a couple of minutes. I will see you on Sunday."

"Love you."

"Love you too."

***

The private jet touched down at the Grand Bahamas International Airport for the second time within the month. The pilots steered the aircraft once again to the private hangar owned by the family. David was greeted by a small man with a strong Bahamian accent in a Hawaiian print shirt two sizes too big for him.

"Hello, sir, my name is Bob. It's nice to have your family back on our island again so soon."

David had to listen carefully to decipher what the man was saying as he spoke with such a distinctive island accent. The contrast of his speech and his name Bob, such an American title, brought about a smile.

"Bob, what do you mean by so soon?"

"I'm sorry, sir, I just meant it was only a few weeks ago I prepared your hangar."

"We own a hangar here."

"Yes, sir. I believe your family is part owner of the airport itself. I apologize, sir. I wish not to speak out of place."

We own this airport. He made a mental note to spend more time with Jacob to learn just exactly what else the company owned. Someday, he and Sandy may have to deal with the inner workings of the business. He wondered who of the family had been here recently.

"Sir, I have communicated with the tour company Mr. and Mrs. Watson are travelling with, and we expect them to be arriving in two hours."

"Thank you, Bob. I will remain here for the time being, but could you return in an hour or so to direct me to the waiting area in which they will be checking in for their flight?"

"Absolutely, sir. Would you care to visit our VIP lounge, or we could arrange a beverage be brought to the hangar?"

"No, thank you. I will see you in a while."

There was no customs clearance, no questions with regards to reasoning behind the visit or departure. He had been an integral part of the McGinnis family for many years, even prior to their marriage. Yet, just when he thought he had a grip on the influence Jacob wielded, he was surprised by another unearthing.

David made his way up the aircraft's ladder and informed the pilots of the estimated wait time before they would return home. He wasn't sure why he took it for granted that Jacob's recent day trip was stateside. Little thought had gone into it, but it did surprise him to learn his father-in-law had flown to the island, or at least that is what he presumed Bob was making reference to.

He adjusted himself into one of the luxury leather seats. It was a much more comfortable place to relax until his parents' arrival, a perfect time to check in with his wife. The call went to voicemail. He listened to the message urging a call back number, then hung up without speaking and tapped another number.

Renée answered. "David, I thought you were on your way to meet your parents."

"I am. I have an hour or so to kill."

"Did you need anything from me?"

"No, I was just checking in. Is anything going on?"

"Everything is under control, boss."

"Good."

"Actually, there is an update. The vet says Belle is doing well. Let's keep our fingers crossed."

"That's excellent news."

Belle was a seven-year-old mare that was in her ninth month of pregnancy. It was a familiar occurrence around the ranch and the staff was well-schooled to properly care for the animals bearing a foal. However, Belle was carrying twins. The odds were one in ten thousand that a mare becomes pregnant with twins and the odds of one or both foals surviving was a great deal less. But from all accounts, Belle was doing fine. All checkups and ultrasounds gave hope to her giving birth to two healthy little ones.

"Do you think we should put her on twenty-four-seven?"

"I think she's fine. We're still a couple of months, and as of today we believe she will go full-term."

The magic number was eleven months and five days to birthing. Three hundred and forty days was the average time frame, but having twins gave concern to a premature delivery. Today all was well by the sounds of it, and David would discuss it further with the doctor when he arrived home. It brought a smile to his face at the thought of his father having an opportunity to meet the horse. His dad would most definitely have some words of wisdom, and that was okay, as he valued his opinion.

"We'll monitor her closely, then," he said.

Both ends of the conversation went silent for a longer than normal time.

"David, everything really is good here. We can catch up tomorrow or the next day. I should be getting back to work. Is there anything else?"

"Not really. You're right. We should catch up later."

"What's wrong, David?"

"Nothing. Listen, I've got to go."

"*Au revoir.*"

"See you soon."

***

After his calls, he stepped back down the stairs to the tarmac and walked in the direction of the hangar. Apparently, they owned it, or more correctly, Jacob's company retained ownership. Why not check it out while waiting for Bob's return?

Once inside, the reality of its immense size sank in. From a frontal view it looked like a typical smaller airport structure, but once inside, he could see it extended lengthwise. It was much larger than would be required to house a private aircraft. The square footage was sizable enough to shelter four or five planes.

He neared a small office and opened the unlocked door. There was very little in the room, but he did notice a company's health and safety manual which he picked up and scrolled through. The title page read, **Health and Welfare, GBIA, McGinnis Enterprises.**

He laid it back on the desk and began rifling through the drawers when he noticed another manual marked **Aircraft Service Log.** David felt guilty for snooping around. He wasn't sure why, but that didn't stop him. He leafed through it and noted a number of entries, each pertaining to a particular aircraft. There was no indication of ownership, as they were listed by model and their FAA registration number. He did recognize the identification of the one he'd just disembarked.

David took out his cell and snapped a picture of the index page, which listed each of the ten or so aircrafts. He wasn't sure why, but curiosity got the better of him. In his spare time he might Google to see who they were registered to.

As he exited the room, Bob entered the hangar.

"Mr. Watson, we should make our way to the main terminal. I have been informed your parents' transportation bus is expected to arrive within a half hour."

"Sure. Thank you, Bob."

They hopped into the opened doors of a small car which shuttled them to the main terminal. It took all of three minutes before they were stepping out onto the warm, tarred surface. He could see the heat rays rising from it. They soon found themselves inside the terminal, which was beginning to fill up with tourists sporting their newly purchased Caribbean attire and sun-kissed faces.

Bob excused himself, then went out the front door, where he would remain on the walkway until David's parents' bus arrived. He would stay in the background but make sure the family connected before they could board the scheduled charter home.

It wasn't long before David watched a new wave of people enter the terminal. Bringing up the rear was Bob, who looked directly at him and nodded to his right, silently informing him that his parents had entered the airport. They were dressed so out of character he hadn't recognized them in the crowd.

He eased his way through the lines, and as he closed in on them, noting how refreshed they looked. They were talking to some others and everyone seemed so happy, all smiles and laughter.

"Mom, Dad," David said as he came up behind them.

The whole group turned and looked. It hadn't crossed his mind that they were probably all moms and dads. Since it was such an unexpected reunion, it took his parents a moment to recognize him. They were startled by his presence.

"David," his mother said. "What are you doing here? Is everything okay?"

"Yes, Mother, everything is fine."

He gave them both a hug.

"Since we couldn't convince you to come down for a visit, Sandy and I came up with a new plan. I flew in to snatch you away for a few more days and then we will fly you back home."

"David, we already have a flight paid for," his mother said.

"I have Jacob's plane, and it is available to take you home whenever you want to leave. Capella is growing up so fast, and I'm certain she would like to see her grandparents."

His father weighed into the conversation. "I really should be getting back to the farm. I promised your brothers I would be home."

"Dad, I talked to them and they want you to stay. Everything is running smoothly. It's only a three hour flight when you do decide to leave. There's a lot more leg room on Jacob's aircraft. Besides, it will give a couple of people on the charter a little more arm room."

David knew he had them at the mention of Capella. He could see they were still trying to grasp his presence, but recognized they were excited about the opportunity to visit with their grandchild, who was growing up far too fast.

"Charles, I would love to spend a couple of days with Capella. David said the kids have the farm covered."

"Okay, then, but what about our luggage? It's probably already loaded."

"Dad, it's been taken care of. I've had it transferred to our plane."

"How did you...?" His father started, then stopped halfway through the sentence. "Never mind. We should tell the others."

At that, Charles looked over to a small group of travelers.

"There's been a change in our plans. We won't

be flying back home with you. My son has flown down in his jet to take us back to his ranch for a few days."

"Your son owns a private jet?" one of the vacationers asked.

The tone of Charles's reply was one expressed by a proud father. "Yes, his wife's family does. It was wonderful to meet all of you. Patricia and I will keep in touch. We're going to hold you to that promise about visiting us up at the farm," he said to one of the couples. "You have our number."

They all shook hands and said their goodbyes before Bob escorted the family to the aircraft.

The conversation on the flight back to Kentucky was mostly split between the highlights of stories about Capella, and the vacation nobody in the family thought would ever take place.

***

"Breaker, I'm proud of you, but I'm not a spy. I'm special ops," Blake said.

"All I'm asking is that you meet with me and hear me out. I'm not going to turn you into a spy." Sandy was reaching out to one of the few people she had an unabridged trust for. He was one of the special eleven. They had stood side by side while enduring that year of training which turned each of them into dangerous human instruments, the level of which outsiders could not possibly understand. She needed someone of his intelligence and skills in the field as her go to, one who was capable of executing those assignments that might not be perceived as the agency's official business.

"I can arrange the transfer. Please, Blake, come in and hear me out. That's all I ask of you."

"All right, Sandy. For you. I'll be in touch."

She left it at that. Confident he would join her, there was no sense in pushing him with regards to a timeframe. They wished each other goodbye.

Sandy ignored the couple of beeps indicating an incoming call on her cell phone while talking to Blake. Noting the tiny screen displayed a missed call from her husband caused her train of thought to switch back to her personal life, which she spent much too little time reflecting upon. Before she could activate her husband's number, the unit displayed another incoming call. It wasn't David. It was Fyad. Her husband's return call would have to wait.

"Fyad, a pleasant surprise."

"It's nice to hear your voice, Sandy. Thank you for being patient with me. As I promised, I wish to detail my Cuba visit and I am flying in tomorrow. Will you be available?"

As he mentioned, she had been patient. Many others hadn't and deflecting the ongoing requests from a number of government departments on the incident seemed to materialize every second day. She was eager to meet with her friend and was prepared to rearrange her schedule allowing for the inquiry, but hesitated with the realization of her plans to return home the next morning.

"What will be the duration of your stay?" she asked.

"I will be spending two days in Washington then

I must attend business on the West Coast before returning. I would appreciate our gathering tomorrow evening. I am departing within the hour."

She took a moment to weigh her options of delaying her return home or propose to Fyad they reschedule for a later date. Maybe she could fly out to the coast after a couple of days at the ranch, yet in reality she knew there was only one choice. "That sounds perfect. Please contact me when you land. I will free up my day."

"Excellent. By the way, how does it feel occupying such an influential office?"

"I will tell you all about it when you arrive."

"Until tomorrow, my friend."

Next on the agenda was a return call to David. He wasn't going to be pleased with her, but it couldn't be helped.

"Babe, operation Mom and Dad was a success. We just got home and we are all looking forward to your arrival."

"I'm so glad, Wattsy. I can't wait to see everyone."

"What time do you land tomorrow? I will pick you up at the airport."

Her stomach tightened as she took a deep breath.

"I'm sorry, David, but something of grave importance has materialized. I won't be able to leave until the day after tomorrow. I hope your parents will understand and stay. I would love to see them."

Sandy knew the family recognized her position was not of the norm, and that when situations arose, as Director she would be required to put all else on the back burner. That being said, she was also aware they were not fond of her separation. What they didn't know was the unwavering devotedness expected from those safeguarding the country. She survived on four, maybe five hours of sleep per night, with every other waking hour spent overseeing the agency's business. Since arriving, she had yet to eat a decent meal outside of work.

Although she earnestly missed her family, in particular Capella, she found herself smiling, anticipating a dinner with Fyad.

"That's disappointing. Can't it be put aside for a few days?"

"It doesn't work that way, David. Please bear with me. I will be home as soon as possible."

"Let me know when you want me to pick you up," he replied.

"I'll find my way. Please enjoy your time with your parents and tell Capella I will be home soon."

"Okay then."

"David, I love you. Please give her a kiss and tell her Mommy is always thinking of her."

"I will. Love you too."

"Talk to you soon."

Chapter Nine

Sandy crammed in her duties, trying to free herself up for Fyad and the trip home. She worked straight through, substituting a few catnaps for a night's sleep. The activity of the agency never slowed. The citizens it protected were nestled into their comfy warm foam forming beds as the intelligence agency was operating full speed ahead. While one side of the world slowed in darkness, the other was bustling in the glow of daylight and she had operatives placed in all corners.

By mid-afternoon, the most pressing issues were mostly dealt with. Since her conversations with Fyad and David, it was the first time she realized it might actually be possible for her to break away. Tonight she would meet with Fyad. Tomorrow, she would reunite with her daughter. Her goal was to press on to finalize as much as possible until she needed to leave.

"Sandy, you will need to discover how to pace yourself," Christopher said. "We will always have an intense situation to deal with. I have built an extraordinary team. Please take advantage of them. You will not survive going solo. I have you covered, and when you return, I will be vacating my office. The ship will be yours to do with as you please."

"I'm taking the week. I may need to lean on you from time to time."

"I wouldn't have it any other way. After all, I do owe this accelerated retirement to you."

His comment was a shot at being forced out of the Directorship for ordering Sandy's accident, among other questionable choices.

"Yes, I do believe you owe me, but we need to let sleeping dogs lie."

"Agreed. Take as long as you want. Go cherish the little time you have with your family and continue to make room for them. If you become versed in anything from me, it is that you will want them there when this is all over. In my case, a lesson learnt the hard way. Now off you go, I will see you when you get back."

Shortly after leaving her future office, Fyad made contact. It was agreed upon to meet at his hotel suite. Dinner would be served by way of room service. They were quite certain there was a good chance any public appearance would most certainly be documented by the press. Both anticipated the interrogation of the rescue would be brief.

Sandy knew all too well every action he executed in his mission would have mirrored the precise movement she would have deployed. Her examination of the facts was a necessity, a going through the motions to satisfy others. An eagerness to initiate the onset of paving a foundation for the uncharted era of intelligence sharing was at the center of her attention. Both privately contemplated how this would affect them. Only the future held the answer.

***

Brooklyn, Jacob, David with Capella at his side, along with his parents, sat at the ranch's dining table.

"Jacob, I understand you have twins on the way?" David's father, Charles, inquired, referring to the pregnant horse.

"That's what we're told," Jacob said. "The vet says all is fine so far. That still remains the diagnosis, isn't it, David?"

"Yes. So far so good."

"Charles, we should take a walk down to the barn after dinner. I would like your opinion on the horse's progress."

"Absolutely. I've only come across this once. It can be a tough go for the mare."

"Did they both survive?"

"Unfortunately, only one made it."

There was a break in the chatter as the food was served.

"Patricia, how in the world did you get this guy away from the farm?" Jacob quizzed her about convincing Charles to agree on taking a vacation.

Before she could answer, her son voiced his surprise.

"We all couldn't believe it. The only time I can

remember my father leaving our home was for supplies or for one of us kid's activities, like my games. We never thought this day would come."

"To be honest, I can relate with Charles's reluctance. It wasn't until Brooklyn…"—he paused, smiled at his wife and rubbed the back of her hand—"guided me out of my cocoon that I realized what I was missing."

"Truth be told, Jacob, you were the one who knocked on my door," his wife interjected.

Everyone smiled. They were having a pleasant time. All would have preferred Sandy be present, but she wasn't, so they forged ahead, not allowing it to dampen the evening's spirits. After a short lapse in the vacation talk, Patricia offered her side of the story.

"I must commend you, Brooklyn. I've been hinting and I believe most recently threatening him with regards to my craving about taking a week or two vacation each year, a needed break from our well-worn routine. But you know he gets a bit grumpy when I bring up the subject."

"Excuse me, everyone," Charles said jokingly. "If you haven't noticed, I'm right here."

"So you are," his wife acknowledged his presence.

"Mom says he really enjoyed the trip and is already planning next year's."

"Son, I can speak for myself. Yes, I must admit I was halfhearted about agreeing to this sort of trip. I've always thought it a waste of hard earned money. But to be truthful, I think I was a bit uneasy about lying around not having enough to keep me busy, and I might add I'm not a big fan of the heat."

"Well, I'm glad you enjoyed yourself," Jacob said. "When Brooklyn and I found ourselves in Europe last year, I discovered the important things in life aren't necessarily provided by one's daily routine. We must push ourselves to explore a bit."

"I get it now. I have agreed with Patricia that we will attempt to get away once a year."

"Excellent. Maybe the two of you should join Brooklyn and I someday. Keep in mind we have our own transportation, so the world is ours to be had."

"Thank you for the offer. That does sound wonderful. However, I do think next year's vacation might already be prearranged by my husband and his newfound friend."

"Look at you, Father—one trip and you already have a new travelling companion?"

"He does, son. There was this man your father met at the pool bar. Come rain or shine, anytime of the day, every single day, this gentleman would be perched in the exact same chair, in the exact same spot. For the first few days, I didn't think he had a proper name as everyone referred to him as the pool guy. At first we just took it for granted he was employed by the resort doing some sort of work pertaining to the pool area. Although I found it odd they would allow him to drink alcohol on the job. We later learned he was a frequent visitor, a Canadian, and he knew all the staff by their first names.

"We kept to our own for the most part, but then one day your father was introduced to him while buying a beer at the bar and that was it. From that point on, whatever we had planned for the day was rushed so your dad could get back to the resort and hang out with his new friend. Charles was up and out the door first thing in the morning. He'd gulp down our meals, then hurry away to see his buddy. In all my life, I've never seen him take to someone like that. I was really happy to see him enjoying himself. We ended up spending most of our second week with this gentleman and his wife, who I might say is a lovely lady. I believe the two men solved all the world's problems during our stay. We promised each other to keep in touch and organize a rendezvous next year."

"It sounds like you have a man crush, Dad," David teased.

"I'm not sure what that even means, son, but I assure you I don't have that."

The remainder of the evening's conversation went from vacations, to a discussion on horse racing, and of course, a major amount of time was spent bringing David's parents up to date on Capella. Everyone avoided the topic of Sandy's arrival. There wasn't a great deal of confidence around the table as to when she would be making an appearance.

Jacob and Charles eventually made their way to the stable. They enjoyed each other's company and the few times they got together, they made the futile promise to visit more often.

Charles did pose a one sentence inquiry about Sandy's well-being. He was reassured she was fine and the obligations of her newly appointed position would lessen as time passed. David's father frowned upon her frequent absence, although he would never voice his opinion.

Brooklyn poked her head into the opened barn door to offer a goodnight, then headed for their chalet. David and his mother found their way to his suite, where Patricia insisted on preparing and laying the child down for the night. It was a comforting sight, one David wished could be replayed more often.

An enjoyable evening for all, David thought. No matter how old he found himself, his parents' presence made him feel good. They were his security blanket. When they were around, he felt taken care of, that life would work out just fine.

***

The hug was a little longer than it should have been. With the door closed, she could take a breath, let her guard down. This was the only place in the world she could be one hundred percent herself. Fyad was the only person she'd never lied to, and she never had to. He knew her as well as she knew herself. A complete trust both were aware would never exist with anyone else in their lifetime.

"Fyad, I miss you so much," she said as they leaned in for a repeat embrace.

"I look forward to our getting together. We do so far too seldom."

"We should make more of an effort. I believe from here on in, we will speak more frequently."

"Yes, that would be nice."

In the sitting room, they began to chat about each

other's families and their spouses. Fyad was particularly interested in Capella's well-being. He was looking for reassurance that the kidnapping had not negatively affected her. Without him coming right out and saying it, Sandy picked up on his concern. She put him at ease, noting Capella showed no signs of stress from the ordeal and would retain no memory of it. Maybe someday in the distant future, she would decide to explain to her daughter what had transpired, but that would be many years away, or maybe never. She once again thanked him for his intervention, reiterating that if it wasn't for his swift engagement there was a real possibility of a grievous outcome.

Fyad's preordered dinner arrived at the precise time of his request. It included a special bottle of wine and a twelve pack of beer, both the choice drink of his guest. The delivery cart supported an abundant array of food, enough to feed many. Fyad wasn't known for overindulgence, but he didn't hold back when it came to eating. For as long as he could remember, nightly dinners at the palace provided a fulsome amount of choices and it must have stuck with him.

"Wow, Fyad, I don't think I'll ever get used to how you eat. This is quite the spread."

"My taste of the day is always a difficult decision, isn't it? I strive not to be disappointed, so I order a nice variety."

"Well, I doubt there is little remaining on the menu. We should eat. I can't recall the last time I had an actual meal."

During the past three weeks, she hadn't enjoyed

an adequate meal. She ate on the run or in front of her computer screen. Tonight's serving was to be savored.

"Fyad, although I have appeased those overseeing the abduction, I do have to finalize my report. We will only review this once. Would you mind detailing the events?"

"Of course. That's the purpose of our gathering. Nevertheless, we shall eat first."

"And drink."

"And drink, yes." He held up his glass, proposing a toast.

Sandy was on her second beer without even noticing she'd downed the first. During the meal, the conversation flowed easily, mostly about family.

Selena, Fyad's wife, was the main focus. Born privileged, there was little need for Sandy to dream about anything money-oriented. Yet, she was still fascinated with the vision that many young girls had to be a princess. Selena was just that, and the more she heard, the more Sandy wanted to take it all in. Maybe it was a diversion from reality, but she was intrigued.

"I'm surprised you show so much interest in Selena," Fyad commented.

"Every little girl's fantasy is to marry the prince."

"Unlike fairytales, the prince and princess live similar lives to all others."

"I don't know, Fyad, I think the prince is pretty special."

This time, she raised her glass of wine and tapped his. That was just about when she felt the effects of the alcohol settle in from the three beers she drank. In addition, she was sipping on her third glass of wine and they hadn't made it to dessert yet.

"I think I should slow down."

"Why? Do you have somewhere to go?"

She was certain his words were accompanied by a devilish smile, but then again it could have been her heedless consumption clouding her perception.

"Fyad, are you flirting with me?"

"No. What I may be alluding to is that, on occasion, an evening of seclusion can be good for one's mind. Leave the demands brought upon you on the other side of the door for a night."

"You have a point." She held out her glass to be refilled. "The night is ours."

She made a conscious effort to drink slower, but it tasted so good she was losing the battle.

The serving table was eventually retrieved by the hotel staff and they settled on one of the sofas.

"Sandy, I think it best if we review your daughter's release."

The mention of Capella hit her hard. Life was on the other side of the door but the culpability of not being there for her daughter found its way in.

"I don't think I can do this tonight, Fyad."

"I do have to leave in the morning, and I'm not sure when I will be returning."

"Let me ask you this. Would I have handled it as you did?"

"I believe you would have."

"That's all I need. I will take care of it from here." She hurriedly changed the subject. "Fyad, I'm not sure I should have started a family. I love them so much, but I'm not there for them. We are a far cry from being anywhere near normal."

"Sandy, you are a wonderful mother. You have taken on this new role to make sure all mothers can rest knowing their children are safe, and I am going to help you do that. Capella will be proud of you."

"You really think so?"

"I do. When I held her in my arms down in Cuba, it was such a special moment. I vowed that I would do everything in my power so this never happens to another child. She is special."

"You held Capella?"

"I did."

"Thank you, Fyad. I love you. I mean…I do love you, not in *that* way. You know what I mean. Damn, I have to stop drinking."

"It's all right, Sandy. I know exactly what you're saying."

She finished her wine and added one more bottle of beer to the party. It had been many years since she felt tipsy. Being a public figure, her behavior was scrutinized more than most, and she never allowed herself to drink in excess. But tonight, with Fyad, the world needed to be washed away and the cleansing was working.

"I'm pretty sure we should refrain from discussing any further business this evening," she said. "It is highly unlikely it will be remembered in the morning. I cannot recall the last time I felt like this."

"There will be plenty of time for us to save the world. We will start tomorrow, and the evening remains ours."

She finished off what was left of her wine and chased it down with another beer.

Fyad switched his beverage of choice to water after realizing he may need to be the voice of reason. Sandy stood, excused herself, then made her way to the powder room. The line she walked was not perfectly straight but no furniture was damaged. On her return, she sported a Mona Lisa smile.

Fyad watched her pick up her jacket off a chair and attempt to put it on. "What are you doing?"

"I really need to leave."

"Exactly where are you going?"

"Home."

He pushed off the sofa and gently removed her jacket.

"Sandy, you can't leave in this condition. The last thing we need is for someone to snap a photo of you wobbling down the hall." He chuckled.

"I apologize. I must look awful."

"On the contrary, you have never been so beautiful."

"Fyad, are you flirting with me?"

"My friend, I think it best that you spend the night here," he said. "You can rest in the bedroom."

"Are you suggesting we sleep together?"

At that point, they both broke out into laughter. Under the influence, her gestures and speech were comical. They were accustomed to being together during serious situations, some life and death. Few times were as sociable as this evening.

"Sandy, I don't recall witnessing this carefree approach to life."

"You know what, Fyad?"

"What?"

"Someone else can take care of this damn country for one night. I'm just too drunk."

Another burst of laughter filled the room.

"Speaking of saving the world, I think I'd better get you to bed. I believe tomorrow you will want to resume your notability."

Fyad came to her side, put his arm around her, and led her into the bedroom. Concentrating on not stumbling, she took hold of him while leaning her head on his shoulder. As they neared the mattress, she twisted and fell onto her back with her legs dangling over the side. Fyad gently took hold of her ankles and positioned her legs to the center of the bed. He then attempted to ease half of the comforter over her. As he did so, Sandy locked her arms around his neck and pulled him onto the bed.

"Breaker, what are you doing?"

"I want to be with you tonight."

"That's not a good idea."

"Come on, Fyad. It will be like old times."

He struggled to get up, but she had a pretty good grip on him and he didn't want the physical element to escalate. The resistance stopped as he eased her to one side where she lay with her head on the pillow. Fyad sat at the top of the bed, leaning on the headboard.

"It's not like we haven't done it before, Fyad."

"Those were different circumstances."

"You enjoyed it." She nestled closer.

"Might I remind you we were trying to keep warm during survival training in the Malaysian Rainforest."

"We sure did turn up the heat."

Even with the room a little blurred, Sandy was mindful of the banter and reveling in it. Fyad was the one becoming uneasy. He instinctively inched away from her.

His awkwardness was uncharacteristic. The only person on the face of the earth with the prowess to trigger it was lying next to him. He'd been tempted by her from the very first time they met. Due to their chosen field, it was imperative to suppress one's emotions, which they did...except that one time.

"Sandy, we promised never to speak of it again."

"We haven't, until now. You'll forgive me. Hell, I'm drunk."

"That was another time in our lives. We are both married now. I'm certain our spouses wouldn't appreciate our closeness."

"They're not here and I'm pretty sure if mine knew, he would be relieved because he could feel less guilty about his indiscretions."

"We can't do this, Sandy." He attempted to move off the bed, but she took hold of his arm.

"Just stay a few more minutes, please. I promise I won't bite."

"Okay, for a minute."

He settled back and with some awkwardness, Sandy raised herself to sit next to him with her shoulder snuggled against his.

"Fyad, no one has ever made love to me as attentively as you. It is the one day that will never be equaled. Selena is a lucky princess."

Her head rested on his shoulder. She sat silently

reflecting on their relationship. They understood each other's every move. Sandy knew the same thoughts were occupying his mind. Seldom, even in the best of relationships, did two people fall into sync like the two of them.

"It was special. I will give you a pass tonight, but you must promise that we never speak of it again."

"Are we going to have sex?"

"No, Sandy, your pass pertains to this conversation. But since this night never happened, I would like you to know I will also never forget. It was the most memorable intimacy I will ever experience. Few days go by without thought of it."

"Come here." She guided his lips to hers.

After the kiss, she lay down and turned her back to him, gripping his arm and resting it on her side. With him cuddled behind her, she held his overhanging hand with both of hers. So many nights they had positioned themselves like this, seeking out warmth from the damp evening chill of the jungle.

"Please hold me."

The memories floated in her head as she fell asleep, and so did he.

***

As their visit to the barn was winding down, Jacob received a call on his cell.

"I'll be right with you," he answered. He then addressed his companion. "Charles, I'm sorry, but business doesn't seem to know how to tell time. I must take this. You stay as long as you want, but I think I'm going to call it a night. We will see you in the morning."

"Have a good night, Jacob. I think I will hang out here for a while."

Jacob walked out into the darkness.

"Kristof, this better be good," he said into the receiver.

Kristof then told him he'd spoken with most of the others and they all wished to extend their apologies for the group's ill-conceived plan.

He went on to explain relatives should've been exempt, and a policy would be implemented immediately. The onus would be on the family member to deal with it internally, should the need arise again.

"Kristof, an apology is meaningless," Jacob shouted. "The others have been advised as to my vacating, so I'm unsure as to the reasoning behind your contacting me."

"I'm afraid we cannot accept your withdrawing," Kristof said grimly. "Jacob, you of all people should know one's death is the only exit from our undertaking."

"My dear friend, do you listen to yourself? For the final time, our ties are severed. I'm out. I wish you all well, but please be warned if I even have an inkling of retribution, before you can blink an eye, your world will come crashing down on you in the most unpleasant way. That goes for the others too."

Jacob ended the call and touched the flashlight icon on his cell. The ground lit up. His vitals began to fluctuate, not in a good way, so he altered his course in the direction of Hanna's memorial. He felt in safe hands exposing his inner concerns with Sandy's mother.

Brooklyn would understand.

***

Charles didn't sleep much. He was still roaming about the stable, knowing full well everyone else was fast asleep. Back home, he could be found meandering about his property at all hours. He was about to call it a night when he was unexpectedly startled.

"Excuse me. What are you doing in here? This is a private facility. I'm going to call security."

"Oh, hello there." Charles approached and offered a handshake. "There's no need to call anyone. I was just heading back to the ranch to retire for the evening."

"You are not supposed to be here. You're going to have some explaining to do," the girl said. "We do not allow anyone, even neighbors, into this stable without authorization. I'm calling security."

"My name is Charles," he said, somewhat enjoying the confrontation. "Charles Watson. I'm David's father."

The girl appeared puzzled. "You're David's what?"

"Father. Everyone has one. David's mother and I have come to visit for a few days. By the way, maybe I should be the one asking, who are you? Do you work for my son?"

"I do. I'm so sorry. I wasn't aware we had company."

"Might I ask what you mean by *we*, and why are you wandering around the stable at this hour?"

"Well, there are only a few of us at the ranch, and I wasn't expecting anyone else. Yes, I work here, or mostly at the track stable. Sometimes when I work late I like to visit these guys before bed. Sleep comes easier after spending time with them."

"A girl your age should be at home this time of night."

"I am. Oh, sorry, I'm staying here at the ranch. I'm on a summer apprenticeship and your son's family offered me accommodations. Mr. McGinnis is a friend of my father. My name's Addison." They shook hands.

"Charles." He nodded. "Now I understand. Well, young lady, this work is tough but gratifying. It can be a good life, so listen and learn this summer."

She chuckled.

"Did I say something to amuse you?"

"You're definitely David's father. He's always addressing me as *young lady*. Sometimes I think he forgets my real name. I see where he gets his good looks from."

"Well, I must admit it's not often I hear that."

The two of them hit it off. They hung around the animals for another half hour before tiredness began to set in. The age gap never came into play. Their conversation was on a level playing field. Charles did most of the talking and Addison sucked it in like a sponge. She instantly realized how much knowledge David's father had acquired by spending his entire life operating a farm.

"I think it's time to saw off some logs," Charles

decided.

"I don't quite understand what that means, but I do know I'm tired."

He laughed. "It means going to sleep, snoring."

"Got it."

They walked back to the ranch house and she listened intently to his farmstead stories. As they entered the majestic foyer, they said their goodnights. But before Addison was two steps up the staircase, her new friend made her an offer.

"Addison, I have an odd nightly routine. Once David's mother is sleeping, I sneak into the kitchen for a little nip of the good stuff. It helps my forty winks."

"I have no idea what that means. You're funny. Sure, why not? I'll give your technique a try."

They settled at the breakfast bar, and true to his word, Charles smelled out the whiskey stock. He poured a shot of each into two glasses.

"Mix?"

"Whatever way you take it works for me."

He set the drink down in front of her. "So, young lady...sorry, *Addison*, are your father and Jacob good friends?"

"I would say business associates more than BFFs."

He gave her an inquisitive look, not understanding the wording.

"BFFs, best friends forever."

"Now I understand. Why don't you just say *best friends*?"

They both had a giggle as they sipped their drinks.

"What does your father do?" he inquired.

Addison knew as soon as someone learned her true identity, the fun would end. People were either star-struck or scared off. Nevertheless, she was appreciative of her father's achievement and always proud to inform others of his appointment.

"He's the President."

"Odd. I thought Jacob held that position."

"He's not the President of McGinnis Enterprises."

"Then which company does he head up? Would I know of them?"

"He's *the* President."

"I understand if you would prefer not telling me."

"Charles, this isn't a trick question." She leaned closer, tilted her head, and gave him a wink. "Think for a minute. You can get this."

He wasn't catching on.

"I'll give you a hint. My last name is Tucker. Addison Tucker."

He still shook his head, indicating he didn't get it. Then he had a light bulb moment.

"The President of the United States? Your father is the President of the United States?"

"That's the one. You win, Charles."

"Holy mackerel."

"Really, Charles? Holy mackerel. That's all you've got? What does that even mean?"

"Addison, I think we were raised on different dictionaries."

Another laugh, another sip.

"Shouldn't you have some people with you?

Security?"

"You're referring to the Secret Service. I do have one detail with me, but she thinks I'm already snug as a bug. Over the years, I've become a master illusionist."

"Well, then, Miss Tucker. It is an honor." He offered his hand once again.

"Don't go all weird on me like most people do when they find out who I am."

"You have my word. I think we should celebrate our new friendship with another little…" He made a hand motion, indicating a drink. "I'm enjoying your company. You are a nice young lady." He held up the bottle and she gave him an accepting nod. "Two is my limit, so after that, we will call it a night."

He replenished their glasses and passed one on to his new drinking buddy.

"You know you're providing a minor with alcohol," she pointed out.

"How old are you?"

"Twenty."

"Correct me if I'm wrong, but the legal drinking age is eighteen."

"You're wrong, Charles. In the United States, the age is twenty-one."

"Holy cow. We'd better keep this to ourselves. It's eighteen where I live."

"It will remain our secret."

"I don't understand how kids can be sent off into battle, asked to put their lives on the line, and those lucky enough to return home can be arrested for drinking. Doesn't make any sense."

"I like the way you think. I'll pass it on to my

father."

The two of them sat for another few minutes flipping the chatter from horse racing, to school, farming, and life in general. Charles was intrigued not so much by what was being said but rather from the realization that his new friend possessed a brilliant mind. She didn't voluntarily display it. To him, it seemed as if she held back, trying to come across as a typical teenager. He recognized her upbringing was one whereby she would not think of herself as better than others, and he admired that personality. Charles wanted to spend more time with her to get to know her better, at least for the next few days.

He had crossed paths with too many people over the years who tried hard to portray themselves of being someone of importance, and it irritated him. Those who looked down upon another due to their financial status, employment, or any other eminency, was his number one pet peeve. He garnered a true respect for someone of a modest demeanor purposely playing down their intellect. The evening provided a simple but stimulating exchange.

"We'd better retire for the night before your Secret Service person, or worse yet, my wife, comes looking for us."

"Young lady." She appeared to be pondering something.

His expression suggested he required an explanation.

"Young lady. You didn't refer to me as young lady," she explained.

"No, I'm convinced you are far more than a young lady. I will address you as Addison from this point on."

"Thank you, Charles."

"I hope we can sneak in another get-together before I leave."

"You got it."

She got up and headed for the door.

"Addison, if David doesn't offer you a job when you graduate, give me a call. I'm always on the lookout for a farmhand."

She smiled. "Why, Charles, you hardly know me," she replied in a Marilyn Monroe flirtatious tone.

"I think I get you. Now, you should find your way to your room."

With that, she gave him the tiniest wink on her way out.

***

Sandy eased into an awakened state bearing the burden of too many, too fast. It took a second to realize she wasn't alone. She was cuddled onto her right side under a comforter with her legs curled up. Head to toe, she felt the warmth of Fyad's body snuggled in behind her, spooning style. His arm was on her side.

As inappropriate as it was, her first cloudy observation of the new day was his morning growth nudging her bum. She instinctively pressed her backside ever so slightly against him. After a quick examination, the next detail she took note of was they, or at least she, was fully clothed. In an effort to open her eyes, it quickly became evident that payback was a bitch. There'd be a few hours of hurt before an acceptable level of norm was restored.

The split second she adjusted herself to look over at Fyad, he was instantly up and sitting on the edge of the bed with his back to her. He was also dressed.

"Good morning."

"Good morning. I apologize. I must have been more fatigued than I realized. Jet lag, I suppose."

"Thank you, Fyad. I needed you last night."

He made no reference to the past evening.

"I will order breakfast." He stood.

"Please." She sighed. "No food. Coffee, please. Spiked."

He gave her an understanding smile.

"Fyad, did we—"

"No, we didn't."

"Did we want to?"

"That, I cannot honestly answer."

"You seemed excited to be with me a minute ago."

Unaccustomed to her bluntness, he gave her a blushing smile before proceeding to place a room service order, extra heavy on the coffee.

Sandy was hurting. She was the poster person of self-control. Mental, physical, emotional, and all other aspects of life were always kept in check. She could slow her heart rate to near death. She could hold her breath longer and swim farther than ninety-nine point nine percent of the population. Sandy excelled at being in control of every waking hour, but not today. The beer and wine had its own mystical power of inflicting pain.

She gave up the fight and lay back down on the bed. It seemed the safest way to avoid the hurt. With another hour or so of rest, her stomach and head would dispense with the internal festivity.

Fyad was soon to bring relief in the form of a coffee pot. After a few sips, she closed her eyes.

Ninety minutes later, he gently woke her. Showered and shaved, he was ready to get on with his day. Sandy felt a little behind.

"Do I look as bad as I feel?"

"Yup."

"I have to go home today. My husband's parents are visiting. They're going to think I'm a terrible person, and I probably am, or at the very least an awful parent. I know I sound like a broken record, but there is something wrong with us, Fyad."

"I'm not going to argue that point."

He handed her a cup of black coffee along with a small plate of fruit and pastry. She took hold of the cup and pushed the other aside. Fyad sat in the chair at the side of the bed. He handed her a brown envelope which he retrieved from the side table. "A detailed account of my every move. Please relay that my actions were initiated solely because it involved your family. I have no desire of over-stepping my boundaries with your country. I know you would have acted similar if reversed."

"Thank you, Fyad. I plan on putting this to rest."

He had contemplated including the names of those he was convinced ordered the attack, but didn't. He knew Sandy better than anyone and was well aware she would come to the same conclusion

217

on her own.

"Sorry about last night."

"Sandy, as coldhearted as I may seem, few days pass by without a reflection of our history. I love you, and this unconventional relationship we have. My affection for you runs deeper than all others. Yet, when we leave this room, we must resume our indurate character."

"Then let's stay."

"I depart for the airport in an hour."

"This is what we have always wanted, isn't it, Fyad? We now have the power to alter the world as we know it. This will be the first time in history our two sides of the world can find trust in each other. We do trust each other, don't we?"

"We will accomplish greatness. Keep in mind, though, all good is accompanied by some bad."

Sandy dragged herself into the shower and returned within twenty minutes. Fyad was packed and ready to leave.

"Fyad, can you wait a few minutes? I'd like to hitch a ride to the airport."

"I can fly you home."

"Thank you, but I have a chopper waiting."

***

It wasn't long before they arrived at the airfield. To the right of the vehicle sat Sandy's ride, a mean looking Sikorsky Black Hawk helicopter. To the left was Fyad's sleek private jet. The crews of each aircraft had filed their respective flight plans and were prepared to guide their machines into the clouds once their passengers were on board.

An hour passed as they talked. Ground work for the unprecedented exchange of intelligence between the two countries was being laid out. Of the many active threats around the world, their initial focus would be terrorism, in particular those groups housed in the Middle East, but with increasingly far-reaching arms. They sketched out a schedule of briefings which would find the two of them in contact much more frequently than in the recent past. With the plan in place, Fyad was about to get out of the car when Sandy gripped his arm.

"Fyad, thank you for what you and your men did to rescue Capella and Brooklyn. I will always be in your debt, but please let it alone. If any further action is required, I will handle it from my end."

He relaxed in the back seat, taking a deep breath. With one hand, he touched her shoulder, leaned in and gave her kiss on the cheek, as a friend would to another.

"We should be leaving. I'm sure Capella is anxious to see her mother."

At the mention of her daughter, a smile disguised the guilt of her absence. It was time to leave and put all else aside.

"You're right. I will be in touch when I'm back at Langley. Say hello to your father."

"I will. Please give that precious child of yours a kiss for me."

They gave each other a hug and the quickest of a kiss, near but not actually on the lips. A little bold for friends…but restrained.

William C. Cole

***

During her flight to Kentucky, Sandy received a call. The craft she was flying in was of military grade customized for VIP transportation. She sat alone in one of the six plush leather seats isolated from the other two occupants, the pilots. Her headset and foam covered microphone was connected to a secure frequency synced to her remote, assuring conversations remained private. The person on the other end wasn't excluded from the wake vortex being fed by the rotor blades, so communications were kept to a minimum during these flights.

"Hello."

The incoming call was from her friend Blake. He was prepared to meet and listen to her proposal. It was welcoming news. Having someone on your side whom you had absolute trust in was crucial, especially in Sandy's case when many personnel were faithful devotees to the outgoing director.

"I'm extremely grateful for your consideration, Blake. Together, we will achieve a greater good."

The communication ended with a promise to connect once she was back at Langley. The discussion made her consider how best to set in motion Blake's official transfer to her agency. In this particular case, she felt it best to have the President issue the movement order, quashing any need for explanation. Exposure of his true identity was not an option.

The fluttering clatter of the aircraft jogged her memory of Marine One landing in her yard, which

220

seemed so far in the past. In reality, it had only been a couple of months. Then it struck her that she hadn't informed anyone of her arrival. No one at home knew that within an hour or so this machine she was enclosed in would be landing on the center lawn of the ranch. After all the recent activity, the arrival would be alarming and most certainly distressing to the animals. She tapped out David's number on her phone.

"Babe, you coming home soon?"

"I'm headed there now."

"When do you land? I will pick you up."

"I'm being transported directly to the ranch. We should be setting down within the hour. I thought you might want to shield the animals from the noise."

"You're flying in by helicopter?"

"You got it, and this thing is noisy, as you know. See you in a bit."

They said their goodbyes, then disconnected.

She closed her eyes, and for the remainder of the flight wished away the headache and unease in her stomach, hoping the punishment of the past night would subside prior to being reunited with her family.

***

Renée walked next to Gabriela, who held the reins of Star Power, one of the stable's premier horses. They were guiding the elite athlete down the beaten path toward the racetrack. The trainer was reviewing how she would like her jockey to pace

221

the workout. It was a redundant exchange, as they were so in sync with one another that ninety-nine percent of the time their strategy was exact. This particular session would be the colt's last full workup before his weekend's race.

Gabriela was soon easing the horse into a routine pace with Renée taking in every stride from the back rails of the track.

"Renée, you wanted to see me?"

An hour had passed since she had sent word to have Addison contact her.

"Yes, Addison. How's your day working out?"

"Everything's fine."

"I know you haven't been with us long, but I wanted to pass on that we are pleased with your progress. You seem to be taking your position seriously."

"Thank you. It is a magical place."

"That it is. I'm moving you from feed to stable hand. There are some not so pleasant duties that come along with the position. However, I think you'll find working up close with these guys will make the unpopular tasks worthwhile."

"Thank you. I appreciate it. I won't let you down."

Renée glanced out to the track to watch the wizardry of her jockey. Having not been instructed to return to the stable, Addison eased herself up beside her boss. She rested her elbows on the top rail and one foot on the lower.

"It's like watching Picasso's gliding brush galvanize a canvas."

Giving her an inquisitive look, Renée replied,

"I've never heard it put that way." She returned her focus to the track. "She certainly is spellbinding, isn't she?"

For the next ten minutes, nothing was said as they stood there in a state of serenity, transfixed on the horse and its rider. The repetition of the hooves thundering by and then fading into the backfield was hypnotizing. Renée was aware Addison was still by her side and opted not to direct her back to work just yet. She felt the young apprentice had earned a few minutes of witnessing the end result of the entire team's dedication and hard work.

Gabriela soon brought the horse to a rest directly in front of the small gallery, vaulted to the track's dirt surface, holding his reins as she confirmed with Renée the training was complete. They were both satisfied with the outcome of the day's run.

"Addison, what are you guys feeding this big boy? He's pretty energetic today," Gabriela said.

"Just following instructions," she replied.

"He feels ready for this weekend," Gabriela said to her boss.

"Good. I want this one."

Being on opposite sides of the rail, they moved toward the open gate. Once through, they stopped while Gabriela gave the horse a tug of the reins, coaxing the animal to settle down, as he was still a bit anxious. Addison moved alongside and rubbed the imposing figure gently along the backside. He let out what could have been construed as a sigh and began to settle. The jockey and trainer looked at each other with pleasantly surprised expressions.

"Looks like I might have made the right decision

by switching you to a ranch hand."

"Congratulations, Addison. Not everyone gets that opportunity. She runs a tight ship." Gabriela looked over at Renée, giving her a wink.

"I think she's earned it."

"Well, in that case, here." Gabriela handed the reins to Addison. "Deliver this guy to his groom."

Addison's legs began to shake and they nearly gave way. Her whole body quivered as she took hold of the thousand pound thoroughbred. She looked at Renée, who nodded her approval. Terrified, she purposely began to walk ever so slowly in the direction of the stable. When far enough away that no one could hear, she quietly started talking to the horse.

"Oh, please be good. Please. Let me get you to the barn and we will give you a nice wash down and a treat. Please don't pull. This is my first time. We can do this. Easy now. Good boy…"

***

"What were you thinking?" Renée asked Gabriela.

"I thought I'd add a little entertainment to our day."

"If he bucks, she's going to pee her pants."

"I think she may have already."

They had a laugh, but in reality their philosophy was similar to the old school method of learning how to swim. Throw them in, and they have no option but to survive.

To everyone's relief, the short trek was a

success, although it would probably be an hour or so before Addison's heart rate and shivering settled down.

"Why don't you come over tonight?" Renée asked Gabriela.

A couple of months had passed since they'd last spent personal time together.

"Sure, I'd like that."

Renée was in need of some company. She wanted to stifle the emotions surfacing from her recent encounters with David. Gabriela might be a good remedy—an intimate evening with someone she truly liked. While they shared an alluring desire for one another, it wasn't as absolute as her longing for David. Still, it was a compelling relationship in its own right.

As they entered the stable, Renée added, "Why don't we meet at my place? Say, eightish?"

"Perfect, but remember, if we're eating, we need to keep it light," Gabriela said. "I have to race this weekend."

"I wouldn't worry. When I serve up dessert, you'll lose a few pounds."

Gabriela remained silent, letting her sultry smirk speak for itself.

Renée spotted Addison through the opening at the far end of the stable, where she was assisting one of the grooms with washing down Star Power. The clear outside view from one end to the other reminded her of an old covered wooden bridge that crossed a small river near her home in France. The timbered structure was a pleasant reflection of her homeland. It wasn't just the similarity in construction that brought back memories. The bridge was a gathering spot for local kids. It was where she'd experienced one of her earliest sexual encounters with the opposite sex.

"Renée. You with us?" Gabriela asked. "You seem lost."

"I'm fine," she replied. "Sometimes this place brings back old memories."

"I'd like to hear about them sometime."

"Maybe someday."

"Listen, I need to run a couple more sessions before taking off. Is there anything else you'd like me to cover today?"

"I don't think so. I am looking forward to tonight, though."

"Can't wait."

Gabriela left. Renée stood at one of the stalls, brushing the crest of the horse that stood there. She had to force herself to clear the past from her head. She patted the animal's neck, then walked towards the sunlight beaming in from the far opening.

"I see this guy is settling in nicely," she said. "Good job, Addison."

The girl shrugged, acting as if it was all in a day's work. "Thanks."

"I think you've earned a race day. How would you like to join us at the track this weekend? We have three entries, so we could use an extra hand."

"Absolutely."

"When you finish up here, go home and rest. Those late night shifts eventually catch up to you. I'd like Ellie here to begin your training in the morning. You okay with that?" She directed the question to Ellie.

"Sounds good to me," the groom replied.

"Be here tomorrow morning at eight, and Ellie will fill you in on what needs to be done."

"Thanks, Renée."

"Ellie, are you scheduled for this weekend?"

"No, but I'll come and hang out with Addison. I love race day."

"Perfect. I'll check in with you girls tomorrow."

"Renée, I won't let you down," Addison pledged.

***

Sandy's ride windswept the splendor of the courtyard for less than five minutes before rising back into the blue sky. Its grounding was long enough for her to depart. There was no suitcase, security personnel, no assistance. It was just Sandy, alone, with only a backpack hanging off her shoulder. She despised briefcases and opted to run around Langley looking like a university student. It contained a few personal items, a quick change of clothing, and her smallish laptop. Although it resembled something out of the Second World War, the rucksack was a logical choice.

Teardrops blurred her vision once Capella was nestled in her arms. The self-discipline instilled in her did little to ease the heartbreak that came with being an absentee mother. It vanished with the warmth of the child's body snuggled against her. After David handed over their daughter, all else was suspended in time. The welcoming committee backed off, allowing privacy for the mother and daughter. It took a few minutes before Sandy acknowledged the remainder of the family.

With Capella close to her side, the remainder of the day was spent getting reacquainted with her in-laws. The story about the pool guy made her laugh. She offered little about her new appointment and no one perused their own curiosity. What was becoming clear to her was the sweeping distinction between the two worlds she lived in. A short helicopter ride thrust her into what seemed like another planet. She knew that during her visit, not a single hour would pass without second-guessing her choices. Fully aware she may be clutching at straws, she'd been reflecting on the day David would agree to make the move to Washington.

***

The two security officers, both of whom were enthusiastic sports fans, buzzed Gabriela through the lobby doors of the condominium without hesitation. They were a little star-struck, as anyone interested in horseracing, or for that matter anyone who watches one of the many sports channels, knew her. She was the jockey everyone bet on. Seldom was she mounted on a horse that wasn't favored in a race. She was the superstar of the industry.

Gabriela was thrilled when time allowed her to mingle with fans. She spent the next ten minutes talking about her past rides, which included wins at the most prestigious races throughout the world. The one rule she had was to refrain from discussing

Who Lies Beside Me

any future race cards in public, as it might be construed as passing on insider information.

Once she broke away from the conversation, she made her way up to Renée's unit.

The instant Gabriela entered the condo, she picked up on the mouth-watering aroma of dinner being prepared. It was killing her knowing how delicious the food would taste if only she could eat it. Race weeks, her daily calorie input was eight hundred, and during off weeks, she maxed out at one thousand. Today's count was already half consumed.

"Renée, you're killing me here. That's not salad I smell."

"Chicken and vegetables Risotto served with a touch of love."

"I like the love part, but you know I can't eat it."

"Oh, yes you can. How many calories have you eaten today?"

"Three hundred and fifty."

"Perfect. This special recipe is a jockey's dream. Three hundred calories max. That leaves you enough room for a glass of my finest."

Renée brought the wine bottle and placed it in the center of the table. The food would remain in the oven warmer until the two decided to eat.

"You're my main asset, Gabriela. I wouldn't chance being a contributor to your tipping the scales at weigh out. I have no intentions of signing off on an overweight ride. After all, it wouldn't look good on my résumé if I was the one responsible for America's leading jockey being issued a suspension. Besides, I have an idea of how we can work off a couple of pounds tonight."

"Sounds intriguing."

All joking aside, the two women and everyone else involved in the horse racing industry knew the significance of a jockey's weight. Prior to handing over their saddle and equipment to the trainer or assistant, the riders were required to weigh out inclusive of the gear before each race, only permitted to be one pound underweight. If greater, they were required to add lead bars to equalize what each horse carried. If overweight, suspensions and fines could be levied. Should the scale tip upward of more than two pounds over, the trainer or owner had to sign off their approval. The maximum overage was five pounds. If more than that, the horse would be disqualified. These rules could be tightened by the race steward based on track conditions. He or she had to sign off their approval that no entry had an advantage over another.

At the conclusion of the race, they once again weighed in before the race could be deemed official and the public was allowed to collect their winnings. If there was a variance from the beginning of the race, the horse would likely be disqualified. Those responsible, the jockey and trainer, would most likely be heavily fined. Food intake was on the athletes' minds twenty-four-seven. Renée would never jeopardize her rider, and she had meticulously scrutinized every minuscule ingredient they were about to eat.

They sat and talked about the upcoming weekend races. Little needed to be discussed as they knew each other so well, but just to be cautious, they ran through a few scenarios. It wasn't long before they decided to dine. Seldom did Gabriela eat anything after seven in the evening. Their plates were emptied before they knew it. This particular night, she was tempted to go back for seconds the meal tasted so good, but she didn't. They began to clear the table when Gabriela steered the chat away from the upcoming weekend.

"You know, Renée, from how you described her, I thought we might have issues with Addison. But she has been working out just fine."

"I know. It scares me. I still think somewhere in that mischievous mind of hers, she's up to something."

"I haven't seen signs of anything. She's fitting in. You might be reading too much into it. It seems she heard your warning loud and clear."

"Let's hope so. I invited her to the upcoming races. I want her to see the end result of the stable staff's hard work."

"Good idea."

They tidied up the kitchen before settling onto the same sofa. There was a lull in the conversation until something Renée said back at the stable earlier in the day came to Gabriela's mind.

"Where were you back at the stables?"

"Not sure what you're referring to."

"After today's workout, back at the barn, you got lost in your past. You said maybe one day you'd tell me the story. No time like the present. We don't talk much about our past. It would be nice to know some of the things that contributed to you being who you are today."

"I'm not comfortable talking about that stuff."

"Okay, I'll start." Gabriela pressed on. "My father was abusive."

"We don't have to do this. I'm really not good with this kind of conversation."

"That's okay, just hear me out. He was abusive when he drank. I never saw him hit my mother, but I'm sure he did. Their arguments were so intense it terrified me. He would scream at both of us, degrade us at the top of his lungs. Many times the police would show up because the neighbors were concerned about our well-being. Then one day in the middle of one of his rants, he went silent, grabbed his chest, and that was it…he died. The paramedics said he was gone before he hit the floor."

"I'm sorry, Gabriela, I had no idea. You really don't have to do this."

"No, it's okay. Apparently, it's healthy to talk about the parts of your life that occupy your nightmares. Anyway, as terrible as it may seem, I couldn't have been happier seeing him lying there. I felt like giving him a kick, saying, 'There, you deserve it.' I didn't. My mother never would have forgiven me. Neither of us shed a tear for him. Does that make me a bad person?"

"You're special, Gabriela. By the sounds of it, you went through hell. Nobody should have to experience such hostility."

"I often wonder what life decision I would have made were it not for him. He was the reason I do what I do. We had a small barn out back which housed my horse. I was the sole proprietor of it, and it was my refuge. During their spats, I would sneak out, saddle up Sam, and we would ride full-out until he was exhausted or I fell off, the faster the better. Being a jockey is all I ever wanted to do. It's strange how a person's life is molded. There you go…the tragedy behind the jockey. Might make a good book someday."

"Again, Gabriela, I'm sorry. It must have been very difficult."

"The stable…where were you?"

After being the recipient of her best friend's baring of the soul, Renée felt impelled to unmask a bit of her background.

"When I was a kid, there was this wooden bridge back home that we used to hang around. The structure of the stable reminds me of it. That's it."

"I would venture to say there is more to the story."

Renée had one, maybe two people, close enough to her that she felt comfortable enough to discuss the intimate side of her life, and she was fine with that. But after hearing her friend's heartrending admissions, she felt it was not the time to relive one of her fond memories.

"Gabriela, you don't want to hear me recount my teen years."

"I do. We spend so much time together and yet, we really don't know that much about each other."

Renée gave in and agreed to expand on her flashback after explaining it was a nice memory. Truth be told, she couldn't recall any negative thoughts of her childhood.

"It was a late, sunny summer day. A friend of

mine, a boy, was walking with me after an afternoon of hanging around with some of the other commune school kids."

Gabriela looked a little confused, picturing her friend being raised in some hippy kibbutz and Renée picked up on it.

"A commune in France is equivalent to say, a township here in the States."

Gabriela felt silly for letting her imagination take over as she smiled her acknowledgement.

"As we approached this covered wooden bridge, it began to rain, a sun shower. We ran into it to shelter ourselves. Unfortunately, the old structure's roof had developed so many leaks it didn't provide much refuge. My companion suggested we wait out the downpour underneath the bridge. Many of us had been under it, fishing, swimming in the river. It was a common gathering place for the youth of the area, so it sounded like a logical suggestion. That day, we were alone and knew due to the weather there was little chance of others showing up. So down the bank we went.

"Soon after we settled on the secluded riverbank, my friend put his arm around my shoulder. We had been together this way before. Kissing was the extent of our intimacy, lots of kissing. Whenever we found ourselves alone and out of sight, we kissed. That particular afternoon was no different for us, so it wasn't long before our lips were locked on one another.

"Back then we had no computers, Internet access. The only knowledge we gained with regards to sexual activity was learned through the educational system, parents, reading, or at the town's movie theater on the odd Saturday night. So basically it was nonexistent. Although, I must admit that having an open relationship with my mother I understood more than most of my peers, at least in theory. But you know there is something to be said about learning first hand by experiencing it. Do you really want to hear this, Gabriela?"

"You've got my attention. Who needs a movie when you have Renée?"

They both got a chuckle out of the comment.

"Okay then, after a few minutes of our lip-sucking, his hand cupped my...what I would describe as petite breasts in the making, and it felt good, really good. I might have let out a slight moan. It wasn't long before his hand found its way to the outside of the zipper area of my jeans. He clumsily began rubbing his fingers between the legs. I was starting to feel my panties become wet so I thought, what the hell, let's find out what a cock feels like.

"I eased my hand across his stomach and soon rested it on the bulge in his pants. I started to laugh, I don't know why. It just struck me as being comical, touching his member which was trying to escape his jeans. I probably gave the poor guy a complex as he pulled away. I had to reassure him it was me, not him, that it was just the shock of being my first time that brought on the giggles.

"We soon resumed the caressing and vocalizing our pleasure. I decided I wanted to see that harnessed monster firsthand. I rubbed a bit more, then took control and unzipped his pants. Once his denims were opened, I pulled them down along with his underwear just far enough that it popped out and straight up. I again began to laugh but quickly composed myself. At that point I removed my hands from him, hoisted my hips, then unbuttoned and unzipped mine. I took a hold of his hand and guided it onto the outside of my panties. He began to caress me as I returned to stroking him up and down.

"I'd never been this close to a penis. I even moved in so I could really have a good look. He was probably scared to advance his fondling, but it felt so good I guided his hand underneath my undies. His fingers found their way inside me. I was so soaked. I think he was a bit bewildered, as he pulled them out quickly and it seemed as if he was wiping them off on my stomach. He probably thought I had peed myself.

"I navigated him back into me and whispered, 'It's okay, this is what happens when I get excited.' Not to be selfish, I returned the indulgence and dove right in once again, taking a hold of him. Thinking back, it makes me laugh. I felt so sorry for the guy. I probably stroked him no more than four or five times before he started spurting all over my hand. He began to jerk back and forth, making some strange noise that I wouldn't label a moan.

"We never discussed it, but I would venture to say it was his first orgasm, at least one brought on by someone of the opposite sex. To this day, I've never experienced so much…well, you get the drift. The explosion found its way to my face, my hand, my arm. He was so embarrassed, his reaction was to hastily zip up his pants without cleaning off.

"I really had to hold back from cracking up again." Renée started to laugh. "The only thing going through my mind was, I hope he does his own laundry, or his mother was about to get the surprise of her life.

"Anyway, I thought he was going to die, yet I must admit it felt really good. I was hooked."

"*Oh mio.*" Gabriela reverted to her native tongue as she sank back into the sofa. "I've never been with a guy, nor desired to be with one, but here I've become excited after listening to your adventure. How old were you?"

"I'll leave that to your imagination."

Renée got up and stood directly in front of her guest and took hold of Gabriela's hand.

"Now, let's see if we can think of some way to cure that."

The two petite, accomplished, astutely alluring young women hastily found one another au naturel, tangled in the silky coverings of Renée's king size bed. The evening found its purpose as each, in succession, skillfully eased onto the other's mouth in quest of that transcendent orgasm.

***

The week seemed to fly by in the blink of an eye. There were family dinners and it was early to bed and sunrise mornings. Capella was glued to her side the entire time. She dropped a hint or two to David about his relocating, but knew it was only wishful thinking.

Sandy wasn't alone in her decision to remain housebound. David's parents didn't stray far from the ranch, as their son had to attend to some business during their stay.

Charles did sneak out for his nightcap, twice meeting up with Addison, whose exchanges he found intriguing. He could have talked to her for hours. To him, she was twenty going on forty. The fact that he was engaging in a meaningful exchange with the President's daughter added to his captivation. The two hadn't consciously kept their talks secret, but as it stood, they had gone undetected.

For the first time in years, the family decided to attend the weekend's races as a group. They strived to remain in the background, void of the publicity that came with being a McGinnis. The decision was made to enjoy the last few days they would be together, as it was expected to be quite some time before both families gathered again. Capella was about to experience her first race day.

***

They arrived at a VIP parking lot and soon found themselves settled into a private owners' booth reserved for the family. Jacob used to secure the suite year-round when he attended the majority of the events. But in recent years, it was David who represented the family for the most part, and he preferred viewing the races ground-level by the stables. Today was no exception. He was intent on checking in with his staff.

"Would anyone care to join me? I should be heading down to the stables. Jacob, Dad, Mom?"

"I'm fine here, son," his mother answered, then addressed Sandy. "We can watch over Capella if you would like to join David."

"I think we're comfortable here, Patricia, but thank you."

"David, our team will be all right without us. Let me get you a drink," Jacob suggested.

"I'm sure they will, but if it's just the same, I'll feel better if I drop in."

"Well, son, I'll join you for a race or two."

"Charles, don't spend the whole day down there," Patricia told her husband.

"We'll be back shortly," David promised.

During the walk, Charles was beaming with pride as a number of supporters and a handful of media wished David well. The jaunt took longer than it should have as David politely made time for the encouragers.

When they finally arrived, it was Renée who first noticed them. She broke off a conversation with one of the hands and walked towards them.

"I thought you were going to be taking in the day up there." She motioned to the grandstand.

"The view is always better down here in the real world."

Renée turned and smiled at Charles, then looked back at David before her boss realized they'd never met.

"Sorry. This is my father, Charles. It just dawned on me that after all this time you two have never met."

"Charles, I'm so glad to finally meet you. David talks about you quite often." She held out her hand.

"I hope it's all favorable."

"He tells me you taught him everything he knows."

"Don't believe a word he says, Renée. I can tell you this, few conversations I've had with him about these animals take place without your name being mentioned. He refers to you as the horse whisperer."

A smirk came over her face as she directed her attention to David. "He does, does he?"

"I'm happy you can now put a face to the name since I go on and on about her," David needled them.

"Renée, do you mind if we go in and have a look at today's entries?" Charles asked.

"Of course not." She led the way.

Gabriela and a handful of staff were preparing for their first race. So as not to disturb the readying of the horse, they stayed clear and went on to the second. Again, a couple of grooms kept the animal company. It was policy to never leave a horse alone during its race day. The staff moved aside, making room for the threesome. Charles brushed the animal ever so slightly with his hand, not wanting to disturb him on an important day.

Renée and David backed off to discuss the upcoming races. The head trainer assured him all was well. They were basically going through the motions, knowing full well everything was taken care of. It was pleasurable swapping the business at hand, but the true meaning of it was what hadn't been said. A fulfillment of their weakness for one another was taking place, indifferent of the words spoken.

The third and final horse of the day's race card had been out for a gentle walk in an attempt to keep him relaxed until it was his time to shine. To the surprise of Charles, the duo guiding the thoroughbred into the stable was Ellie, who he wasn't familiar with, and his new friend, Addison.

A little too enthusiastically, Charles blurted out, "Tucker!" referring to her last name as a good friend might.

Surprised by his appearance, she also responded a bit loud. "Charles."

"Addison."

"Charles!" She spoke a touch louder in a higher octave.

He left the side of the other two and walked towards her.

As he distanced himself, David turned to Renée and whispered, "What the hell?" He gave her a baffling look.

"Don't look at me. I didn't even know they had met. Sad our trainee was introduced to your father before I was."

"I didn't introduce them. She better not—"

"David, don't be ridiculous. They're staying under the same roof, so they probably bumped into each other."

"They sound like they're lifelong friends. I don't like this. We need to find a way to send her packing."

"Easy now, she's really putting an effort into

this. There have been no reports of her overstepping her boundaries. Everyone's really taken to her."

"That's the problem, she's too damn likable."

"We're not going to throw her to the wolves because she's got a warm personality. I told you I'd deal with this. Now go on and enjoy your day."

"I don't trust her."

He was soon standing beside his father and the two girls. Ellie seemed nervous in the presence of her boss. He picked up on it and tried to put her at ease.

"Ellie. It is Ellie, isn't it?"

"Yes, sir."

"Ellie." He offered a handshake. "Please call me David. I hope you're enjoying working for us. Renée tells me you are a vital part of our team. Please keep up the good work. We do appreciate it."

"Thank you, sir," she shyly acknowledged.

David's attention turned to his impish young house guest.

"Addison, how's it going with you?" He questioned her to some degree in a harsher tone.

"Everything seems to be working out perfectly, David, just as I promised. Did I do something wrong?"

Ellie appeared surprised by the straightforwardness her trainee had towards the boss.

"No, all's good. I wasn't aware you and my father were acquainted."

"We've bumped into each other a couple of times," his father informed him.

"Okay then, everything seems good here. Dad,

we should head back and join the others."

Learning that his father and Addison had become friends caught him off guard. His speech was tentative, the decisiveness in his demeanor removed. He enjoyed watching the race at ground level, but the unearthing deflected his train of thought to keeping his father clear of the young lady.

"You go ahead. I'm going to hang around here for a while. After all, we're heading home tomorrow and I'd like to chat with Addison some before we leave," Charles answered. "If that's okay with you?"

Not sure how to reply, David agreed. He didn't know what to do. Should he hang around or join the other family members? Renée would be close by most of the day, so she could keep an eye on the improbable pairing. He advised his father he was heading back and they would meet up later, and then went in search of Renée.

She was outside around the corner talking to Gabriela.

"Everything okay, girls?"

"Hello, David," Gabriela offered.

"Hi. Listen, Renée, my father would like to stick around for a while. I'm joining the family up in the grandstand. Would you mind keeping an eye on him, or maybe I should say Addison? You would think they are lifelong friends."

"Sure. David, you have nothing to worry about. They'll be fine, but we will look in on them. Your father is a grown man."

"You're right, it's just he leaves tomorrow and

I'm a little concerned about this newfound friendship. Gabriela, get us over the line first."

"You got it."

He left their side, but didn't get far before Renée, who excused herself from the jockey, caught up with him. She called to get his attention.

"David, wait up."

He stopped.

"What's going on?" Renée frowned. "Is there something you're not telling me about Addison? If not, you need to stop this."

"Forget it. The summer will soon be over."

"Everything will be fine here. You should go spend the day with your wife."

She didn't wait for an answer before she turned and went in the opposite direction.

*   *   *

When David returned to the private seating area, he explained Charles wanted to spend a little more time down at the stables. He didn't mention Addison.

Gabriela was true to her word, winning all three outings. The first two she won by more than a length, leaving the third and final race for the nail biter. It was a photo finish that took the officials an uncomfortable amount of time to declare a winner. The McGinnis Ranch prevailed as they did the majority of times.

Charles did find his way back to the family before the intense last race. The day went off without incident for all except David and his paranoia. It was decided they would dine out for the last evening of his parents' visit. The next morning, they would board the McGinnis aircraft and soon after be home. David decided to accompany them for the flight and spend an hour or two with his siblings during the refueling of the jet. A couple of days after, it would be Sandy's turn to depart.

After an exquisite meal, the family arrived back at the ranch and with the uncertainty of when they would all have an opportunity to come together again, it was decided to stretch the enjoyable day out a little longer. The only casualty was Capella, who slept through most of the restaurant stay and was captured by the spell-casting of the ride home. Sandy did excuse herself from the partaking, and with her child in arm, retired to their suite.

The night neared its end and everyone began to make their way to their respective rooms. As they were entering the foyer, the front door swung open and there stood Ava, holding up Addison, literally dragging her into the lobby. They all stood motionless, witnessing the young girl's undoing, not immediately knowing what to make of it.

It was Charles who first reached for one of her arms to assist the Secret Service agent. David was next to come to her aid. Unfortunately for him, as he approached and centered himself in front of her, Addison threw up on him.

Even without understanding the circumstances leading to her condition, there was a great deal of sympathy for the girl.

"Ava, is she drunk? What happened?" David gave little attention to his clothes being soiled.

"Please forgive us. I have this under control. At the moment, I would like to get her to her room."

"Ava, I want to know what's going on here."

"David, that can wait," Jacob overruled his son-in-law in a commanding tone. "Let's just help Ava get Addison upstairs."

The three men assisted her, and it wasn't long before Addison was placed on her bed. Brooklyn and Patricia took it upon themselves to clean up the floor. Ava asked the men to wait in the hall, as she wanted to discuss the situation, but first Addison required her attention.

David found the nearest bathroom and wiped down his clothing with a damp towel. When he emerged, he blurted out, "I think we may have to consider she may not be the right person for the job. I know she's the President's daughter, but I can't put the horses in jeopardy."

The incident gave him the out he was looking for. She had gotten to him, and every time he was near her, he felt uneasy.

"You're being a little harsh, David," Jacob began. "From all reports thus far she has been exceeding everyone's expectations."

"With all due respect, this is my call. I select who I want representing our stable."

"I am aware I've entrusted you with this authority. However, all I ask is that you give her the benefit of the doubt until we learn more. Let's hear out Ava, then sleep on it before making any rash decisions."

"Son, I think Jacob makes a good point."

David was avid about letting her go, but before

the discussion escalated, Ava appeared.

"She was drugged, I think. Seabiscuit—sorry, *Addison*. I'm so used to referring to her by her code name. Anyway, Addison was invited by a group of her peers to a bar and grill to celebrate a co-worker's birthday. I authorized the outing as I have done before. She can be a handful at times, but is always true to her word and refrains from drinking alcohol in public. The girl is always within my reach, and I'm certain no liquor was involved here. Her drink is always lemon water.

"She was cozying up to a young man. I have the FBI reviewing the security footage. But in the meantime, there is an agent on the way. I will be handing off a blood sample I have just taken, and we should have the results within the hour. At the moment, I must ask you not to come to any conclusions until the results are official."

"I think we can agree to leave it in your hands, Ava." Mr. McGinnis took charge of the situation. "I would like a briefing in the morning."

"Absolutely."

"Out of curiosity, why Seabiscuit?"

"Our Communications Agency assigns the code names. Word has it Addison insisted on the name Seabiscuit. She does have a winning way when she zeros in on something. As for the reason, I believe she took to the book. The girl has a tender spot for an underdog. Gentlemen, I ask you not to judge her on tonight's incident. I have been assigned to her for two years now and she is a brat at times, I'll give you that, but she truly has the biggest heart."

"We will leave you to your duties," Jacob

concluded.

Ava slipped back into Addison's room and the men went to their respective suites.

Jacob and Charles assured their wives all was well. On the other hand, David was of the opposite opinion. When he finally found his way to his suite, Sandy was cuddled under her comforter reading. The baby was fast asleep.

"Burning the midnight oil, are you?" she asked.

"You didn't hear the commotion?"

"No, what's happening? Oh my God, David, you reek."

He enlightened her on the girl's behavior, adding that he'd seen it coming from day one and was determined to send her home. From Sandy's perspective, his explanation was a touch melodramatic. She recognized there was more to the story than the night's incident, but it was late and she wasn't in the mood to delve into it any deeper. It was her husband's call and whatever was happening in the backdrop was his to deal with. Her plate was full.

"David, she's just a kid. I'm sure your parents could tell a few stories about you coming home drunk. I think you're being a little tough on her. But it's in your hands. Now, please go clean up and come to bed. We only have a couple of nights before I head back."

***

Sunrise burned away the blackened sky. A farewell breakfast was being prepared by the staff and it wasn't long after that the group met in the dining room. As David began to dig into the spread, Ava appeared at the door.

"Ava, please join us," Sandy offered.

"Thanks, but I'm fine. David, could I have a word?"

He put down his utensils and stepped out into the hallway.

"Again, I would like to apologize for last night. Addison is my responsibility and I should have caught it."

"Caught what?"

"We found gamma-Hydroxybutyric acid, otherwise known as a club drug, in her blood samples. She was drugged. I ordered a review of the security footage and subsequently we have arrested a young man. Addison was engaged in a short conversation with this person at one point during the evening. We know what his intent was, but we are certain he did not know of her true identity. The situation has been dealt with swiftly and has been resolved."

"Okay. Was this person an employee of ours?"

"No. Neither was he in any way involved in the horseracing industry. He was not acquainted with any others in Addison's party."

She went on to explain that while everyone was sound asleep, the mysterious exclusive arm of the law identified, arrested, and prosecuted the man responsible before daylight. The case would not be pursued in a public arena, concealing any link to the White House. With his lawyer present, who was abruptly wakened in the middle of the night, he was given, not offered, one year incarceration at a military facility rather than a state prison. The solicitor did recommend the arrangement, as the alternative painted a bleak picture. He would serve the complete sentence, at which time all records of the incident would be destroyed. Officially, it didn't happen. If ever caught with illegal drugs again, the charges would void the impunity of the Secret Service and it would be a long time before he found himself on the right side of the bars.

"Even so, I think it might be best for all if we bring her employment to an end."

"As you wish, sir, but may I say something off the record?"

"Absolutely."

"I would appreciate your taking the day to reconsider before your final decision is made. Addison's choices are at time a bit precarious, but I tell you from the bottom of my heart I have never seen her as passionate about something as she has been these past weeks. Please keep in mind, here's a brilliant girl who graduated from college three years earlier than most. Every breath she takes is scrutinized. There are few opportunities to blow off steam. She's a good kid growing up in demanding surroundings. Being the President's daughter presents many challenges most girls her age never have to encounter. Please keep this in mind."

"Everyone seems to be rooting for her, so I tell you what, if you feel that strongly about this, I will give it some thought and discuss it further with Renée. For the time being, I don't see any harm in her resuming work as soon as she feels well enough."

"Thank you."

***

It wasn't long after the wistful goodbyes that David and his parents were buckled into the company aircraft taxiing down the runway. Once the jet was leveled off, Charles relaxed. He wasn't thrilled about sitting in a chair some thirty-thousand feet above the ground. It was an unnecessary evil that he found a way to deal with.

"Dad, would you like anything to drink?"

"Thanks, son, but I'm okay."

"Mom?"

"A bottle of water would be nice."

He walked to the small refrigerator at the rear of the plane and grabbed three bottles of water. After handing one to his mother, he sat down beside his father, who did accept the drink with a smile.

"David, you had a chance to speak with the Secret Service agent this morning. What did she say?"

"I did, and it looks like Addison was drugged against her will at an outing last night. It has all been taken care of."

"That's terrible, the poor girl. So everything is forgiven. Your decision to send her home without learning exactly what happened was harsh. You shouldn't jump to conclusions without all the facts, son. Unless there's more to it than meets the eye."

"Dad, why are you so concerned about her, and when exactly did you two become such good buddies?"

"I know I'm not an educated man and most of my life has been spent in the field or in a barn. But I've always been able to see through the outward behavior of someone, and believe me, this young lady is special. She may be going through a stage of finding her way, but she is a brilliant, caring person."

"I don't even want to ask how you came to that conclusion. The jury is still out on whether we will be keeping her around."

Charles raised his voice slightly. "Son, I don't get in your face often, but I'm telling you, she stays. I'm not suggesting or asking, I'm telling you. Blame it on me if it doesn't work out, but it will. Someday you will thank me."

David didn't want to argue so he changed the subject to talking about how his sister and brothers were doing. Before they knew it, they landed at Calgary International Airport. The remainder of the family was waiting for them on the tarmac as they disembarked.

After a three hour layover, David was headed home only to see off his wife once again, thrusting him into single parenthood.

***

Upon his return, David's first order of business was to meet with Addison. At the time he summoned her to the stable's office, he was still unsure of his decision. It took two seconds after she walked through the door for him to become conscious of his verdict. She entered the room with her head down, avoiding eye contact. This wasn't the bold Addison he'd become accustomed to. With a demeanor of defeat, she stepped a couple feet in before stopping. He couldn't help noticing how pale she looked and that her hands had a slight shake to them.

Seeing her in this state struck a chord with him. He'd witnessed the same scene play out many times throughout his hockey career. Whether it was him, which it was on a number of occasions, or a fellow player, the walk into the coach's office with the knowledge of being cut from the team was gut-wrenching.

Deep down, David was too soft-hearted to send her packing. Despite her willful disposition, there was no upside of making her a casualty of an unwilled mishap. Doing so would only tarnish her self-confidence. Asking her to leave was the easy way out. Keeping her on, working with her, digging deep and trying to draw out all that good others were seeing in her was the proper direction to take. Witnessing her like this stirred his sensitivity, causing a lump in his throat.

"Addison, please come in and have a seat."

"David, I'm so sorry. I know I screwed up. Just let me go grab my things and I will be out of your hair."

"Please, Addison, take a seat." He indicated one of the two chairs.

She did so, but with her head still facing towards the floor.

"Addison, you can look at me. I'm not going to

bite." He immediately regretted his choice of words.

As her face came into sight, he noticed a tear drop grazed her cheek. These situations were not his strong point, so he decided to dispense with the small talk.

"Addison, please, you don't have to cry. I'm not firing you."

The gloomy look remained as she sat there and said nothing.

"Addison, did you hear me?"

"Sorry."

"I said I'm not going to fire you."

"Why wouldn't you? I'm an idiot. I screwed up. I've been acting like a spoiled kid."

She wiped her face with the back of her hand. David opened a drawer, but found no tissue, so he got up and tore off a couple of strips of paper towel from the table supporting the microwave. He returned to his seat, then handed it to her.

"Thank you," she said.

"Addison, listen. Everyone should be given a second chance. It's what you do with it that will expose your true self. You are surrounded by many who believe you have a future in this industry, should you decide this is the path you wish to pursue."

"What about you?"

"I'll be honest with you. I haven't witnessed your progress, but Renée has only good things to say. My problem is with us." He pointed back and forth with his index finger. "Your actions are not okay, and we've talked about it before. I'm just about old enough to be your father and I'm a married man. Add to that, I'm your employer. If we can find a way to curb your flirtatious ways, I'll provide you with every opportunity to grow in this business, if it's something that interests you."

"I'm sorry. It's just that I find you such an attractive man. It was wrong, I know. Sorry. For the past few years, I've been surrounded by a bunch of adolescent university guys. It clouded my judgment being near a real man like you. It won't happen again. You have my word."

David didn't let on, but he was a little flattered by being referred to as attractive. Wanting to end the meeting so both of them could move on to their responsibilities, he tried to lighten up the mood by spurting out something which he again kicked himself for saying. It was a recent acquired trait which was recurring far too often for his liking. He needed to keep it in check.

"Are we on the same page?"

"Yes."

"I don't even want to be in your dreams."

"David, that might be a little difficult to control, but I'll see what I can do." A sheepish look replaced the bleak expression she'd arrived with.

"Okay, time to get back to work. We're done here. Check in with Renée."

"Thank you so much. I won't let you down...promise."

* * *

With that bothersome plight momentarily put to rest, he contacted Renée to inform her of his talk before tracking down his wife and daughter. All other business was put aside until Sandy's departure two days later.

Until then, he and his wife talked about pretty much everything going on in their lives. While Capella was awake, their daughter commanded their outright attention. While the baby was asleep, their intimacy was visited a number of times during those forty-eight hours. Then, just like that, Sandy was gone.

***

It was Jacob who drove Sandy to the airport, where a private government jet waited to whisk her off. David decided to stay back with his daughter, and Brooklyn stayed put in the office attending to the business at hand.

Upon his return, because it was nearing sunset, Jacob bypassed the office and went directly to the chalet. He was surprised to find their house unoccupied. At the thought of his wife being bogged down by the company's dealings, he made an about-face and walked up the path towards the ranch house.

Closing in on the office, he could hear Brooklyn talking. He presumed she was speaking to someone on the phone, but her tone of voice was concerning, bordering on a holler. Jacob remained out of sight as he caught the end of the conversation. He heard her raise her voice even louder. "I don't care what it costs. Just get it done."

Silence fell.

"What was that about?"

"Nothing. You're home."

"Should I be concerned for the person on the other end? You didn't sound too happy."

She tidied her desk, stood up, walked around it, and gave him a kiss.

"All in a day's business. I was trying to light a spark under someone who has been trying my patience with too many delays. Everything is under control."

"I would venture to say they received the message loud and clear."

"Let's go home and have dinner." She took hold of his arm and guided her husband towards their rustic retreat.

Chapter Ten

Heartbroken, yet driven by a sense of duty of her commission, Sandy found a way to suppress the heavy heart of being separated from her family as she stepped into her office. Taking a deep breath, she dove right into questioning her assigned executive assistant, Agent Jonathan Martinez, for a prioritization of ongoing matters.

At the top of the list was a request from outgoing Director Young for a meeting immediately upon her return. He handed her one sheet of paper which contained only numbers. Each sequence referred to an action, a situation somewhere in the world—a coup, an assassination, some detail of high classification.

The information had been compiled from communications with the State Department, Homeland, and the White House, among many other sources inclusive of her own domain's agents. To the common eye, it was unreadable, but once entered into her computer along with a series of her own personal generated inputs, which changed hourly, the data came alive. The disclosure of this information was meant for a select few, those who had the country's highest security clearance.

She instructed Jonathan on her day's priorities, along with directing him to delay informing Christopher of her return until midday. He acknowledged her requests without speaking as she stepped into her office and closed the door.

As she neared her desk, there was a sound coming from within her private en suite bathroom. Sandy drew a holstered handgun concealed under her jacket and inched along the wall to the opened door. A split second before she was about to enter and take down any intruder, if that was the source of the noise, her friend Blake emerged.

"Damn, Blake, you nearly got yourself shot."

"Ah, you weren't going to shoot me. You're more of a 'break a few bones' girl."

"How in the world did you get in here?"

"I have my ways. Besides, isn't that what spies do?"

"You're not a spy."

"I always thought it would be cool to be one. So, tell me, why are you courting my services?"

"Come here and give me a hug. I missed you."

They embraced each other as friends do, then took a seat in the chairs situated at the front of her desk. Some time was spent talking about their past and a couple of missions they were involved in together. Blake brought up the unexpected explosion Sandy initiated the last time they found themselves unknowingly on the same assignment. Sandy was his favorite warrior, although together they were seldom assigned to the same conflict. Yet, during that unprecedented year of enhancing their proficiency in warfare, an irrefutable admiration for her was found.

"Sandy, I know you better than most others, and you don't need me. Look around. You have the brightest minds in the intelligence community at your beck and call. I'm a field guy."

"You're here. It must have sparked some interest."

"I'm here because of you. That's what we do. Eleven is one, isn't that what we used to say?"

"We did, yes. Blake, there will be tasks that need to stay below the radar. No paper trail, no reports or justifications, no interrogations. For these undertakings to succeed without repercussions, I need someone who I categorically trust, and you are that person."

Understanding exactly what was being asked of him, Blake smiled while shaking his head in a way that implied *shame on you*.

"You mean, I'm the guy who gets those assignments that might be frowned upon by our judicial system?"

"Hell no. I have a building full of men and women doing that on an hourly basis. What I'm going to ask of you goes beyond that."

"Now you've sparked my interest."

"So you're on board?"

"How can I say no? I'm yours."

"Perfect. I will have the paperwork put in place for your transfer under an assumed identification. Your official classification will be Special Security

Adviser. We can arrange for you to teach a couple of hand to hand combat classes each month as a cover to keep it real."

"That's fine, but Sandy, if things get dull around here, I will want to go back. I'm not a desk guy."

"I hear you. Let me assure you this is going to be far from boring. You will be generously compensated for the rest of your life. Thanks, Blake. Fyad will be happy to hear you're receptive to the offer."

"Fyad? Now you've *really* sparked my interest. Sandy, was that him flying the helicopter that put you down onto our ship that last outing?"

"It was."

"I thought so."

They both took an instant to reflect on the mission he was referring to before Blake broke the silence.

"When do we start?"

"Right now." She leaned in to shake his hand.

Sandy walked behind her desk, where she opened a drawer and retrieved an envelope. She handed it over and asked him to open it. Enclosed was an outline of his first assignment along with a new passport, credit cards, and all documentation required to support his newly fabricated identity. It took him less than a minute to absorb what was being asked of him.

"You like to get right down to business."

"I do."

"Sandy, are my operations in the best interest of this country?"

"Yes."

"That's good enough for me."

Although she trusted Blake with her life, she needed to analyze his reaction once he became aware of what was being asked of him. Only then did she repeat her steps and take hold of a second, more official looking package. She held it to her chest, and took a deep breath before handing it to him. Blake rested it on his lap and looked at her for an explanation of its contents.

"Inside you will find an affidavit signed by the President of the United States exonerating you of all violations of the law committed during your military tenure, past, present, and future. I've got your back, Blake."

"This is getting better by the minute."

"We are going to make this world a better place. Thanks for coming aboard."

A wide grin came over him as he left the office, thanking and saying goodbye to the bewildered agent manning the desk at the entrance.

***

Sandy's next order of business was to walk down the hall to Christopher's office. The door was open, so she walked in. He was standing amidst a couple of boxes which she recognized as his personal belongings. His desk was cleared, the workplace now bare of any official activity.

"Sandy. Good, you're back."

"I am. Christopher, I wasn't expecting this." She gestured to the crates.

He asked his assistant to leave and close the door

behind him so he and Sandy could speak in private.

"I will vacate the office by the end of the day. You can make the arrangements to relocate."

"My understanding was you would be staying on until the end of the month."

"I was, but I've decided that you are prepared, and besides I'm not good at hovering in limbo. The time has come to move on and I need to face up to it. Honestly, Sandy, I'm terrified of what lies ahead for me."

"So am I."

"You'll be fine."

"Christopher, you know this wasn't me retaliating. Truth be told, my actions would have been similar, and I did suggest to the President that he not overreact."

"I'll let you in on a secret, Sandy. I inherited Andrew and he never liked me. You're his girl and you will do great. I promise."

"Thank you, but I felt a lot more confident in my ability knowing you were down the hall."

He asked her to have a seat and went on for the next two hours briefing her on issues of critical substance. He expressed his confidence in her a number of times, so by the end of the conversation, Sandy felt self-reliant. The time to say their goodbyes snuck up on them.

"I need to leave now," he said.

They shook hands.

"Christopher, if need be, may I call?"

"No. This is your ship now. Keep it afloat."

***

"I see you're still with us." Renée acknowledged Addison's arrival at work.

For the past couple of days, Renée had been absent from the track stable dealing with the acquisition of a couple of horses, so this was her first opportunity to speak with the trainee.

"Yes, and thank you. I'm sorry for disrupting things. I let my guard down. I'm so grateful for this second chance. I really am. I plan on making it up to you guys."

"Well, what are you standing there for? Get back to work."

With all the activity of the last few months, Renée's administrative obligations were neglected, big time. It baffled her how that insignificant desk nestled into the corner of the stable's office in its abandonment continued to produce such an increase of paperwork. She made a promise to bury herself in the labyrinth of the assemblage. Today, she was up for the challenge. Many of her daily duties had been tasked out to her employees. Two days, three tops of undisturbed work would return the exercise to its norm. Then, barring anymore unforeseen bizarre sidetracks, she decided to keep ahead of the game. She took in a deep breath, opened the door, walked in, then closed it.

Plopping down into the antique office chair, which featured two seized rollers, she positioned it in place by lifting and shifting. Another gulp of air was in order as she summed up the daunting chore which covered the entire desktop. Rooting herself on, she plunged in. After instructing her staff she was not to be disturbed, she was certain the afternoon would yield a constructive result.

The first half hour passed in the blink of an eye. It may have been an optical illusion, but the pile looked as though it was getting smaller, albeit the wire trash can and the recycling bin were filling up in short order. Impressed with her progress, she forged ahead. Mission impossible was being tamed.

Another forty-five minutes of shredding, sorting, and shuffling flew by before she knew it. The end of the tunnel was in sight. If this pace continued, she might even have enough time to ride a training session before day's end. With every scrunched up piece of paper, she affirmed her intentions of keeping this part of minding the store current on a daily basis.

She smiled at the progress and was thinking that without interruption, she would be up to date by the end of the day, when there was a knock at the door. Before she could call out, it opened and there stood David. Without movement of her lips, she swore to herself.

"*Damn it!* David, I wasn't expecting you."

"Jacob and Brooklyn wanted some time with Capella, so I thought I'd drop by."

"Is there anything I can do for you?"

"Do you have a few minutes? I'd like to talk to you about something."

She really wanted to be polite and hear him out, but she was in a groove. To tell the truth, she wasn't in a listening mood. Engaging in a conversation with him—or for that matter, anyone—was the last thing she wanted. The goal was to clear her desk. Nothing more, nothing less. Was that too much to ask?

"Can it wait, boss? I'm so far behind with this stuff." She motioned to the piles of paper. "Maybe we could catch up later?"

"That can wait." He turned back and closed the door, then took a seat in front of the desk. "Maybe we should consider hiring you an assistant to take care of these things."

She was resigned to the fact that she would have to hear him out. Dropping the pen on the desktop, she leaned back in the chair and asked, "What can I do for you, David?"

"I want a divorce."

"David, I'm not married to you, so I can't help you there."

"You know what I mean."

"Do you even listen to yourself?" Renée took a deep breath. She most certainly didn't want to have this conversation right now or ever. He'd been through a great deal of stress the past couple of months. As a friend, she would put her own agenda aside and let him vent.

"I know exactly what I'm saying. What I have is not a marriage. It's...I don't even know what it is."

"Listen, David, we've had this talk before and you're not going to leave anyone. Sandy is every man's dream. Drop-dead gorgeous, brilliant, and kind. I could go on and on about her attributes. What's keeping her away is extremely important work, and you should be very proud of her. You need to realize her appointment isn't for life, but your marriage is."

"It's no kind of life for Capella or me.'

"You're being selfish. Go for a ride. It will clear your head. Don't throw away everything you've worked so hard for."

Please get me out of this, she silently wished.

"Renée, we should start our own stable, you and me. Leave here, build a life together."

Now it had to end. "That's enough. Forgive me for being blunt, but you need to give your head a shake. The last thing in the world I want is to settle down with you or any other person. You want to leave your wife, be my guest. But there is no future with me."

Sometimes the truth hurt. Renée was being honest. Actually, if and when she was ready to settle down, she wasn't sure whether her life mate would be male or female.

"Renée, I love you. We could have a great life together."

"No, David, we've had great sex together. That's it, that's all, nothing more. You've got to get your head around it."

"It was more than that and you know it."

"Sex, David. Really good sex. You need to understand that, please."

"Whether you want to admit it or not, Renée, I know you care."

"Of course I do, David. I like you and care for you a great deal. You would have never been inside me if I didn't."

He stood, walked behind the desk, and gently took her hand. "I miss it. The sex."

That was the final straw. It was time to do something drastic to shock him out of his delusion and back to reality. She gently pushed him away, stood, and unbuckled her gold horse engraved western belt buckle. Her zipper spread open as her thumbs slowly eased the jeans off her hips. David stood there in disbelief. It all happened within a couple of seconds, but he was seeing it in slow motion.

"What are you doing?"

"Sex. You want sex? Let's do it. Right here, right now. And then you can get back to your wife and child."

With her right forearm, Renée forcefully swiped all the papers off the desk to the floor.

"You're crazy."

"No, David, you're crazy. Now, are you going to take me?"

Stopped in his tracks, he didn't know what to do. It had been such a long time visualizing having her again, and now he stood there, frozen.

"We can't do this now, here."

"Why not? That's what you want, isn't it?"

Resting her bum on the edge of the desk, clad in Victoria's Secret panties, she took hold of his hand and guided it so he now cupped the gap between her legs. Instinctively, David's middle finger straightened out and he felt her warmth.

It was playing out to become an all powerful sexual encounter, over a year in the making. Renée wanted it as bad as he did, but her thinking was that once he satisfied his craving, all would revert back to what it should be.

As quickly as it started, David pulled his hand away. He wanted it. So much of the past year was spent thinking about this exact moment. But he couldn't continue, not like this. How could life be so confusing?

"We can't do this here. We can meet later."

Renée didn't attempt to stop him as David tugged her pants up and began to fumble with the zipper, trying to zip them up.

The quandary was they were both so immersed in the exchange, neither locked the door. So they didn't hear the soft knock before the door swung open by the single person who didn't get the *please do not disturb* memo.

They heard a restrained, high-pitched voice. "Oh my God. I'm so sorry. I didn't know. Shit, I'm so sorry, I'll go. I didn't see anything, I promise. Damn."

All three of them were frozen in time. No one could move. They just stood there looking at each other.

Addison was blocking the partially opened door, her hands cupping her nose and mouth.

"Addison, please. It's not what it looks like." Renée hastily adjusted her still opened jeans, hopping upwards a couple of times and attempting to zip them up.

Addison left, closing the door, but not before making the half-turn on the knob to lock it, safeguarding the two occupants from further embarrassment.

David and Renée remained silent, each thinking their way out of what just transpired.

"You know, I don't care if she exposes us. Maybe it's for the best."

269

"David, shut up. No one is going to find out anything. Go home and let me deal with this."

"This shouldn't be on you."

"I know you're my boss, but I'm telling you to get out of here, now." She raised her voice. "Go home. I will call you later. Now!"

"Okay, but I do want to have this conversation."

Once he left, she took a few minutes to compose herself, then went in search of Addison. It didn't take long. She was standing inside one of the stalls talking to Ellie, her tutor. Witnessing the discussion accelerated Renée's heart rate.

"Addison," she called out. "If you're not busy, can I have a word in my office?"

"Renée, there you are. I was just asking Ellie if she had seen you around. I went looking for you a couple of minutes ago and couldn't find you. We had a question about this week's training schedule."

"Can I see you in my office, please?"

"Sure. Is everything okay?"

"Please." Renée motioned for her to follow.

With the door securely locked this time, Renée asked her to take a seat. Before she could speak, Addison offered her reassurance.

"Renée, you don't have to explain. I can be a brat sometimes, but the one thing you need to understand about me is I respect other people's privacy. I would never speak a word of this. I swear."

"Without getting into detail, what you saw isn't an accurate picture of the situation."

"Renée, with all due respect, please don't sugarcoat it. It is what it is, and I don't judge you.

270

To each their own. To be honest, I don't care what it was. This is yours and David's business, no one else's. Believe me when I say no one will ever hear about it from me, that you can bet your life on."

There was something about the conviction in her voice that made Renée accept her words as true.

"Thank you, Addison. You continue to surprise me."

"Is there anything else?"

"No, you can get back to whatever you were doing. Wait, what was the original reason for your visit?"

"It was nothing. I think Ellie answered it for me."

"Okay, then. Addison."

"Yes?"

"Thank you."

***

It was three weeks before Sandy returned to the ranch. Gravity encased the world's conflicts where they would remain until her return. Now being the solo commander of the agency, she was confident the organization would survive her brief absence. At present there was no second in charge because when Sandy offered the appointment to the existing Assistant Director, he resigned. He felt the job should have been his. She would soon sit down with the President to discuss a replacement. The agency did possess a talented senior management team to oversee the operation when she was absent. Sandy was only a secured call away should the walls come tumbling down. Even the President found time for his family, she reasoned.

The afternoon was spent alone with Capella. David was attending to business somewhere away from the ranch. The evening was reserved for the three of them and that's exactly what transpired. The scarcity of time being allocated to their relationship cried out for them to hold dear Sandy's abbreviated visits.

With the baby fast asleep, David and Sandy took refuge on the sectional sofa. It had been a good day, no drama or disruptions. There was no talk of moving, and he didn't criticize her for being gone too much. It was a glimpse of what could be. David thought if only this was the norm in their lives, everything would be okay.

Sandy curled up under a quilt, electing to read a novel in hopes of impelling herself into someone else's fantasy for an hour or so. David sat near with his arms resting on her upward bent knees. He switched on the television and launched into his dial flicking, but at a low volume so as not to disturb her. The sports channels were the recipient of his interest. Spending half his life on the road, calling hotels home, he mastered the annoying ability to watch four or five channels at the same time. He began watching a couple of ball games, alternating back and forth every five minutes or so. This was the life he craved for—peaceful, relaxing, being in the moment. It was nice. If only she needed it as bad as him, he felt the yearning for another would subside.

A half hour into his viewing, a special news

bulletin streamed along the lower screen. The announcers broke from the game call to narrate the breaking story. He turned up the volume slightly, not wanting to disturb the baby in the next room, but loud enough to hear. As the story began to unfold, Sandy's secured phone chimed. He knew it was too good to be true, an evening without interruption. However, he didn't pay attention to her side of the conversation as his focus was on the broadcasters.

"Russian billionaire Kristof Hoffmann has died in a plane crash. The owner of many Russian sports teams, considered the richest and most powerful man of the Russian Federation, dead at the age of sixty-five. We have few details other than witnesses reported the aircraft disintegrated in midair. More details will follow on tonight's newscast. This will prove to be a devastating blow to the European sports world and the Russian economy. Now back to the game."

David didn't know the man personally, but he was well aware of his sports holdings. A number of David's friends had been enticed to play hockey in the KHL, considered to be the number two rival to the NHL. Hoffmann was well known for his extraordinary financial offers in an effort to tempt the best professional hockey players to play for one of his teams. It was also said that he was a true fan.

David lowered the volume and turned to his wife to see she had laid the book down and was passing on instructions. She soon finished the call, but not before he heard her say, "Do we have eyes on the ground? Good, I want to be updated as we learn more."

Pointing to the TV, David looked at her. "Was that about him?"

She nodded. "Yes, it was."

"Of course it was. Why wouldn't it have been? My wife's the Director of the CIA. Who needs the news when you have…?"

"David, it's my job. When something of this magnitude transpires, I need to be briefed. I'm not saying we get involved in this kind of tragedy, but sometimes these incidents have far-reaching consequences. We initiate our own investigation. Information coming from the other side isn't always reliable." She picked up the book as if nothing had happened. "Did you know him?"

"No, I knew of him. A lot of my friends are on his payroll. He was the king of European hockey. Big shoes to fill."

"We will soon learn the cause of the crash. I hope your friends and their families are not negatively affected by this. You should get in touch with them."

"I might. Sandy, this whole CIA stuff just seems so surreal to me. Here we are enjoying an evening at home, like so many other normal families, and all of a sudden the phone rings and your directing some covert mission halfway around the world. I don't think I will ever become accustomed to it."

"David, it won't be forever. Now, come here."

She pulled him closer and they soon resumed the cuddliness prior to the news report. He refocused on a game, and she again the world within the paperback. Not too long after, they were under the covers, locked into one another. The lovemaking was kind, soft, slow, and absolute, not what might be expected of those deprived of marital intimacy.

***

Capella declared it was time to rise and shine with a snivel. Both parents came to her side only to be welcomed by her ever present smile. The baby's grin was so prevalent David was concerned she might develop cheek wrinkles much too early. Before they picked her up, they beamed as they stood at the edge of the crib, taking in her joy. This had to be the true meaning of life. The search, the hunt, that interminable quest for the purpose of being, lay at arm's reach, the beacon of their souls.

Soon, the baby was fed, as were Mom and Dad. The day's routine was taking shape. David had a short meeting scheduled for early afternoon at the racetrack, and Sandy decided to tag along with their daughter, but not before she attended to some business of her own.

"David, would you mind if I slip down to Father's office for a bit? I shouldn't be longer than an hour. I do need to deal with a couple of issues and then the day is yours and this little one's."

"No, go, I don't need to be at the track until early afternoon. Besides, I wanted to shout out a few texts to some of the guys in Europe. I hope to God none of them were on that flight."

"Okay, back in a bit."

Sandy gave them both a kiss before leaving. David sat on the sofa with Capella in one arm, holding his phone with the other hand.

It was dinner time in Gorky Park, so he didn't expect immediate response as most of his friends were likely in some dressing room in the midst of training camp. In total, he sent out four messages. He knew of more guys playing on that side of the world, but these four were buddies he regularly kept in touch with, two of whom were considered superstars on one of Kristof's teams. Without Mr. Hoffmann's financial support, the league might be in jeopardy. For his chums' sakes, he hoped those who held the man's power of attorney continued the billionaire's passion for sports, in particular hockey.

He set the phone down beside him and smiled as he looked at the toddler who was, what David had coined, baby snoring. His wife disagreed with the label and threatened him in jest, saying she would record one of his sleeps and then he would understand what snoring really was. Capella had developed a habit of dozing off for five or ten minute periods when nestled in the warmth of his arms.

With his now free hand, he picked up the remote and turned on the TV. He flicked his way through the sport channels, landing directly onto a news station searching for reports about the downed aircraft. It didn't take long as the wealthy commanded air time, dead or alive. He felt it a bit of a paradox that here he was so enthralled in seeking information on the crash by way of what a reporter passed on, when his wife was downstairs probably discussing the exact issue with some field agent standing at the scene. By this point, she would have acquired more intelligence about the accident than any journalist. And of course it would be classified. Marry her, sleep with her, be her friend, raise a family with her—but know you will never be awarded one-hundred percent of her. It was a bothersome assessment of his life.

***

Sandy sat in her own small office adjacent to her father's on the phone being briefed about the downed aircraft. The unofficial cause was a mid-air explosion. To the best of the agency's knowledge, four people lost their lives—Kristof and an assistant, along with the two pilots. The wreckage was spread out mostly within a twenty kilometer area. Few pieces were intact except for the rear fuselage with the airplane's undisturbed Certificate of Registration number imprinted on it. The country-specific usage prefix identification of RA allowed for a quick confirmation of its ownership. All aircraft registered in Russia carried a call sign beginning with RA, similar to the United States being the letter N.

Sandy wasn't particularly interested in the minute details of the accident, but rather the political and financial ramifications. She instructed her agents to zero in on any propaganda coming out of radical groups who might be assuming responsibility and what train of thought the crash's investigators were leaning towards. To her, the cause was not as important as the perception it may have on senior government officials. Many conflicts were initiated not by fact, but rather by cultural and social influence. Her job was to keep ahead of international events such as this. Alter the truth if need be, let the investigation play out, but then make it go away. Yesterday's news was soon forgotten.

With the business of the day taken care of, she went in search of her father. She found him and Brooklyn right where the majority of their days were spent. Brooklyn sat at her station outside the office, and her father at his desk.

"How are you this morning, Brooklyn?"

"It's a good day, Sandy. Go right in. Do we get to see that little angel today?"

"Let's do dinner. David has some business to attend to this afternoon and we plan on tagging along."

"Sounds wonderful."

Jacob was buried in his work and didn't notice Sandy's presence until she was dropping into a leather chair directly in front of him.

"Oh, Sandy, you startled me."

"You were deep in thought."

"I think it was more like daydreaming. To be honest, the more I sit here, the less I want to be here. It was my hope that it would be you overseeing my company at this point in our lives."

"Sorry, Father, I'm kind of busy overseeing our country's well-being right now. But never say never, maybe someday I'll take you up on it. Besides, you were the one who said I couldn't say no."

"Yes, I was," he conceded. "So when do you return?"

"I think I can stretch it out a couple of more days. We've had no revolutions these past few hours."

They had a chuckle and the conversation switched to family, plotting out a schedule of meals and times they could enjoy each other's company before her departure. Brooklyn had joined the chat and an hour soon passed before they realized it. Sandy needed to prepare the baby and herself for the afternoon trek, but there was one subject she wanted to touch on before leaving.

"Father, I trust you're aware of Kristof's passing?"

"I am. Such a tragic way to go."

"How is this going to affect you? I know there were dealings between the two of you."

"Sandy, we severed ties some time ago. Most of our few remaining interests will remain unscathed. He was a smart man, but far too eccentric for my liking. May he rest in peace."

"Okay then, I should get going. We will see you this evening."

Sandy was almost out the door when her father asked, "Will you keep me updated on the theorization of those in charge of the investigation? As best you can."

"Absolutely." She knew what her father was asking.

***

During the ride to the track, the conversation was light. It centered on Capella and their plans for the remaining two days of Sandy's stay.

"Are we buying a new horse?"

"No. Why do you ask?"

"The meeting. That's why we're going to the track, isn't it?"

"Actually, it has nothing to do with horses. I'm considering investing in a project with a friend of mine."

"Look at you, spreading your wings. How exciting. Are you going to fill me in or is it a secret?"

"No, Sandy, unlike your dealings, mine is not confidential. I think it is wise for me to look at opportunities beyond the racing industry. You never know. Never mind…" He stopped mid-sentence, hoping she would leave the comment alone. "It's drones."

"Drones what?"

"Drones. I'm investing in the drone business. Actually, its cutting edge software that can be utilized by a drone or even aircrafts, I would imagine."

"Well, this is interesting."

He went on at length, explaining his friend Kale Robinson was a leader in the field of drone software. They had played hockey together. Instead of pursuing the professional route, Kale went on to play in NCAA. They ran into each other a couple of years back. The two exchanged contact information and eventually began to discuss how this future technology could be utilized in the farming industry. He told her the more Kale picked his brain with regards to the needs of today's land management, the more intrigued he became. Never being asked, David eventually offered to invest in his friend's business.

"Besides your typical 3D and so on, his software can pinpoint the ideal location for planting by analyzing soil from the air. It's the future of land management."

"As I said, interesting."

"He wants to take the research to the next level, but it's going to cost. His technology will change many industries. For instance, we can already analyze thirty feet below the ground from the air and we believe in the not too distance future, we will be able to go lower. It works similar to an ultrasound. Can you imagine locating oil reserves without even drilling? Just with a fly by. Dry wells will be a thing of the past."

David went on about how excited he was at the possibility of having a business venture outside the horseracing industries, even if it was only a financial commitment.

The next thing they knew, they were pulling into the parking lot.

"Sandy, you're okay with this, aren't you? I know it sounds a bit farfetched, but trust me, these drone applications are becoming very sophisticated. He had begun to ramble with enthusiasm.

"David, I am the Director of the CIA." She gave him a wide-eyed look. "We have drones."

He took a deep breath, then exhaled. "Of course you do. When you're here, I have a difficult time seeing you in that light. Sorry."

"Actually, Kale's advancements sound intriguing. Maybe I should be meeting with him."

"No, he's mine," David joked as he turned off the vehicle.

***

Capella instantly became the center of attention. Kale hadn't arrived and Renée was nowhere in sight. The work at hand stood still as everyone wanted to catch a glimpse of the boss's daughter.

As David was about to excuse himself and check in to see if the office would be free for his meeting, he was stopped in his tracks by Addison. She was like an on and off switch for his paranoia. He wasn't going to leave her alone with his wife if his life depended on it.

"Hi, Sandy. *Aww*, Capella." She tickled the baby's belly. "I never get see you, you little doll."

"How are you, Addison? We live under the same roof when I'm home, but we rarely meet up."

"I heard you were home, but I presumed you had already returned to Washington."

"I'm still here for a of couple days. You should make time to join us for dinner tonight."

David said nothing. He wished he possessed extrasensory perception so he could telepathically tell her to decline.

"I'd love to." She hung on to the words longer than normal, knowing full well David was uncomfortable with the invitation, then paused before adding, "but I'll have to decline. Gotta work late." She jerked her head at David, implying boss's orders. "Thank you, though. I appreciate the invite."

Maybe he did have special powers.

"Perhaps tomorrow evening."

"I'll see what I can do." She smiled, then excused herself and moved a couple of stalls away to attend to one of the horses.

Kale soon walked into the stable. David introduced him to Sandy. He was aware of her designation, but didn't mention it. Given an opportunity, a meeting with the CIA Director might have produced a lucrative business contract, although that was not the reason for his aligning with David.

Sandy knew a five-minute search would reveal the agency was familiar with his work. The CIA employed some of the brightest minds in the field and what she was to learn upon her return was Kale's advancements in this software was the foundation from which many of the agency's developments were based on. He held the distinction of being the Steve Jobs in this particular arena.

"Let's go see if we can commandeer the office." He turned his attention to his wife. "Sandy, we shouldn't be long. Are you good?"

"Absolutely. I miss this place. We're going to wander about. Take your time. Capella and I will spend some time with the guys," she added, referring to the horses.

The men turned towards the office when Addison once again approached them.

"Excuse me. Sorry for interrupting, David, but

are you Kale Robinson?"

The man nodded.

She offered a handshake. "I'm honored to meet you."

"Why, thank you," he kindly replied. "And you are?"

"Addison Tucker."

David stood in disbelief.

"Addison Tucker, as in the President's daughter?"

"Yes. I'm surprised you know of me."

"I read your thesis. You should be commended for presenting such an in-depth study at such a young age. It was remarkable. Actually, I've decided to incorporate some of what I read in my research."

"Wow, I don't know what to say. How did you even know of it?"

"One of your professors is a friend. He was impressed."

"This is a thrill." She turned her attention to David. "Sorry, boss. I'd better get back to work. Thank you so much, Mr. Robinson. It really has been an honor."

She said her goodbyes, but not before accepting a card from Kale with his private number and email address. He made her promise to keep in contact, mentioning he would love to pick her brain about her research on the social ramifications and sensitivities of technology advancements.

"How did you scoop up a mind like that?" Kale asked David as they walked to the office.

"I have no idea," he replied.

Who Lies Beside Me

***

Renée looked surprised to see them.

"Renée, this is my friend, Kale."

"Pleased to meet you."

"Same here," his buddy replied.

"Had I known we were entertaining, I would have tidied up," Renée joked.

They smiled at her comment.

"Renée, if it's not too much of an inconvenience, could we have the office for a while? Kale flew in this morning and we have some business to go over."

She stood up, grabbing the files from the desk and stacking them on a filing cabinet. "It's all yours. I was looking for an excuse to ride a few training laps."

As she was leaving the room, David motioned to his friend. "Can you give me a second?"

He walked into the hall with Renée and looked around, confirming they were alone.

"Do you need something?" she asked.

"You didn't call me."

"About what?"

"Your talk with Addison."

"I told you I would take care of it. She won't breathe a word of it."

"You sure?"

"Yes."

"She scares the hell out of me. The kid even knows Kale."

"Who is he, anyway?" she whispered.

"A hockey buddy."

"I wasn't aware we had a deal on the table."

"It has nothing to do with the stable. He's a friend and I'm interested in a project of his. I need to diversify a little."

"Okay, is there anything you need from me?"

"No, but it would be nice if you assign Addison some work to keep her as far away from Sandy as possible."

"Sandy's here?"

"Yes."

"Great."

David returned to the office and reassured Kale everything was fine.

***

Renée came out of the hallway and the first person she saw was Sandy. Their talk was brief but cordial. Renée broke it off, quickly explaining she needed to get a couple of rides in before day's end. She would disappear until her boss and his wife were on the road back to the ranch.

In her hastiness, she inadvertently forgot to reassign Addison, although she was less concerned than David. The girl had begun to gain her trust. Worst case scenario, she'd lose her million dollar job and would take up David on the launching of a new stable. It wasn't going to play out that way, but as disturbing as it seemed, a small part of her fancied the thought. Even though it went against all her aspirations, the seed had been planted.

Since there were no more scheduled training runs, she decided to make her way to the trackside.

Maybe she would catch up with Gabriela and invite her over for a night of gladiator sex. That should rid her of the burdensome emotions which had been resurfacing. As luck may have it, there she was, walking towards the barn with her gear in one hand and the reins of a graceful thousand-pound athlete pecking at her shoulders in the other.

"Hi, there, how'd the session go?"

"*Stupendo*," she replied in Italian. "This gentleman—" She rubbed the thoroughbred's neck. "—was an angel. He's ready for next weekend's race. Me, on the other hand, not so good. I'm coming down with something. If you don't mind, I think I'll call it a day. I'm feeling a bit queasy. Must be a cold or flu. Nothing a good night's rest won't cure."

Renée smiled. Inside, she was thinking, *so much for that idea.*

"Why don't you take tomorrow off? It's an important race. You need to be on your game."

"I'll head home and get some rest. I should be okay by morning. We'll keep in touch."

"Good. Now, let me wash this kid down. You get going."

"Thanks, Renée. If we weren't here in a professional capacity, I'd give you a big hug and kiss. Maybe you'd come down with something and we could console each other under the covers. I miss you."

"Go, now. Get better, then we will see what we can do about that. Gabriela, watch your weight."

"*Arrivederci!*"

Less than ten minutes after excusing herself,

287

there she was, horse in hand, entering the stable. She sighed in relief. There was no sight of Sandy and the baby, or Addison. She walked through the barn and through the opening on the other side towards the cool-down area.

As with the food preparation for these elite wonders, cooling them down wasn't as simple as grabbing a hose and spraying water on them. Actually, in doing so, the water making contact with the horse's skin quickly became heated to its body temperature. The water then acted similar to a raincoat, repelling any further spraying. In many cases, the animal would get hotter.

The method Renée instructed all her staff to use was to hold a sponge in one hand and a sweat scraper in the other. Cool water was to be applied to a portion of its body with the sponge and immediately scraped off. The method insured the horse's core temperature was reduced in a safe manner. And that was exactly the process she applied, alone, in somewhat of a tranquil state until she heard voices behind her. She knew exactly who it was and was not thrilled about it.

"Renée, let me take care of him."

Turning, she witnessed Addison handing Capella to Sandy. Renée couldn't fathom why the two of them had teamed up, and to be truthful, she didn't much care. *It is what it is.*

"I've got him," Renée assured her.

"I insist."

Addison took hold of a second set of necessities and began sponging the horse. In an effort not to make a fuss, she relinquished the task to the apprentice and made for a final disappearing act. It wasn't to be. She was having difficulty drawing the curtain on the day.

***

Sandy wasn't completely honest with David about wanting to accompany him to the track. Yes, it was nice to spend her fleeting hours with him, but the main purpose of the ride-along was to haphazardly run into Renée and collar her into a private moment.

"Renée. Come, walk with us."

Sandy directed her to an area of less traffic. All Renée could think of was Addison shooting her mouth off, and now her fairytale career was about to come to an end. She figured her only consolation was that Sandy was holding Capella so chances of her being pounded into the ground were slim. It was midnight of a Cinderella story, except no one was going to be searching for the shoe that fit. It was over.

"I am a tad busy, Sandy. Can this wait? Maybe you could pass it along to David and he can fill me in later."

"Don't be silly. I only need five minutes of your time. You look pale. Are you feeling okay?"

When they were out of reach of the others, Renée figured she might as well get it over with. She stopped and turned to face Sandy, locking eyes.

"What's on your mind, Sandy?"

"David."

"What about David?"

289

"David and you."

"I don't understand."

"Your relationship with David, or rather, his with you."

"I'm not sure what you're insinuating, but I believe this conversation has come to an end." She started to leave.

"Relax, Renée. Just hear me out."

She stopped and again faced Sandy. It took everything she had to mask the trembling inside. Masquerading it with anger seemed logical.

"You stand here accusing me of having a relationship with your husband and in the same sentence tell me to relax? No, I'm not going to relax. You have a nerve."

"Renée, I have a relationship with many of my staff. A working relationship. I didn't make reference to any other type of rapport."

"Sandy, I'm upset and I don't feel comfortable having a conversation with you, especially in front of Capella."

"Oh, don't worry, she can't understand us. Listen. Hear me out. No need to reply, just listen."

Renée nodded for her to continue, but the look that accompanied the gesture said, "Make it fast."

"I know you and David slept together back in Miami, and I can live with that. I understand he has needs and I'm seldom around. Just so you know, he didn't tell me about it. Please understand, David has not spoken to me about this. He would never expose you."

"I'm sorry, Sandy, but I will not stand here and listen to this. How dare you."

Sandy blocked her way. She wasn't finished.

"We both know men fall back into their childhood and they need someone strong to make them feel wanted. In David's case, that's you and me. If you two need to sleep together, then so be it. I'm a big girl and can deal with it. I will eventually be coming home, but until then, I wanted you to know I feel comforted knowing you're looking out for him. He needs you."

Shaking her head in disbelief, Renée replied, "Let me get this straight. You are granting me permission to sleep with your husband, take care of him when you're away, and then hand him back when you fly in on one of your field trips?"

"Well, I wouldn't word it like that. But yes, I'd rather him be with you than someone else. You're a self-assured young lady capable of keeping the emotional side of a relationship in check. I can see why he is attracted to you. You remind me of myself when I was your age."

"Maybe you should reevaluate your priorities, Sandy. But if you're asking me to babysit your husband while you're off saving the world, go to hell."

Renée stormed off to anywhere a McGinnis family member was not.

***

Sandy smiled, mission accomplished. As inappropriate as it would seem to an outsider, Sandy was confident her approval of the extramarital relationship would in turn ensure her husband remain in their marriage. Deep down, she'd always known the call of duty to her country would take priority. This was who she was and wanted to be. Allowing her husband a little indiscretion was a necessary evil, but one that would ultimately save the relationship. It was messed up, but at the moment, that's the way it was.

Sandy slowly walked back to where Addison was still cooling down the horse. She stopped in front of the animal, allowing Capella to pat its nose. The animal instinctively recognized the child's tenderness and returned the gentleness by remaining still.

"Is everything okay?" Addison asked Sandy after witnessing the end result of the conversation by way of Renée's demeanor as she passed by a moment earlier.

"Couldn't be better."

If you knew what I knew, things wouldn't be all that rosy, Addison thought.

Mother and daughter stuck around a few more minutes until Addison completed her duty, at which point they entered the stable guiding the thoroughbred to his stall. Sandy and Capella were standing out of the way, watching the process of settling him into his resting place when David and his friend appeared.

"Hey, baby." He motioned to Capella and Sandy handed her over.

"You boys done?"

"Yeah, I think we got everything covered."

"Good, ready to go home. This little one needs some rest."

David shook Kale's hand with the promise of keeping in touch. Before Kale left the barn, he reminded Addison to send him a text. David had planned to talk a bit more about his buddy's familiarity with the girl, but one thing led to another and he forgot.

With his friend now gone, he acknowledged Sandy. "That sounds good to me."

They were about to leave when Sandy turned to Addison. It was clear she was becoming more impressed with her each time they met up.

"Addison, I'm not sure what your plans are after the summer, but the agency could use a brain like yours. Think about it."

The girl smiled. "I appreciate that, Sandy, but I promised myself not to sign up for anything that requires my father's signature on the paycheck."

Sandy laughed. "Well, at least keep my dinner invitation in mind. Maybe we could talk about it a little more."

"I'll see what I can do."

David was bewildered by Addison's ascendancy. The girl had everyone clamoring at her feet. He didn't get it. She was a brat. Summer's end couldn't come soon enough, and then she would be back at the White House.

***

During the trip home, they discussed David's new venture, which he explained was in the early stages, but he felt it would be a good investment. Sandy gave him a brief account of her visit to the stable and how Capella seemed transfixed by the animals. As the conversation went on, he became increasingly convinced Addison had kept to her word and not mentioned the embarrassing caught in the act episode, until Sandy's next words.

"It was nice to have a laid back day without a crisis."

"This could be your life. I'm sure there are many capable people available to run the agency."

"Someday, David, but not right now. Let's not ruin the rest of it talking about my job, please."

"Okay."

"I will give you this. It was a wonderful break and I want to make a point of doing it more often. Besides, it gave me time to catch up with Renée. You and Father were right. She's very dedicated to her responsibilities. It puts one's mind to rest knowing we have someone with such loyalty and at such a young age. The staff speaks highly of her. We are lucky. The kids couldn't be in better hands."

David didn't reply. He just smiled and began to fiddle with the radio, although it was already dialed in to his favorite country music station. Then the perfectly fine setting of the rearview mirror required an adjustment. Of course, a quick glance at the baby in the back seat seemed appropriate.

Sandy seemed amused by his squirming.

"The fresh air is good for her. She is sound asleep." He again played with his mirror.

"Don't you agree?" Sandy said.

"With what?"

"Renée. Is everything okay between you two? You didn't utter a word to her."

"What are you talking about? I didn't even see her after she left the office."

"It just seems every time I mention her name, you avoid the conversation."

"I have no idea what you're talking about. Yes, she does a great job. She is the best. With you gone all the time, I don't know what we would do without her. I certainly wouldn't have as much time for Capella as I do now, which leads me to another subject. A nanny. I've thought about our discussions on the subject, and I think we should start looking into it. But only if we can find the right person."

"I agree. Why the change of heart?"

David went on to explain when they first discussed it, because of his upbringing, he didn't consider it an option. Where he came from, families didn't rely on outsiders to care for their children. They found a way to make it work within their own group. A sister, brother, uncle, aunt, or some other relative was always there to step in when needed.

"I've come to the conclusion it might be in Capella's best interest. I don't want to burden your father and Brooklyn. They would never say no to taking care of her, but they do have their own lives. I think the time has come for me to resume my duties in a greater capacity. In the last year, I've sat out the majority of our away races. There is a lot of business that can be accomplished on those trips. Putting the burden on Renée is not fair."

"I agree."

"Let's discuss it with your father and Brooklyn at dinner. Maybe she can make some calls."

"Sounds good to me."

They were sitting down for the family dinner when Sandy got a call. Her visit would be cut short. The President beckoned her to the White House for the next day.

Chapter Eleven

A week had passed since Sandy returned to her commission. David stayed close to home, handling his obligations at the ranch. Renée stuck to her routine, preparing the horses for the upcoming races. David had spoken to both women on a daily basis. Sandy's conversations were short, as she always seemed to be dealing with one thing or another, and Renée focused solely on company business. For Renée, the less she conversed with her boss the better. She hadn't said a word to David about Sandy's proposition.

After his nightly routine of tucking Capella in, David laid down on the couch preparing to watch a NHL preseason exhibition game. It turned out to be a close one with the score tied after two periods. With Sandy away so much, and his affection towards Renée, life was confusing to say the least. However, he always had his hockey family. Watching the games gave him a bona fide sense of belonging. Each season, there were fewer players he knew personally. Many of them were now the

297

coaches or head office executives. He wondered what might have happened if he'd stayed in the game. Was it too late to consider an off-ice position?

Prior to the start of the third period, there was a brief news flash of headlines that were to follow the hockey broadcast. He had a sense of déjà vu listening to the reporter say,

"In less than a month, tragedy has struck another one of the world's billionaires. More details after the game."

"Holy crap," David blurted out.

The game went into overtime and ended with a shootout. Normally, he would have called it a night, but he wanted to know more about the headline. He got up and grabbed himself a bottle of water, knowing the news channel would not report on the death until the middle of the broadcast in order to entrap viewers. True to form, he first had to endure stories on the Middle East crisis along with a number of other world issues. They were important events, yet he was tired and preferred to inform himself on the topics by way of his laptop. Watching the news cast brought about an odd synthetic perception of having inside knowledge on world affairs. Although he realized he didn't, his wife was most likely far more knowledgeable about the facts than the correspondent reporting them. For all he knew, the CIA might be fabricating some of the events.

Who Lies Beside Me

"Billionaire Daniel Gonzalez disappeared off his hundred million dollar yacht docked off the coast of St. Tropez, France and is presumed drowned. We're told he was entertaining a small group of friends for the past day or two. According to two of his companions, he woke up before sunrise, told them he was going for a walk, and was not seen again.

"A search of the waters began once it was apparent he was no longer aboard. Early this afternoon, we had an unconfirmed report that one of his slippers was found floating in the vicinity of the yacht. We will update this story as new information comes in. As a side note, the NYSE took a hit due to the uncertainty of how his assets will now be managed. Two billionaires in two weeks. Coincidence or not? We close tonight with an inspiring..."

David turned the TV off and wondered like probably most others watching the broadcast if there was any connection between the two deaths. For him the events took on a weightier significance than most, as there were few of billionaire status and his father-in-law was one. Maybe he was being overly suspicious, but he didn't have a good feeling about what was going on. He would call Sandy first thing in the morning and voice his concerns. Maybe she could shed light on the deaths.

He stood up and went to check on the baby. She was sound asleep, so he washed up, but as he was preparing for bed, the little light bulb in his head turned on. During the second intermission of the game when the news channel showed a clip from the upcoming story, in the background was a flashback picture of Kristof Hoffmann's private jet sitting on a tarmac before it disintegrated mid-air a few weeks earlier. He grabbed his cell phone and turned the television back on.

He replayed the intermission until the aircraft filled the screen. There in bold print was the plane's identification number. He retrieved a pen and paper. Once the number was scribbled down, he turned off the TV and tapped the photo gallery icon of his iPhone. David wasn't one for taking a lot of pictures, so it didn't take long for him to find the one of the aircraft maintenance log. The book he found while snooping about in the hangar office at the Grand Bahamas airport. He looked at the screen, then back at the paper a couple of times and there it was. The serial numbers matched, which meant Jacob and Kristof were at the very least business associates. His interest piqued.

Resting back on the sofa, he sat in silence for a few minutes, trying to sort out what it was about these two deaths that bothered him. It wasn't a surprise that Jacob would have known each of them. There were few people of such wealth, so it stood to reason that they would be acquainted. Maybe it was the association of the aircraft being listed in the log at Jacob's Bahamas hangar. His inquisitive mind kept churning which guaranteed sleep was improbable for the time being. That's when an idea came to mind.

He sat up and flipped open his laptop, which was sitting on the coffee table, and began a search of Daniel Gonzalez, or rather, his private jet. It didn't take long before he was staring at a screen full of small pictures of the man's aircraft. Most were shiny pictures taken from the front, face on, the ladder extended to the ground with someone either boarding or stepping off. He continued to scroll through a few pages until he found what he was looking for. There it was, in bold letters, the registered identification number of the aircraft. He once again wrote it down, then checked it against picture on his phone. Bingo, a match.

David's heart skipped a beat or two. These mysterious accidents were beginning to feel close to home. The two deceased were not only acquaintances of Jacob's, they were business associates. Questions of these deaths not being accidental were transpiring within. If that was the case, could Jacob be in danger? He had to call Sandy.

Five rings before it went to voice mail, and he didn't leave a message. He redialed, receiving the same results.

Frustrated, he left a voice mail. "Sandy, call me. It's important."

It wasn't five minutes before his cell rang.

"Sandy."

"David, what's wrong?"

"I think your father might be in danger."

"What are you talking about?"

"The drowning, the plane crash. I don't think they were accidents. I think these men were targeted."

"David, what drowning and what plane crash? Are you feeling okay?"

301

"Yes, Sandy, I'm fine. The billionaires. They are business partners of your father."

"Wattsy, they were accidents. And why do you think my father had dealings with them?"

"I arrived early when I was picking up my parents in the Bahamas. To my surprise, I learned your father is part owner of the airport and has his own private hangar. I had some time to kill, so I roamed around, and on the desk in the office was an aircraft maintenance log. For some reason, I took a picture of the first page which listed the identification of the planes authorized to use the hangar. I remembered seeing the wreckage of the Russians and the number was intact. After watching the news tonight, I looked up pictures of the private aircraft of the gentleman who drowned. Luckily, there it was, and guess what? Both are listed in your father's log. Your dad must know these guys well, and if it wasn't an accident, he could be in danger."

Sandy took a second to respond. She didn't want her husband to worry and certainly didn't want him to run off and start his own investigation. She knew he was stubborn, so she chose her words carefully.

"Okay, listen, David. There are a number of agencies throughout the world analyzing every tiny detail of these two deaths. If there was any foul play, they will find it. And if they do, I will be one of the first to be advised. If for one second I believed my father's well-being is in jeopardy, I will immediately take the necessary steps to protect him. You have my word. Just so you know, I can tell you this, all reports thus far lead us to believe they were accidents. The timing is a bit of a coincidence, yes, but you know my sources know a great deal more than any news outlet. I promise you I will have my team keep me updated hourly and I will let you know if anything changes. Are you okay with that?"

"Yes. You should have one of your..." He rethought what he was about to suggest. "Forget it. You're right. This is what you do. I'll leave it in your hands."

"I promise. How's my baby?"

"She's perfect. I've been with her twenty-four-seven. When are you coming home?"

"I have meetings at the White House for the next couple of days, so maybe in a week or so. Everything here went smoothly last time I was home. I'm working with some extremely talented people and they seem to be coming around quickly with how I want things to run around here. It is a bit of a stretch from what they are used to."

"That sounds good. Sandy, keep an eye on this. I'm going to hit the sack now. Capella will be up early. Love you, babe."

"Back at ya, Wattsy. Talk to you tomorrow. Love you."

David sort of fibbed. He wasn't at all tired. What he wanted to do was contact Bob in the Bahamas, who was employed by one of Jacob's companies. That would have to wait until morning. It was one thing to call your wife late in the evening but another to call someone you barely knew.

***

Six in the morning, Sandy was in the back seat of a chauffeured limousine on her way to the White House. During the ride, she made one phone call. It was to Blake. She had another assignment for him. He informed her he was already in the air and would have the pilot alter the flight plan. The uncapped budget Sandy afforded him along with priority for air flight and security clearance allowed him to travel from one location to another swiftly.

"Blake, keep this under the radar."

***

Sandy was soon in the Oval Office along with the President, the Directors of Homeland, the FBI, and the Secretary of Defense. It wasn't long before the Chief of Staff and Press Secretary joined them. More would fall in place as the day rolled along. For the next hour, they touched on domestic and international issues requiring their attention. They refrained from going into details because the heads of all related government departments were to spend the next two days at the White House developing and implementing strategies to best handle each policy. The majority of the participants would have preferred to be at their respective offices directing their own agendas. However, the President championed cooperation among all bureaus.

By noon, everyone had a grasp of what was expected of them. Secured space was allocated for each individual and their staff to work along with three separate boardrooms for the joint effort segment of the endeavor. The President dismissed them. The marathon had begun.

As Sandy was about to walk into the hallway, President Tucker called out to her. "Sandy, can I have a minute of your time?"

She walked back in and the President nodded to the Secret Service, indicating he wanted to be alone with his guest. They closed the door behind them and stood guard outside.

"Sorry to have put you through this, but I can't show favoritism. Come here, sit, let's have a drink." He poured a glass of scotch. "Would you prefer a beer?"

"Scotch will do just fine."

"How is your father and Brooklyn?"

"They're busy as always, but I believe they are finding time to enjoy life."

"An attribute we should all pursue."

"Are you hinting at something?" She gave him an inquiring smile.

"How is David holding up with all this?"

"He'll be fine."

"Sandy, I completely understand your thought process, but I would like to see you fit in a little more family time. I know it's early in your term. Let's not get stuck into a pattern that becomes increasingly hard to pull away from."

"I hear you. Let me get my feet wet first, then I promise I will heed to your advice."

"Good. Are we expecting any backlash pertaining to the deaths of Mr. Hoffmann and Mr. Gonzalez? Their holdings reached far and wide."

"The explosion of Kristof's plane was caused by

a leak in the fuel line. The official reports coming in confirm there was no foul play. Our friend Daniel was entertaining three hookers in his stateroom when he decided to take a leak off the portside and fell. The ladies of the night witnessed him consume a large amount of drugs and alcohol. He got drunk and over he went. Maybe he realized he couldn't get it up anymore and jumped out due to embarrassment. Sorry, a little of that street girl coming out."

"Be my guest. I like it when you sensationalize our briefings. Everyone is so formal around me. It becomes mundane."

"You're welcome. The official bottom line is again, no foul play. As far as the financial repercussions, we will be fine. There is always someone there to pick up the pieces."

"Again, good. Let's sit here and sip on this for the next fifteen. A break from reality."

To the remainder of the inner circle's dismay, that's exactly what they did, and the fifteen turned into forty-five minutes.

***

By the time David fed himself and the baby, put in a couple of calls in regard to the horses, and cleaned up best he could with Capella awake, it was noon before he contacted Bob. What he asked of him was to take a picture of each page in the log, then email the photos to him. Without stipulating it, he led Bob to believe the information was required by the family business in an attempt to reconcile an accounting issue. He stressed it was imperative that the information be forwarded as soon as possible. David offered to compensate him nicely if he could put aside any other obligations he might have for the day. In his Bahamian mannerism, he pledged to be en route to the airport the second they hung up. He declined the offer of payment, explaining Mr. McGinnis's company held him on retainer and already compensated him handsomely.

Not wanting to sit around, David packed up a baby bag and with Capella in arm, walked down to Jacob's office. As was always the case, Brooklyn jumped up at the sight of the child.

"How's your day going, Brooklyn? Any luck in our nanny search? Sooner or later, I need to resume taking care of the business your husband pays me for."

"I've narrowed it down to two candidates. One young lady from Sweden and the other is American. I've been in contact with Sandy, and as soon as she advises us as to when she will be home, I will set up the interviews. They both seem perfect. I hope you don't mind, David, but I gave Sandy their names so she can look into their background a little deeper, although I believe I've left no stone unturned. But we can never be too careful when it comes to this little one." She gave the baby a little tickle.

He didn't mind Sandy utilizing her position to vet the nannies. What he found odd was that she hadn't mentioned a word of it to him during their daily chats.

"David," Jacob called out from behind his desk. "Got a minute?"

"Let me." Brooklyn held out her arms, offering to take care of her grandchild.

David handed her over along with the bag, then entered the office, taking a seat facing his father-in-law.

"How's things?"

"Everything is fine, Jacob."

"Good. I miss our morning meetings."

David thought, *I'm glad you do, because that's the last thing I miss.*

"As do I."

"David, how's it going? I am not referring to business. I mean you. How are you holding up? My daughter has left a lot for you to shoulder."

"We're in a good space, Jacob. Brooklyn says she is closing in on finding help. I'll ease into the nanny thing, which should free me up to get back to my routine and take some of the burden off Renée."

"I know it is none of my business, but if you ever decide to get back into the game, I could put a call in to the Washington Capitals and see if they can do me a favor."

"Thanks, Jacob, but we're not moving to Washington. We've been through this. I like what I do here. If your daughter decides our family needs more time together, she can move back home."

David was low key with his reply, but wanted it known he really didn't appreciate Jacob prying into his life.

"Point taken. Enough of that. I understand we have a Canadian race this weekend at Woodbine in Toronto."

"We do. The transportation crew and horse will

be leaving this afternoon."

"Brooklyn and I were thinking maybe it would be good for you to take a couple of days as a break from fatherhood. We'd like to offer our sitting services for the weekend. You take the jet, fly up to Toronto, and enjoy the race. Think about it. You deserve a break and we love to spoil Capella. Besides, Toronto is a great city. Maybe you could catch up with some of your hockey buddies."

"I'll think about it. Thank you."

He hadn't given any thought to attending the race, for that matter any race, until it was offered. *What the hell, I do deserve a break.* But first he wanted to get to the point of his visit in the first place.

"Jacob, how well did you know the two gentlemen who recently passed away?"

"You're speaking of Kristof and Daniel."

"Yes."

"We weren't golfing buddies. However, we did have some mutual investments."

"Their deaths…have they affected you negatively?"

"I'm curious of your concern. Their interests will be well managed by others, in some cases better, and any joint ventures we have with their organizations remain unaffected. Why the concern, David?"

"It's just, if…and I stress *if* their deaths were not an accident and someone is taking out billionaires for some strange reason, it wouldn't hurt for you to beef up your security. Which I might add is nonexistent at the moment."

"Look, I appreciate you're looking out for me. I really do. It's nice knowing someone has your back. But although the accidents may look suspicious, they were just that, accidents. I'll be okay, David, but thank you, it is appreciated. Now, back to my suggestion."

"You know, you might be right. Maybe I should take in the race. I can book a commercial flight. Are you sure you don't mind watching over Capella?"

Jacob didn't say a word. All he had to do was nod in the direction of Brooklyn, who held the baby in her arms. If she had her way, she would spend every day with the child.

"Take the plane. It's sitting there and I have to pay the pilots whether in the air or not. Sandy employs government transportation now, and I'm afraid the aircraft will rarely be used. You'd be doing me a favor. Then I can justify paying the crew."

"Okay, then. Are you sure you two want to do this?"

"There is nothing in the world we would rather be doing," said Brooklyn, who now stood in the opened doorway.

If he was going to attend the race, he thought it best to discuss it with Renée in person. It made sense that he be brought up to date on any potential business his trainer might have scheduled. Since the birth of his daughter, he had authorized Renée to carry out any transaction she felt was in the best interest of the stable. In addition, he would suggest she cancel her flight plans and join him.

"Jacob, would you mind if I ask Brooklyn to

watch over Capella this afternoon? I would like to take a run to the track and check in with the staff."

"Absolutely, we'd love to pamper her. David, in regard to the other subject, please don't be concerned. I have some very gifted people looking out for me."

"I just thought it was something that needed to be discussed."

***

As he was pulling into the parking lot of the track, his phone vibrated.

"Mr. Watson, after we spoke I went directly to the hangar. The log book is gone. I looked everywhere. It is nowhere to be found. This is very strange, sir. I have made many of the entries myself and in all the years I have served your family, the book remained in the exact same spot. I have requested a copy of the security footage of the hangar's monitoring system and expect it shortly. I wanted you to know right away. I'm so sorry. I trust Mr. McGinnis will forgive me."

"This is not your fault, Bob. Please get back to me as soon as you have reviewed the tape."

"Yes, sir, I will."

David wasn't all that surprised the log book had disappeared. He hadn't thought about it before, but once Bob told him, he realized it was a mistake mentioning it to Sandy. His mind didn't normally function in a scrutinizing manner. Yet, it was possible his wife ordered one of her operatives to retrieve the log so she could commence her own investigation.

Sitting in the parking lot with the engine turned off, he gave some thought to it. Maybe her having possession of it was the prudent way to handle the evidence. She had the entire agency's resources at her fingertips. Even if he was successful in retrieving it, what in the world would he do with it? Probably hand it over to Sandy, anyway. Bob could have been mistaken and the damn thing might have fallen on the floor or some other simple explanation. After giving it more consideration, he supposed his imagination was running wild.

Promising himself to visit the matter later, he focused on the purpose of his visit. Stepping out of the vehicle, the anticipation of spending a weekend in the same hotel as Renée quickly invaded his mind. He wasn't exactly sure how the personal side of the trip would unfold, but the thought of what might happen had become as tantalizing as the physical fulfillment in itself. Maybe that was enough. Maybe not.

It didn't take him long to track her down.

"Renée, can I have a couple of minutes?"

Her back was turned to him, so his voice caught her off guard. Nevertheless, when she swung around to face him, she was sporting a welcoming smile.

"David, you are full of surprises these days."

"I try not to be boring. Do you have a few minutes?"

"Sure." She instructed one of the stable hands to finish off and motioned to the walkway leading to the office.

"No, not there," he said. "Let's take a walk."

"Okay."

Although his visits often developed into a complicated exchange, she was still fond of his company.

"What's up, boss?"

"I'm coming to Toronto this weekend."

"I've got it covered. We only have one horse on the card, and to be honest, there's no business to take care of. It's going to be a quick trip."

"I need a break. Cancel your plane ticket. We'll fly up in Jacob's jet."

"That doesn't sound like you."

"He's insisting, and you can't argue the fact that it eliminates a lot of hassle. Maybe it's time for me to take advantage of such luxuries."

She couldn't argue his point, so after giving the idea a few seconds of consideration, she agreed. What would it hurt to revel in the perks of the job once in a while? Every other trainer she knew did.

Renée wasn't going address it at this instant, but the trip needed to stay on a professional basis. She knew they couldn't or at least shouldn't fall back into the past. Although being with David was a pleasant thought. It made her feel good. After all, she did have permission from his wife to do as she pleased with him.

"Why not. Sure, I'm in. We need to offer Gabriela a ride. She was going to fly up with me."

"Absolutely. Did you have Brooklyn book the trip?"

"No. She's got enough on her plate. I've been taking care of our travel arrangements."

"When you cancel your flight, would you mind booking me a room?"

"Consider it done. Is there anything else, David? I need to attend to a few things."

"You go ahead. I think I might stick around for a while. We'll catch up later."

"*Bon!*"

"On second thought, there is one more thing I've been meaning to ask you. On the way home from our last visit, Sandy seemed pleased with the outcome of a conversation she had with you. She wouldn't expand on it, but said it was nice to finally chat with you. Is there something I need to know?"

Renée hoped Sandy would have kept their little talk to herself but wasn't surprised to learn it had been discussed with David. Actually, his wife was most likely counting on sparking a dialog between them. It was Sandy's way of indirectly putting them both on notice the physical embroilment would be overlooked but anything more would be met with grave consequences. And Renée thought she had given up babysitting when she was a teenager.

"I'm not sure what you're referring to. I did see Sandy for a couple of minutes before your meeting ended. We chatted about the horses and she asked about Addison. That's about it. I've got to get going. I'll see you before you leave?"

"Yep."

***

They touched down at Lester Pearson Airport in Toronto at three in the afternoon the day before the

314

race. Renée arranged for the horse to be transported the previous day, along with the grooming team. The three of them decided to head to the track, since it was at most a fifteen minute ride. David spent some time in the city during his hockey years, so he was comfortable navigating the rented vehicle on its streets. In addition, with GPS or Siri, how could a person not be confident in finding their location?

Upon arrival, they checked in on the horse and staff. To David's surprise, the ranch hand on duty was none other than Addison. Before being enlightened about her boss's decision to join in on the trip, Renée assigned her to the traveling team. Renée felt Addison earned the opportunity, and with summer soon coming to a close, she felt it was a nice perk. David's expression revealed his being surprised by it, but he offered no remark.

Gabriela prepared the horse for an easy canter around the track. She would ride a few laps to feel out his disposition. Once she was convinced there was no jet lag, he would be brought back to the stable and pampered until race time.

She was soon mounted and guiding the animal onto the turf. David and Renée stood at the rail watching.

"Renée, is everything all right with Gabriela? She was quiet on the plane and she looks pale."

"She's had a bout with a flu bug, but says she's starting to feel better."

"Is she going to be okay for tomorrow?"

"Her weight's good. She's a pro. She'll be good to go."

Their attention went back to watching her and

the horse glide around effortlessly. A hundred pound women commanding a thousand pound animal was a thing of beauty. The union was a mystical force of nature. Hearing the horse's hooves slap the ground with such power as they neared only to listen to the brawn disappear into the backstretch. It took on a mesmerizing aura.

"Nothing compares to this."

"You're right, David. We are fortunate."

"You know, it may sound a bit odd coming from a guy but…" He lost his thought momentarily.

"What's odd?"

"It's romantic. Every time I stand here watching these kids," he explained, referring to the horses, "it gets me right here." He tapped his heart. "It melts me. Romantic is the only way I can explain it. And you know what, Renée?"

"What?"

"I never want to lose that feeling. I crave it and I've missed it. I want my daughter to know it. With each year gone by, I've realized how short life is. We should not waste a single sunshine, as there are far too few."

Renée's legs went weak. Listening to the softness in his voice, witnessing him expose such intimacy tugged at her heart. He was a good person, torn about by circumstances. It was no wonder she had become so attracted to him over the years. At the moment, she just wanted to grab him, take him, hide from the world with him, cradle him. *Stupid Sandy.*

"God, this does something to me." He turned to her with a gentle smile.

316

"*Oui,* David, it does." She held on to the rail a bit tighter so as not to lose her balance. *He's killing me here.*

They returned their attention to the track until the session soon came to an end. Gabriela dismounted and handed the reins over to Addison, who had discreetly kept her presence undetected from her superiors—though she'd been witness to their exchange.

"He's ready," Gabriela told them.

"Are you?" Renée questioned, as she looked like hell warmed over.

"I'll be fine after a good night's rest."

"All right then, let's grab an early dinner before heading to the hotel," David suggested.

"If you two don't mind, I'm going to pass. I can hitch a ride. You guys go enjoy yourselves."

"Nonsense. We'll go check in, and then if you care to join me, Renée, we can search out some food."

***

The front desk clerk directed them to the elevator. Their accommodations were located on the top floor. Renée originally reserved two junior suites, one for her and one for Gabriela, but later booked an additional one for David. The grooming staff were booked into rooms located a few floors below.

When the clerk handed over the hotel key cards, she informed them each suite was identical. Neither of them gave room preference a second thought and randomly grabbed a small envelope, then waited for the ping of the elevator.

A second ding was heard as their floor came into sight. Their eyes searched for the sign with arrows to direct them. As it turned out, the three rooms were side by side, facing the rear and overlooking green space, which was preferred to the other on the traffic side. Gabriela's card indicated the first suite, Renée's the middle, and David's the last door in hallway.

"I'll see you guys in the morning." Gabriela disappeared into her room.

"Goodnight," David said awkwardly, as it was still daylight.

"If you need anything, call me," Renée offered.

"You still up for grabbing a bite?"

"I'm famished. Give me a minute to clean up."

"Let me know when you're ready."

Now in separate rooms, they mirrored each other by kicking off their shoes and placing their suitcase on the luggage rack. Making their separate ways to the washroom was cut short when they realized the hotel had issued them joining rooms.

David sat down on the edge of the bed. Staying on the same floor as Renée was going to be difficult enough. Now with the only barrier between them being an interior door and a half turn of the handle, his self-discipline would be put to the test. On the opposite side of the door, Renée faced the same quandary.

He retraced his steps to the washroom, but stopped at the door, and without contemplating the reasoning behind his actions, he deliberately opened his portion of the two-way ingress. He swung the door until the hinges stopped its movement and left it that way.

The shower felt good. The water pressure and temperature were a pleasant surprise. Not seeing any reason to rush, he put his head to the wall and let the water pound on him, almost falling asleep. He realized it had been some time since he'd enjoyed one of his lengthy showers, because he was always hurrying through just in case Capella needed to be attended to. If he didn't hear Renée knock, she would recognize that he wasn't ready.

By the time he stepped out, it looked like a steam room. The haze seemed to roll out into the suite. David quickly dried off and tossed the towel on the counter, deciding to allow the mist to subside before finishing up. As he walked out naked, he noticed that he could see clear through into Renée's room.

There, sitting on his bed with a smirk bordering on laughter, sat Renée. David didn't attempt to cover up. He just walked past her to the unoccupied side of the bed and lay down on top of the covers.

"Thanks for the invite," Renée said, referring to his side of the door being left open.

"I should be saying this is awkward, but it's not. It's kind of cool."

"Lying around a hotel room nude can be cool. Now are we going to dinner?" She tossed a pillow over his private parts.

"Are you sure you don't want to hang out here?"

"You wish. I'm not doing you, boss, at least not right now. Now, go get dressed, I'm hungry."

He threw on a pair of jeans and a t-shirt. They

decided it best for each to enter the hallway from their own respective room's entrance. The interior doors remained open.

"By the way, I didn't request joining rooms."

David smiled without a reply. It made no difference whether she requested it or not. It was a pleasant surprise.

With wonders of modern technology such as Google, they selected and made reservations at their restaurant of choice by the time they stepped outside the hotel lobby. Once in their vehicle, David tapped the address of his buddy Wayne Gretzky's restaurant into the GPS. He had convinced Renée they served the best poutine and burgers in the city. She was sold.

During the drive, Renée was being educated on how David and Wayne became good friends over the years. The story in itself wasn't particularly interesting to her, but the enthusiasm by which he was telling it engaged her. He told her the year he played his first NHL game was the same year Wayne retired. David went on to say it was because of his awe toward "The Great One" that he practiced day in and day out.

His father rigged up an area in the barn for him to practice his shots off a piece of Plexiglas. He would be alone with stick in hand shooting pucks into a net pretending to announce his own make-believe game: "Gretzky passes over to Watson, Watson shoots, he scores, history in the making, they are Stanley Cup Champions."

Every kid who grew up in Alberta, or for that matter anywhere in Canada, idolized Gretzky. To any boy or girl interested in hockey, he was a hero, a god. They had become friends during the summer breaks, playing together in many golf tournaments. They both loved hockey, golf, and later David learned Wayne was fascinated with the horseracing industry. Their friendship developed early in David's career and remained as strong today.

"I hope he cooks as well as he played."

"Renée." He chuckled. "He doesn't work there. He lives in California."

"Why does he have a restaurant in Toronto?"

"It's an investment. He has some good people running it for him."

"Okay."

***

Supper equaled the hype, delicious and filling. It wasn't one that would receive a five star endorsement by a nutritionist, yet to a great burger and fries lover, it topped the charts. With the excuse of wanting a clear head for race day, both of them refrained from drinking any alcohol. If they dug deep enough, the real reason would reveal neither wanted liquor to cloud their judgment on what may or may not transpire later.

How the night played out was in the back of their minds, but wasn't discussed. David had a mind to touch on the subject during the ride home, but didn't. It wasn't until they were securely in their suites by way of the separate entrances did Renée initiate the conversation. She walked directly into David's room and plopped down on the bed.

"We should talk about this."

"That we should."

"David, you know what alarms me about our relationship?"

"What?" He sat beside her.

"When we're alone, we interact like a married couple. The ease in which we exist, we've bared our souls to one another. We complete each other's sentences. There are secrets between us that we will never share with others. You walked in on me masturbating, eased beside me and respected my space, not judging but rather becoming a part of the experience. I sat here earlier when you strolled out of the washroom naked and neither of us flinched, nor did you make any attempt to cover up. It was like an everyday routine. We are so at ease with one another's behavior. It's a bit concerning because, David, we are not married. You are."

"We do seem as one. I believe that is how you describe many married couples."

"That's what I'm saying."

"Where do we go from here? Do we want to change anything?"

"I don't know."

They sat in silence for a minute or so before Renée continued.

"David, whether by design or not, we have become close friends, lovers. But tonight let's not engage in the sexual aspect of our relationship. We can revisit it another time. You did say you wanted to start traveling to more races. I've really enjoyed your company tonight. I've missed you that way. Let's just be satisfied with the lovely evening we've had and not complicate it any more than it is. You okay with that?"

"You're probably right. Renée, it's good to be back."

She bent over and gave him a quick, friendly kiss on the cheek, then stood up and retreated to her room.

"Goodnight, David."

"Goodnight."

Renée made no effort to close the joining doors.

Soon, they had cleaned up and were nestled into their respective beds as the rooms surrendered to darkness within seconds of each other.

"Goodnight Jim-Bob," David called out as he tucked in with a smile on his face.

"*Quoi!*"

"Never mind. Go to sleep." He almost added, "Love you," but caught himself just in time.

"Goodnight, David."

***

Blake walked past Agent Martinez, who was sitting at his desk outside Sandy's closed office door. Unlike executive assistants of the real world positioned to filter access to corporate head honchos, Sandy's guy sported a gun and knew how to use it. Blake didn't even acknowledge the words.

"Sir, the Director is in a meeting at the moment. If you would have a seat, I will advise her you are here."

The directive brought about a smile to Blake's face as he opened the door and entered the office.

323

"I'm sorry, ma'am, I explained you were busy," the agent said, following Blake in.

"It's okay, Jonathan. Please close the door behind you."

"I don't think the poor guy cares for me too much."

"He'll come around."

"Here."

Blake slid the logbook from the hangar in the Bahamas across her desk. Sandy didn't take the time to look at it and placed it into a drawer.

"Any encounters?"

"Nope. Security cameras will confirm no one entered or left the building. Do we have anything on the go?"

"We do, but take the rest of the day and we will meet up tomorrow."

Blake lifted out of his chair. "You know where to find me." He closed the door and disappeared, but not before thanking the agent at the desk.

Sandy picked up her phone and put in a call to Fyad. There was no answer, so she left a message for him to make contact. She then called David. No answer. Another message was left, this time telling her husband that she had an evening meeting and would call him first thing in the morning.

***

With his lower half concealed by the bedding, David sat up, resting his back on the pillows as he answered his cell phone.

"Hey, how's it going? Sorry I didn't catch your

call yesterday."

Sandy was also apologetic about not calling more often. The majority of the conversation pertained to Capella and the search for a nanny. Although David was originally opposed to the idea, they were now on the same page and agreed it was best. Sandy informed him she was planning a trip home within a few days.

"Sandy, did…" David was about to question her in regard to the missing log, but was stopped mid-sentence when Renée appeared in the interior door frame.

"Rise and shine, boss." She froze when she noticed David cuddling the phone to his cheek, holding his index finger to his puckered lips, signaling for her to be quiet.

"Do you have company?"

"No, that was the cleaning staff. I just left the room. I'm out in the hallway. Yes, I'll be checking out," David added, trying to make his story believable.

"David, I love you. I need to go. Call after the race."

"Talk to you later."

Sandy smiled, knowing full well the cleaning staff's name was Renée. David's omission of the words, "I love you," or "Love you too," confirmed it.

"Sorry, I didn't know you were talking to Sandy."

"It's okay. Isn't it a little early to be leaving?"

"Actually, we're not leaving. We have a bit of a problem and we are working the phones. Gabriela is too sick to ride today. She's been throwing up all night. Even if she felt better, she will never clear weigh-out. We need a jockey. Between the two of us, we should be able to find one."

He jumped out from under the blankets stark naked and freely pranced by Renée, who was now sitting on the base of the bed. Her reaction was a long drawn out, "Okay then," with an emphasis on the O, as she shrugged her shoulders and smirked. Renée's eyes were perfectly positioned and did follow his midsection until he was out of site.

David poked his head out of the washroom, "I'll be ten minutes."

Renée went back into her room and began placing calls to contacts who would know if any jockeys might be available. Their drawback was being in Toronto. They weren't as familiar with those who rode at Woodbine as they were of the riders in the USA. David joined her in less than ten.

A decision was made to grab a coffee and breakfast sandwich by way of the drive-through at a Tim Hortons, which were on every second corner in Canadian cities. They would then head to the track and resume their search. With any luck, they wouldn't have to scratch their entry. Gabriela elected to stay back at the hotel and rest until the flight home.

"Sandy will know it was me in the room."

"No, she won't."

"I would bet she does."

"Doesn't matter. We weren't doing anything. Now, back to the problem at hand. If you want, I can scratch out and we can head home."

"No. I want this race. Let's see who's available."

***

They parked and went their separate ways, David to the racetrack offices, and Renée to the stables. She wanted to check in on their horse before asking around the grounds. David would inquire with the track's race officials.

An hour passed before they came together in front of the stall. Renée gathered the staff who made the trip. All attempts to secure a jockey proved to be of no avail. They knew it wasn't that the jockeys who were present at the track today wouldn't have loved to jump onto a McGinnis Stable entry, but the issue was they were all committed to their rides for the day. When a jockey prepared his or her day, a rescheduling was difficult. There was a weight-out factor in addition to many other issues. Weight loss in an extra three minute race could jeopardize one of the planned rides. Most of the jockeys were Canadian, and that wouldn't sit well with the owners who provided the majority of their rides.

The staff was briefed and informed that if a jockey was not secured within a half hour, they were to prepare the animal for transportation back to Kentucky. David would arrange to have the cargo plane readied.

Everyone nodded their understanding as they all walked back into the barn. They were about to return to their duties when Addison spoke up.

"Renée, why don't you ride this guy?" She patted the horse's nose with her right hand while holding his cheek strap with the left.

"I can't do that, Addison."

"You know him better than anyone. I hope I'm not out of line here, but I've watched you ride and you're as talented as it gets."

"Thanks for the vote of confidence. There is a difference between riding a training run and jockeying a race."

"She makes a point, Renée." David broke into the exchange. "Your jockey license is valid in Canada."

"Listen, I appreciate it, but my foremost responsibility is the safety of our horse and me riding alongside ten experienced jockeys is unsafe. We have thirty minutes to find a qualified rider or we scratch and head home. Sorry, David, but this is my call."

He knew she was right, but believed, as Addison did, that besides Gabriela, Renée could be first over the finish line.

"Let's get back to work," Renée instructed.

David and Renée reverted back to their phones in a last effort to find a replacement. Addison and the remainder of the staff stayed with the horse. There was little they could do until receiving final word on the decision to race or go home.

***

"I'll be right back," Addison informed her co-workers and was out of the stable before they could inquire why she was leaving.

Ava recognized the panic on her face. Other than

the issue of the drugging episode, the summer was without incident, so she allowed Addison plenty of space. For the most part, the agent went unnoticed. In this case, the urgency she displayed called for close monitoring.

Addison made a beeline towards a building a hundred yards from the cluster of stables, a red brick structure with a walkway lined with flowers. There were no horses housed here. It was the jockeys' clubhouse.

With the agent close behind, Addison's entrance mirrored one who might have owned the place. She ignored the security personnel at the front desk and before they could jump up to intervene, Ava flashed her badge, urging them to leave it alone.

Addison stopped halfway down the hallway, looking to her right, then to her left, then back to the right. Without knocking, she opened a door and entered. Ava followed but stopped and stood just inside the door which read, '*Jockey Room-Men.*'

As in any sports dressing room, the occupants varied from being dressed, half-dressed, in the shower, and of course naked. Since this impromptu visit from two females was unforeseen, the majority were near naked. Their state of undress didn't even faze Addison as she stood in the center of the room. It made Ava smirk.

"Gentlemen, I apologize for the intrusion. I only need a moment of your time."

"Young lady, I'm not sure if you're aware that you are not supposed to be in here. As you can see…" He referred to the other jockeys scrambling to cover up. "It is a male only dressing room."

"Don't worry, I'm not into jockeys. My name is Addison Tucker. I'm an apprentice with the McGinnis Stables in Kentucky. As many of you are already aware, we have an entry in today's seventh race and our jockey, Gabriela D'Angelo, has taken ill. She will not be able to ride today. We are in need a replacement."

Half a dozen of the men in the room were already scheduled for the seventh race and without Gabriela and her horse, they had a much better chance of winning.

"If one of you could do us a favor and squeeze in an extra mount, we would greatly appreciate it. I am not in a position to offer any more than the expected pay, but as you know, we are favored to win the race. I will, however, do everything in my power to convince my ownership to provide you with quality rides if you are ever down our way."

Everyone in the room knew Gabriela was North America's leading jockey, and an opportunity to get in good with an organization of such stature as the McGinnis Farm didn't come along often. That didn't change the fact that their day was already structured to their own commitments. To alter could negatively affect the outcome of another race.

"Gentlemen, I have little time to spare. Do I have any takers?"

The guys looked back and forth at each other and a couple of them began to show some interest but not before a young man in the back held up his hand as if he was seeking permission from his elementary teacher.

"What's your name?"

"Santiago Cruz, ma'am."

Addison couldn't recall ever being called *ma'am*.

"Are you saying yes, Santiago?"

"Yes, ma'am. Today I race only in the fourth."

"Are you any good?"

"Yes, ma'am."

"Put your pants on and come with me. Thank you for your hospitality, gentlemen. If you're ever in Kentucky, drop by and say hello."

Addison and Ava left the room and waited for Santiago, who was with them within a minute. During their hurry back to the stable, Addison asked the jockey, who actually looked younger than her, "How long have you been licensed?"

"This is my first year, ma'am."

"Great. Well, at least you have your own colors." She referred to his riding uniform.

Entering the barn, Addison noticed the crew was once again gathered around David and Renée.

She called out, "Wait, don't scratch! We have a jockey."

Everyone turned to her and the young man at her side. Ava again faded into the background.

"This is Santiago Cruz. He only has one ride today, in the fourth. Santiago is touted as the next superstar this side of the border. We're extremely lucky he is available today."

David and Renée introduced themselves to the jockey. They were curious as to how their apprentice came upon him, but that conversation would wait until later. As Renée mentioned earlier, her first priority was the horse's safety. Unless she was one hundred percent convinced the person mounting her animal possessed the ability do so with unwavering professionalism, it wasn't going to happen.

"No disrespect, Santiago. We do appreciate your offer, but I believe we will be scratching our horse from the race." Renée put an end to the offer.

"I understand, ma'am. Should you change your mind, I would be honored to help out your stable. I must go now and prepare for my race. Addison knows where to find me."

The jockey turned and thanked her for considering him, then went on his way.

"Thanks for caring, Addison. I'm not comfortable hiring someone I know nothing about."

"You're welcome. We tried," Addison said.

"Let him rest right now. We're going to check in with Gabriela and see how she is doing. We'll be back in a bit," David instructed the staff as he urged Renée to accompany him outside.

Once alone, Renée spoke up. "I'm not running Gabriela. Let's just go home. It's only one race."

"I wasn't planning on calling her. We don't have to make it official until race time, so why don't we watch this kid run the fourth? We're always looking for talented riders, and if he is the new up and coming, as Addison says, we might have a spot for him at the end of their season up here."

"I thought you were skeptical of everything that comes out of Addison's mouth?"

"I am. Come on, let's go have some fun and watch a couple of races."

That's exactly what they did. Not up in the private area reserved for the well-to-do, but down on the main floor where they could walk to the fence and hear the thunder of the hoofs rumbling down the home stretch. Even though David had been witness to thousands of races, the thrill of each rider trying to maneuver his or her mount across the finish line before the others was as exciting as the first time he experienced it as a child.

The fourth race was quickly upon them. Santiago was in the saddle of a horse handicapped about mid-field with the number one post position. The bell rang as the starter's gate opened and the riders jockeyed for position.

Santiago's horse belonged to a respected Canadian stable which elevated him one notch up in Renée's book. David and his trainer learned a little about the jockey by the information provided in the program. He had ridden the horse he was now on a number of times with some success. One win and a couple of seconds and thirds were respectable outings.

Today he seemed to have made a rookie mistake and remained blocked in along the rails by the others. As they paced the three-quarter mark of the race, Santiago made a sly maneuver to position the animal, allowing him to challenge the leaders. Coming around the last turn, they were looking like contenders until Santiago pulled up on the horse's reins to slow him down and steered him to the right, away from the others. He slowed to a stop, dismounted and held him still until the trainer arrived on the track.

All horsemen had seen this before. An experienced, caring jockey put winning second when it came to the horse's health, or at least that was the hope of all owners and trainers.

"A skeletal fracture," Renée said to David. "A class act."

When a racehorse's legs hit the ground at racing speed on the straight stretches, its legs took three times its body weight. Around the turns, which was the case here, the animal was bearing five to ten times his weight. More than not, a jockey or trainer wouldn't recognize the fracture until after the race or never. Renée wanted to hear the reasoning from the jockey himself, so she flashed her security clearance ID to gain entry to the parade area in order to speak to the young rider. David followed.

Santiago and the horse had moved off the track. He stood with the animal's trainer while both rubbed its leg to assess the injury. David and Renée stood aside, not wanting to intrude. A groom soon had hold of the horse and guided him to the stalls. The trainer in question was a veteran in the field and recognized David.

"David Watson, I was hoping to cross paths with you today. It's been a long time." He offered his hand. "And this must be the one and only Renée."

She smiled. "Very nice to meet you."

"I'm looking forward to watching Gabriela in the feature. We get excited when the best roll in town."

"Sorry to disappoint, Thomas, but Gabriela has come down with a nasty flu and is not able to ride. We plan on scratching."

"That's too bad."

Renée noticed Santiago making his way back to the jockey's clubhouse. "It was very nice to meet you, Thomas. Would you two excuse me?"

"Your jockey has offered to fill in for Gabriela. I doubt Renée will approve it, but if so, would you mind?"

"He's a talented kid, David. You know how picky I am. If he wasn't up to my standards, he wouldn't be sitting on my horse. Case in point, he recognized the fracture and immediately put the animal's health first and foremost. That's the guy I want. He will give you an honest ride, but don't go off stealing him from me."

"I wouldn't do that to you, Thomas. Send him down when your season's over. I'll keep him working."

They promised to stay in touch and David went in search of Renée. He took notice of her walking away from talking with the rookie.

"David, I've asked Santiago to join us so he can meet Star Power. If I feel comfortable with their interaction, I will sign off on him riding today. That is, if it's okay with you."

"It's your call. Thomas only had good things to say about him."

It wasn't more than fifteen minutes before the jockey returned and he instantly hit it off with the horse. To most, the animal's reaction to the young man wouldn't seem out of the ordinary. But Renée read the horse's behavior like few others and immediately sensed the connection. She authorized the ride and David made the call to race officials, informing them of the jockey change.

Most races Gabriela rode, her horse's odds went off as the favorite. She was named North America's top jockey for the second year in a row. People bet on her because of her talents along with the fact that she only rode the best. In addition to her winning percentage, she was also named North America's top female athlete of the year. As was predicted, Star Power was the early favorite in the morning lines. Handicappers unanimously picked her to win. When the bell rang at the start of the seventh, the horse's odds had fallen to third due to the jockey change.

Santiago rode the race exactly as Renée instructed him to. When the dust settled, the McGinnis entry lost in a photo finish and placed second. A respectable outing, taking into consideration horse and jockey had only met an hour before race time.

David exchanged information with Santiago, leaving open an invitation to join the stable when his season was complete. The horse looked energetic enough to be still running around the track, so Renée made the decision to transport him home early that evening. With the race behind them, David and Renée slipped by the hotel to retrieve their sick girl before heading to the airport. All things considered, it had been a good trip.

Chapter Twelve

It was early evening before Fyad returned her call. He apologized, then went on to explain he was hidden away with his wife, Princess Selena. Sandy listened to him mimic her own life. Because of his responsibilities, there was little time for romance, so a promise to spend three uninterrupted days at a secluded retreat was far overdue. Hamza was left in charge and instructed not to contact him unless Fyad's father felt it warranted. It had been a long time since Sandy remembered hearing her friend so relaxed.

"It seems like the hiatus worked. You sound reinvigorated."

"I believe it did enliven me. A practice you might consider."

"I agree, soon. But for now, the President has asked me to arrange a meeting with you. There is something he would like to discuss with both of us in private. It will only be us three."

"Sandy, with all due respect I would prefer you hear him out and pass it along."

337

"Fyad, I think it important he sees firsthand the benefit arrived from our collaboration."

"I'm not entering the White House."

"I will suggest a neutral location."

"All right, for you I will do this."

They agreed to put aside a block of time and he would fly in for the get together as soon as Sandy made the arrangements. Their conversation continued for a while longer, mostly centering on their personal lives. As was common practice for the two of them, an evening's dinner would be worked into their visit. Sandy promised there would be no repeat of their last encounter.

"Fyad, I have to run, but before I do, are we comfortable with our actions thus far?"

"I believe we're good for now. Let's talk at our next dinner."

"You take care and say hello to your father for me."

"Will do. Talk to you soon."

The call ended with friendly goodbyes. Sandy then called the President on a private number and was surprised when he picked up on the first ring. He seemed pleased that Fyad agreed to the briefing, assuring her the scheduling would allow for plenty of lead time.

No matter what position a person held, if the President requested your attendance, little stood in the way. She was, however, curious as to the reasoning behind the inclusion of Fyad, knowing that the president himself understood the Prince's lack of enthusiasm towards the administration, so she thought she would ask.

"Sir, may I ask the premise behind such a meeting?"

"I prefer to discuss it in person. You two seem to work so well together. I have a special project I would like to share."

"Okay then, I'll wait to hear from you."

"And you will."

Sandy read into it that the meeting would take place sooner rather than later. Getting the impression the assignment would demand a great deal of her time, she would arrange a trip home sooner than planned. She would call David later to tell him.

***

With Gabriela a few steps ahead halfway down the aircraft's stairs, Renée leaned in to David and said, "Thank you. That was fun. I hope you join us more often."

"I'd like that."

David offered to give the women a ride, but Gabriela's vehicle was still parked at the airport and she would chauffeur Renée home. Just as they were about to go their separate ways, Renée remembered something she'd been meaning to ask David.

"I think it's time to put Belle on twenty-four-seven. Do you want me to arrange it?"

"I'm going right home, so I'll get someone on it for a couple of days. You can work it into the staff's next schedule."

She was concerned about Belle, the mare who was carrying twins and nearing her eleventh month of pregnancy. It was time to keep her monitored around the clock. A group decision was made earlier in her term not to reduce to a single pregnancy. The stable had success in the past with a similar parturition and it didn't hurt that they employed the best veterinarians available. In addition, the stable was outfitted with the finest state of the art equipment money could buy. Statistics stated a mare had only a ten percent chance of birthing two healthy foals. However, a mare housed within the McGinnis system bettered its chances to a probability of more like twenty-five percent.

"Good. Will I see you tomorrow?"

"I'm not sure. I'll give you a call." He paused. "Renée, it was a nice weekend."

David jumped into his jeep with his mind focused on seeing his daughter. He asked himself how in the world his wife was capable of repressing her need to be with Capella for such lengths of time. He was absolute in his belief that their daughter was the single most important part of Sandy's life, but still couldn't fully understand the path she had elected to lead the family down.

***

He found his little bundle of joy at the chalet with Grandma and Grandpa.

"Well done, David."

Capella was showing signs of wanting to walk, but at the recognition of her father's voice, she came barreling out from amidst of her toys on all

340

fours. David picked her up, planting a few kisses on her cheek.

"Daddy's home," Brooklyn gave her a little poke on the side of her belly.

After David cuddled his daughter for a couple of minutes, he responded to Jacob.

"It was an interesting weekend. I'll fill you in tomorrow."

"How's Gabriela?"

"She looks like hell but she'll be fine."

"Good, and what about my daughter? It's been a few days since she's checked in. Have you heard from her?"

"I have. She's trying to break away soon. Brooklyn, as soon as we get a date, can you arrange for us to meet the nanny candidates?"

"Absolutely."

Brooklyn read it on his face that he didn't want to stick around and chat, so she packed up the baby's bag and strapped it onto his shoulder. He thanked them for watching over Capella for the weekend and stepped down the wooden steps of the porch with his daughter clinging to his grip. David elected to pass through the stable. It wasn't until he laid eyes on Belle did he recall Renée's request to have the mare monitored. Being that it was the end of the weekend, there was a skeleton staff on duty, but he was able to secure volunteers for the next two midnight shifts of pregnant horse sitting.

It wasn't long before Capella was showing signs of weariness. He assumed the onset stemmed from Jacob and Brooklyn playing her out the last couple of days. A quick bath and she was down for the count. Although it was the child's time for rest, it was far too early for him. He sat down on one of the sofas, pondering how to spend the remainder of the evening. In the kitchen area he prepared a snack, then opened the refrigerator and snatched a bottle of beer. It was decided a distraction to the complications of life was in order, so he was soon munching down a sandwich with one hand and a novel in the other. Reading make-believe did wonders for putting reality on hold for an hour or so. He wasn't through the first chapter when a call came in. It was Sandy.

"Hey, babe."

"Are you home, Wattsy?"

"I am, and you?"

"I'm at work. What's my little one doing?"

"She's in la-la land. I think your parents wore her out this weekend."

"I'm coming home tomorrow. I'm clearing my schedule tonight and will be there in the morning. Did you have plans?"

"None. I'm all yours."

"I like the sound of that. I gotta go, I love you."

"Love you too. See you tomorrow."

He disconnected and texted Jacob to inform him his daughter was coming home.

As the pages turned, he couldn't help but drift off into a daydream, thinking his life story would make for a good book. He was rich, living the dream, somewhat of a celebrity status, in love with two amazing women, both of whom were preeminent in their respective fields, but as kindhearted, understanding, and caring as anyone he'd ever known. He was father to the most beautiful child in the world, son to wonderful parents, and yet here he was, so screwed up. Yes, it would most definitely make for a bestselling narrative. Maybe someday he would write it.

***

Sandy came through the door at seven the next morning. She worked until midnight, then grabbed a couple of hours' sleep before flying in by way of one of the agency's private jets. To her surprise, David and Capella were still asleep. She tiptoed into the baby's room, and stood over the crib, staring at the bundle of joy she so dearly missed. A tear eased its way down her cheek. Her position demanded she suppress her emotions so deep she feared they might never resurface, but the tear garnished some reassurance.

Call it mother-daughter sixth sense, but she was looking down at her child for less than a minute when the baby woke without a fuss, and laid perfectly still while looking up at her with the most beautifully innocent smile God could have blessed her with. Sandy picked her up and cuddled her against her chest, feeling the warmth of the baby's body. Capella instinctively reached for her mother's earlobe with her tiny fingers.

Carrying the baby, Sandy went to the bed where David remained fast asleep. Sandy gently wiggled his toes, hidden under the bowed comforter. He mumbled a low noise not found in any dictionary and adjusted to his side while curling up. She repeated the fondling of his foot, this time a bit more convincingly. He once again incoherently uttered something as his eyes focused on mother and daughter. The beautiful vision manifested a split second before he realized they'd brought a glow to the room. Smiles were reflected back and forth.

"Good morning."

"Good morning. Why don't you get up, Daddy, and we'll whip up some breakfast?"

David's feet found the floor, and he slid into a pair of slippers positioned at his bedside, then followed them into the kitchen area. Sandy first mixed up a small plate of food and poured juice for Capella, who was secured into her high chair. The child was beginning to grasp the concept of getting the food from her plate to her mouth. David had placed a small plastic painter's sheet under her chair, as he expected half the serving to be flung onto the floor, and that was okay with him. If they felt too little had actually reached her mouth, David would hand-feed her more.

"Do you have a lot on the go today?"

"No, I plan on wiping my schedule while you're here. How long can you stay?"

"Two, maybe three days."

"We should make the most of it."

"Are you okay with the three of us just hanging out here at the ranch? I'm really not up for any field trips."

"Sounds perfect." He leaned in to give her a kiss.

After breakfast, Sandy slipped downstairs with the baby in hopes of seeing her father and Brooklyn.

She was pleased when she found them settled into their daily routine. The delight of her surprise appearance was mutual. Dinners were promised and planned. Catching up on the recent past, present, and future agendas of the ranch were bounced back and forth. Little was discussed with regard to her CIA projects and successes. It became too awkward of a conversation, being that ninety-five percent of her work was classified top-secret.

***

Meanwhile, upstairs, David made a couple of calls, cancelling his itinerary for the next two days. Renée was his first. She would again be asked to bear the brunt of the management workload.

"How long is she home for?"

"A few days. You never really know with Sandy. Listen, Renée, I arranged Belle's watch last night and tonight. Can you take it from there?"

"Not a problem. Will you be traveling with us to Saratoga in a couple of weeks?"

He took a deep breath, then exhaled. "Oh man, I love that track."

"It is your favorite. I'm making arrangements for the crew. Should I book you in?"

"I don't know if I can do it. Go ahead and take care of you guys, and I'll let you know."

"*Bon!*"

"We should touch base at the end of the day. If you need anything, I'm staying close by."

"Goodbye, David."

He threw on a t-shirt and a pair of jeans, tucked

the cell into his rear pocket, and went in search of his family, distracted by thoughts of Saratoga.

***

Downstairs, the gathering moved from the office to the kitchen.

"Breakfast?" Jacob asked David as he entered the room.

"I'm good. We just ate."

"Coffee?"

"Sure."

The four adults and Capella sat around the island. There was never a shortage of topics to discuss when they got together. David didn't spend much time with his in-laws during Sandy's absence and early morning meetings were becoming a thing of the past. David wasn't going to drag his daughter to the office at that time of day, so Jacob took the impromptu gathering to get an update on the racing scene, in particular the previous weekend's race.

It brought an amusing smile to David's face when he explained how it was told to him by other riders about Addison bursting into the jockeys' clubhouse. Jacob questioned whether or not it was wise to run the horse with a rookie aboard. Having his decision second guessed rubbed him the wrong way, but he attempted to disguise the fact.

"It was all on Renée, her call. And I agreed. She knows what she's doing." He tried not to use a forceful tone, but he had.

"Well then, I guess that's what we pay her for." Jacob brought the subject to an end, then reverted

346

back to discussing the President's daughter. "I've had the opportunity to get to know Addison a bit. We've run into each other a few times as she was making her way in and out of the house. She even shared a couple of lunches with me when she was working nights. The more time I spend with her, the more I appreciate her candor. She's a very bright girl. David, not trying to butt in, but are we offering her a full-time position at summer's end?"

David shrugged. "Again, that's solely Renée's decision, but I will pass along your sentiment."

The better part of the morning was spent in the kitchen catching up. The only topic left untouched was Sandy's work. Around noon, the grandparents returned to the office area. Mom and Dad entertained their daughter with a leisurely stroll about the homestead until it was time for her midday nap, at which point they returned to their suite. The baby was soon asleep.

David was itching to question Sandy on whether or not she was responsible for the removal of the aircraft log. He was about to get into the conversation, knowing full well it would prove to be of no avail, when Sandy walked out of the bathroom naked.

"We have about an hour. Let's make the best of it. I've missed you."

She walked up to David, who had gotten comfortable lying on the couch with his head slightly raised and resting on the arm of the sofa. That was exactly where Sandy positioned herself. She stood there, seductively looking down at him. He wasn't making eye contact. He focused on her newly styled bikini wax, ever so close to his face. He was accustomed to her clean shave, but had to admit the tiny half-inch wide strip of tightly shaven blonde hair, extending up an inch or so from where his fingers were about to disappear, was a turn-on.

Before his arm could reach up for her, she gently moved his head forward on the armrest. Sandy lifted, then bent her left leg and rested it on the edge of the side table while straddling her husband's face. Buried between her legs, David knew exactly what to do. Her excitement was felt the moment his lips met her. His arousal quickly became evident.

It wasn't long before Sandy took notice of his growth and stretched out to free it. They readjusted their positioning with her chest resting on his stomach. The oral caressing deepened his need as he felt his wife's well-versed lips, tongue, and teeth fuse together, flawlessly swallowing him up.

The sofa dance came to a powerful climax just shy of an hour, the intensity magnified by the usual extended period of separation. They laid on the narrow surface tightly embraced, supported by David's bent leg bearing down on the floor.

"There is something to be said about your homecomings."

Sandy didn't reply, just pulled his lips to hers and kissed him.

Spent, they both drifted off into a near sleep when David's leg gave way, suddenly jolting them awake.

"Let's go shower."

"I'm perfectly fine here. You go and I'll keep a listen for you know who," Sandy responded.

"Okay, but you don't know what you're missing."

"Oh, believe me, I do, and I can't take anymore right now. We still have tonight."

"Rookie," he teased, turned and disappeared into the shower.

Sandy threw on a pair of track pants and a t-shirt. She saw no need for bra and panties. She brushed through her hair with her hands and went into Capella's room. Her daughter was still ever so quietly snoring. Not wanting her to nap the day away, she decided to make herself a beverage and relax for another fifteen before waking her. After all, her superhuman conditioned heart was beating a wee bit faster than it had recently been accustomed to. Time to wind down was welcomed.

***

The afternoon flew by and the next thing they knew, dinner was being served. As was the case during David and Sandy's mid-afternoon conversation, the exchange remained light, steering clear of any in-depth talk. They did, however, touch base in regard to the nanny candidates Brooklyn scheduled interviews with the following day. David reserved the upcoming evening for questioning his wife as to the whereabouts of the log.

Brooklyn looked over at Jacob, who gave her his nod of approval before speaking.

"Sandy, David, Jacob and I have been talking about hiring a nanny. We understand your situation and recognize the necessity of being afforded time to pursue your careers. After all, that is what the majority of parents do. We would like to offer our assistance in caring for Capella. Jacob and I would like to propose that you allow us to provide the same assistance as a nanny. Please go forward with the interviews tomorrow, but we ask you give it some thought."

"Brooklyn's correct. We would love for Capella to be part of our daily routine. For the past few months we have been restructuring the company's operations and are now at the point where a couple of morning calls and the odd board meeting is all that will be required of us. A great deal of thought has gone into this and we genuinely want to make her inclusion into our lives our number one priority. We would want you to go about your responsibilities as you would if a nanny was caring for her. As Brooklyn said, give it some thought."

Sandy and David didn't know how to respond. The suggestion came out of left field. A scenario neither one had considered.

"Daddy, I don't know what to say. We were gearing up to introduce a nanny into Capella's life. I appreciate the offer, but I'm sure you two have far too much on your plate already."

David didn't offer his opinion, because he didn't have one. It wasn't something he would immediately write off, as he knew how much their daughter meant to Sandy's parents, so it was best to discuss it in private with his wife before speaking.

"Meet with the ladies tomorrow, and then we will talk. Please give it some thought. Now we should have some dessert."

It was late once dinner and an evening of catching up finally came to an end. Jacob and Brooklyn insisted on cleaning up as they had given the staff the night off. David and Sandy retreated to their suite.

David knew his wife could be called back to Washington at any given time, so he was going to have a conversation with her before the night's end.

"Can we talk about a few things?"

"We have so little time together, are you sure you want to talk?"

"Yes, Sandy, I do."

"What's on your mind?"

Sandy joined him on the couch. There was no television on or music playing, so the room was quiet. She said nothing, allowing him the opportunity to air his thoughts, which she predicted would once again relate to their frequent separation.

"I'm finding it difficult thinking about our daughter being raised by a nanny. I know we agreed, but as we get closer to actually doing it, the more worrisome it becomes."

"David, I don't want to get into an extended conversation and rehash our choices again, but we need to continue our work. Capella would be disappointed in us if she learned later in life that her father and mother turned their back on the importance of our careers."

"Sandy, your work is important. Mine, not so much."

"Are you kidding? Our ranch staff relies on you to make all the right choices so they and their families have food on their tables, a house to live in.

Each decision you make touches many lives."

"Are we ever going to be a normal family?"

"We will, I promise. I truly believe I can make a difference. Stick with me for the next few years and let me pave a path for my successor. I've been given such a great opportunity and the freedom to curb the atrocities of our world in any way I see fit. I can do this. As clichéd as it may sound, I want to bring about world peace. Or at least contribute to a solid foundation for it. I understand how difficult this is for you, but I believe my team can make a difference. We will leave this planet a safer place for our children and theirs."

She gave his arm a squeeze, then got up and walked into the kitchen area to prepare a cup of tea from the shiny machine sitting on the counter.

"Can I get you something?"

"I'm fine."

It took from the time she stood and walked to the counter for what she'd said to sink in. She'd said 'our *children*,' not 'our child.' Given their lifestyle, he had written off any additions to the family. But she said *children*. Maybe he heard wrong.

With drink in hand, she nestled back onto the sofa. "David, what was it you've been meaning to talk to me about?"

His mind was clouded by his wife invoking a chimera. It was best to replay her words over a few times before asking for clarification. Besides, he wanted to know about the log book, so he refocused.

"Remember when I…" His phone began to play a country tune.

Sandy sat there listening to his side of call.

"Okay, Ben. That's not a problem. I'll take care of it. Listen, you go home now. Family comes first. Now get going, I've got you covered."

"Is everything okay?"

"Yes. We have Belle on around-the-clock watch and Ben volunteered to stay on tonight, but his son hurt himself playing ball and his wife called him from the emergency room. He broke his collarbone. It's best he be with them."

His employee's situation made them think of their own concerns. What if Capella hurt herself? Would it be the nanny rushing her to the hospital, frantically trying to contact them with the news? Hell, they failed to protect her from the kidnapping. Sandy was rarely home and now they were considering hiring someone so David could increase his time away.

"He should be with them. You were saying? Remember what?"

"Sandy, would you mind if we talk about this later? I'm sorry, but everyone else has gone for the day. I think I should spend the night at the stables. Her estimated due date is still a few weeks off, but if anything happened to her and we weren't there it would be..." He stood. "You know what I mean. I'll be back as soon as the early shift gets in."

"You go. I've got a ton of correspondence to review. Washington never sleeps. I'll be here when you get back."

He leaned over to kiss her, then grabbed his jean jacket and left.

Sandy opened her laptop and entered a series of

codes, then placed her thumb on the bottom right portion of the screen. Before the screen produced information intended for those few with the highest of security clearance, the process of identification took a few minutes.

***

On his way out, he noticed a glimmering of light escaping from the kitchen. He thought by this time Jacob and Brooklyn would have been settled in at the chalet. Maybe something was wrong. He went down the hall to have a look.

As he came to the doorway, he was surprised to see Addison seated at the breakfast bar. Not that he should have been, but nevertheless he was.

"David, a pleasant surprise. You're up late."

"It's not that late. I'm old, Addison, but not that old. I can still make midnight, on a good day."

They had a chuckle and Addison was delighted to witness her boss in a witty mood. Their encounters were, for the most part, strained by the circumstances surrounding them.

"How was your trip home?" he asked.

"Everything went smoothly. David, I apologize for butting in on the weekend. I just wanted to see if I could help out."

"There's no need to apologize. You did great. I must say you do have lady-balls."

"Why, thank you," she said as a smile flushed her face.

David looked down at her food. "That looks good. What is that?"

"It's a Bean Kale burger. Do you want one?"

Before he could reply, Addison was off her chair and had the refrigerator door opened. He was going to decline, but it looked so good. The frying pan was being heated on the gas range and in no time she placed a delicious looking snack in front of him.

"Thank you. I'm impressed."

"I'm just a girl who likes flowers on the table sometimes."

"What's that suppose to mean?"

She laughed. "Sorry, it's a lyric from of an old country song that I found in my dad's record collection. It had a catchy flair that stuck with me."

"You might be growing on me. I've had my concerns."

"I know." Addison took deep, apologetic breath. "I guess I've been a little overassertive towards you."

"You think?"

"I was just so tired of the…never mind. I once again apologize."

"Addison," he began, then stopped to take a bite of the burger. "Oh my God, this is so good."

"Thanks."

"I was going to say you can't go around playing ass grab with people you don't know. It could be a dangerous practice."

"When I met you, it was like meeting the man of my dreams. I knew my actions were wrong and I wasn't thinking. I wish I would have been more mature about it. Sorry."

"Good enough for me. All is good. And for the record, you are a beautiful young lady who I and everyone else who comes in contact with you believe will achieve great things with your life."

Her smile remained. Seldom had anyone other than her father and mother complimented her. She was always seen as the President's daughter, not Addison. It felt nice.

"David, you didn't mention why you were up this…" Hesitating, she said, "early."

He laughed. "Renée feels the time has come to have Belle on twenty-four-seven watch. Ben was sitting tonight, but needed to go home. A family issue. That leaves me."

A moment went by while each of them munched on their food.

"I've got tomorrow off. I can spend the night at the stable. The horses are better company than my computer. Besides, I understand Sandy is home. You should be with her, David. I know it's none of my business, but really, you should be spending the night with her, not Belle."

It hadn't dawned on him that Addison was an option, and he liked it. Going back upstairs and crawling in beside his wife was a pleasant idea.

"You know, I just might take you up on that. Are you sure you don't mind?"

"Boss, you'd be doing me a favor. Don't get me wrong, it's a beautiful room you've so graciously provided for me, but no matter how comfortable it is, it becomes lonely when you're getting into bed by yourself every night."

"Okay. She's not due for a few weeks, so there's no chance of you having to deal with anything. However, we want to be cautious. Let's finish this sweet burger, then I'll walk you down to the stable." He took another bite before adding, "Maybe I should have hired you as a chef."

It wasn't long before they wiped down the table and washed the dishes.

"Do you need to grab anything from your room or inform Ava?"

"I'm good. I'll text her and let her know where I am."

With that, they were out the door and walking down the dirt trail adjacent the rustic fence.

"It must be difficult having someone looking over your shoulder. At what point do you no longer require the Secret Service?"

"It's not as bad as it might seem. I've been fortunate. In a way, it is reassuring knowing someone's got your back. When children of past Presidents turn sixteen, they no longer are provided with security. I guess when he leaves office, Mom and Dad will continue to have agents assigned to them for life. I would think if I made a big enough fuss about it, I might be able to lose them now."

They entered the stable and each gravitated to different animals that were roused by the company. Soon they found themselves standing together in front of Belle's stall. The horse looked healthy. It certainly did not appear as if she was carrying two one hundred pound foals in her belly.

"Is it safe to be in here alone with you?"

"You have my word, boss."

David went through the protocol should something happen. First, call the vet, who would be on sight within an hour. Second, call him, and third, try to comfort the horse. He showed her where all the numbers were listed. Anxious to return to Sandy, he cut the conversation short and bid her a goodnight.

"You're sure you're okay with this?"

"David, I'm fine. Please go."

"Okay then, have a nice night. If you have any questions, don't hesitate to call me, anytime."

"Goodnight, David."

"Goodnight."

***

He followed the same path back to the ranch. When he entered their room, he found Sandy sitting upright in their bed with her back leaning against the wall, her computer resting on her lap. She was sound asleep. He removed the laptop and turned it off, resisting the temptation to view what flickered on its screen. How could someone who looked so peaceful be capable of taking down governments? Although he had no knowledge of it, there was more than a better chance that assassinations were etched into her job description. The only chance of his marriage surviving was to stifle those thoughts.

Sandy sensed his companionship as she slipped down, curling up under the covers and whispered with her eyes squinting open, "You're home. Is everything okay?"

"Everything is perfect. Now go back to sleep." He leaned in and kissed her on the forehead.

Sandy drifted into dreamland before David reached the washroom.

When done, David checked in on Capella, who was sleeping like an angel. Then he snuck under the bedding and nudged up against his wife. It wasn't long before he fell asleep.

***

For the first hour, Addison unloaded all her deep dark secrets onto the apathetic animals. Finding no solace in the stall area, she retreated to the bunkroom. After David's explanation, she was convinced Belle would not be inaugurating into motherhood on her shift, or at least not tonight. In any case, she set her cell phone alarm to chime every hour on the hour.

After taking off her cowboy boots, she fluffed up a pillow and rested her head and shoulders on it. The glow of her cell phone illuminated her face as she laid there with her legs curled, knees facing upward. After five minutes of thumb typing onto the device, she set it aside, cupped her hands around the back of her head, and stared up at the bottom of the top bunk.

The alarm jarred her from near sleep. Up she got, tugged on her boots, and looked around the stable. All the horses were as she left them, so she returned to bed. When the next hour's notification arrived, a repeat of the previous walk around rendered the same results.

It was on the fourth tour she noticed that Belle's neck and head were drooping towards the floor. The mare was making a low, barely audible gravelly gargling sound. Addison stepped into the stall and

359

rubbed the horse's forehead and neck. The moaning subsided and the thoroughbred raised its head. Addison's heart began to race and she was relieved when she felt everything had returned to normal. She figured the mare must have been having a bad dream while sleeping standing up. Five minutes passed before she exited the stall and locked its door.

The second she turned her back, the horse's discomfort grew louder. She looked around and witnessed Belle lie down on the hay covered floor. Addison swung open the door once again and knelt down, facing her.

"What's the matter, baby? Are you okay? I'm going to call the doctor. Everything's going to be fine." She patted her on the nose.

Addison stood and grabbed her cell from her rear pocket. With phone in hand, she mulled over whether she was overreacting to the horse's plight. Maybe the mare wasn't experiencing any abnormal symptoms. After all, it was carrying an extra two hundred pounds. She went to tap in David's number two or three times, hesitating at each attempt. At that moment, Addison wished she knew more about horses and their actions. She spent the better part of the last few months surrounded by the animals, but was barely scratching the surface. She made a mental note to start asking more questions and read more about them.

As the minutes passed, Belle's condition worsened. A decision was made. She would reach out to David first, not the doctor. After all, he did say to get in touch with him at any time of the night.

For some reason, she stepped to the side of the horse, as if not wanting it to hear the call. She thought about how silly that was, but did it anyway.

Just before she pressed her finger on the screen, she noticed a small white piece of material at the rear of the horse. At first she thought it to be a sheet of paper that might have made its way into the stall. Maybe the mare was acting out of the ordinary because it was lying on something. But it only took a second for her to realize what she was looking at was the amnion, the white bag of the equine placenta, as the shape of a foal's nose began to appear.

Being a prey animal, a horse gave birth quickly to escape predators in short order. A newborn foal could stand and nurse almost immediately. It could trot or canter within three hours and gallop in a day. She knew a doctor would have no chance of helping her. It was happening now.

With the realization of what was transpiring, she tried to keep a cool head, but wasn't succeeding. Her heart rate was maxing out and her hands were trembling. When she tried to call David, her phone fell in the hay. In her panic, instead of bending over to pick it up, she somehow kicked it out of sight. It was now hidden somewhere on the grassy floor.

There was no time to search for it as she instantly became conscious of the fact that it was her and Belle. They were going to have to go it alone. Time had run out to summon someone.

"Okay, babe. It's you and me."

Trying hard to keep her composure, she moved around to the mare's rear. The head of the foal was already pushed out, or at least she presumed it was the head, as it was still covered in the white bag. It wasn't long before her supposition was confirmed, as now half the offspring's body was visible and tears in the amnion sac exposed a gorgeous chestnut colored baby horse. Addison's panic gave way to the rapture of being party to the birthing.

Now with a smile on her face, she sensed everything was moving along as it should and nature would nurture the delivery. Her reverie was short-lived when she noticed a leg of the twin awkwardly appearing. The progress of the parturition came to a halt. Foal number one was not advancing, and to Addison, it looked as though the leg of the second was wedged into the side of baby one, bringing the proceedings to a standstill. Recognizing something needed to be done, with one hand she gripped the foal and pried the intruding leg in an effort to assist the flow.

Her aid succeeded as foal number one was soon free of his or her mother's birth canal. Addison needed to make a choice: assist the newborn or enter the passageway with her hands to grip and gently pull the other. She knew there was a very good chance the second would be a stillbirth. Directly beside her, the foal was floundering about, looking to be in good health. She quickly cleared the remnants of the white bag off the fresh arrival that that stood wobbling back and forth in one place. Her attention turned to rescuing number two.

With her hands and part of her arms now buried, she could feel the leg which had slipped back into the canal. Once a grip was established, she tried to compact the body by pressuring its legs to its midsection. She had no idea if the foal was alive, but she was going to do everything humanly possible to make sure it met its sibling. At that moment, she recognized something was drastically wrong. The head appeared, but it was enclosed in a red bag, not white. Addison had a slight concept of what this meant. It was briefly explained to her when she inquired about it after noticing a birthing bulletin on the stable wall. From what she could remember, and nothing at the moment was very clear, it spelled trouble.

She recalled a mare's placenta was made up of two parts, the amnion or white bag, and the chorioallantois, otherwise known as the red bag. The white bag surrounds and protects the fetus. The red bag attaches to the uterine wall, allowing for the exchange of nutrients. The danger with the red bag carrying the fetus down the birth canal meant it had probably broken away from the wall too early and the foal might be short on oxygen.

Whether by instinct or subconsciously recalling the illustration on the stable wall, she knew it was imperative that she cut away the red bag immediately. Addison threw caution to the wind and tugged as hard as she could to pull the newborn out into her arms. Within seconds, she held the enclosed lifeless fetus. She tried to rip it free, but the jacket was too thick. What was needed was a pair of scissors or small knife, which she didn't have access to. Her only hope was to tug on the small opening where a leg had punctured it. Addison worked on it feverishly until it began to rip away. She soon cleared the foal of both bags, but it lay there inert. Once again, tears replaced her smile. The foal standing beside her was oblivious to the surroundings, trying ever so hard to balance on its four legs. Belle lay on her side in an attempt to regain energy.

Addison had no clue what to do. Her first thought was find the phone and call David. The tears were pouring off her trembling face. Then, without further thought, she laid the foal in the hay, bent over and pried its mouth open and began to blow air into it. She held its upper lip open with one hand while driving air into its dormant frame, and with the other she pumped up against its chest. Whether basic CPR would work, she had no clue. But what she did know was that she would make every effort to revive it.

A minute which seemed like an hour passed and still there was no sign of life. Maybe it was another minute or so, even seconds, but all of a sudden she was blessed by a miracle. The offspring expectorated to life. It pushed away and began the unbalanced ritual of fending for itself and wiggling to its beginning.

Addison sat there in shock, near collapse, powerfully crying tears of joy, fear and gratefulness. She witnessed a gift from God. Never had she seen anything so beautiful in all her life. The completeness of the experience would remain with her and her alone, as she could never articulate the words of properly describing not only the visual but the emotional.

With Belle now standing, she shook off her

bewilderment and recognized that David needed to be informed immediately. On all fours, she weaved between the twelve legs vying for floor space until the cell phone was retrieved. Instead of leaving the stall, she plopped back down against the wall, bending up her knees, embedding a mental image of it forever. Before she laid a finger on his contact number, she snapped a picture.

***

It was just past four in the morning when a tune resonated from his iPhone. He shook off the grogginess of being awakened in the middle of the night.

"Addison, what's wrong?"

Hearing the first few words that came out of her mouth was enough to have him jumping off the bed, hopping around in search of his clothing.

"David, what's going on?" Sandy inquired after being awakened by his urgency.

"It's Belle. I've got to run."

He was down the staircase and out the door within seconds. The night was bright enough whereby he didn't require a flashlight as he sprinted full out in the direction of the barn. When he arrived, he was in awe of what he was witnessing. There stood Belle, looking as she did on any other day. Rustling about, contending for the mare's teat were the two new chestnut colored members of the family. He'd witnessed birthing more than he could count in his lifetime, but the magic of it never ceased to amaze him and in this case even more so because of the twins.

He was so taken aback by the view, he momentarily forgot about Addison, who was still crouched up against the wall. When David entered the stall, she stayed put, so he walked over and without uttering a word, sat down beside her. She began to cry. The buildup of every imaginable emotion a person could endure came pouring out of her.

With one look at her, David knew all too well what she had experienced. There she sat beside him, her clothes soaked from the delivery. Her arms and hands were sodden. A river of tears rolled down her cheeks. She couldn't speak, but could only weep. He knew it was not the time to question her as to why she hadn't called earlier. What was needed now was consolation. The animals seemed healthy and didn't require his immediate attention.

He wrapped his arm around her shoulder and she responded by laying her head on his.

"Thank you," he whispered.

Between her shuddering inhalations, she cried out, "David, I'm so sorry." She paused, trying to control the sobbing, "I didn't have time to call you."

He pulled her tight. "Addison, you're amazing."

They sat there in awe for a minute until David put in two calls, the first to the veterinarian and the next to Renée.

***

Within the hour, word spread about the ranch's new arrivals. The day shift staff began to arrive, a number of them much earlier than scheduled. Everyone was anxious to witness the marvel. Chances were they would only be part of such a wonder once in their lifetime.

First to join David and Addison was the doctor, followed shortly after by Renée. The huddle of onlookers respected the space of those attending to the animals and stayed well back. There would be plenty of time during the course of the day to snap a couple of pictures.

The vet's examination was soon complete. He removed his gloves, and after he put away his instruments, he turned to the other three who were grouped in the corner of the stall.

"David. Oh hello, Renée. Your new family seems to be in excellent health. I see no reason why their progress should be anything out of the ordinary. Addison, I don't believe they would have made it if it weren't for your inventiveness and caring. You should be proud of yourself."

Addison smiled, but had no words. Still comforting her with his arm around her shoulder, David pulled her nearer as she continued to shed tears.

"I might be overstepping my bounds here, David and Renée, but it might be fitting that this filly carry the name Addison."

Renée was first to respond. "You make a valid point. Let's see." She covered her mouth with her fingers. "Addison's Pride. I can hear the track announcer calling her across the finish line. What do you think, David?"

"Addison's Pride, it is."

It took an hour or so before things returned to normal. Renée bid them goodbye, promising to return after her duties were taken care of at the track. David escorted Addison back to the ranch. Once inside her room, she disrobed, showered, and crawled under the covers. No one saw her for the remainder of the day.

Sandy was thrilled to hear about the new additions. They planned to spend part of the afternoon introducing Capella to the twins.

Chapter Thirteen

"Sandy, do you have plans of returning to the ranch within the next couple of weeks?" The President questioned her during an early morning call.

"I'm not certain. I believe it might be a few weeks before I can fit home into my schedule. Is there something of concern?"

"My sources tell me Fyad and his father plan to visit their Embassy in the near future. Am I correct?"

"I'm not aware of their scheduling, sir."

A month had passed since the birthing at the ranch. Sandy had stretched out her stay a couple of days longer than she'd planned and again returned this past weekend for a quick three day visit. She was burning the midnight oil trying to catch up on her workload and hadn't been in contact with the Prince for as many weeks.

"I would like my meeting with you and Fyad to happen during his stay. I trust that can be arranged. The subject matter has become time sensitive."

"I will contact him immediately. Is there anything else, Mr. President?"

"How is Capella?"

The mention of her daughter brought a smile to her face.

"She's wonderful, sir."

"She will be very proud of her mother's achievements. Have a nice day, Sandy."

"You also, sir."

She leaned back in her chair, mulling over the reasoning behind the urgency in the President's voice. For now, she had little time to dwell on it. A call to Fyad was in order and once the gathering was secured, it was back to a world of conflicts.

***

President Tucker's information was accurate. Fyad and his father arrived as expected a week and a half later. With some persuasion by Sandy, Fyad reluctantly agreed to free up time to meet with her and the President. To the best of Sandy's knowledge, the sit down was exclusive to the three of them. The Prince was steadfast on not stepping into the White House, so it was agreed upon to convene under the radar at Sandy's condo.

"Why does your President require my presence?"

"I have no idea. Fyad, I only ask that you hear him out. He's insightful to your distrust of the American way, so the matter must be of significance."

"I'll behave…for you. By the way, he is late."

"He's the President."

"See, I told you."

Sandy gave him a friendly jab on the arm. They both laughed it off and changed the subject to a more personal note.

An hour passed before they heard a faint knock on the door. He had arrived. Sandy welcomed him, surprised to find only two Secret Service agents positioned in the hallway. It was considerate of him to locate the others out of sight. That being said, Sandy was comfortable with their presence, as most of her neighbors were well aware of her title. She, herself, had two agents securing the perimeter of her whereabouts twenty-four-seven. The only exception was when she traveled home to the ranch. She insisted on keeping the two lives separate.

"Sandy." He shook her hand. "Fyad, I've been looking forward to meeting you in person. We've crossed paths many times, but I have not had the pleasure." He offered his hand.

Fyad rose with purpose, delaying his response, but did extend a polite greeting.

"I really do appreciate you taking time to sit down with me, Fyad. I understand your reluctance, but I assure you my one and only goal is to rid our world of its hostilities. I am certain the two of you share the same beliefs."

"Would you care for a drink, sir?"

"Thank you, Sandy, I'm fine. I know how busy you two are, so maybe I should jump right in. However, before I do, this coming Sunday I am hosting a small dinner and would like to extend an invitation to each of you. I've taken the liberty of inviting both of your fathers, along with Brooklyn, and they have accepted. It would have been nice if your mother could've joined us, but I understand she did not make the trip." He turned to Sandy. "Please invite David."

Fyad remained quiet. There was zero chance he would attend. His father liked the President, so it came as no surprise he'd accepted. The commerce exchanged between the two countries was immense and the King could not afford to ruffle any feathers. That diplomacy would remain his father's forte. He would concentrate on his country's security issues which brought his train of thought back to the rationale behind him sitting there being audience to the President of the United States. The answer was about to become apparent.

"Thank you, sir, I will see what I can do." Sandy was warm to the idea.

Fyad did not reply.

"Sandy, please ask David to bring Capella. Emma would love to meet her. Layla is home and I'm sure she would be happy to help out."

"I will see what he says."

"Good, now down to business. The two of you seem to have been busy these last few months. Contrary to what you may think, Fyad, I put a lot of weight behind what can be achieved through cooperation with others. You two are testament to that.

"During my term, we have developed a form of weaponry which I now wish to employ. Few, and I mean few people, are aware of its development. I entrusted this project to a handful of men and women of our most skilled personnel. It has now been brought to completion. The funding was, let's say, filtered in through other means.

"I now want you two to assemble a Special Forces Infiltration Unit of your choosing. Bring together twenty or thirty of the best. Some of our people, some of yours, Fyad...whomever you decide to select. The two of you will have one hundred percent control of the operation. Do I have your interest?"

"Mr. President." Fyad was first to question him. "You are being vague with regards to this armament you have developed."

"I am. First, I would like to know if you are attracted to this joint venture. I will say that if you accept, should the operation go south, our government will deny any knowledge of it. Let me add, if my plan is successful, both our countries will have made great strides in ending the unrest in the Middle East."

"Please continue," Sandy interjected, after receiving a nod of approval from Fyad.

"Lights Out. That's what we have labeled it. LO. The device will shut down anything which relies on a source of energy or electronics. It can be transported and deployed in many ways. For this mission, we would utilize a drone. When hovering, we can pinpoint a designated area. It can be anywhere between a yard to a hundred miles. The wave it produces will penetrate everything within the determined radius. All weaponry relying on an electronic chip, utilities, vehicles, batteries, communications devices, and so on will be disabled. Unless a device is one hundred percent mechanical, it will be rendered inoperative. Any resistance would be equivalent to that used in World War One.

"Sandy, your recent briefing indicated a gathering of terrorist principals was scheduled for within the next few months."

"Yes, sir."

"If we can remove the upper leadership of this group in one clean sweep, we can cripple the organization. I propose three simultaneous incursions, the mentioned meeting, their major training facility, and finally their central financial bunker."

"Sir, the reason we have not penetrated these assemblies is the many innocent targets they shield themselves behind. All of our scenarios estimate the loss of hundreds of civilian lives if an attempt is made to infiltrate one of these gatherings."

"I am aware of the challenges. However, with this technology, I believe we can keep innocent casualties to a minimum. Unfortunately, we need to factor in some civilian loss."

He pressed on. "Each weapon issued and each piece of clothing our forces will wear during this mission will have a chip implanted in them which neutralizes all effects of the wave. Compare it to our modern day military up against a town in the old west."

Not much more needed to be said, as the details would unfold once a decision was made. The covert operation was going to take place one way or the other.

"Why us?"

"Fyad, I can't think of any other pair better suited to oversee this. Together, the two of you are capable of pooling the elitest of assault units. You know the topography, the environment better than anyone. When I took office, I made a promise to surround myself with the very best. For this, I don't believe there is anyone more qualified. Sleep on it. I will need your answer by morning."

Fyad and Sandy knew each other so well all it took was one quick glance and the decision was made.

"We're in," Sandy said as Fyad nodded his approval.

"Excellent." The President offered his goodbyes. He motioned to Sandy to remain seated. "I can find my way out."

As he reached the door, he stopped and turned. It took him a few seconds of thought before he spoke. "With regards to another matter, as you are aware, our economy is delicate and I don't believe it would be in the world's best interest if we lost another billionaire. The shifting of power can be destabilizing. Would you by chance have any insight on whether this retaliation towards the so-called Bonanza Club has concluded?"

Sandy shrugged. "Sir, I'm not sure why you would pose that inquiry to us. However, that being said, I do believe the world will retain the remainder of their wealthy to frolic their money away as they see fit."

"Thank you. I would like to turn this over to you soon. I hope to see you Sunday for dinner."

With that, he was gone. Sandy and Fyad leaned

back without speaking for a bit.

"Field trip," she joked.

***

Back at the track, another meeting was taking place between David and Renée. The focus of the discussion was Addison. Her summer apprenticeship was at its end. After her recent actions and the compassion presented towards the horses, they arrived at a decision to offer her full-time employment. If she accepted, the details would be hammered out. Everyone within the organization was extremely impressed with her. In the back of David's mind, he believed even though Addison's attachment to the ranch was genuine, she would choose to follow the path of her schooling as a lifelong career. They would soon know as she walked through the door.

"Addison, please come in. Have a seat."

"Is there something wrong, David?"

"Not at all. We want to have a little chat with you."

"First, let me say it has been a pleasure working with all of you this summer. Everyone has treated me like family. Friday is going be a sad day. I want to thank both of you from the bottom of my heart. I know I've been a pain in the butt at times, but this has been the best few months of my life."

"What are your plans, Addison?" Renée jumped into the exchange.

"I'm not sure. If I follow my heart, a career that allows me to care for animals will be first on my list. Spending time here has changed my whole outlook on life. If ever a full-time position should open up with your stable, I would definitely be interested."

"Perfect. We are prepared to offer you an assistant trainer's position. In addition, we would also like to take advantage of your technology skills and ask for your input on fine-tuning our existing data system. Renée and I have discussed this at length and feel you will be an essential part of the team. Take some time to think about it."

"I don't need time to consider it. That's all I've been thinking about. Yes, yes, I would love to stay."

"Remember, this isn't the greatest paying job."

"What good is money if you're not excited to get up in the morning? I accept."

"Well then, welcome aboard."

They sealed the deal by shaking hands before Renée added, "Is your father going to be okay with the decision?"

"He'll have to be. It's my life."

"You're welcome to continue staying at the ranch or if you prefer, I'm sure Renée can assist you in finding other accommodations. To be honest, it's nice having someone else taking up occupancy at the main house. For the most part, it is only me and Capella."

"I'd love to for the time being, thank you. My room is starting to feel like home."

"Settled. Renée will work out the details and discuss them with you later in the week."

Addison thanked them again, then left to resume her day's work. David and Renée went on to discuss some of the upcoming races.

***

Before long, he was sitting in his vehicle preparing to make the trip home. There was one more item of business he wanted to take care of before retrieving Capella from the in-laws and resuming his fatherly duties. During Sandy's last visit, the nanny matter was revisited and it was decided by all that for the time being they would take Jacob and Brooklyn up on their offer to care of the child.

As he pulled onto the road, he recited Dr. Ricky's number to his vehicle's imperceptible assistant. The doc was a psychologist recommended to him by a good friend. He decided to take the leap or at least explore it. What could it hurt? Although it would be a challenge, as throughout his lifetime, when things got tough he found a way to fight through it. On a farm or at the rink, you sucked it up and dealt with it.

His love for Capella was the singular important aspect of his life and it was driving him to be better. That was undeniable, clear as day. No uncertainty there. She was number one. What he couldn't grasp was his love for Sandy and Renée. His feelings were straightforward in their own way. The troubling factor was the equal love he shared for both at the same time. How was he to decide? How was he to move forward? For the first time in his life, he recognized that maybe, just maybe, he needed help to understand how it was tearing him apart. Hence the call.

The conversation with the doctor's assistant was quick, polite, and non-judgmental. An hour long appointment was scheduled for the following week. Although he was somewhat nervous about baring his soul, he felt relieved there was someone of neutrality who would hear him out. Clarity was becoming more important to him than the situation itself.

***

Arriving home to an empty house meant his in-laws had Capella at the chalet. He turned and headed off in the direction of the log home. As he approached the rustic stained surround porch, he first noticed Jacob sitting on one of the wooden swings held up by golden chains bolted to the beams. His father-in-law's eyes were closed. At the bottom of the steps, he became aware that Capella was snuggled onto Jacob's belly, motionless but wide awake, and staring into the sky. David stopped to take in the peacefulness of the moment, only to be snapped out of it by Brooklyn. She stood centered within the screen door opening.

"I've never seen him so happy, David."

"Thank you, Brooklyn. Knowing Capella has such loving grandparents looking out for her means the world to me. I'm very lucky to be part of this family."

"There is little in life we want more than to care for her."

The chat was of a whispered volume but loud

enough to wake Jacob. It took him a second to zone in on who was present. He didn't speak or move, so as not to wake the baby. Brooklyn eased towards them and gently took Capella in her arms and quickly disappeared into the house.

"Hello, David. I think our little one has me wrapped around her finger. Damn females in my life always know how to get to me."

"Tell me about it."

They chuckled, knowing the statement was full of truth.

"Come in for a beer."

"David, why don't you stay and join us for an early supper. I made a mean lasagna."

He thought about it for a split second. "I don't think I can pass up an offer like that."

"Wonderful. Have you talked to Sandy today?"

He actually had to delay his answer momentarily to think about it. "No, no I haven't. She called me yesterday. I expect we will touch base tonight. Have you?"

"No. But I had a call from the White House a little while ago." She turned to her husband. "I didn't want to wake you, Jacob. We have been invited to dine with the President and a few guests this coming Sunday. King Saud and his son Fyad are visiting Washington. My understanding is the King has accepted the invitation and the President thought you would like see him before he returns home."

"Well, that sure came out of the blue," Jacob commented.

"It would be a pleasant evening, Jacob. I haven't

seen Emma in a long time. How nice it would be to catch up."

There we go, Jacob thought. Brooklyn had made the decision for the two of them. Truth be told, he wouldn't have it any other way. He couldn't refuse. When the President reached out to you, declining wasn't an option.

"That does sound like a captivating Sunday evening out. His chef is the finest."

"You two should definitely go. Make a weekend of it. Leave early and spend some time with your daughter. I've got this place covered."

"Actually, David, my understanding is you and Sandy are also invited. Apparently, the First Lady is insisting you bring Capella. The message was she would not take no for an answer. She wants to meet your daughter. I thought Sandy might have mentioned it. We'll take the jet. If you do talk to Sandy, I think it would be a lovely idea if we leave early and spend a day or two with her."

"I don't know. It's all so sudden. I'll get in touch with her tonight and let you know in the morning."

The invite was left at that. After dinner, David packed up Capella's things and walked back to the main house. The following couple of hours were focused solely on the baby.

***

With this time-sensitive operation squeezed into their already twenty-three hour days, it didn't take much for Sandy to convince Fyad to have his luggage delivered to her condo. There was literally not a spare minute to waste. They would be briefed in the morning and from that point on, they would be fine tuning every minute detail of the covert undertaking. It only made sense for him to bunk in one of the spare rooms while in Washington. After all, in the weeks leading up to the attack, she would be taking up residency at his Palace. For the next couple of months, they were going to become inseparable.

"Need I ask if you would reconsider the dinner invitation? After all, by the sounds of it, your father is attending."

"And yours."

"Yes, he is. And unlike you, I am not brave enough to say no."

By the time weariness took hold of them, the majority of their preferred team was established. With two of the world's brightest counterintelligence minds in the same room, it didn't take long for the perfect plan to take root. Although the President's briefing was vague, they each grasped exactly how the assignment would unfold. Preparation, preparation, preparation.

"We should get some shut-eye, Sandy. Our days are full, but tomorrow night we will take up where we left off."

"Since I'm not drunk, I guess I'll sleep in my own bed tonight."

"Your call."

"Fyad, are you flirting with me? So out of character."

He smiled and disappeared into the guestroom. Sandy closed her bedroom door and slid under the covers. There was that something when two grown adults who care for one another find themselves sleeping under the same roof. Albeit in separate rooms, both were sensitive to the warmth.

***

Morning fell upon them hastily. For most of their adult lives, lack of proper rest was the norm, yet each found a way to function flawlessly. An aptitude they attained only by way of extreme mind management. A study so intense few people could fathom its depth.

"Will it be a late day?"

"I do have much to oversee."

"Fyad, here's a key if you should get back before me. I will meet with the President this morning and confirm our decision. We are in?"

"We are."

"It's nice having you here," she whispered on her way out the door.

***

Sandy's day kicked into high gear the second she left the driveway. The Secret Service preferred those in such positions be chauffeured in secured vehicles, but being the rebel, she insisted on driving her candy apple red Corvette. There was little resistance from those in charge of security as upon her arrival in Washington, she made it clear her choices were not to be questioned.

The first call during the ride in was usually to her assistant. As she was about to prompt the car's voice directory, it dawned on her she neglected to call David last night.

"David," she commanded the voice recognition.

The incoming call broke the silence and woke David from a deep sleep. It took him a second to adjust before answering.

"Wattsy, are you there?"

"Sandy."

"Were you still sleeping?"

"I was. What time is it?"

"Six. Sorry, I presumed Capella would have you up by now."

"Sandy, I thought you might have called last night."

"I'm sorry, David. I got caught up in something. How are you two doing?"

"We're fine."

The small talk continued for a couple of minutes until David questioned her on the invite to dinner. The subject had completely slipped her mind. She really hadn't given a second thought of David attending, let alone bringing Capella. As soon as the President suggested it, she took for granted her husband would have no interest in making the trip. So it came as a surprise when he was receptive to the idea and that maybe they could make a weekend out of it.

"Are you sure, David? You've never been the type for these things. I was actually hoping to excuse myself out of it."

"Your father and Brooklyn have accepted. After

all, you keep encouraging me to spend more time there. I think Capella would be up for a get together with Mommy."

"I'm surprised but excited to see you guys. I'm meeting with the President this morning and will let him know."

They continued the conversation, promising to get in touch with one another by day's end. It wasn't until the call ended did she think about the complications of having Fyad moved into one of the spare rooms. She would discuss it with him tonight. If he was comfortable with it, they would leave the arrangement as is. They were the best of friends, and that's the way it was. Besides, after jumping Renée's bones, David should be the last to oppose the accommodations.

***

Sandy packed a week's work into her day. Meetings with the President, a number of department heads, and the CIA's top brass consumed the sunlight hours and it wasn't until nine-thirty that she found her way back home.

The instant she entered, the aroma of what could only come from a home cooked meal filled the room. Sandy placed her bag on a hallway stand and made a beeline for the kitchen. She took note of Fyad by the stove, but more shocking was the eloquent setting of the petite dining table sparkling in candle light.

"Are we expecting company?"

"No, Sandy, we are not. Sometimes warriors

need to feel special."

"Fyad, I believe married life has had an effect on you. In a good way, I might say."

He prepared one of his favorite Middle Eastern dishes, one his mother would serve on those private occasions when her instincts told her life needed a bit of a boost.

Sandy savored every bite. The offering was far too delicious to overshadow it with conversation of work and the world. They touched on family and some enjoyable times shared in the past. The serious stuff didn't come to light until the dishes were cleared and the wine bottle recycled.

Earlier at the White House, Sandy was briefed about their upcoming operation. Schedules were drawn up that would see the majority of the mission's development take place at Fyad's palace. It was the logical choice since the attack would be launched from his country. They agreed that Blake would be sent overseas to coordinate the initial preparation. Sandy and Fyad would become more involved as soon as they entrusted their existing commitments.

It was nearing two in the morning when Sandy became to some extent distracted at the thought of not seeing her daughter for a full month or more while executing the attack. Fyad was quick to pick up on it.

"Blake and I can take care of this, Sandy. You'll be as valuable supporting us from this side of the world."

"I know, Fyad, and thank you. But I need to be there. I want to be there. I'm going to be there."

They soon called it a night, but not before Sandy mentioned that David and the family had accepted the dinner invitation and she felt obligated to attend. She explained they were planning on arriving a day or two early and insisted that he remain as a guest. Fyad appreciated the offer, but informed her that he would be heading home the day after tomorrow. He was accompanying his father to a number of appointments the following day and would bunk in tomorrow night but fly out early the next day.

***

Midday Friday, the McGinnis jet set down in Washington. Sandy sent a car to transport the family to her residence. Anxious to hold her baby, she was striving to hurriedly wrap up her day.

Capella and mother were reunited early evening. Brooklyn took it upon herself to prepare a supper. It was an enjoyable evening for all, as was the following day. They decided to spend the day inside. Sandy couldn't remember doing so since making the move. They watched a ball game, a couple of movies, and consumed enough food to warrant the loosening of belt buckles.

David took notice that on the unoccupied guest room's bed sat a zipped up piece of luggage. He presumed it must have been Sandy's, one prepared for that unexpected demand for an overnight task. Once Capella was settled down for the night and they were alone in the room, David questioned her on it.

"Is that your suitcase sitting on the bed in the

spare room?"

She hadn't given a second thought to the fact that Fyad's meetings the previous evening ran late and he elected to stay at the hotel. He was to send someone for his things. By now he would be on the other side of the world.

"It belongs to Fyad. It is to be picked up at some point. We are overseeing a project together and felt it best if he stayed here. We worked late the past few evenings. He flew home this morning."

To her surprise, David accepted the explanation without further qualification.

They cuddled and talked about their daughter. When the conversation soon became one sided, David realized Sandy was fast asleep. The lovemaking would wait until tomorrow.

***

Arriving at the White House around three, they were escorted to the President's private quarters. The visit was not going to be a formal event. Other than King Saud, it would only be members of the two families. They were greeted by Emma, the First Lady, and their daughter Layla.

Drinks and hors d'oeuvres were served. Sophia Foster, the Press Secretary, soon arrived, welcoming everyone. She asked Jacob and the King if they would be kind enough to join the President for a drink in the Oval Office. David felt a bit excluded not being invited, but nonetheless realized it was most likely more than a social gathering.

"The President promises to return with them

shortly."

***

As it turned out, for the most part the men had a couple of drinks and discussed the thoroughbred horseracing industry. The President let it be known he was interested in investing in the business once his final term came to an end. He had always loved the sport, and now with Addison immersed in it, the idea of establishing a family stable intrigued him. Maybe Layla would follow the path of her sister. The two guests pledged their support at any time.

"Off that topic, I wanted to personally apologize for occupying so much of your daughter's time." He looked at Jacob, then to the King. "And your son's time. I have enlisted them to oversee a delicate matter which will consume them for the next couple of months. I can't go into the details, but if I didn't consider it of the utmost importance for the safety of our countries, I would have delegated it to others."

The King would soon know every detail, given the attack would be initiated from his country. Jacob withheld any reaction, knowing full well what was being said without further explanation.

"Enough of that. We should join the others."

They stood, but before leaving the room, the President added, "Gentlemen, your children have assured me that for the time being, our billionaire population will remain alive and in good health. Would you agree with their assessment? Our economy is fragile, and this kind of shift in wealth can weigh heavily on it."

The King looked at Jacob, conveying his silent blessing for his friend to field the inquiry.

"Sir, we certainly trust that is the case."

They were soon at the dinner table with the others, thoroughly enjoying the chef's special plate of a Southern Kentucky cuisine in recognition of the guests. Paying respect to their Middle Eastern visitor, a side dish of Fattoush Salad was served.

It would have been thought the allurement of such an occasion be centered on the White House and the presence of the First Family. But that wasn't the case. The spotlight belonged to Capella. She was the center of attraction and simply stole the show.

Chapter Fourteen

Throughout the weeks to come, Sandy made it back to the ranch twice, five days in total, before leaving for the Middle East. She would not be home for a minimum of four weeks and knew the trip weighed heavily on both her and David. However, it was necessary. If all went as planned, the world was about to rid itself of many threats.

With Sandy's long distance approval, Fyad and Blake selected each participant, thirty in all. The team consisted of Americans, Fyad's personnel, along with a handful of private militia with close ties to all three of them. Each a deadly instrument capable of singlehandedly destroying any rival, against any number of aggressors.

Together, armed with the finest weaponry, there would be no defenses capable of stopping them. In addition to the fact that the majority of their targets' weaponry would be rendered useless, the expectation was nothing short of one hundred percent success. However, sixteen hours a day they trained, scrutinizing every infinitesimal facet of the mission. Over and over again until every move, every step they took would be guided by instinct not thought. Hell was about to descend on those soon to occupy it.

Upon arrival, Sandy joined in on the rigorous preparation. Although she remained in immaculate condition, it had been a while since she participated in one on one combat. Fyad and Blake urged her to refrain from breaking anyone's bones, emphasizing the need for all thirty to be in peak condition entering into the covert-op. She heeded their advice, but the men unfamiliar with her ability soon became aware of it.

The President entrusted every detail to Sandy and Fyad. His only condition was when the day arrived, the two of them would direct it from afar. They were not to be on the ground. He did not want the Director of the CIA to be a known participant.

The United States would not take credit for its success or failure. If things went south, they would suggest it was an act of some other radical group. There was no lack of those wanting to seek acclaim for such a brave act. It was expected collateral damage could not be avoided due to the militants heavily shielding themselves with the innocent, as they do when a congregation of them were required to gather in one location. If casualties were avoided, the White House might consider issuing a statement of its success as a joint mission if its allies wished to be party to it. Either way, it didn't matter to the President. His only goal was to inflict as much damage as possible on the insurgents.

Sandy and Fyad understood his logic, but

nevertheless decided to partake in the advance. The White House would have no knowledge of their choice until it was too late. The attack would be transmitted real-time from monitors attached to each member. The President wouldn't be happy, but they guessed in the back of his mind he was expecting it.

***

The morning of the covert operation, Sandy put in calls to her father and then David. She talked to both longer than normal, only ending the conversation with her husband and child after receiving a nod from Fyad indicating everyone was aboard the helicopters. Capella's voice brought on tears. She promised David that upon her return, somehow they would find a way to spend more time together.

***

The assault was designed not for the purpose of taking prisoners or collecting intelligence. Its sole purpose was to destroy as many terrorists as possible. That's exactly what this force of twenty-nine men and one woman accomplished. Between the three locations, their wrath descended upon the radicals. Hundreds were killed. The hierarchy of the fundamentalists was no longer. Their choice fighters were obliterated. It would take years for them to rebuild. Yes, mankind still needed to be vigilant to the group's silent cells placed throughout the world, but soon their financial support would dry up due to the blow. It was sure to cause a self-dismantling.

The President would be pleased with the outcome, Sandy thought. In time, maybe he would give her a pass on disobeying his order. However, she and Fyad felt the choice was of necessity. Truth be told, she missed the game, the adrenaline rush. There was never going to be anything in her life that would match it.

It was a good day. The damage inflicted was achieved without casualty of their soldiers and minimum loss of civilians, until they were about to climb aboard the waiting helicopter.

Out of the corner of her eye, Sandy detected a reflection, then a flash. She instinctively knocked Fyad to the ground, shielding him from the enemy's bullet. Before she could take aim, one of her men put down the sniper with a single shot.

She began to lift off her friend and then she felt it, a burning sensation in her side. Her world went dark.

Chapter Fifteen

A funeral was as always a gut-wrenching occasion. It was a time to mourn, to celebrate life, an emotional roller-coaster. A day everyone prayed would never come, but always would.

"Today, we pass on a true hero. We will meet again, that I promise. Until then, our prayers will always be with you." The President of the United States spoke eloquently before stepping aside to make way for the final eulogy from Fyad.

The stately military setting was fitting, but did little to mask the sadness for which it was being staged. A sea of black clothing stood on the immaculately manicured grounds flanked by the formality of statuette soldiers. The eerie silence was only broken by the restrained sobbing of grief.

Capella stood between Jacob and Brooklyn, supported by one hand of each. She had been fidgety in her stroller, but now seemed content kicking at the grass. David was positioned beside them.

"I'm a man of few words. However, today many

wonderful memories flood my mind, some of which I wish to share with you."

His voice crackled as he went on, looking over at his mother, who could barely stand. She struggled to put on a brave face. And standing to her right, with her arm around her shoulder wasn't his wife, his sister, or another relative.

No, it was the one person in the world who always had his back. She'd saved his life on more than one occasion. It was Sandy.

At that moment, he was filled with the most powerful love he imagined a human being could experience. His father may have been right. She was the one.

"My father...may he rest in peace." Fyad's recollection of his father's virtue brought tears to all.

Chapter Sixteen

It had been six months since the family returned from their flight overseas to pay respect to Fyad's father, who passed away quickly after being diagnosed with a rare form of cancer. Unbeknownst to Sandy or her family was that the King and his son's last visit to the United States had been an effort in procuring an experimental treatment. Sandy's heart went out to Fyad learning he had traded precious hours with his father for their operation.

***

Life as they all knew it was for the most part back to normal. At the family's insistence, Addison remained bunked up at the ranch. She was living up to all expectations, assisting in the revamping of the stable's software while becoming an integral part of the organization.

Brooklyn and Jacob were as close as they would ever be with delegating the daily operation of the business to their trusted associates.

The racing world was starting to tout Renée and Gabriela for rewriting thoroughbred history. They were unstoppable, breaking record after record. Their faces were paired on every sporting publication conceivable.

With life becoming a bit easier to understand, David kept up with the monthly baring of the soul sessions with his therapist. At his in-laws' insistence, he was beginning to attend more races than he had since his daughter's birth. During those overnight stays, he and Renée refrained from intimacy, although that familiarity was always present in their flirtatious kinesics. David began to trust that time would be the sole determining dynamic in his future choices. He would embrace patience.

The one single most important aspect of the family remained Capella. So young, yet the glue that instilled hope in everyone. She was going to achieve greatness. There was no doubt in anyone's mind.

The doctors were astonished at how quickly Sandy recovered from the wound. A pair of broken ribs seemed to be the worst of it. The bullet miraculously hit her in the side, through the smallest of openings in her protective wear. A fraction of an inch to the left or right and she would've been dancing with death. They removed the projectile and stitched her up. Sandy tore up the pain prescription sheet as she dealt with the discomfort the way she had been trained to do.

Following the mission, the White House insisted

the Director take two months off. She agreed. Her injury went without public notice and the mission was hailed as a successful joint undertaking. The press described it as the single most important accomplishment of the President's occupancy of the White House.

Sandy acknowledged that in the near future, there would be some difficult decisions. The President's term was nearing its end. Those jockeying for the Oval Office were crisscrossing the country, drumming up support. In the relatively short period of time she became resident of the city of deals, she commanded the admiration of many unfamiliar with her tenacity. Now she was being lauded by highly influential insiders to take the next step and throw her name into the hat.

The one certainty in her life was Capella. She was evolving into an exceptional child at the blink of an eye. Missing out on it wasn't an option.

In addition, she was reflecting on David's subtle shift in demeanor. He was calmer, becoming distant. She hadn't put her finger on it yet, but knew her next choice would solidify his search.

And now, her best friend in the world was a King.

For better or worse, she knew the significance of her resolution would affect all the lives she held dear.

The only absolute was that life would never be the same again.

The End

William C. Cole

To be continued….

Acknowledgements

I owe a debt of gratitude to Diane, for so patiently reviewing the countless drafts I threw your way. This book would not have happened without you.

A special thanks to my family, for their continued support and encouragement. It is comforting knowing so many wonderful people are in your corner.

About the Author

Author of 'LOVE LONELY' and
'WHO LIES BESIDE ME'

Born in Toronto and raised in Northern Ontario, Canada. My wife Diane has been by my side for the past 37 years, which I do believe should propel her directly into sainthood. I have been blessed with an amazing and supportive family.

Creativity has always played a role in my journey. I suspect writing novels is a natural extension to my years in the music industry, where I had the pleasure of listening to songs I penned being played on the radio.

When not out and about earning a living, writing or biking, I'm on the golf course attempting to keep up with my sons Aaron and Lee.

Facebook:
www.facebook.com/williamccole

Twitter:
https://twitter.com/_WilliamCCole

Goodreads:
http://www.goodreads.com/user/show/33782347-william-cole

Website:
http://www.williamccole.com/

Linkedin:
http://www.linkedin.com/pub/william-c-cole/a5/76a/779/

Instagram:
https://www.instagram.com/williamccole/

Made in the USA
Columbia, SC
21 July 2020

14432958R00245